Court of Scotland, John Fleming, J. Irvine Smith

Report of Proceedings in Causa Her Majesty's Advocate v. Fleming and Others

SALZWASSER VERLAG

Court of Scotland, John Fleming, J. Irvine Smith

Report of Proceedings in Causa Her Majesty's Advocate v. Fleming and Others

Reprint of the original, first published in 1864.

1st Edition 2022 | ISBN: 978-3-75259-275-7

Verlag (Publisher): Salzwasser Verlag GmbH, Zeilweg 44, 60439 Frankfurt, Deutschland
Vertretungsberechtigt (Authorized to represent): E. Roepke, Zeilweg 44, 60439 Frankfurt, Deutschland
Druck (Print): Books on Demand GmbH, In de Tarpen 42, 22848 Norderstedt, Deutschland

In the Court of Exchequer (Scotland).

REPORT OF PROCEEDINGS

IN CAUSA

HER MAJESTY'S ADVOCATE

v.

FLEMING AND OTHERS

FROM THE SHORTHAND NOTES OF MR. J. IRVINE SMITH.

WITH AN APPENDIX.

1864.

CONTENTS.

APPENDIX.

INFORMATION OF SEIZURE.

THE LORD ADVOCATE *v.* FLEMING AND OTHERS.

BEFORE LORD ORMIDALE IN EXCHEQUER.

Thursday, 11*th February* 1864.

A BRIEF preliminary discussion took place, the result of which was that the defenders (owners and builders) agreed to put in a Minute denying the said Information as 'untrue in fact, and bad in law,' and throwing themselves on the country—namely, by appeal to a Jury. Some conversation took place on the question whether, according to the usual form of process in this Court, all questions of relevancy should be discussed and made the subject of an interlocutory judgment, open to reclaiming note and appeal, or be taken up at the trial, on motions that the presiding Judge should charge the Jury to the effect of the pleas then to be maintained. It was resolved, in the first place, to allow the Crown to make an incidental correction of the Information, and to allow the defenders to lodge a Minute of denial, the case to be called on Saturday for the purpose of arranging preliminaries, with a view either to debate on the relevancy, or to proceeding to trial at an early date, as should be resolved.

Mr. Gordon, for the builders, who had a lien over the vessel for part of the price, which would be defeated by forfeiture of the vessel, said there were several objections which occurred to them with reference to framing the counts, and they wished distinctly to understand that while they were ready to go to trial, and anxious there should be no delay, it should be open to them at the trial to state those objections to the relevancy of the counts as laid, and to ask that they should be withdrawn from the Jury. If, however, the Crown and his Lordship thought the other the preferable course—namely, to have a discussion on the relevancy before going to the Jury, they were ready to adopt that course; it was one, however, which would be attended with much delay. The Crown had ninety-eight counts, but would probably ask a verdict only on one or two; in the Alexandra case a verdict was asked on eight counts. He would give his learned friend notice, however, that if the first count was one of those insisted in, it was one to which the defenders would state serious objections.

Mr. Gifford said the defenders must put in their pleas and take their stand upon them; and until he saw them, he could not pledge himself to any particular course, but he could assure them that no obstacles would be thrown in the way.

Lord Ormidale said that perhaps it might be desirable that the preliminary points should be to some extent opened upon, so as to see whether they could be disposed of at once, or whether the whole case should not go to the Jury.

Saturday, 13th February.

Mr. Gordon said that, when the case was last called, his Lordship thought that some plea should be put in by the defenders. They had communicated the terms of the proposed plea, and he now asked his Lordship to allow him to lodge it.

Lord Ormidale.—What does it say?

Mr. Gordon.—It is in substance that the Information is untrue in fact, and bad in law.

Some conversation then took place as to whether any minute should be put in, stating that all questions of relevancy are reserved for the trial.

Mr. Gordon.—The general rule in Scotland is that if you go to trial you are understood to have waived your objection to relevancy.

Lord Ormidale.—That depends on what you call relevancy. It is now an established rule of practice in the Scotch Courts that matters of relevancy which may be in some degree affected by evidence stand reserved for disposal at the trial. But if you take the question of relevancy in this sense, that even upon the pursuers' averments, in any reasonable view that can be taken of them, there is no case, that is a different matter.

Mr. Gordon.—That is our case.

Lord Ormidale.—If that is the contention of the defenders here, is it not a point that should be raised now?

Mr. Gordon.—If we are all agreed that these points should be reserved, why should we not express it, so as to prevent the Court, who are not parties to this arrangement, from being afterwards hampered by an order for trial, which they may think has the effect of precluding us from raising any objection to the relevancy? I should be satisfied with what has taken place, if your Lordship were the final Judge in the case, but a different view may be taken elsewhere, and whatever confidence I may have in the personal assurance of my learned friends, I think it is more satisfactory to express in writing that which is understood, so as to prevent any difficulty afterwards.

Lord Ormidale.—I think that is a matter in which the Court is concerned. Any other course would look as if, perfectly blindfolded, and knowing nothing about what the pleas are, I am to reserve them. According to Scotch pleading, no such interlocutor as that could be pronounced without the Court knowing what is reserved.

Solicitor-General.—It appears to me that the practice of the Court is worthy of attention here, because the stating in an interlocutor that matters are kept open, when they are really reserved, or kept open without any such expression, is introducing a very dangerous practice. I should think it clear that all legal objections to this Information are kept entire, and not prejudiced by sending it to trial in point of fact. If any record of the understanding of the present Crown counsel to that effect is desired, the defenders may have it in any way they please. Your Lordship may note it, or we shall express it in writing, the agent on the one side to the agent on the other side, that it is quite understood by the parties that all legal objections to the Information are kept open, notwithstanding the case being sent to trial. But it has not been usual in this Court to reserve questions of relevancy expressly; if they are not disposed of they reserve themselves; the legal objection is there, and it has not been decided.

Mr. Gordon.—I shall be quite satisfied if my learned friends will give in a minute.

Lord Ormidale.—You must keep in view that when you put in anything judicially, you must have regard to the views of the Court. Now I am not prepared to allow any minute of that sort to be lodged.

Lord Advocate.—The Solicitor-General has said, that as matter of practice the pleas are reserved, and we are ready to express our opinion to that effect.

Solicitor-General.—And to minute it extrajudicially.

Mr. Gordon.—A letter from one agent to the other would not be satisfactory, because it would not bind the parties in the same way as a judicial minute.

Lord Ormidale.—I would suggest to you that this matter is important, and all the more important that we are only in the commencement of a course of practice in connexion with Crown cases under the recent Statute. There is no form of process yet established; and I would suggest that perhaps we may consider this question till Tuesday, by which time I should consider how far the Court is concerned in the question.

Lord Advocate.—I should have no objection to your Lordship noting that you send the whole case to trial, and that all objections to the relevancy are kept open.

Lord Ormidale.—When do you propose that the trial should take place?

Lord Advocate.—We are not quite ready to name the day, but certainly within a very short time.

Lord Ormidale.—Would you propose that the trial should take place in session?

Lord Advocate.—We were proposing to have it about 10th March, but we are not quite certain whether we shall be ready by that time; and if not then, about the first week of April.

Lord Ormidale.—There can be no harm in allowing the pleas now tendered to be received.

Lord Advocate.—I think not.

Lord Ormidale.—I think the correction of clerical mistakes in the Information may be done without an interlocutor.

Mr. Gordon.—Your Lordship will understand that we should like the question of relevancy disposed of, unless the Court is clearly of opinion that all questions of relevancy are reserved.

Lord Ormidale.—The Court probably will not give you any opinion.

Mr. Gordon.—My friends have given us an assurance, but that assurance is not binding on your Lordship. Now I may be put in prejudice by this matter being postponed till the trial, when your Lordship may hold that we are too late; and that is the importance of having the matter determined now.

Lord Ormidale.—But there is a difficulty in the way of the Court saying anything about it, because at the present moment the Court is in entire ignorance as to what your plea means. All I can say is, that if both parties are agreed, it is not likely that the Court will be inclined to take any objections. I don't know that I can say anything more.

Mr. Gordon.—My friends can relieve us from difficulty by putting in a judicial minute.

Lord Advocate.—With a view to the general practice, nothing would induce me to do that.

Mr. Gordon.—Probably your Lordship will hear us further on Tuesday. What we wish your Lordship to determine is whether it is of advantage in the present case, and in similar cases, that all questions of relevancy should be reserved for the trial, or whether questions of relevancy should now be disposed of. If they are now disposed of, I can see that it would give rise to a good deal of delay, because any judgment your Lordship may pronounce will very probably be taken elsewhere. Now we have no interest to cause delay; our wish is to come before the jury as quickly as possible, and therefore we are perfectly ready not to adhere to the ordinary practice in civil and criminal causes in Scotland, of having questions of relevancy disposed of before trial. We are anxious rather to adopt the course followed in the Alexandra case, as I understand, of having the counts as framed by the Crown sent to a jury, subject to this, that it is in the power of the Judge to direct them that some of these counts are irrelevant, not being consistent with the terms of the Statute.

Lord Ormidale.—No question of relevancy was raised in the Alexandra case. The case can stand in the roll till Tuesday.

Tuesday, 16th February.

Mr. Gifford.—The case was continued from Saturday to see whether there should not be a Minute consenting to the whole question of law being left open for the trial. I have not had an opportunity of seeing the Solicitor-General this morning, but so far as my impression goes, I don't know that there is much objection to that course.

Lord Ormidale.—I may mention that the Court cannot be a party to any such minute. You may make any arrangement you please, but the Court cannot be a party to any arrangement of that kind, so as to tie up the hands of the Court at the trial. The Statute appears to me to be pretty plain as to the course of procedure. In the 11th section we have the preliminary matters about the case being in the roll, and about an order for an Information. That has been done. Then the Statute goes on, 'And 'upon such Information of seizure being lodged, the procedure 'shall thenceforward be conducted, as nearly as may be, in the like 'manner as in ordinary causes commenced by *subpœna* and Infor- 'mation, in terms of this Act.' Then section 9 provides that all cases commenced by *subpœna*, so far as not expressly regulated, 'shall be conducted, as nearly as may be, in conformity with the 'procedure before the Court of Session in ordinary actions.' In section 6 we have a special regulation, that after the Information shall have been served, if the defender shall appear, and shall not admit the truth of it, the Lord Ordinary shall appoint a day for hearing the parties upon the Information, where this may appear to him to be necessary, or shall appoint a day for trying the matters put in issue by such Information, without any adjustment of any separate issue or issues, or shall take such other course as to him may seem proper. Now, should we not just appoint a day for trial at once?

Mr. Gifford.—There is no objection to that, excepting that we are not quite ready to fix a day yet. My friends on the other side have stated that they have objections to the Information both in fact and in law, and they wish it agreed, or at least understood, that these points should be left open for the trial, and we think they will be left open for the trial.

Lord Ormidale.—I believe, in all Exchequer cases formerly, all these points were left open for the trial; but I cannot and will not pronounce any judgment on that at present. On inquiry, I think it will be found that all these things were left entirely open under the practice in the Exchequer Court.

Mr. Cook.—Did your Lordship pronounce an interlocutor allowing the plea for the defenders to be put in?

Lord Ormidale.—There is no harm in that, because it shows that the parties have not agreed to the Information.

Mr. Gordon.—Then I am afraid that we must have a discussion now, so that we may know how we are situated.

Lord Ormidale.—I am quite resolved at present, unless I hear a great deal more than I have heard, not to tie up my hands; and the way to keep the Court at liberty to do what is right, is not to have any of these reservations.

Mr. Gordon.—They are reservations which are inserted in interlocutors in the Court of Session.

Lord Ormidale.—I never in my life saw a case sent to trial under reservation.

Mr. Gordon.—I think the Court have found it inexpedient to dispose of a question of relevancy before trial, and that is just reserving it. All we want is an interlocutor sending the case for trial without determining anything. That was done in the case of Gill, 20 D.

Mr. Gifford.—We on this side of the bar concur in the view that it is inexpedient to dispose of questions of law before the trial, and if your Lordship should find that, there can be no objection to it on this side. But I now move your Lordship to appoint the case to be tried on a day to be afterwards fixed.

Mr. Cook.—We oppose the motion in these unqualified terms. We wish the reservation.

Lord Ormidale.—I am quite ready to hear you on that.

Mr. Cook.—Perhaps your Lordship will consider whether you will give us an interlocutor.

Lord Ormidale.—No, I cannot. I must be guided by the Statute as nearly as possible. My own impression is that you are perfectly safe, and I think the previous practice in Exchequer causes should satisfy you of that. How could I direct the Jury to find a verdict for the Crown if I were perfectly satisfied on the arguments in law and otherwise that there was no ground for such a course?

Mr. Gordon.—Then you would direct them to find a verdict against the Crown?

Lord Ormidale.—I would direct the Jury to find that, if I were satisfied that on no grounds of law or fact was there any case for the Crown. I wish you quite to understand that I threw out that observation in perfect ignorance as to what your pleas are; and you must clearly understand that the Court is not limited or tied up in any way as to the proper course to be taken at the trial.

Mr. Cook.—Our plea must be disposed of in some way. We must either have a discussion on it before or after the trial.

Lord Ormidale.—If you wish to be heard, I will hear you upon it.

Adjourned.

17*th February* 1864.

Mr. Clark.—I attend your Lordship on the part of the owners, Messrs. Fleming and others, who are defenders in this Exchequer process, and this folio volume of sixty-six pages, with a relative explanation and abstract, contains ninety-eight charges against these owners of having contravened the Foreign Enlistment Act. Your Lordship has directed that we shall bring under your consideration any objections which we have to the different counts of this Information, in so far as we think these objections may be disposed of, or, at all events, are properly fitted for consideration before the case is sent to a Jury trial; and without attempting to go into the whole questions which may and indeed will arise at the Jury trial when it takes place, if it takes place at all, I shall confine my attention to those objections which may be disposed of, or, at all events, are properly fitted for consideration before we go to trial. The first thing to do, and I confess it is by no means a very easy thing, is to ascertain what are the charges which are made against the owners. I think I may say, that taking it in its broadest sense, there are only ten charges which need be at all considered. The first eight are a type of all the rest, except the ninety-seventh and ninety-eighth, and therefore I shall confine my attention entirely to the first eight, and to the ninety-seventh and ninety-eighth. I believe there is no doubt that we have in these ten charges a full statement of the whole of the different charges which are made in this Information, and the Abstract explains the differences in the different charges,—I mean, other than the eight. The first count makes this charge, that certain persons, viz., John Fleming, &c., 'without any leave or license of Her Majesty for that purpose first 'had and obtained, did equip the said ship or vessel with intent 'and in order that such ship or vessel should be employed in the 'service of certain foreign states styling themselves the Confederate 'States of America, with intent to cruise and commit hostilities 'against a certain foreign state, with which Her Majesty was not 'then to wit, on the day and year last aforesaid, at war, to wit, 'the Republic of the United States of America, contrary to the 'form of the Statute in such case made and provided, whereby 'and by force of the Statute in that case made and provided, 'the said ship or vessel, together with the said tackle, apparel, and 'furniture, became and was forfeited.' The offence as stated consists in three things—1st, in the equipment of the said ship or vessel, whatever that may be; 2d, in the equipment of the vessel with intent and in order that such ship or vessel should be employed in the service of certain foreign States; and 3d, with intent to cruise and commit hostilities against a certain other foreign state. The three things therefore which go to constitute the statutory offence charged in the first count, are equipping with two separate intents libelled, the first being the intent that the vessel should be employed in the service of a foreign state, the other being with intent to cruise and commit hostilities against a certain other foreign state. The next count is not materially different, except in making certain alterations in the name of the foreign states, for instance, 'did equip the said ship or vessel, with intent and in order 'that such ship or vessel should be employed in the service of certain foreign states, styling themselves the Confederate States of 'America, with intent to cruise and commit hostilities against 'citizens of a certain foreign state, with whom and with which 'respectively Her Majesty was not then at war.' Throughout, the things which are charged as constituting a statutory offence are precisely the same in the first and second counts, with an alteration in the description of the foreign states against whom it is said the ship was to be used. The third count varies considerably from the two first, and it is very important to notice this difference, because it goes very materially into the question which I shall immediately bring under your Lordship's consideration. The allegation of the offence is this, that the claimants 'did equip 'the said ship or vessel, with intent to cruise and commit hostilities 'against a certain foreign state with which Her Majesty was not 'then at war, viz., the Republic of the United States of America.' Here the structure of the Information is altogether altered, and the offence charged, which in the two previous counts consisted of three things, is in this count reduced to two, the equipment of the vessel contrary to the Statute, with the intent to cruise and commit hostilities as against a foreign state, the words, 'with intent that such vessel should be employed in the service of a foreign 'state,' being in this count altogether omitted. One of the elements which go to constitute the offence as charged in the 1st and 2d counts is omitted in the charge of the offence in the 3d count, leaving the 3d count stating the offence as consisting only of equipping the vessel with intent to cruise and commit hostilities. I need not go minutely over the 4th count, except to say that it is framed in precisely the same form as the 3d, viz., the equipment of the vessel with intent to cruise and commit hostilities. The variation consists in using the term 'citizens of a foreign State,' instead of using the words 'a certain foreign state.' In the 5th count the Crown goes back to the form of libelling adopted in the 1st and 2d counts, and it is said that the offence consists in equipping 'the said ship or vessel, with intent and in order that 'such ship or vessel should be employed in the service of divers 'and very many persons exercising the powers of government in 'and over certain foreign states, styling themselves the Confederate 'States of America, with intent to cruise and commit hostilities;' that is to say, the equipment of the ship or vessel with the two intents is libelled in the 5th count in precisely the same manner as it is libelled in the 1st, with an alteration in the manner of describing the foreign states in whose service or against whom the ship may be employed. I think, with the exception that there is a difference in the description of the foreign states, there are substantially only two counts against the owners in all these ninety-six counts. The 6th count is, 'did equip the said ship or vessel, with 'intent and in order that such ship or vessel should be employed 'in the service of divers and very many persons exercising the 'powers of government in and over certain foreign states, styling 'themselves the Confederate States of America, with intent to 'cruise and commit hostilities.' Two intents are again libelled. It is the same as the 1st and 2d counts, with a difference in the description of the foreign states. The 7th is, 'did equip the said 'ship or vessel, with intent and in order that such ship or vessel 'should be employed in the service of divers and very many 'persons exercising the powers of government over part of a 'certain foreign people, to wit, part of the people of the United 'States of America, with intent to cruise and commit hostilities.' The double intent is libelled in that charge, and it is the same as the first, with a difference only as regards the States in whose service the ship is to be employed, or against whom it is to be employed. The 8th count is framed upon the model of the 1st, and describes the offence as an equipment of 'the said ship or vessel, with intent 'and in order that such ship or vessel should be employed in the 'service of divers and very many persons exercising the powers of 'government over part of a certain foreign people, to wit, part of 'the people of the United States of America, with intent to cruise 'and commit hostilities,' &c.; the only difference, as compared with the 1st count being a difference in the description of the foreign states.

These are the whole of the first eight counts, which are the type and model of the next eighty-eight. The next eighty-eight counts are all the same as these, with trifling exceptions, which your Lordships will see set forth in the Abstract; as, for instance, the substitution of the word 'furnish' for 'equip,' the substitution of the word 'fit' for 'equip'; and whenever a new word is substituted, that causes eight variations to be played upon the tune. This is the short and easy form of pleading which is introduced for expediting the business in the Court of Exchequer. I think I may say, therefore, that there are two charges made against the defenders:—1st, there is the charge, of which the 1st count may be taken as an example, of the equipment of a vessel with the two intents—with the intent that it should be employed in the service of a foreign state—with intent to cruise and commit hostilities against another foreign state; and the 3d count gives the form of the other charge, viz., the equipment of the vessel, with intent to cruise and commit hostilities as against a foreign state, dropping in that charge the element contained in the first, of the employment of that vessel in the service of a foreign state. The equipment of the vessel with the two intents, is the first offence; and the equipment of the vessel with the one intent, is the second offence.

The next matter I notice is the 97th and 98th counts, which, though they will not figure very much in any subsequent proceedings that may be taken in this case, are nevertheless of importance to notice with reference to the argument which I shall immediately submit. The 97th count charges that the claimants 'did attempt 'to fit out the said ship or vessel, with intent and in order that 'such ship or vessel should be employed in the service of divers and 'very many persons exercising the powers of government over part 'of a certain foreign people, to wit, part of the people of the United

'States of America, as a transport or store-ship against a certain 'foreign state with which Her Majesty was not then, to wit, on the 'day and year aforesaid, at war, to wit, the Republic of the United 'States of America, contrary to the form of the Statute in such 'case made and provided, whereby, and by force of the Statute in 'that case made and provided, the said ship or vessel, together with 'the said tackle, apparel, and furniture, became and was forfeited.' The element is there brought in, for the first time, of the employment of the vessel as a transport or store-ship. The 98th count is, 'did equip, furnish, and fit out, and did attempt and endeavour to 'equip, furnish, and fit out, and did procure to be equipped, fur'nished, and fitted out, and did knowingly assist and be concerned 'in the equipping, furnishing, and fitting out of the said ship or 'vessel, with intent and in order that such ship or vessel should be 'employed in the service of certain foreign states, styling themselves 'the Confederate States of America,' &c., 'as a transport or store'ship, against, and with intent to cruise and commit hostilities,' &c. This is a variation on the 97th, but it is an important variation to notice with reference to the construction which you will be asked to put upon the Statute. It does not charge equipping merely, but it charges equipping, furnishing, and fitting out, attempting and endeavouring to equip, furnish, and fit out, and procuring to be equipped, furnished, and fitted out, and knowingly assisting and being concerned in equipping, furnishing, and fitting out. That is all charged in one charge, somewhat contrary to our notions of what would form a proper charge, because the same persons who are charged with actually fitting, furnishing, and equipping, are charged with attempting and endeavouring to do that, with procuring it to be done, and with assisting and being concerned in its being done. Then there is the charge of being employed in the service of a foreign state as a transport or store-ship, with the words, 'and with intent 'to cruise and commit hostilities,' inserted. That is the material difference between the 97th and 98th counts, that the store-ship is said to be employed with intent to cruise and commit hostilities. These are the material words in that charge.

And now, to go over the different charges again shortly :—The 1st is a charge of equipping a vessel with the intent that she shall be employed in a foreign state, with intent to cruise against another foreign state ; 2d, the equipping of a vessel with intent to cruise or commit hostilities against a foreign state ; 3d, the attempting to fit out a vessel as a store-ship, with intent that she shall be employed as a store-ship for a foreign state ; and 4th, the fitting out a vessel with intent that she shall be employed as a store-ship by a certain foreign state against and with intent to cruise against another foreign state. That is the substance of the different charges contained in the Information.

I shall now consider whether the 1st count is libelled in the statutory form so as to contain a statutory charge against the defenders, and I shall maintain that it does not, as stated, contain any statutory charge. The Act of Parliament is 59 Geo. III. cap. 69, and the preamble is, 'Whereas the enlistment or engagement of His

'Majesty's subjects to serve in war in foreign service, without His 'Majesty's licence, and the fitting out and equipping and arming of 'vessels by His Majesty's subjects without His Majesty's licence, for 'warlike operations in and against the dominions or territories of 'any foreign prince, state, potentate, or person exercising or assum-'ing to exercise the powers of government in or over any foreign 'country, colony, province, or part of any province, or against the 'ships, goods, or merchandise of any foreign prince, state, potentate, 'or persons as aforesaid, or their subjects, may be prejudicial to and 'tend to endanger the peace and welfare of this kingdom,' &c. It appears from the preamble that the mischief which the Statute was intended to prevent consisted in two things, 1st, the enlistment or engagement of His Majesty's subjects to serve in war in foreign service without His Majesty's licence; and 2d, the fitting out, equipping, and arming of vessels by His Majesty's subjects without His Majesty's licence, for warlike operations in or against the dominions or territories of any foreign prince. These are the things which it was intended to prevent, and I understand that the immediate cause for passing the Act was that a very perfervid Scotchman, who assumed the name of Sir Gregor M'Gregor, had fitted out and armed a fleet consisting of some vessels, with which he engaged in the service of the Spanish colonies in 1818, or about that time, against the mother country of Spain, with whom her colonies were then at war, or in a state of revolt. The purpose for which I refer to the preamble is to show that it is a Statute which, from the preamble, appears to be directed against His Majesty's subjects to prevent them from enlisting or taking service in a foreign state, and to prevent them from fitting out or arming ships for the purpose of engaging in war, or aiding in the hostilities of a foreign state. The 2d section deals with the first part of the preamble, viz., enlistment. It is directed against the enlistment of British subjects in foreign states without His Majesty's leave and licence.

Lord Ormidale.—We have nothing to do with that.

Mr. Clark.—Except so far as may be necessary for construction. The next part of the Statute to which I have to refer, and which deals with the case in hand, is the 7th section, the terms of which I must bring under your Lordship's notice.

Lord Ormidale.—That is the clause on which the Information is laid.

Mr. Clark.—Yes.—(*Reads 7th section.*)—These are the words enacting the offence, and the question comes to be what is the offence, or what are the offences, enacted by the Statute, and which the Crown, or any person suing under the Statute, may competently libel against any individual? Now, getting rid of some of the numerous alternatives which occur in this Statute, and which to a great extent prevent the ease of reading it, let me read the first part of it again:—'That if any person within any part of the 'United Kingdom shall, without the leave and license of his 'Majesty for that purpose first had and obtained as aforesaid, equip 'any ship or vessel with intent or in order that such ship or vessel 'shall be employed in the service of any foreign prince as a trans-

'port or store-ship, or with intent to cruise or commit hostilities 'against any prince, state, or potentate with whom his Majesty 'shall not be then at war.' I have taken the word 'equip' as the word which expresses the act, and I have thrown out the different alternatives, which I think to some extent obscure the sense. Now, it seems to me that in that part of the Statute which I have just read there are two distinct offences and not one—two distinct acts, each creative of an offence, and a separate offence, and not creative of one; for there is, in the first place, the equipping of any ship or vessel with intent that such ship shall be employed in the service of any foreign prince as a transport or store-ship, and secondly, there is the offence of equipping any ship or vessel with intent to cruise or commit hostilities against any prince, state, or potentate. I think these two offences are quite distinct, and I object to any Information which is laid against me upon the ground of endeavouring to combine these two offences. I may mention that this was a point which was taken at the trial of the 'Alexandra' in the opening of the case, but it did not come to be much considered by any of the Judges in giving their opinions when the case came to be argued on the motion for a new trial in Exchequer, because the argument there turned almost entirely on what was the meaning of the words 'equip, furnish, and fit out,' in the sense of the Statute,—whether it was an armed fitting out or equipping, or whether something short of actual arming would be sufficient to constitute the statutory offence. And therefore this, though not raised for consideration for the first time in this case, at all events comes up for the first time for judicial consideration. It was mentioned in the Alexandra case in this way, that if it was a well-founded objection, the objection would be reserved,—would indeed reserve itself, and in the event of the jury finding for the Crown, the defendants would then move in arrest of judgment. Whether that is a course which is open to us in this Court or not I cannot say, but at all events it is competent for us to state this objection now, and it is one on which I greatly rely, because I think the Crown, in laying this Information, have attempted to create a new offence which is not under the Statute at all.

Lord Ormidale.—Where do they combine the two?

Mr. Clark.—Take the first count: 'did equip the said ship or 'vessel with intent and in order that such ship or vessel,' &c. (*reads.*)

Lord Ormidale.—That is one charge.

Mr. Clark.—No; there are two intents, with intent that the vessel should be employed, &c., and with intent to cruise. Then look at the third charge,—and I don't say that the third charge is not, at all events as regards this matter, quite well charged under the Statute; it is 'did equip the said ship or vessel with intent to 'cruise and commit hostilities against a certain foreign state.' That is keeping it quite separate and distinct, and that is, as I contend, a perfectly good libelling of the statutory charge second mentioned in the Statute. So far as I can judge, this is a somewhat plain matter depending upon the construction of this section of the

Statute. Your Lordship, in construing this Statute, will keep in view what I referred to at the outset, that it is a Statute directed against things done by British subjects, and not by persons in foreign states at all; it is intended to be directed against certain unlawful acts on the part of British subjects, or persons in the United Kingdom,—against their enlisting in foreign service, or fitting out or equipping vessels of war, or vessels for the purpose of cruising and committing hostilities against foreign powers. It may be said no doubt that the Statute, to some extent in its enacting part, went beyond the preamble; for the preamble does not in any respect, so far as I see, refer to transport or store-ships, but the use of a transport or store-ship for the purposes of war, and of course a transport or storeship intended for the purposes of war, is a thing which is fairly within the matter mentioned in the preamble, and therefore the Legislature enacted that it should be unlawful to equip any vessel with intent or in order that such ship should be employed, and, as I read the words of the Statute, employed by the equipper, in the service of any foreign prince, as a transport or store-ship. That is the meaning of the Statute; that it is an illegal act on the part of any person within the United Kingdom to equip a ship which shall be employed by him in the service of any foreign prince, state, or potentate, or in any foreign colony. I need not say that the employment must be by him, and that the intent to employ must be an intent by him, because it was quite conceded in all the discussions which took place at the Bar and on the Bench in the Alexandra case, that notwithstanding the Enlistment Act, it is a perfectly lawful thing for a person to arm and build a vessel of war, and send it to a foreign port, being the port of a belligerent power, and to sell that ship there as an armed ship. That has been decided over and over again. It was admitted, I think, in the course of the discussion in the Alexandra case by the Attorney-General, and it was assumed as good law on the Bench. The cases in which it was decided were American cases, but they were adopted as being good law, having reference to the American Statute, which is much the same as this, and there were two cases in which that point was separately decided, one of these being the *Santissima Trinidada*, 7 *Wheaton's American Reports*, p. 283; and the passage in the judgment of Justice Story, which is important in this matter, is at p. 340: 'The sending of armed vessels or of munitions of war'—(*reads to*)—' by the other belligerent.'

Lord Ormidale.—Any contraband of war is subject to that.

Mr. Clark.—Any contraband of war is subject to capture—from the neutral port to the belligerent port. This judgment was pronounced in 1822, and at that time the Act of Congress of 1794, which was repeated in 1818, was then in force. The case, shortly stated, is this, that a vessel was fitted out at Baltimore, in the United States, which were then at peace with Spain, and was sent to Buenos Ayres, and put into the hands of certain persons assuming to be citizens of the United Provinces of Rio de la Plata; at all events, it was sent to a port then in the hands of a belligerent power with whom the United States were at peace, and the question came to be whether that ship was carrying on war legally, and whether the prizes which she took in the course of that war were capable of being condemned, and it was maintained that she was an illegal vessel, and not a vessel entitled to come within the laws of war, and to make lawful prizes, in respect she had been fitted out and armed contrary to the Act of Congress which regulates this matter. Mr. Justice Story disposes of that question in these words:—'The 'question as to the original illegal armament and outfit of the '"Independencia" may be dismissed in a few words. It is ap'parent, that though equipped as a vessel of war, she was sent to 'Buenos Ayres on a commercial adventure, contraband, indeed, but 'in no shape violating our laws or our national neutrality. If cap'tured by a Spanish ship of war during the voyage she would have 'been justly condemned as a good prize, and for being engaged in a 'traffic prohibited by the law of nations. But there is nothing in 'our laws, or in the law of nations, that forbids our citizens from 'sending armed vessels, as well as munitions of war, to foreign 'ports for sale. It is a commercial adventure which no nation is 'bound to prohibit, and which only exposes the persons engaged 'in it to the penalty of confiscation. Supposing, therefore, the 'voyage to have been for commercial purposes, and the sale at 'Buenos Ayres to have been a *bona fide* sale (and there is nothing 'in the evidence to contradict it), there is no pretence to say that 'the original outfit on the voyage was illegal, or that a capture 'made after the sale was for that cause alone invalid.'

Lord Ormidale.—Everything turned on the intent.

Mr. Clark.—No doubt; but the fact which there occurred was, that a citizen of the United States of America who had fitted out the 'Independencia,' had fitted her out as an armed vessel for the purpose of selling her to a belligerent power, with which belligerent power the United States were then at peace. He therefore had the intent, in the first place, of arming her, which he carried out, and of giving her over to a foreign power for the purpose of being employed, of course, by that foreign power in the committal of hostilities against a power with which that belligerent power was at war, and the question came to be, whether that was struck at by the Act of Congress, and the Court unanimously held that it was not so,—that subject to the chances of confiscation in the course of the voyage, it is quite a lawful act to fit out a ship of war, and sell it to a belligerent power.

Lord Ormidale.—Would they hold that now, do you think?

Mr. Clark.—I think the Judges would, whatever the people might say. Indeed it was decided in another case, where other points were raised,—the case of the *United States* v. *Quincy*, 6 *Peters' Reports*, p. 445.

Lord Ormidale.—Is the Act of Congress under which these cases were determined precisely the same as the Act of Parliament here?

Mr. Clark.—No, it is rather more strict. The case is stated on p. 62 of the Appendix to the Report of the 'Alexandra' case, and the Act is quoted at p. 22 of the Appendix. It is the Act of 1818, but it was merely a repetition of that of 1794. Section 3 is the section which is similar to that on which our case turns. It is, 'That if any persons shall, within the limits of the United States, 'fit out and arm, or attempt to fit out and arm, or procure to be 'fitted out and armed, or shall knowingly be concerned in the fur-'nishing, fitting out, or arming of any ship or vessel, with intent 'that such ship or vessel shall be employed in the service of any 'foreign prince or state, or of any colony, district, or people, to 'cruise or commit hostilities against the subjects, citizens, or pro-'perty of any foreign prince or state, &c., or shall issue or deliver 'a commission within the territory or jurisdiction of the United 'States, for any ship or vessel to the intent that she may be em-'ployed as aforesaid, every person so offending shall be deemed 'guilty of a high misdemeanour, and shall be fined not more than 'ten thousand dollars.' These words are almost the same as the words in our Statute, with the exception that the words, 'as a transport 'or store-ship' don't occur. Therefore there are in this American Statute only two offences, viz., the fitting out of a ship with intent to cruise or commit hostilities, and the issuing or delivering a commission for any ship or vessel, to the intent that she may be employed as aforesaid, *i.e.*, to cruise. On this matter I am entitled to refer to the case of the Alexandra for the opinion of the Judges that the construction of that Statute was correct, and therefore that the same construction is to be put on the Foreign Enlistment Act. It was held that the fitting out and arming of a ship of war in a port of the United States, and selling her to a belligerent power, in a port of that belligerent power, was not an offence against the Statute. Now, your Lordship will observe, that in fitting her out, and carrying her to that port of the belligerent power, it was impossible but that in a certain sense the person so fitting out the ship had the intent that that ship should be employed as a ship of war.

Lord Ormidale.—He might or might not.

Mr. Clark.—It was at all events a question for the Jury whether that intent existed; but the Court said, That cannot be a question for the Jury, because it is a perfectly lawful thing in any of our citizens to fit out a ship of war, and take it and sell it to a belligerent power, and he is subject only to the risk of the ship being captured in the course of the transit between the neutral port and the belligerent port.

Lord Ormidale.—But supposing there was an antecedent contract under which all that was done?

Mr. Clark.—I don't think that would in the least degree vary that matter. I am perfectly entitled to construct a ship for the purpose of selling it to a foreign power, in order that it may be employed by that foreign power as a ship of war. I am not within the Statute if I do so. I don't think that the mere existence of a contract by which I contract to build a ship for that foreign power will in the least degree vary it, and for this reason that I think the Statute means that the employment of the ship shall not be an employment by a foreign power, but an employment by the person who equips the ship. The preamble shows that the Statute was intended to prevent British subjects, wherever they were, from enlisting in the service of a foreign power then at war. The Crown has a personal jurisdiction over all its subjects, and the enactment was, that any British subject who should enlist or take foreign service in a state at war, was committing a breach of this Act, which the Legislature of this country thought fit to pass. It also thought proper to prevent any persons in the United Kingdom fitting out or arming vessels of war, with the intent that they should employ them in the service of a foreign state. The cause of that Act was the famous Sir Gregor M'Gregor. He fitted out ships of war for the purpose of himself employing them in carrying on hostilities against a country with which this country was at peace, and it was to prevent that mischief, as the preamble of the Statute itself says, that the Statute was passed, and therefore we read the 7th section in the light of the preamble, and with the light thrown upon it by the construction of the American Act, sanctioned by the Court in the Alexandra case. The reason, I think, why the acts referred to in the two cases I have quoted were not contraventions of the Act of Congress, was simply this, that there was and could be no allegation, that the intent to employ the vessel was an intent to employ it by the equipper, but it must have been merely this, that she should be sold to the foreign power, with the intent that the foreign power might themselves employ her. Now, let me again look at the 1st count in connexion with the Statute. The words of the count are, 'did equip the said ship or vessel, with intent and 'in order that such ship or vessel should be employed in the service of certain foreign states styling themselves the Confederate 'States of America, with intent to cruise,' &c. Whose intent is that? No doubt it may be said that these are the statutory words, and that in using the statutory words it must be held that the statutory intent is libelled; but what I object to is that the statutory words are not used, and that your Lordship, in considering this Information, would naturally hold that there is a totally different intent libelled than the intent which alone the Statute recognises as sufficient to create the statutory offence. In the Information the intent is that such foreign ship should be employed in the service of certain foreign states with intent to cruise, *i.e.*, with the intent upon the part, as I would read it, of the foreign states to cruise and commit hostilities. At all events, it does not in any respect connect the intent to cruise with the persons who equipped the vessel, as the Statute directs that that intent shall be connected. Now let us see what are the statutory offences. I think they are these:—to equip any ship or vessel, with intent that such ship shall be employed in the service of any foreign state as a transport or store-ship. There is an end of that offence; that is one intent—an intent to employ her in the service of a foreign power as a transport or store-ship. Of course, in connection with the words, 'as a transport or troop 'ship,' I read, 'against a foreign state with which this country is 'at peace.' But the intent, and the only intent which constitutes the offence, of employing the vessel in the service of a foreign power, is an intent that she shall be employed as a transport or store-ship. The offence consists in the employment in the service of a foreign prince, but the only intent and employment which will create the statutory offence is an employment as a transport or store-ship against another power, because you instantly come to another part of the Statute, which creates a different crime by reason of expressing a different intent, and I therefore read the Statute thus: I read, 'to equip any ship or vessel with intent, or in order that 'such vessel shall be employed in the service of any foreign prince 'as a transport or store-ship,' as meaning one offence, and the equipping of any vessel, with intent to cruise or commit hostilities, against any prince with whom this country is at peace, as a different offence altogether, not connected with the other.

Lord Ormidale.—Then you read it that you may arm a store-ship or transport to be employed in the service of a foreign power?

Mr. Clark.—Surely, as a transport or store-ship. I have an observation to make on that, but taking that construction of the Statute, I have no objection that they should so charge.

Lord Ormidale.—In the ordinary case a transport or store-ship is not armed.

Mr. Clark.—It may be. Generally it is armed.

Lord Ormidale.—That gives rise to another suggestion. You may be right or not in regard to a transport or store-ship being armed, but that may be matter for inquiry, and the construction you are now contending for may depend on evidence in some degree.

Mr. Clark.—As I read the Statute, the one offence consists in equipping the ship with a view to a certain employment, and the other in equipping the ship with intent to use it as a cruiser. These are the two things. The Statute was intended to prevent persons in this country from engaging in the service of foreign states, either by helping them in actual warfare, by enlistment or otherwise, or by becoming the carriers of ammunition, &c., or becoming their allies as cruisers. You shan't enlist, you shan't enter their employment for the purpose of transporting the ammunition and provisions necessary for their campaign, and you shan't become their allies for the purpose of privateering. Sir Gregor M'Gregor was their ally as a cruiser; he fitted out ships for the purpose of cruising and becoming a privateer, not necessarily in the service of a foreign state, but on his own account probably, so that he might make a fortune as a privateer. But the Act of Parliament is intended to prevent any citizen of the State or any person over whom it has jurisdiction, acting in any respect in a hostile way to a foreign power, and to prevent the ports of this country from being used for the purpose of fitting out vessels to be used in that way against a foreign power. There are, therefore, I think, plainly these two offences: you shall not fit out a ship to be employed by you in the service of a foreign power as a transport or store-ship, nor shall you fit out a ship with intent to use it as a cruiser. The Crown just slip out these words 'as a transport or store-ship' altogether, and add on the second, 'with intent' to the previous words 'with in-

'tent.' There are two intents against which the Statute strikes, both the intent of the equipper—the first is an intent to employ the ship as a transport, and the second an intent to employ the ship as a cruiser. The Information, on the other hand, has two intents; the one may be the intent of the equipper of the ship to use her in the employment of a foreign state, but the other is necessarily the intent of the foreign power with whom that ship is placed, 'with intent to cruise and commit hostilities,' or of anybody else; at all events, it is not in any respect the intent of the person who equips the ship. Now, if a Statute is so framed that one act coupled with a certain intent is a crime, and the same act coupled with another intent is also a crime, is it an ordinary construction of such a Statute to say that you will combine, or try to combine, these two intents and purposes so as to make one new crime? It seems to me that this 1st count under the Information is a perfect monster, not in any respect authorized by the Statute, but an attempt to combine the two crimes under the Statute, by leaving out a portion of the first crime, and putting in the other intent. The 97th count is a very good illustration of the way in which they purpose to send this Information to trial—(*Reads it*). That is the actual charge which I think the Statute permits; that is a perfectly good charge of employing the ship as a transport or store-ship against a foreign state. The 1st count does not in any respect charge the proper statutory offence, and therefore what I have to submit to your Lordship on that 1st count is, that it in no respect charges any statutory offence, and that your Lordship is now entitled to hold that no statutory offence has been stated; and therefore that the 1st count, and all the other counts which are like unto it, shall be dismissed as irrelevant under the Statute.

There is another point to which I have to direct attention, and it has reference to what your Lordship said as to the use of the word 'arm.' The preamble of the Act refers to fitting out 'and' arming, not 'or' arming. At the same time, in the enacting clause, you have the transport or store-ship, which is not necessarily an unarmed vessel; and one consideration is this, that there are two offences as I submit,—the employment of the transport or store-ship, and the employment of the ship as a cruiser. The words 'equip,' 'furnish,' 'fit out,' are the words which apply to the transport or store-ship, and the word 'arm' is the word which applies to the cruiser. I don't say that the Statute is by any means a specimen of legislation. You take the transport-ship as being perhaps a word introduced here in contradistinction to a ship of war or cruiser—as being a ship not intended to be in itself a means of offence, but as offensive and within the scope of the Act, in respect that it gives material aid to a belligerent power by having its materials carried by transport-ships or store-ships fitted out and employed by persons in this country. You have the word 'arm,' which does not in any respect naturally refer to a vessel which is to be employed as a transport or storeship. On the other hand, you have the words equip, furnish, and fit out, which, if read as excluding arming, don't naturally connect themselves with a ship which is built with intent to cruise, because a ship with intent to cruise, however well equipped, furnished, or fitted out, if not armed, is not very much worth for that purpose; and therefore, if you read the words as the Crown contend that they shall be read, as exclusive of arming (because they have not ventured to insert in this Information any count charging arming), the natural construction of the Statute I think is this, that if any person shall equip, furnish, or fit out any ship or vessel with intent, and in order that it shall be employed in the service of any foreign prince as a transport or store-ship against any foreign state,—there is the one offence; or, if any person shall arm any ship or vessel with intent to cruise or commit hostilities against any prince, there is the other offence; in short, upon the principle of *reddendo singula singulis*, you refer the words, 'furnish, equip, and fit out,' to the transport-ship with which they naturally connect themselves, if they do not include arming, and you refer 'arming' to the other vessel, which is an armed vessel intended to commit hostilities. Therefore, what I submit to your Lordship on this matter is, that this Information, so far as it does not charge arming, is not an Information within the Statute, except, of course, so far as regards the 97th count, in which the words, 'employed as a transport-ship,' are inserted. Therefore, I have to submit that the only way of charging any offence under this Statute which does not involve a charge of arming the ship, is to charge the employment of the vessel as a transport-ship, and as that has not been done, and as arming has not been charged, there is no relevant charge under the Information at all, except perhaps the 97th. These are the two objections which, I think, plainly arise upon the Information as it stands.

Lord Ormidale.—Did that last point not arise in the Alexandra case?

Mr. Clark.—It was stated in the Alexandra case at the opening, as a question which would arise in the event of a verdict being returned for the Crown.

Lord Ormidale.—Was it not one of the great points in the application for a new trial?

Mr. Clark.—No; the defendants had got a verdict, and therefore there could be no motion by them in arrest of judgment, because there was no verdict against them. It was a motion for a new trial with reference to evidence which had been led, and the direction. The direction upon which the discussion almost entirely turned was this, that equipment in the sense of the Statute meant warlike equipment—complete equipment—for the purpose of war.

Lord Ormidale.—But would it not have been a complete answer to the whole argument for a new trial, that no armament had been proved, and that they had no case in any view?

Mr. Clark.—They would not allow the party merely answering the motion for a new trial, to found on anything except the mere question of what was the direction of the Judge.

Lord Ormidale.—Perhaps you are right there; but according to my recollection of what I read in the newspapers at the time, a good deal of the argument in the Court of Exchequer touched the passage you are now at.

Mr. Clark.—Sir Hugh Cairns just touched the points on which I have been commenting in a very few sentences, and then the Lord Chief Baron says (foot of p. 143),—'I think the proper course 'would be,' &c.—(*reads*)—that is to say, supposing the Jury to affirm these counts, it is open for the defendants who have had a verdict against them to say,—These counts are not within the Statute at all, and, therefore, there must be an arrest of judgment.

Lord Ormidale.—It is not the discussion at the trial I allude to, but the discussion in the Court of Exchequer on the motion for a new trial. You may be quite right that that did not properly come into discussion there, because the defendants had a verdict; but I think the Judges all adverted very much to the point in regard to the word 'arm.'

Mr. Clark.—Yes, because the point they really had to consider on the motion for a new trial was whether equipment was in the sense of the Statute a warlike equipment, that is, an equipment of such a kind that when completed it would enable the ship to be used as a means of offence. The Crown held that equipment, fitting out, or furnishing, was something short of arming, and that, therefore, the offence might be committed, though there was no arming. On the other hand, with reference to the two matters which were alone before the Court,—the direction of the Chief Baron, and the evidence,—Sir Hugh Cairns and the defendants maintained, that unless the equipment came up to arming,—to such an equipment that when equipped the ship could be used for warlike purposes, so that it could cruise and commit hostilities, there was not equipment in the sense of the Statute, and that, on the evidence as it stood, taking the direction of the Chief Baron as right, no new trial could be granted, because the Chief Baron had simply held that the equipment meant a warlike equipment, and there was no evidence to show that the Jury were wrong in holding that there was no warlike equipment. These were the only two questions raised, and they were raised without any reference to the counts, but with reference simply to the direction which the Judge gave as to the meaning of the Statute, and the evidence which had been taken at the trial.

Lord Ormidale.—My impression is that all or some of the Barons held that it was not necessary to charge that the ship was actually armed.

Mr. Clark.—Yes; two of them held that.

Lord Ormidale.—Did they not all go to that extent?

Mr. Clark.—Here is the judgment shortly stated: 'Held by 'Pollock, C. B., and Bramwell, B., that the equipment meant is 'such an equipment as will enable her to cruise and commit hosti'lities.' That is what we contend for. I don't think there can be the least doubt that the Chief Baron and Baron Bramwell meant an armed equipment capable of enabling her to be used as an instrument of offence; whereas Baron Channel held that any equipment is illegal which will be of use to her when cruising. I read from the *Weekly Reporter*.

Now I have stated the two points which I think the leading points in this question—1st, whether the combination of the charges was a statutory offence at all; and 2d, whether it was competent under this Statute to charge as an offence equipment with a view to commit hostilities without the word 'arm.' That goes to the whole counts in this Information except the 97th and 98th. Now these are questions which are raised, I think, on the face of this Information, and being so raised, they are susceptible of immediate judgment by your Lordship. My objection is an objection to the relevancy of the indictment, as we would say in Scotland, and your Lordship does not require information or inquiry to enable you to dispose of such an objection. The question whether two intents can be combined so as to make one offence is a question arising upon comparison between the Statute and the Information; and so I think also with reference to the other.

There is a third point which I shall only notice very shortly, because I am sensible that, with reference to it, the observation that inquiry may be better had before any decision upon it is come to, has more force than as regards the other two. Your Lordship will observe that throughout this Information the Statute is split up into parts, so that the word 'equip,' for instance, occurs in one set of charges, the words 'fit out' in another set, the word 'furnish' in a third, and the word 'arm' never occurs throughout the Information. Now that is an Information which is prepared, not according to our usages, nor according to the style in which I think an indictment would be drawn, supposing the Lord Advocate had chosen to proceed by indictment under this Statute. Suppose, for instance, that any of the gentlemen for whom I appear had been indicted in the Justiciary Court for committing the offence under the Statute, it appears to me that the indictment would have read in this manner,—'That you, the said so and so, are guilty of the said crime of contravention of the said Statute, actor or art and part, in so far as upon a certain day, you did, at Glasgow, equip, fit out, furnish, and arm a ship called the "Pampero," with intent that she should be used by you in the employment of a foreign state, as a transport-ship, as against another foreign state.' That is one form in which the indictment might charge the offence. 'Or otherwise' (it would then proceed), 'in so far as, time and place above libelled, you did equip, fit out, furnish, and arm the said ship called the "Pampero," with intent to cruise and commit hostilities against a foreign state, viz., the United States of America.' I think that would be the indictment, closing with the usual words, 'all which, or part thereof, being proven, you shall be sentenced to such and such a penalty.' Your Lordship will see, therefore, that if you are to follow that procedure, which is the procedure usual in our Criminal Courts, you have the whole words charged in the indictment,—I don't say charged in the indictment so that it shall necessarily be incumbent on the prosecutor to prove all of these words, because he takes refuge under the alternative with which his indictment closes, 'all 'which or part thereof;' but it will be incumbent on him to prove under that indictment what in the opinion of the Court will amount to a contravention of the Statute on which the indictment is laid, and the importance of that style is this, that you have all the words inserted in the indictment so that you read the one as in the light of the other, and so that you may say that 'arm' is merely exegetical of equip, fit out, and furnish, that is, that it must be an armed equipment, fitting out, or furnishing, and that equipment, fitting out, or furnishing, is not in any respect different from arming. It may be more or less complete. Arming may mean something more in the sense of completeness for the commission of hostilities, than equipment, fitting, or furnishing, but still equipment, furnishing, and fitting out must all mean, in the sense of the Statute, and in the sense of that indictment, as we contend, an armed fitting out, an armed equipment, and an armed furnishing. But then the Crown here have broken up this Information into these monstrous ninety-six charges, and they have taken the word 'equip,' so that it shall not be read in these different charges alongside of the other words with which it occurs in the Statute, and we may therefore be deprived of that aid which we should have in reading the word 'equip,' in consequence of the omission of the other words with which it is associated in the Statute, and which we say mean substantially the same thing. I don't say that we will be deprived of it, if it is clearly understood that we shall be able to raise that question to your Lordship, and if your interlocutor reserves all these questions to be raised at the trial, but if we proceed to trial under this Information as it stands, and having regard to the fact that this is a Scotch Court, regulated to a certain extent by Scotch procedure, it may be held that your Lordship would be bound to direct the Jury what is the meaning of the word 'equip' in the Information as it stands, segregated and separated from the word 'arm,' which does not occur in the Information, but which stands alongside of the word 'equip' in the Statute, as explaining its meaning.

Lord Ormidale.—In order to that, all the words in the Statute might be fairly enough and necessarily looked at.

Mr. Clark.—That is what I am not quite sure of. In the Court of Exchequer Act, which regulates the procedure here, Schedule B. is referred to as the style which the Legislature has laid down. We have got an Information of Seizure, Article 8, p. 133. 'I, the 'Right Hon. A. B., Her Majesty's Advocate, inform the Court, &c., '1st count, that the said malt was fraudulently deposited, concealed, 'or conveyed away from the sight of the officers of excise, contrary 'to the Statute, &c., whereby the said malt became forfeited.' That is just the kind of indictment which I was imagining might be prepared if it was charged under an indictment. And the 40th section of the Statute on which that Information is supposed to be laid is this,—'Be it farther enacted, that if any maltster or maker of 'malt, or other person, shall fraudulently deposit, conceal, or con'vey away from the sight of the officers of excise any malt or corn, 'or grain making into malt, every maltster, &c., so offending, shall, 'for every such offence, forfeit and lose the sum of £200.' They don't break this up into three different charges, charging a fraudulent deposit, a fraudulent concealment, and a fraudulent conveying away, which would be the form if this English style of Information were adopted. If the Information in England were drawn under this Statute, there would be three counts in the Information at least, and probably a good many more; there would be first a 'maltster,' then a 'maker of malt,' and then 'or other person' would likely be put in, so that twenty-four counts would be about the thing. But what I think we might be prejudiced by is this, 1st, this Information is not charged in the ordinary way directed by the Statute.

Lord Ormidale.—But it is not specially directed by the Statute.

Mr. Clark.—I think it is.

Lord Ormidale.—Then your point is, that it is directed by the Statute in this case, and that it is not in conformity.

Mr. Clark.—The 7th Section of the Exchequer Act is, 'Every 'information to be lodged in terms of this Act shall be in the form, 'as nearly as may be, of the Schedule B. hereunto annexed.' I am not making the point that it is incompetent necessarily to take any one of these words. Equipment, in the sense of the Statute, with the intents libelled, may, I think, constitute the statutory offence without putting in the other things, but I am raising this more for precaution than otherwise, for the purpose of showing that we are entitled to have this guarded, that the meaning of the word equipment must not be equipment as it appears in the Information, separated from the rest of the words which occur in the Statute, but that equipment must be read in the light of the Statute, so that the Jury shall be directed by your Lordship that the equipment they are to find proved, must mean equipment in the sense of the Statute, which may be an armed equipment, if your Lordship thinks that the only equipment meant in the Statute is an armed equipment.

Lord Ormidale.—I suppose it will not be contested on the other side, that in order to construe and arrive at the proper and true meaning of the word equipment in the counts here, the whole Statute must be looked at.

Mr. Clark.—I don't know. That is a matter which we think must be guarded, though when I mentioned this point I said that it did not so imperatively call for decision in the meantime.

Lord Ormidale.—I could hardly by any interlocutor, I should think, that could be supported by any precedent, in any Court, say what may or may not be looked at in the argument upon what the Statute means.

Mr. Clark.—It is not in any degree to specify what may be looked at, but it is to reserve for future discussion all questions of that kind which may be raised.

Lord Ormidale.—That is unprecedented also, according to my view of it. It is unprecedented to reserve all kinds of imaginary questions that may or may not be raised.

Mr. Clark.—I have stated all those questions which I think can be usefully discussed now, and without going into farther detail upon that last matter, I stand upon the construction of the Statute which I have said I maintain, not by reference to any foreign law, or even to the history of the Statute, which I don't think it is proper, at all events at this stage, to refer to, though it may be very important, and I think it is fair, to refer to that in ascertaining the meaning of 'equipment;' but I refer to the Statute for the purpose, not of showing what is the meaning of equipment there, but of ascertaining, as far as I can, what are the statutory offences.

I had forgot to notice the 98th count, which I think is very objectionable. It brings out the objection as to the 1st very prominently indeed. If the 1st is a monster, this is still more so. They charge—'did equip, furnish, and fit out;' then they charge—'did 'attempt to endeavour to equip, furnish, and fit out;' then they charge—'did procure to be equipped, furnished, and fitted out;' and then they charge—'did knowingly assist and be concerned in 'the equipping, furnishing, and fitting out.' I rather think it 'should be 'aid' and assist, because wherever the word 'knowingly' occurs in the Information, 'aid' is always put in before 'assist.' Now there are these four things which I think are altogether inconsistent. They are not the same charge, and they are all charges against the same persons. I think they are inconsistent charges in themselves, and cannot be cumulatively charged in one count as against the same party; they could not be so in an indictment; they would form alternative charges under the indictment, but they are here charged cumulatively. However, that is not the most important objection to this 98th count, for after stating all these things they say, 'with intent and in order that such ship 'or vessel should be employed in the service of certain foreign 'states, as a transport or store-ship, against and with intent to cruise 'and commit hostilities against,' &c. So that your Lordship has here charged, 1st, being employed in the service; 2d, as a transport or store-ship; and 3d, with intent to cruise and commit hostilities. What is the warrant for that in the Statute? The 97th count charges quite rightly the equipment of this vessel to be employed as a transport-ship in the service of the Confederate States against the United States, but here you have a charge of the employment of the ship in the service of the Confederate States as a transport-ship with intent to cruise. Now I think that the intent to cruise and the employment of the ship as a transport-ship are quite distinct and separate charges, and that this only brings out more clearly the misconception of the Statute upon which this Information has been framed; and therefore I submit to your Lordship that the 1st objection should be sustained, which would dispose of 72 charges. There are 72 charges which, if this objection is right, would be disposed of, and then your Lordship, if we went to trial, would have this great advantage—and I fervently trust your Lordship will give us the advantage—of having the Information limited to 26 counts. If your Lordship sustains the 2d objection, you dispose thereby at one swoop of 96 counts, leaving the 97th and 98th charging about the transport-ship. I would not object to go to trial on the 97th, but I think the 98th is a bad one. I think the 97th is the only good one, which charges the fitting out of this vessel with intent that she should be employed in the service of the Confederates, as a transport or store-ship against the Federals.

Lord Ormidale.—I suppose you don't seriously ask me to sustain the 1st and 2d objections, in respect that we will thereby get rid of 96 counts?

Mr. Clark.—I think it is a relevant argument, but I would not like to plead that.

Lord Ormidale.—What plea have you on which you raise this argument?

Mr. Clark.—I think it is the second. The first is a plea of not guilty; the second is that the counts are all and each of them bad in law.

Lord Ormidale.—Did you ever see such a plea in this Court?

Mr. Clark.—Oh, yes! in the Court of Exchequer.

Lord Ormidale.—I thought they were always in the shape of demurrers where it was intended to object to the case going to trial.

Mr. Clark.—The first plea is that there has been no forfeiture, and I think that is quite sufficient to raise it, because there is no forfeiture if the counts are not well laid under the Statute. All the counts conclude with this, 'whereby and by force of the Statute 'in that case made and provided, the said ship, &c., was forfeited.' That is what I deny, or, to use the English expression, demur to. We may amend our plea to the effect of stating that the counts are irrelevant, but it does not seem to me that that is different from saying that they are bad in law, *i.e.*, assume the facts of the case as stated, the legal consequence of forfeiture does not follow.

Lord Ormidale.—You say that the being employed in foreign service is only applicable to the transport or store-ship; but supposing that were so, how is it inconsistent with its being a war vessel? Suppose a vessel of war armed and equipped for hostilities, with the intent, in terms of the Statute, to cruise or make hostilities against one of the belligerents with whom this country is at peace, then must she not, in committing these hostilities, be in one and in not an unnatural sense of the Statute, in the service of the belligerent power for whom she is acting?

Mr. Clark.—Not necessarily, and that is not said by the Statute.

Lord Ormidale.—I don't mean so as to form a part of the navy of that belligerent power; but if she is really acting for and assisting that belligerent power by committing hostilities against the other power, is she not truly acting in the service of that power in a not unnatural and unfair sense of the Statute?

Mr. Clark.—The objection is an objection to the mode of libelling these charges, and in order to ascertain whether or not the different counts of the Information are well libelled, you must see in what language the Statute itself charges the offence, because in order to libel the statutory charge well under the Statute, you must use in the Information or Indictment the language in which the Statute expresses the offence. You are not entitled to use other language than the language the Statute uses, whether it is equivalent to it or not. You are bound, if you found upon a Statute, to charge the offence in the words by which the Statute creates the offence. There are two offences, as I submit, and two only, viz., the fitting out a transport-ship, and the fitting out a ship to commit hostilities. If you are going to charge me with fitting out a transport-ship, then you must use the words, 'equip a ship with 'intent that it shall be employed as a transport-ship against a 'foreign state.' If you resort to the other offence, it is 'equip a 'ship,' not with the first intent mentioned in the Statute, which is the intent of employing the ship as a transport-ship, but with the second intent mentioned in the Statute, viz., 'with intent to com-'mit hostilities.' The one alternates with the other. But when you come to try to join on the two intents in the Information, as, for instance, in the first count, you create a perfectly different meaning in the Information than that which occurs in the Statute, because under the Statute each of these intents is the intent of the equipper; whereas under the Information, the first intent may be said to be the intent of the equipper, but the second intent is the intent of the person or state in whose service she may be employed.

Lord Ormidale.—Then I am driven to this, according to your argument—I must hold that the 'with intent and in order that 'such ship or vessel should be employed as a transport or store-'ship, and with intent,' must also apply to the latter part of the clause. I must either do that, or hold your plea to be well-founded.

Mr. Clark.—My argument is this, that there are only two charges, putting out the alternative words, which can be charged under this part of the Statute. The first is, that you did equip a ship or vessel, with intent that the same should be employed in the service of a foreign power as a transport ship against another foreign power. That is the 97th count, and that is well libelled. The other is, that you did equip a ship, with intent to cruise or commit hostilities against a foreign power, but you cannot charge well under this Statute any offence which combines, or attempts to combine, these two things.

Mr. Shand.—I attend your Lordship on behalf of the Builders of this vessel, who are resisting this forfeiture, and have lodged in process a claim, the effect of which is to resist the application of the Lord Advocate; and I have only a very few observations to make in addition to those of my friend Mr. Clark, for I adopt the argument which he has submitted. But I desire that your Lordship should clearly apprehend at the outset, that the effect of these objections, if they are well founded, necessarily is to dispose finally of a number of these counts without the slightest necessity for inquiry. Your Lordship is just in as favourable a position for finally disposing of these counts now, as you could possibly be after the longest trial of the facts, for our contention in law amounts to this, that although the Crown were to hold that they had proved every word of what they averred in point of fact in these counts, —though we were to put in a minute now admitting that the facts as there alleged are true, we are in a position to say that the legal effect of forfeiture does not follow. If that be so, your Lordship sees how plainly this is raised as a question of relevancy, which it will be an advantage to have disposed of now, for though the case may go to trial on one or two of these counts, if it should be ultimately held that one or two of them are relevant, that is no reason why we should be taken before a Jury on 96 counts which, on the face of them, are irrelevant. Our plea is, that these different counts are bad in law. Is not that just the plea which is stated in a criminal case, before the trial, that the indictment is not relevant, and is it not the practice of the Court at that stage to clear away what is not relevant?

Lord Ormidale.—We are not in a criminal case.

Mr. Shand.—Quite true, but it is a case where the Statute charges misdemeanour. In like manner, in our civil procedure, if a case is presented where the defender says, 'admitting every fact 'alleged, you can never obtain the result asked,' then the Court will not send parties to an inquiry into the facts, and they will give a judgment of irrelevancy.

Lord Ormidale.—But according to the practice in civil causes in this Court, if there is any relevant issuable matter at all, they will send the case to trial.

Mr. Shand.—Yes; but they will extract the issue, which is relevant in the cause, and allow it to go to trial, and nothing else. Now, I think the plain common sense of it is this, that if your Lordship is satisfied that whatever the Crown can prove under these charges cannot lead to the result which the Crown asks, surely we are in as favourable a position now for disposing of the matter as we would be at the trial. If the whole cause is sent to a Jury, each count is practically an issue, and in sending them all to the Jury, your Lordship may be practically affirming the relevancy of these counts. On what footing is it that you allow them to go to the jury? It is on the footing, that if the informer shall prove the facts he alleges, he shall be entitled to the forfeiture which he asks. Now, I meet him upon the threshold, and I say—If you prove every one of those facts, they don't come up to the statutory charge. If it were in the Criminal Court, all irrelevant matter would be cleared away before trial; in the Civil Court, I think the same course would be followed; and on this point I appeal to your Lordship's own practice, in a case where, with two or three counts libelled, your Lordship held one of them not relevant, and allowed the case to proceed on the other.

Mr. Rutherfurd.—There was no objection to the relevancy in that case. It was a question whether there was sufficient specification.

Lord Ormidale.—It was an objection to the relevancy, and nothing else. There were two counts in the case, and I dismissed one of them as not corresponding with the *subpœna* under which the defenders were brought into Court; the other count I held to want the specification necessary to make it relevant, but I allowed the Crown to amend; and the Crown might amend here for all I know.

Mr. Shand.—The peculiarity of this case is, that no amendment of these counts that can be suggested will make them relevant without altering the substance of them. I cannot see any legitimate interest on the part of the Crown to resist the course which I propose. If the various counts are bad in point of law, is it not better for the Crown as well as for us that that shall now be ascertained and fixed? We are quite ready to go to trial on everything averred which constitutes a good charge under the Statute; but we ask the Court to protect us against going to trial on 96 counts, which we undertake to show are bad in point of law. And we ask your Lordship for a judgment upon these objections now, since the matter of relevancy has been raised. We were willing, if there had been a distinct reservation, so as to save us from any risk arising from the previous procedure and practice of this Court, to have had these objections distinctly and unequivocally reserved, so as to put us in a position to say before the Jury that your Lordship should not allow these counts to go to trial; but that was rejected. We had no assurance that we should be safe without such a reservation, and therefore we follow the ordinary practice of the Court, and ask your Lordship for a judgment whether these counts are good or bad, and we submit that they are bad.

Lord Ormidale.—Supposing I was to take the course of appointing the trial to take place, without saying anything about the relevancy—that is to say, if my inclination were not to dismiss the Information—would you desire that I should pronounce to that effect?

Mr. Shand.—Yes. I was willing to have put the case in another position formerly, but we now ask a judgment on these objections. We are in as favourable a position now as we ever can be for disposing of them; and if so, it is plainly expedient that we should have eliminated from this case those counts which are not relevant, and that we should be left to go to trial with the real questions between the parties; and we maintain that in asking the judgment, we are following the invariable practice of the Court in dealing with questions of this kind, while it appears to us that we might be prejudiced if the case were to go to a Jury without these objections to relevancy being disposed of, because it might be said that the counts being practically issues in the cause, the very fact of their being sent to trial was an affirmance of the relevancy of them in point of law.

If the objection which has been stated to the first and second counts is well founded, I ask your Lordship to observe its effect upon the Information as a whole. From the Abstract you will find that the first and second counts charge what Mr. Clark called the double intent, which we say is objectionable; the third and fourth charge the single intent; all the others printed at length in this Abstract charge the double intent. At p. 6, the 9th count is stated to be the same as the 1st; if the objection is good to the

1st, the 9th goes; if the objection is good to the 2d, the 10th goes. The 11th is said to be the same as the 3d, and the 12th the same as the 4th; so that in the group of counts from 9 to 24, the only two charges which are not open to the objection which I am now referring to are the 11th and 12th. Taking the next group, the 25th to the 40th count, I make the same observation in regard to them all, except the 27th and 28th, which are stated to be the same as the 3d and 4th. In short, taking the Information as a whole, if this is a well-founded objection, it will leave standing two counts in each group, but nothing more; in short, we shall strike out seventy-two counts, leaving only twenty-five free from this objection, but liable to the other objection which Mr. Clark urged. Now surely it is very desirable to strike out so large a number of counts.

Lord Ormidale.—Although there were 5000 counts, is that any reason why I should dismiss the Information?

Mr. Shand.—If there were 5000 counts, and I could show that 4000 of them were bad, that would be a good reason for striking them out.

Lord Ormidale.—And if you can show me that only one is bad, your argument is just as strong.

Mr. Shand.—I think my argument is a good deal stronger if I find no less than seventy-two irrelevant counts proposed to be taken to the Jury.

Lord Ormidale.—You will never persuade me of that. I will give your argument as much effect if you can show me that one count is bad as if they were all bad.

Mr. Shand.—As your Lordship has announced that no reasoning will alter your Lordship's view on that matter, I say no more about it. And I now come to the question whether these counts are bad. The first thing to do is to ascertain distinctly what it is that is alleged. My friend Mr. Clark has stated that double intent is alleged, and with the appearance of taking a double *onus* by charging a double intent, the Crown has practically lessened their *onus* very considerably. With the appearance of libelling a double intent, they are truly libelling one intent against one party, and another against another, which there is no warrant for in the Statute.

Lord Ormidale.—The one applicable to British subjects and the other to foreigners?

Mr. Shand.—Yes. Taking the first count, it is a charge against the persons there named as having equipped the ship with intent (and it is quite plain that this intent refers to the persons said to have equipped it), 'and in order that such ship or vessel should be 'employed in the service of certain foreign states, &c., with intent 'to cruise and commit hostilities,' &c. Now I say that that intent applies not to the equippers, but to the Confederate States.

Lord Ormidale.—But supposing it were proved at the trial that, *de facto*, it was the intent of the owners and of the builders of the ship also, not only that the vessel should be employed in the service of the belligerent state, but also that she should commit hostilities, would not that count be sufficient to cover that?

Mr. Shand.—I should certainly say not for this reason, that if it is intended to connect me with the second intent, it should be said.

Lord Ormidale.—Is it not sufficiently said?

Mr. Shand.—I decline to go to trial with the Crown on an ambiguous charge. This is a penal Statute. If it were stated against me as a misdemeanour, the effect would be to put the party in the position of a criminal, and practically he really is so. The Statute provides that the very act now charged implies that the person offending is guilty of a misdemeanour, and may be punished by imprisonment. Now, is not the Crown bound to make their indictment distinct? It is proposed to forfeit and hand over to the Crown, property of immense value, on the footing that my clients have been guilty of a misdemeanour. I know nothing more settled in our law than that where a penal action or a criminal complaint is brought, it is the duty of the person bringing it to make his meaning distinct, and the Court will require that it be made distinct. First, it is a bad complaint if it is ambiguous, but second, it must be made clear on the language of the complaint that it comes up to what the Statute requires. I say farther, that in such an action as this, it must be made clear upon the very statement of the charge that it is a charge which the Statute warrants, and I submit that if the Crown mean that that second intent is in any way to attach to the persons complained of, they must say so. But as they have avoided saying so, I think I am warranted in maintaining that their meaning is that if they shall make out to your Lordship's satisfaction before a Jury that this vessel was equipped with intent on the part of the equippers that she should be employed in the service of a foreign state, and if that foreign state had another intent, viz., to cruise and commit hostilities against another state, they shall get a verdict on that count.

Lord Ormidale.—I can fancy that that would be very fairly and properly raised at the trial.

Mr. Shand.—It cannot be one whit better raised at the trial than now. Am I not right in reading this as distinctly averring an intent against the owners, that the vessel should be employed in the service of the Confederate States? I read that as the only intent attaching to the owners.

Lord Ormidale.—It is questionable whether it is the only complaint against them.

Mr. Shand.—My construction of it is, that that is the only intent charged against the owners. When they do want to charge a further intent, viz., the intent that the vessel shall cruise, and that her owners had that in view, you have that in the 3d count. The statement there is that they did equip the said vessel with intent to cruise and commit hostilities. But the case that the Crown want to present under the 1st, 2d, and other charges is, that the vessel was fitted with the intent that she should be employed in America, and being employed there that the Confederate States intended to cruise and commit hostilities. Is there anything in the Statute, or any implication under the Statute, inferring that the owners are connected with the intent of the Confederate States?

The language appears to me quite plain, and that language must be interpreted against the Crown. They are bound to make this distinct; they are not entitled to take ambiguous words, or words which don't come up to the Statute. I don't think the words are ambiguous. I think it is as plain as such language can make it, that the first intent attaches to the equippers, and the second to the foreign state, viz., the Confederates, and that the second intent does not in the slightest degree attach to the equippers. If it is intended to be maintained that the equippers intended both of these things, 1st, that the vessel should be employed in the service of the Confederate States, and, 2d, that she should cruise and commit hostilities, that should be stated; but it is quite plain they don't mean that, for they have all that under their 3d charge.

Lord Ormidale.—They may mean that what they charge in the 3d count is in itself a part of the charge in the 1st count, and perfectly sufficient under the Statute, if made out, to support the forfeiture,—that they don't require to charge everything in the Statute, and that it is enough if there is sufficient charged under the Statute.

Mr. Shand.—The 3d charge is a charge of equipment for the purpose of cruising.

Lord Ormidale.—Well, they may say that is quite enough, whether there is proof that there was intention also to employ or not.

Mr. Shand.—I think so, and we have no objection to the 3d count. The Crown may make out a case of intent to cruise either by the owners themselves cruising or cruising through others. But I want to know what the thing in the first charge is.

Lord Ormidale.—It is that and something more.

Mr. Shand.—It is a great deal less. Upon that reading of it your Lordship assumes that the Crown mean to say there, that the equippers had that vessel in their possession with intent to cruise themselves.

Lord Ormidale.—That their intent was that she should be employed for that purpose.

Mr. Shand.—If it is something else, I want to know what it is, and if it is not something else, it should go out of this count. I decline to go to a Jury, and I ask your Lordship's protection against going to a Jury, on a count which is not distinct in itself. If it means the same thing as the third, it is unnecessary, for we have the third. But it cannot mean the same thing. The meaning is, that the vessel was equipped with the owners' intent that it should be employed in foreign states, and being in the hands of the Confederate States, their intent is next given,—'with intent to cruise and commit hostilities.' I submit that that is the only meaning which this count will bear; but if the Crown maintain that that is not their meaning, then I ask your Lordship to require that it shall be made distinct what their meaning is. Now, I turn to the Statute, and I ask, Is there any warrant for a charge which infers forfeiture, where the intent is the intent of the owners, that the ship shall be employed by a foreign state, and it is the intent of that foreign state that she shall then be employed against a belligerent power with whom we are at peace? My friend Mr. Clark showed that, under this Statute, there are two separate things which amount to a misdemeanour, and either of which will infer a forfeiture of the vessel. The first is, if any person shall equip, &c., a vessel with intent that she shall be employed in the service of a foreign power as a transport or store-ship. That clause of the Statute plainly stops there. It does not provide that the vessel shall be employed as a ship of war; whether that was omitted by accident or mistake, or by intention, we don't know; but in point of fact the Statute deals with only one case so far as the equipper is concerned, viz., his equipping a ship to be employed as a transport or store-ship against a foreign power. But observe how distinctly the other branch of this Statute deals with the other matter as a separate and alternative matter.

Lord Ormidale.—There must be some antecedent words, and the question is, how many are there?

Mr. Shand.—The whole of them are antecedent, leading to the word 'or.'

Lord Ormidale.—Why should you stop at 'equip?'

Mr. Shand.—I don't stop at 'equip;' I take in the verb and the substantive. I say the Statute introduces two alternatives; and each is a separate alternative and a separate intent: you have the verb 'equip' and the substantive 'ship;' in the first branch of the Statute it is with one intent, viz., with intent to employ her as a transport against another power; in the second branch you have a separate and distinct and clearly expressed intent, viz., to cruise and commit hostilities. It may be that you may reach the equipper by showing that his true intention, among others, was to commit hostilities. If that is a good view of the Statute, it will arise on the 3d count, which charges that this vessel was held by the equippers with intent to cruise, and if something short of themselves intending to cruise will make a good charge, the Crown will get the benefit of it. But they don't take either of the alternatives which the Statute gives them, though either will infer forfeiture. The first branch of the Statute is to the effect that if a person shall equip a vessel with intent that she shall be employed as a transport or store-ship against a foreign power, there is to be forfeiture. Now that is not averred. There is not a word in any of the seventy-six charges about a transport-ship. Therefore, in dealing with those seventy-six charges, I ask your Lordship to deal with them as not falling under this branch of the Statute. The other branch of the Statute is the intent to cruise or commit hostilities. But whose intent? Surely that intent attaches to the equipper. He may build the vessel with intent to employ her in the transport service of a foreign state, or he may do so with intent to cruise or commit hostilities against the foreign state. The Statute says if he does either of these things the vessel shall be forfeited. But it does not say that except for one or other of these things there shall be forfeiture. But your Lordship is asked to introduce, as a statutory misdemeanour, a new charge altogether which is not within the Statute at all. The count is that the equippers of the vessel equipped her, not with intent that she should be used as a transport-ship, not with intent that she could cruise or commit hostilities, but with intent that she should be employed in the service of the Confederate States, with intent to cruise and commit hostilities, that is, with intent that they should cruise and commit hostilities. I say that the Statute introduces, as plainly as language can do, just two different misdemeanours, which admit of easy separation. The Crown does not lay its Information under either of them. My learned friend does not aver that we have violated the first branch of the Statute, or the second branch of the Statute, except in the 3d and 4th counts. But as far as the ninety-six counts are concerned, I submit that there is nothing in the Statute to entitle them to go to a Jury as to these. My friend Mr. Clark went so fully into the other charges, that I don't propose to do so. If the argument submitted in regard to the effect of the word 'arm' is the sound argument, and the word 'arm' applies to ships intended to cruise, and sent out for cruising purposes, then the whole of these charges are bad except the 97th and 98th, and I submit that that is a sound argument. Finally, I submit that the 97th and 98th counts are really open to the objections stated against them. There is another objection which Mr. Clark did not urge, but which I submit is a serious one, and it is this, that there are no less than 98 counts in which there is a marked change of the verb used; one being 'equip,' another 'furnish,' and another 'fit out.' Now, do these mean different things, or the same thing? If they mean the same thing, and are merely used exegetically, I don't think this complaint should be sustained in the shape of separate complaints as to these things. Is your Lordship to tell the Jury that thirty of the ninety-eight counts mean exactly the same thing? If they mean different things, I can understand why there are separate counts; but if they mean the same thing, should they not be charged cumulatively? My argument is that they mean the same thing.

Lord Ormidale.—You don't say that 'arming' means the same thing as these other words?

Mr. Shand.—No.

Lord Ormidale.—That goes far to show that the other words mean something different; and whether they mean the same thing or something different may depend on the evidence. Suppose shipbuilders tell us that it is perfectly well known among them that to furnish a ship is quite a different thing from equipping it—

Mr. Shand.—It would then come to this, that the words did not mean the same thing, and the basis of my argument being that they do mean the same thing, my argument would be gone; but I don't think that the words 'equip,' 'furnish,' and 'fit out,' can mean different things, and if so, I don't understand the use of ringing the changes by a series of counts, one with 'equip,' another with 'furnish,' and another with 'fit out.'

Lord Ormidale.—They want to catch you on one or the other of them.

Mr. Shand.—But I am entitled to know what they mean, and I want nothing but what is fair and reasonable.

Lord Ormidale.—And what you think is fair and reasonable is, that the whole Information should be dismissed except the 97th count.

Mr. Shand.—I adopt Mr. Clark's argument. I have submitted that 72 of the counts are utterly objectionable. If the Statute requires intent to cruise on the part of the equipper, then I say that intent to cruise is not charged in these counts, except in the 3d and 4th. I think nothing short of intent to cruise will do under the Statute, and if they mean something a shade less or different, I decline to go to trial with them under the Statute. Now, on the grounds which I have stated, I submit that the Information is bad.

Lord Ormidale.—Supposing that after hearing all parties, and considering the matter, I should not be disposed to separate the case at present, but to send it to trial, would it be any advantage to the defenders, or would it not rather be a disadvantage to them, to find expressly, in reference to any point, that their plea is not sufficiently supported, and is not tenable? Wherever there is the least ground for thinking that the pleas of irrelevancy may be raised sufficiently at the trial and disposed of then, the Court have always most properly been averse to pronouncing at all on the subject before the trial, because it is a great disadvantage not only in separating the case, and creating one course of litigation on preliminary matters, and then a second course of litigation on the merits, but it also places the party against whom the finding is pronounced in a disadvantageous position.

Mr. Shand.—Of course, if the finding becomes final it is a great disadvantage; but whichever way the point is decided, it being pressed for judgment, neither party will rest satisfied with your Lordship's decision.

Lord Ormidale.—That is what I want to avoid if I can, consistently with justice to the parties. A good many of the points at present raised appear to me to depend in some degree on evidence.

Mr. Shand.—I don't see that the seventy-six counts which I have referred to are in that category.

Adjourned.

Thursday, 18*th February* 1864.

Mr. Rutherfurd.—I appear for the Crown in answer to certain parties who have lodged claims in this Information. Your Lordship is aware that this is a proceeding *in rem*, in which it is open for any parties having interest to lodge a claim and appear in the process as contradictors of the Crown. Two claims have been lodged, one of them being for certain parties who are not expressly mentioned in the Information, but who design themselves as Messrs. J. and G. Thomson, shipbuilders, Glasgow; and it is averred by the counsel who have appeared for them, that these parties were the builders of the 'Pampero,' an averment which I shall at present assume to be the fact. There is also a claim put in for certain parties, who are among those expressly mentioned in the Information, viz., the partners of the firm of Smith, Fleming, and Co., who claim to be interested in the vessel. But the Information applies also to persons who are not here. There is one person expressly named in the Information for whom no claim has been made, viz., George T. Sinclair; and there are others included in the general expression, 'other persons whose names are to me, Her Majesty's 'Advocate, at present unknown.' These parties are not represented; but that there may be other parties who, by their actings and conduct, have brought themselves into connexion with this case is quite likely, because a claim has been lodged by parties alleging themselves to be the builders, though they are not expressly mentioned in the Information. My object in making these observations is to show that the Information applies to parties who are not here, and therefore, that even if the objections stated on the other side are well founded *quoad* them, it would not necessarily follow that they would apply to the case of other parties who have not appeared and claimed, but who are covered by the terms of the Information, and in respect of whose actings and conduct the forfeiture of the ship might competently be claimed by the Crown, though they have not appeared. What the defenders must show, as I maintain, is, that the acts charged in the counts objected to, cannot by any possibility amount to a statutory offence, not only as against them, but also as against any other parties who may be covered by the terms of the Information. It is quite possible that, assuming all the facts as stated in the Information to be correctly set forth, none of the counts objected to might set forth a statutory offence; if, for instance, we were to charge murder or theft, it would be for your Lordship to order these counts to be struck out, and that the Information should proceed upon others with which the Act plainly deals. My learned friends must show that on no possible construction of the terms of the Statute can the offence charged in the counts to which they object, amount to a statutory offence. If I can satisfy your Lordship that any or all of the counts to which they object can, on any possible construction of the terms of that section of the Statute, amount to the statutory offence, then that is a matter which must go to trial, because, whether the circumstances so stated in these counts apply to the parties claiming here or not, they may apply to other parties who are mentioned or covered by the terms of this Information, but who have not appeared or lodged claims.

The 1st objection stated refers to the 1st and 2d counts of the Information, and all that are framed on the same principle—72 in all; and it is, that whereas the 7th section of the Statute deals with two offences, the counts in question charge only one. My friends read that part of the 7th section upon which this question of double intent arises, as enacting two offences—1st, equipment with intent to employ the vessel equipped as a transport or store-ship against subjects of any foreign belligerent with whom Her Majesty is not at war; and 2d, equipment of the vessel with intent to cruise or commit hostilities against any prince, state, &c. I don't understand that the 3d count and the others framed on the same principle are alleged to be improperly framed as regards the question of double intent, though there is another objection to them to which I shall afterwards refer. As to the 1st offence which they take this section of the Statute as creating, viz., equipping a transport-ship to be used against a foreign belligerent, they hold that the 97th count deals with that, and that that is properly there charged; but they maintain that except in the 3d and relative counts and in the 97th, no other view can be taken of this section as creating an offence different from that which they say is set forth in these counts. But I submit there is another possible and rational view which may be taken of the section under which the offence is charged in the 1st, 2d, and relative counts, and that is, that if any person in any part of the United Kingdom or Her Majesty's dominions, without the leave of Her Majesty, do equip any ship or vessel with intent or in order that that ship or vessel shall be employed in the service of any foreign prince, state, &c., with intent to cruise or commit hostilities against any prince, state, &c., or against the subjects of any prince, state, &c., that is an offence; that is to say, we read this part of the section as if the words 'as a transport or store-ship 'or' were put within parentheses; and read in that way, we have exactly the offence set forth in the 1st, 2d, and relative counts. There would therefore come to be three views which might be taken of this section, each creating a separate offence. We have, *1st*, that which my friends on the other side concede to have been relevantly set forth in the 97th count, *i.e.*, equipping any ship or vessel with intent or in order that such ship or vessel shall be employed in the service of any foreign prince as a transport or store-ship against any prince, state, or potentate. We have, *2d*, that which they don't dispute is well set forth in the 3d and relative counts, viz., that if any person shall equip, fit out, arm, or procure to be equipped, &c., any ship or vessel with intent to cruise or commit hostilities against any prince, state, or potentate, &c. And we have, *3d*, that which is dealt with in the 1st, 2d, and similar counts, and which is made plain by reading the words 'as a transport or 'store-ship' as if in a parenthesis, and which consists in the equipping of any ship or vessel with intent or in order that such ship or vessel shall be employed with intent to cruise or commit hostilities against a belligerent. My friends say there is here a double intent, and they demand whose intent it is. That will appear at the trial. But take it that the words 'with intent' are equivalent to 'for the 'purpose of,' 'for the object of,' or 'in order that,' and see how the section reads,—If any person equip any vessel with intent or in order that such ship or vessel shall be employed for the purpose of cruising or committing hostilities. Is not that a plain reading of the Statute by which an offence is created, which is relevantly charged in those counts of the Information? We have a key to the meaning of the words 'with intent' furnished by the Statute itself, for where these words first occur in this section of the Act, we find the words thus, 'with intent, or in order that.' The Statute therefore takes the phrase 'in order that' as an equivalent for 'with 'intent,' and if we substitute these words, I say we have the offences which are charged in the counts objected to by the claimants clearly provided for by the Statute, or at least, I maintain that as a possible construction of the Statute. I don't say it is the only one. My friends may be quite right in supposing that the proper construction is that which is provided for in the 3d and relative counts, or in the 97th; but what I now suggest is at all events a possible view which may be taken of the construction of the Statute; and if so, are we, before any investigation into the facts, and while we don't know which charge in the Information will be met by the evidence on the trial, to say that such a construction of the Statute is impossible?

Lord Ormidale.—If the evidence is not to affect the construction, you are just in as good a situation now to say what the construction is as you can be at any time.

Mr. Rutherfurd.—I say this is a possible view of the Statute, which may be met by the facts, and if so, then I should be entitled to the verdict of a jury on these counts. Notwithstanding all the ingenuity which my friends have exercised in criticising this Act, it does not appear to have occurred to them that in the case of the 'Alexandra,' where the Information was in precisely the same terms, *mutatis mutandis*, this objection was not for one moment insisted in, and the judgment did not turn on that at all.

Lord Ormidale.—It was said, on the other side, that Sir Hugh Cairns, before addressing the jury, started these very points for the consideration of the Court, but that the Chief Baron suggested that the trial should proceed, and that the defenders would have their remedy by arrest of judgment.

Mr. Rutherfurd.—I shall refer to some expressions of the Chief Baron in giving judgment on that case, which showed that he had this objection before him, and that he contemplated the construction which I am now contending for, as one which might possibly be put on the section of the Act. What was decided in the 'Alexandra' case was, that to constitute the offence created by the Act, the equipment must be intended to be so completed that the vessel, when she leaves port, shall be in a condition at once to commence hostilities, and they held that the evidence showed that there had been no such equipment of the Alexandra. In dealing with the 7th section of the Act, the Lord Chief Baron is reported to have said:—'I now come to the 7th section itself, and to the 'terms in which the Statute enacts that persons doing certain acts 'with a certain intent shall be deemed guilty of a misdemeanour. 'It is not necessary carefully to separate the act itself from any 'attempt or endeavour to commit it, and to simplify the inquiry as 'to how the Statute should be construed. I will take (as the In-'formation does) one of the prohibited matters—"equip," for 'instance—and examine that alone, without reference to the 'others, and without reference to attempting, procuring, aiding, 'assisting, &c. The clause would then run thus:—"If any person '"within any part of His Majesty's dominions, in the United King-'"dom or beyond the seas, without the leave and license of his '"Majesty, shall equip any ship or vessel with intent or in order '"that such ship or vessel shall be employed in the service of any '"foreign state or government as a transport or store-ship, or with '"intent to cruise or commit hostilities against any state or govern-'"ment with whom his Majesty shall not be then at war, every '"such person so offending shall be deemed guilty of a misde-'"meanour." Two questions obviously arise upon the construction 'of these expressions:—1st, Whose intention is it which is meant 'by the Act? 2dly, What is the meaning of the word "equip?" 'It is difficult to make out what was the intention of those who 'framed this clause as to the manner in which it should be broken 'up into parts and then be put together, so as to present all the 'alternatives contemplated. Probably it could not mean that '"with intent and in order that such ship or vessel should be '"employed in the service of any foreign prince, state, &c., as a '"transport or storeship," should stand alone without some subse-'quent matter being added, for that would make it a misdemeanour 'to permit a transport or store-ship to be equipped for any foreign 'prince, &c., without any regard to his being at peace or at war 'with any state or government with whom the sovereign of this 'country should not then be at war. It is probable that the words '"against any prince, state," &c., should follow the word "store-'"ship," and then the effect of the clause would be this,—it would 'be a misdemeanour to equip a ship or vessel with intent and in 'order that such ship should be employed in the service of any 'foreign prince, &c., as a transport or store-ship against any prince, 'state, &c., with whom our sovereign should not then be at war, or 'with intent to cruise and commit hostilities against any such 'prince, state, or potentate. And some 24 of the 98 counts are 'founded on this view of the section. Or the alternative may be 'as a transport or store-ship, or with intent to cruise or commit 'hostilities against, &c.; and then the effect of the clause would 'be to make it a misdemeanour to equip a ship with intent or in 'order that she might be employed by one belligerent as a trans-'port, or with intent to cruise or commit hostilities against another.' That last paragraph is precisely what I am contending is a construction which might possibly be taken of the terms of this Act. The Chief Baron goes on to say:—'When two intents are men-

'tioned, and they are put in the alternative thus, with intent to do 'such a thing or with intent to do another, the obvious and the 'grammatical mode of reading the clause would be, to make the 'two intentions the alternatives; but most of the counts in the 'Information (about 72) combine the two intents together, and, in 'effect, turn "or" into "and," and charge the defendants with 'equipping, &c., the ship with intent that the ship should be em-'ployed in the service of one belligerent with intent to cruise and 'commit hostilities against the other belligerent with which her 'Majesty was not then at war. If this mode of reading the 7th 'section be not correct, 72 of the counts are improperly framed, 'and the Statute does not warrant any such charge; but as-'suming it to be correct, then the question arises, whose intent 'does the Information mean? Who is it that the Informa-'tion charges with an intent to cruise and commit hostilities?' He then goes on to deal with the evidence, taking it as a question that must arise on the evidence, that it must be the intent of the person who committed the act. But I refer to that to show that this view of the Statute, which I am contending is a possible interpretation, suggested itself to the mind of the Chief Baron. He no doubt said that if it should turn out that this mode of reading the Statute was not correct, 72 of the counts were improperly framed, but he does not find that in point of fact it was not correct, or that that is not the construction which the Court would be inclined to put on that section. That was not necessary for the decision of the case, which went upon this, that to constitute the offence created by the Act, the equipment must be intended to be so completed as to put the vessel in a position to commit hostilities, and that the evidence showed that the equipment had not been carried out so far. In reference to this matter, I may also refer to what passed at the motion for a new trial. At p. 350 of the Argument on the motion, Mr. Baron Channell observed to the Attorney-General, 'I understand your argument upon the 7th section to be 'this—you read the section, equip, and so on—"in order that such '"ship or vessel shall be employed in the service of any foreign '"prince, state, or potentate, or of any foreign colony, province, or '"part of any province or people, or of any person or persons exer-'"cising or assuming to exercise any powers of government in or '"over any foreign state, colony, province, or part of any province '"or people," "with intent to cruise or commit hostilities," leaving 'out for this purpose, "as a transport or store-ship."' And the Attorney-General said, 'I do. I may observe, upon those second 'words, "with intent," which no doubt are awkwardly introduced, 'we are all substantially agreed that the sense is just the same as if 'those words were not there; for two reasons, first of all, the words 'which follow must be words of qualification applicable to "trans-'"port or store-ship," as well as to "cruise or commit hostilities," 'otherwise there would be this absurdity, that furnishing a ship for 'the purpose of being used as a transport or store-ship, not to be 'used for belligerent purposes, would be indeed illegal. But that 'is not all. Your Lordships will find a conclusive proof that the 'Legislature so used the words; for a little lower down, when you 'come to that part which relates to commissions, "or shall within '"the United Kingdom, or any of His Majesty's dominions, or in '"any settlement, colony, territory, island, or place belonging or '"subject to His Majesty, issue and deliver any commission for '"any ship or vessel, to the intent that such ship or vessel shall be '"employed as aforesaid," it is clear that must apply both to the 'case of a "transport or store-ship," and to "cruising and com-'"mitting hostilities," the employment governs both.'

Lord Ormidale.—The Attorney-General says they were all agreed that the sense of the section was the same as if the second words 'with intent' were not there.

Mr. Rutherfurd.—That that was so appears from the opinion of Baron Channell in giving judgment. At p. 329 of the New Reports he says:—'It has been assumed in the argument on both sides 'that this may be read as if the words "with intent" were there 'omitted, as they are in the American Act. Whether this is right 'or not, their insertion certainly causes great confusion. In the 'first place it provokes comparison with the other clause commenc-'ing "with intent," causing one, at first sight, to read them as 'showing alternative intents, either of which would, with the re-'quisite act, constitute the offence. This, on looking into it, is 'agreed on all sides not to be the right construction. But they 'create a further difficulty. This intent now spoken of is neces-'sarily, from the collocation of the words "shall be employed with 'intent," an intent of the employer, and not of the equipper, which 'is, as it were, engrafted upon the intent of the equipper; and it 'is very difficult to see how one man can intend that another man 'shall intend something or other. It is probably this difficulty 'which has prevented the counsel on either side from founding any 'argument upon these words.' Both parties assumed that the words 'with intent,' where they occur the second time, should be held *pro non scripto*, because of the difficulty which Baron Channell points out. I trust I have now satisfied your Lordship that, taking this view of the 7th section in reference to the matter of double intent, we have, under the 1st and 2d and relative counts, a relevant charge of what may possibly be construed as an offence under the Act; and my learned friends on the other side have pointed and can point to no authority to show that that is not the proper reading of the Act. I don't say that it is. I say it is equally likely that the offence charged in the 3d and in some of the other counts may be an offence which may more properly, more easily, and more intelligibly be construed as falling within the provisions of the 7th section. But that is one view which may be taken of it, and we have no authority to show that it is not a correct view; and therefore I am entitled to go to trial with this and the relative counts, and if the facts then disclosed shall amount to the offence there set forth, I shall then ask your Lordship for a direction to the Jury that a statutory offence has been committed.

Lord Ormidale.—Supposing your view of the 1st count is the correct one, can the charge in the 3d count be maintained consistently with it?

Mr. Rutherfurd.—I think so; but it need not be consistent. I may charge a great many offences inconsistent with one another, and at the trial, when the facts are disclosed, I shall be prepared to state which I proceed upon.

Lord Ormidale.—You think that though the 1st count charges perhaps a larger offence, there is a good offence in the 3d count as well.

Mr. Rutherfurd.—I think so. The offence charged in the 3d count may not amount to the whole offence charged in the 1st count, but it is still an offence under the Act, and whether they are consistent or not, I am entitled to go to trial, with both offences charged, and when the facts are disclosed, I shall be prepared to state to your Lordship under what count I ask a verdict. I cannot ask a verdict on all the counts, but when we get to the Jury, I shall be able to state upon what count I mean to insist.

The second objection urged by Mr. Clark refers to this, whether it was competent under the Statute to charge as an offence equipment with a view to commit hostilities, without using the word 'arm?' He could only arrive at the result which he pointed at by reading the Statute as showing that the words, 'equip,' 'furnish,' and 'fit out' refer only to the transport or store-ship, or that if used as regards a ship intended to cruise or commit hostilities, they must be used in conjunction with the word 'arm,' and, in short, that the equipment in that case struck at by the Act, meant a warlike equipment. But even assuming that this was so, there may be warlike equipment without arming, and if there is a warlike equipment, furnishing, or fitting out, short of arming, that is an offence relevantly charged under the Statute. Mr. Clark referred to the preamble of the Act, in which undoubtedly all these things are set forth conjunctively, but in the 7th section they are set forth disjunctively, for the word 'or' is used; and the reason is obvious; the preamble narrates the things which were struck at by the Act. The Act did not strike at the equipment without Her Majesty's license, or the fitting out or the arming or the furnishing of vessels, but it was intended to strike at each and every one of these things, and therefore we have in the preamble the conjunctive form used, but in the 7th section we find 'equip, furnish, fit out, or arm,' showing that these words are plainly used disjunctively, and that each or any one of them, if it be a warlike equipment, though it may fall short of arming, necessarily constitutes an offence struck at by the Statute. This view is supported by the dicta of the Judges in the Alexandra case. At p. 321 the Chief Baron says:—'There can be no doubt they [the Legislature] did not mean to 'permit a ship or vessel to go away armed, for they have said so 'distinctly; but "arming" admits of many degrees, and a doubt 'might arise, if the word "arm" alone had been used, what degree 'of arming would constitute the offence. But the degree is settled 'and determined by taking the whole sentence—the ship is not to 'be equipped, &c., in order to cruise or commit hostilities. If the 'equipment amounts to that, the law is broken; if it does not, no 'offence has been committed.' And Baron Bramwell, at p. 323:—

'Again, the title and preamble both show that the Statute was 'directed against fitting out and arming for warlike purposes. 'Section 2 is in the same sense. It is said that this construction 'requires the vessel to be armed to be within the Act, and that so 'the words "fit out, furnish, and equip" are superfluous. I agree 'they are not to be so treated if it can be avoided, though I strongly 'incline to think that the persons who used them attached no very 'definite idea to them. In the title it is "fit out or equip," with- 'out "arm;" in the preamble it is "fit out, equip, and arm." In 'section 2 it is used, "fitted out, or equipped, or intended to be '"used for any warlike purpose." In section 7 the words are '"equip, furnish, fit out, or arm." Surely no precise idea was in 'the mind of the author of the varying though similar expressions. 'The probable intent was to use sufficiently comprehensive words, 'and to avoid such a question as whether a ship was "armed," 'strictly speaking, and make it enough if she was equipped for 'warlike purposes. Such a case may well be, that the ship, though 'not armed, is equipped for warlike purposes. By "armed," I sup- 'pose it would be meant ordinarily that she had cannon; but if 'she had a fighting crew, muskets, pistols, powder, shot, cutlasses, 'and boarding appliances, she might be well said to be equipped 'for warlike purposes, though not armed.'

Lord Ormidale.—If she had a fighting crew and a ram probably she would be armed, but it might fairly enough be said to be an armed ship thoroughly equipped for warlike purposes, though she had not cannon or fire-arms, if she had a ram and a fighting crew.

Mr. Rutherfurd.—I mean that there may be an equipment, furnishing, or fitting out, or any one or other of them, for warlike purposes, which may be short of arming, and therefore that the use of these words alone, without 'arm,' constitutes a relevant charge under this section of the Statute. At p. 328, Baron Channell says: 'What did the Legislature mean by the words "equip, furnish, fit '"out, or arm a vessel with intent or in order that she should be '"employed in the service of a foreign power as a transport or '"store-ship, or with intent to cruise or commit hostilities against '"a power with whom we are not at war"? Arming is not 'charged in the present information; we may therefore leave out the 'words "or arm." The words "transport or store-ship" are also 'immaterial, now that the 97th and 98th counts, charging the '"Alexandra" to be a transport or store-ship, are abandoned, ex- 'cept that we must adopt such an interpretation of the words com- 'mon to both clauses as they would be capable of bearing when 'combined with the words "as a transport," as well as when 'combined with the words "with intent to cruise." The words '"equip, fit out, and furnish," seem to me to mean nearly the same 'thing. Throughout the whole course of the argument in this 'case little stress was laid upon any supposed difference between 'the words "equip, fit out, and furnish." We may therefore still 'further reduce the words we have to construe to these, "equip '"with intent or in order that the vessel shall be employed in the

'" service of a foreign power, with intent to cruise or commit '" hostilities." It is admitted, I think, on all sides, that these are ' the words upon which the main question turns.' Therefore he, like the other Judges, considered that any one of those things, equipping, furnishing, or fitting out, though short of arming, might be done for a warlike purpose, and if so, constitute an offence struck at by the 7th section.

There were two other objections dealt with by Mr. Clark. The first was, that if the words 'equip, fit out, and furnish,' mean the same thing, why are there so many counts charging them separately? My answer to that is, that it is impossible for me to say that they do mean the same thing. If they mean the same thing, as I can only obtain judgment for the Crown upon one count, the claimants cannot be put to any disadvantage by the fact that there are a great many other counts charging the same thing, under which I cannot recover. If they do not mean the same thing,—if equipping is different from fitting out, and fitting out is different from furnishing and equipping—then the Information is undoubtedly properly framed, and these things are properly charged in separate counts. But the words, I think, are plainly different. I think it would be difficult to say that to equip was the same thing as to fit out or to furnish. In the argument on the motion for a new trial in the Alexandra case, the Queen's Advocate quoted the following definition of 'equip' from Todd's Johnson's Dictionary: —'It is properly a naval term, *equippe* being the old French for ' a sailor, and so used in the thirteenth century, derived, perhaps, ' from the barbarous Latin, *eschipare*, to furnish or adorn vessels, ' whence *echipper* or *equipper*, as Junius has observed, was easily ' formed. See also Du Cange in *eschipare*. And thus our own ' word was also first written *esquippe*, and used in the naval sense, ' as by Barret in 1580, to equippe or furnish ships with all able- ' ments.' And it has been held, in some cases referred to in the motion for the rule, that 'equip' included the manning and rigging of the ship. Furnishing may be applied to the fitting up the internal appliances of the ship, which may or may not be warlike. It is a valid word applied to a transfer, and it may likewise be used with reference to a sale; and if there was a contract in this case between the parties claiming—let us suppose the Confederate States of America, in which they asked the claimants to furnish them with a ship, that is to sell them a ship, or transfer to them the property of a ship—it is something quite different from equipping. Therefore it is plain these words cannot be taken to have the same meaning, and the counts in the Information in which they are separately used are therefore proper charges under the Statute.

One more objection was stated by Mr. Clark applying to the 98th count—the objection being that it is cumulative. This is rather inconsistent with the other objection, according to which he wished to get all the words, 'fit out, furnish, and equip' put together into one count. But according to the proper style in which informations are framed, whether *in rem* or informations in ordinary excise cases,—and your Lordship will find abundance of authority to this effect in Bateman or Douglas' Excise Law—the proper form, though it sounds somewhat abhorrent to the Scottish ear, is not that an information charging different offences should be in the alternative form, 'or otherwise,' as we would say in an indictment, but that it should charge them in the cumulative form. Thus you don't charge a man, as I understand, in England, with the offence of forgery or otherwise with the offence of theft, but you charge him with forgery and theft. The 98th count is laid against a great number of persons—(*Reads it*). My friend, Mr. Clark, says this is cumulative and inconsistent in itself, as charging a variety of offences. I say that that is not an incorrect form according to the English system of libelling these charges, but that in any view the charges are there laid for the acts and conduct of a great number of people. It would be competent for me under that to prove that some of the partners of the company of Galbraith were perhaps concerned in the equipping, furnishing, or fitting out; and I might show at the same time quite consistently, that George T. Sinclair was a party who did knowingly aid and assist in the equipping and fitting out; or in like manner, that the parties who have appeared here to claim as the builders, Messrs. Thomson, assisted, and were concerned in the equipping, furnishing, and fitting out. I could prove all these things as against any one or other of these parties. I could prove that some of them did one, and that others were concerned in another, and that without the least inconsistency under this count. That such a mode of stating an offence was not contemplated as being incompetent, is seen from the 7th section of the Exchequer Act. My friend referred to the form of the Information appended to that Act, but in the 7th section it is provided that notwithstanding the terms of any Information brought under that Act, it shall not be incumbent to prove against the defender in order to recover under such Information, any matter stated therein, except only such matters as are by law required to be proved in order to the forfeiture, &c. In enacting that, the Legislature plainly had before them the possibility and the competency of the Crown including in one Information or one count of the Information a variety of charges or different matters stated therein.

I have only to add that on this side of the bar we object altogether to this discussion going on at this stage. We have here undoubtedly an Information with 98 counts, and we can only hope to succeed upon one of these. There is one, viz., the 97th, which has not been objected to by my learned friends. Now put the case, and it is not an impossible case, that we should only ask a verdict from the Jury upon that 97th count, which has not been objected to, then all this discussion which has taken place would go for nothing. Mr. Clark states that his fear was that he might be foreclosed,—that we might seek to obtain a verdict on some of the other counts to which he has objected; and that while in England the remedy of the party consists, if the verdict is against them, in making a motion for arrest of judgment, he is not sure whether any such remedy is competent to him in this case. No such remedy is required. It will be perfectly competent for my friends at the trial, after the evidence has been led, and after we have stated upon which of the counts we mean to insist, to ask your Lordship to direct the Jury that that count cannot be competently insisted in by the Crown in respect it does not contain the statutory offence. Your Lordship would either give effect to that motion or not. In either case they would have a remedy. They could apply to the Court for a new trial on the ground of misdirection, or on the ground of the verdict being contrary to evidence. Therefore, I say that this whole discussion is unnecessary and premature at this stage of the proceedings, because we are not yet in a position to say which count of the Information we intend to ask a verdict upon, and we cannot do so until the evidence has been led. Therefore, I conclude with this motion, that your Lordship shall appoint this case to go to trial, on a day to be afterwards fixed, superseding in *hoc statu* all further consideration of the objections which have been urged by my learned friends.

Lord Ormidale.—Are you not prepared to tell me the day that you desire to be fixed for the trial.

Mr. Rutherfurd.—Hardly at this moment.

Lord Ormidale.—The Statute says, 'The Lord Ordinary shall 'appoint a day for the trial,' &c.

Mr. Rutherfurd.—We shall be subject of course to your Lordship's appointment, but we would crave some little indulgence in point of time to enable us to get ready our witnesses.

Lord Ormidale.—Supposing I were to take your view, and to think that there ought to be a trial here before any positive decision on the relevancy and competency of so many counts, don't I require to name the day under the Statute.

Mr. Rutherfurd.—I think if your Lordship were to pronounce an interlocutor appointing the trial to proceed on a day to be afterwards fixed, we should be able within a short period to name a day.

Lord Ormidale—The Act says, 'or shall take such other course 'as shall seem to him proper;' probably that gives me a discretion, but, for the convenience of all parties, I think the sooner we come to an arrangement when the case is to be tried, the better.

Mr. Gifford.—At the previous discussion two days were mentioned, 10th March and 5th April, the one before the other, after the ordinary Jury sittings. Perhaps we are too near the 10th March now to fix that day, but the 5th of April might be fixed.

Lord Ormidale.—You had better not begin it on the 1st! but why the 5th more than the 2d?

Mr. Gifford.—There may be extra sittings till the end of March, but we are in the hands of the Court.

Lord Ormidale. While I am quite ready to accommodate the parties as much as I possibly can, I am not going to leave it in an indefinite way, or to take the case in the middle of the vacation, if I can as well take it in the beginning of the vacation. I don't see any reason why the 5th of April should be fixed instead of the 2d.

Mr. Gordon.—The 2d is a Saturday.

Mr. Gifford.—And the 5th was mentioned in order that the witnesses might come forward on the Monday.

Lord Ormidale.—Well, probably that will be about the time, and I suppose you will not be prepared on both sides sooner.

Mr. Gordon.—It is not yet decided that there is a relevant case against us.

Lord Ormidale.—But that does not commit you or me or anybody.

Mr. Gordon.—Except that it indicates rather an opinion on your Lordship's part to overrule our objections.

Lord Ormidale.—You must not take it in the least degree as indicating that I have formed any opinion.

Mr. Cook.—Probably your Lordship will not be able to pronounce any interlocutor till you are told by the Crown on what day they will be ready to proceed to trial; but before your Lordship pronounces any interlocutor sending the case to trial, we humbly think your Lordship must determine what is the case to be sent to trial. I attend your Lordship for Mr. John Fleming of London, and all the other parties mentioned in the 1st count, with the exception of Mr. Geo. T. Sinclair, and I am to submit to your Lordship, following the same line of argument as was adopted by my friend Mr. Clark, that none of the counts of this Information are so expressed as to warrant your Lordship in sending them to trial, except perhaps the 97th.

Now the position in which we appear technically is that of claimants of the property of this vessel which has been seized by the Crown; but our real position is that of respondents in answer to this Information—I had almost said, in answer to this indictment—at the instance of the Lord Advocate. I apprehend there can be no doubt whatever of our title to appear as claimants of the property of the vessel. My friend Mr. Rutherfurd seemed to doubt that, but he ought to recollect that the Lord Advocate, on his own showing, has nothing whatever to do with the property of this vessel, and has no right to interfere with it at all, except upon the footing charged in the Information, viz., that we, the persons who, he says, were concerned in the equipping and furnishing of the vessel, did so with certain criminal intents. No other person, with the exception of my clients, has appeared to claim the property of the vessel. The Lord Advocate has nothing to do with it, unless he can show that the vessel has been legally seized; and therefore I apprehend that beyond all doubt I am entitled now to appear and show your Lordship, that unless sufficient and good ground is stated in this Information for the seizure, I am entitled not only to insist in my claim for the property of the vessel, but to have my claim allowed. No other person is claiming the property. *Primâ facie*, on the Information, I am the equipper and furnisher of the vessel, and therefore *primâ facie* I am the owner and proprietor of the vessel, and entitled to have her delivered up to me, unless the Lord Advocate has stated sufficient legal ground for divesting me of my right, by the process of seizure. I apprehend therefore there cannot be the slightest doubt about our title to appear and maintain the present argument. And what does the argument come to? We say that there are no relevant grounds stated by the Lord Advocate why we should be divested of our title to the property of this vessel; and we say that for three reasons. We say that in regard to 72 of the counts, they are irrelevant, and do not describe anything which is made an offence in the Statute, upon one ground, viz., that while the Statute declares the equipping of a vessel, with one or other of two criminal intents, to be an offence which shall infer forfeiture, these 72 counts charge us with equipping the vessel with an intent which is not made criminal by the Statute. In the second place, we say that the whole of the counts, with the exception of the 97th, are irrelevant; because in describing the acts which we have done in the way of equipping and so forth, the Crown have omitted to use one word which was essential, viz., the word 'arm;' and our argument in regard to that matter is, that unless we have done something here which was equivalent to arming, or attempting completely to arm this vessel, with intention to cruise and commit hostilities, no good count is stated against us. And that applies not merely to the 72 counts to which I have already adverted, but to all the counts of the Indictment, with the exception of the 97th and 98th. My friend stated some technical objections to the 98th, on the ground that it accumulated offences which ought to be kept separate; and he also stated some objections in point of pleading, to the structure of the Information, as stating in 98 counts what might have been very well, according to our practice, stated in one; but with these matters I don't know that I shall trouble your Lordship at any length.

The first question which we have to determine is what is the true construction of the Statute. If we can come to a right understanding in regard to that matter, there ought to be very little difficulty in ascertaining whether the Crown have in the Information stated against us anything which the Statute makes a crime. The first thing, then, to determine is, what is it that the Statute, and in particular that section of the Statute upon which the Information is more immediately libelled,—what is it that it makes criminal? My learned friend, Mr. Rutherfurd, laid down some principles which took me wholly by surprise. If one thing more than another is clear on the face of this Information, it is that it is a highly penal action; it is almost of the nature of a criminal indictment, because, beyond all doubt, the Lord Advocate cannot prevail in his conclusions to have the vessel declared forfeited, unless he shows that these gentlemen have committed a crime; and I say he is bound to tell the Court and the parties what the crime or offence is, in language which, beyond all doubt, describes a crime, if the facts stated in the several counts of the Information be true. But Mr. Rutherfurd says the Lord Advocate is not bound to describe in the several counts something which is necessarily a crime, —he is not bound to tell us under which of these counts he means ultimately to ask a verdict; but if he can satisfy your Lordship that there is a possible construction of the Statute which will warrant him in saying that some one of these 98 counts describe a criminal offence, then he is entitled to have the whole case sent to trial; and he will tell us, forsooth, at the trial, under which of the

98 counts it is that he is going to ask a verdict! Suppose all the others are wrong, and upon my friend's own reading of the Statute don't perhaps describe a crime at all, the Lord Advocate is to be entitled to have the case sent to trial if he can show that there is a possible construction of the Statute which will support one or more counts of the Information! I deny that altogether. I submit that, although the Lord Advocate, if the case is sent to trial, may tell the Jury, after he hears the evidence, upon which count he asks a verdict, he is bound to show us now, and to show your Lordship before he can get the whole counts of this Information sent *per aversionem* to trial, that every one of these counts describes a crime, in respect of which he would be entitled, at the trial, to ask your Lordship to direct the Jury if the facts stated in the count be true, to convict the parties, and to find a verdict for the Crown upon that count. He must show that an offence is described in every one of the counts before he can get them sent to trial. It won't do to say that although one is a bad count, another may be a good one, and that there is a possible construction of the Statute that will support it. He must show that not upon a possible construction of the Statute, but upon the sound and true judicial meaning of the Statute, every one of these counts describes something which, if the facts contained in it be true, is a crime, before he can get it sent to trial. He is not entitled to have anything sent to trial which does not infer the conclusion that the Lord Advocate draws from it. If, taking the facts stated in any one of the counts for granted, there is nothing in the Statute which says that in respect of these facts the vessel shall be forfeited, the Lord Advocate is not entitled to have that sent to trial. It may be that in England the objection I am now stating would be raised in another form. It is the more common practice in England to raise objections of this nature in arrest of judgment, instead of stating them before the case is sent to trial; but the very reverse is the form we usually adopt in Scotland. I am not aware that it is a common practice, or a practice almost known in our Courts, to move in arrest of judgment after the jury have found a verdict on the issues sent to trial in any case.

Lord Ormidale.—I suppose it is not an incompetent course. I think it has been done.

Mr. Cook.—I never saw it done; but unless before sending the issues to trial there had been some such special reservation of relevancy as we rather wished your Lordship to insert in your interlocutor here, I think it would be quite hopeless to state any such objection in this Court. And the reason is obvious, because in England the Record is sent to trial, and any objection which appears on the face of the Record is, in their ordinary practice, raised in arrest of judgment. But with us, the Record is not sent for trial; the issuable matter is extracted from it, and sent to trial, and in every case where issues are adjusted and approved as the issues to try the case, it is almost if not altogether tantamount to a judgment that what is sent to the jury is relevant to infer the conclusions of the Summons, and will do so if proved before the jury. I apprehend, therefore, that we are perfectly entitled to state our objections to this Information in the present form, and I must confess that my impression as to the expediency of stating them in the present form has been very much strengthened in the course of this discussion, because, without depreciating the ability of Mr. Rutherfurd's address, I am entitled to say that my learned friend stated scarcely anything which could be called a sufficient answer to the objections to the Information stated by Mr. Clark. Before going to these objections, I may refer again to the terms of the 7th section of the Statute. A good deal has been said about the ambiguity of that section, and I am very far from saying that it is expressed so as to make it possible to give a very complete or adequate description of the offences which it means to describe, which shall be free from doubt or question. Undoubtedly, a great deal of difficulty has been found in exactly describing the offences which the Statute means to create, and that the Crown have found some difficulty, both here and in England, in describing the offence, may perhaps be inferred from the fact that they have attempted to describe it in 98 different ways. They have not described it in 98 different ways, because it is so easy to describe that it may be described in 98 different ways, each of them clearly and beyond doubt describing an offence. It is described in 98 different ways because the Crown are doubtful which of the 98 ways of describing it is the true description. But there are one or two points which I think this section of the Statute, and the whole of the Statute, make quite clear. Looking at it broadly, what is it that the 7th section meant to make criminal? It is equipping, furnishing, or arming a vessel with certain intents. Equipping is the stock of the crime, if I may so express myself; but equipping a ship being quite possibly, in itself, a perfectly innocent act, if done not for any power at war, and if not done with any intention to violate neutrality, it must be done with certain intents in order to make it criminal. But the intent is nothing at all, unless it is connected with equipment. The Statute does not make it criminal to sell a ship to a foreign power, even with intent that that foreign power shall use it for the purpose of committing hostilities against another foreign power. That is not made criminal. The Statute does not even make it criminal to employ a ship, already built, furnished, and equipped, in the service of a foreign power, against another foreign power with whom that power may be at war. That is not made criminal by Statute. It may be an offence at common law. It might be piracy for any subject of this country to employ a vessel already completely equipped for war, to commit hostilities against another foreign power with whom Her Majesty is not at war. It might be piracy, and it might be a high crime and offence,—a much higher crime and offence than anything described in this Information. But it is not made criminal under this Statute. What this Statute makes criminal is equipping, furnishing, fitting out, or arming a ship with certain intents; and the intent therefore beyond all doubt, being necessarily connected with equipping, and not being criminal under this Statute, unless as connected with equipping, the intent necessary to make any count relevant under an Information laid on this Statute, must be the intent of the equipper. It cannot be separated from the equipping. It must be an intent entertained by the person charged with equipping or arming the ship. The Statute enacts that if any person within any part of the United Kingdom —(*Reads*). Are the intents there not necessarily connected with the equipment, the fitting out and arming the vessel? It is not said if any person shall employ a vessel already fitted out, with that intent; that is not the offence. It was not necessary to declare that to be an offence, because it would have been an offence independent of the Statute. But the previous law had been found insufficient to enable the Government of the country to preserve neutrality so completely as was thought desirable, and as was thought due to foreign states, and a new crime had to be created,—something which would have been perfectly legal before was to be declared in future illegal, in order to give Government larger powers to preserve the neutrality of the country. Therefore not merely the employment of a vessel with a commission to commit hostilities was to be held illegal,—that is already provided for by the law,—but whereas it is now quite legal for any subject of the country engaged in that description of trade to build a vessel and to equip it in any manner he thinks proper, and with any intent that he thinks proper, to sell it to any state whether at war or at peace, the Legislature think it necessary, with a view to preserve the neutrality of the country, to enact not only that the employment of a vessel armed and equipped to cruise against the subjects of another country with whom Her Majesty is not at war, shall be criminal, but that the equipment and furnishing and arming the vessel for that purpose and with that intent, shall in future be held illegal. It is to be held illegal if you equip, furnish, or fit out a vessel, either to be used as a transport in the service of any power against a foreign power with whom the government in whose service it is employed is at war, or if you furnish or fit out or arm it with intent to cruise and commit hostilities yourself against any prince, state, or potentate, that also is to be an offence. The equipping is declared an offence, but it must be an equipping with a certain intent, the intent being inseparable from the equipping, and being necessarily in the sense of the Statute the intent of the equipper, and of no one else. Well, I think it is clear beyond all doubt upon the construction of the Statute, that what is made criminal here is equipping with certain intents, and that those intents must be the intents of the equipper, and not of another party. If that be clear upon the reading of the Statute, I am quite warranted in submitting to your Lordship that if I can find any count in this indictment which charges as criminal against me the equipping of a vessel, not with an intent on the part of me, the equipper, either to employ it as a transport-ship, or to employ it to cruise and commit hostilities, but with an intent, or knowing or believing that it may be employed with these intents by some other party, that is no offence under the Statute. The Statute don't make it an offence for anybody to sell a vessel to a foreign power flagrantly at war with another, though it may be well known that the vendee will employ it to cruise and commit hostilities. You are not responsible for the intents of that other party: you are only responsible for your own intents; and if I find that the counts of this Information, or any of them, impute it to me as a crime that I am equipping, or concerned in equipping or furnishing, a vessel which I know or believe or intend shall be used by some other person with certain intents, that is no offence under the Statute, because it does not charge me with equipping with an intent of that kind myself, but it charges me with knowing or believing that some other person with whom I am dealing may have such an intent. It may be right or not to carry the enactments of the Statute further than has been done, but with that we have nothing to do. It may be that the enactments of the Statute, as they stand, are insufficient to enable the Government to do all that is necessary to observe an absolute neutrality, and to compel all the subjects of the country to maintain what we or some other foreign governments may think an absolute neutrality. That may be, but we have nothing to do with that question. These are matters of policy, and are exclusively for the Legislature. What we have to do with is, what is the right construction of the Statute as it stands, and whatever extension of the law it might be prudent and right for the Legislature of the country to pass, we have nothing to do with that; if the offence charged against us has not already been made a crime by the law as it stands, I am entitled to prevail in my claim for the property of the vessel.

Lord Ormidale.—That argument would strike at the whole Information; indeed it would go very far to destroy the Statute,—to find that there was no statutory offence in it.

Mr. Cook.—I shall now advert particularly to the first count, and the others framed on the same plan; and our objection to these counts comes to this, that they do not describe an equipping of the vessel with an intent in the mind of the equipper alone. That is not what the 1st count charges. All the intent that is charged is an intent that it should be employed in the service of certain foreign states. That is not criminal at all. I am quite entitled to equip a ship in order that it may be employed in the service of certain foreign states styling themselves the Confederate States of America; but what gives the sting to this count is, that it is done with intent to cruise and commit hostilities. All our intent is, that it shall be employed by the Confederate States. The intent, that it shall cruise and commit hostilities, is not an intent in my mind, but it is the intent of the employer of the ship, which necessarily must be the Confederate States of America, because the ship is to be handed over to them. It is to be put by us into the service of the Confederate States, and after becoming engaged in their service, it is to be employed with intent to cruise. I can have no intent with reference to its employment after that, in one way or other. I have no control over the vessel. After I hand it over to the Confederate States, it is their property, and any intent with regard to the employment of the vessel must, after that, be an intent entertained not by the person who equipped the vessel, or who sold it to the Confederate States, but it must be entertained by the Confederate States, or by the persons whom they appoint to the command of the vessel. That is clear beyond doubt. So that if there be any force in language at all, we are charged here with a criminal offence, and our property has been seized, because we have equipped a ship which may in future be intended by the Confederate States to be employed in a certain manner. No such offence is described in the Statute, no such offence is made criminal as against the equipper, and no such offence is made the ground for seizure of the vessel. Now, I submit that that arises clearly upon the reading of the count, and if so, it cannot be sent to trial. If this count is sent to trial, the Lord Advocate will be entitled to prove the probable intent of the Confederate States of America with reference to the use of the vessel after it is handed over to them. I have nothing to do with that. He is not entitled to lead any such proof; he is not entitled to say that, suppose he established such intent by proof, it would infer anything against me. Why then send it to trial? I adopt the observation of Mr. Shand as to this matter, and I submit that you are now in as favourable a position as you possibly could be at the trial, and after hearing the whole evidence that may then be adduced by the Crown, to determine whether this count could possibly infer a seizure or not. If I grant the truth of all the facts in it, what more can the Lord Advocate ask? What is the use of sending it to proof, if I, granting the truth of all the facts charged, am still in a position to maintain to your Lordship, as I do, that they don't infer a forfeiture of the vessel? My objection is to relevancy. I say no statutory crime is described in this count, or in any of the counts formed on the same plan, and therefore I submit that they ought not to be sent to trial. My learned friend says it is very odd that this objection was not stated in the course of the trial of the 'Alexandra' case, and that there is very strong presumption that as it was not stated there, there is nothing in it, because it is not to be supposed that we on this side of the bar could be capable of discovering an objection that had escaped the vigilance and the great legal ability of the eminent persons who were employed for the builders in the case of the 'Alexandra.' For the honour of the bar, I cannot admit that that is a good logical observation, because it is quite competent for us if we can discover any objections that escaped them, to state them to your Lordship. But I don't pretend to such merit, because I am here humbly following in the steps of the very eminent person who conducted the case for the owners of the 'Alexandra,' and I shall show your Lordship immediately that this objection was very carefully and elaborately stated by Sir Hugh Cairns before the Jury in the 'Alexandra' case, and very carefully reserved, although the course that the case took before the Jury rendered it unnecessary ultimately and in the sequel to pronounce judgment upon it. But before I do that, I think it will be as well to advert to the second point touched on by Mr. Clark, because Sir Hugh Cairns, at the same time that he stated the objection which I have already dealt with, stated also the objection which Mr. Clark made his second point. That second point goes not merely to the 72 counts which I have referred to, but it goes to the whole counts of the Information with the exception of the 97th and 98th; and that objection was that in respect the Crown have omitted, and of course we are entitled to assume, because it does not seem to be disputed even by Mr. Rutherford, omitted *ex consulto*, to use the word 'arm,'—to charge us not only with equipping and furnishing, but with arming the vessel, none of these 96 counts describe an offence under the Statute. It is quite true that the word 'arm' was not charged in the 'Alexandra' case, and the way in which the Court got over that was this, the Chief Baron and Baron Bramwell held that the equipping, furnishing, and fitting out a vessel with intent to commit hostilities meant arming,—that there could be no equipping and furnishing a vessel with intent to commit hostilities without arming it, and therefore that the whole expressions in the Statute, equip, furnish, fit out, or arm, in order to commit hostilities were convertible terms; equipment to commit hostilities meant arming, furnishing with intent to commit hostilities meant arming, fitting out with intent to commit hostilities meant arming, just as much as arming with intent to commit hostilities meant arming. That was the way in which the Chief Baron and Baron Bramwell construed the indictment, and therefore it became very immaterial and unnecessary for the Chief Baron to give any directions to the Jury in regard to the structure of the Information on that point. But that is not the plan on which the Information here is framed, and I am obliged to take my objection before the case is sent to trial, and I am now entitled to point out that the Crown here are using the words equip, furnish, and fit out, not as synonymous with arm, but as meaning something else than arm. It cannot be supposed, or so put in argument, that if the Crown had intended and meant that equip means arm, they would have missed out arm. Why should they use an equivocal expression when they had the expression itself in the Statute before them? That cannot be suggested, and is not possible. The Crown has omitted the word arm, because they are of opinion that without charging arming at all,—charging something short of arming, something that does not infer arming at all, they yet describe an offence. Now, is that so or not? Is that the true reading of the Statute? I don't say that the point is not a doubtful point, because there are different opinions upon it in the Court of Exchequer, but I have the authority in my favour of the Chief Baron and of Baron Bramwell, both of whom distinctly say, and put it as the ground of their judgment in that case, supporting the direction of the Chief Baron, that on the fair reading of the Statute, the words equip, &c., meant arming. The Chief Baron, at the close of his opinion, makes that the ground of his judgment. He says there may be degrees of arming, that it may not be necessary to have the complete armament of cannon on board, but that there must be arming. In the *Weekly Reporter*, p. 268, he says, 'The degree is settled and determined by taking 'the whole sentence,—the ship is not to be equipped, &c., in order 'to cruise or commit hostilities; if the equipment amounts to that 'the law is broken; if it does not, no offence has been committed.' There is his distinct opinion, that unless the equipment amounts to arming, no offence has been committed under the Statute. But the Crown, on the plan of this Information, charge us with something short of arming, therefore if the Chief Baron's law be right, no crime has been charged. Baron Bramwell states it a little more at length. At p. 269, he says, 'The section reads thus:—"If any '"person within any part of the United Kingdom shall equip, '"furnish, fit-out, or arm any ship or vessel, with intent or in order '"that such ship or vessel shall be employed in the service of any '"foreign prince as a transport or store-ship, or with intent to '"cruise or commit hostilities," &c. Now to ascertain the meaning. 'On the part of the Crown it is said that if there is an intent that 'the ship shall be employed in the service of any foreign prince 'with an intent to cruise or commit hostilities, any equipment 'with that intent is sufficient, however unfit to accomplish such 'intent; that the rigging, victualling, manning, and other parts of 'equipment are lawful or not, according to the intent with which 'the ship will be used by those for whom they are done. This is 'said to be according to the very words of the Statute. Supposing 'it to be so, it seems to me that the difficulty is only shifted—that 'the question remains, what is the meaning of the words "with in-'"tent or in order that such ship shall be employed in the service '"of any foreign prince with the intent to cruise or commit hos-'"tilities?" Does it mean with intent or in order that by means 'of such equipment she may cruise or commit hostilities, that she 'shall be in a condition for proximate hostilities, so that the port 'she leaves will be a "station of hostilities?" or does it mean, as 'contended by the Crown, that an intent is within the Statute 'where the equipment is in order that she may be employed in the 'service of a foreign prince, though further acts on his part are 'necessary to enable her to cruise or commit hostilities? I think 'this is a correct statement of the question, and it seems to me 'that it must be answered adversely to the Crown's contention. I 'think the fair and natural meaning of the words is, that the 'equipment must be fit for cruising or the commission of hostili-'ties. The word "intent" before "to cruise or commit hostilities" 'seems put there on purpose to show this.' Now, no equipment can be sufficient to cruise or commit hostilities unless it infer arming; I suppose that will not be disputed; no one will set out to cruise or commit hostilities against a foreign power with an unarmed ship. The equipment to cruise and commit hostilities must infer arming.

Lord Ormidale.—Must there be a fighting crew on board?

Mr. Cook.—There may be degrees. You cannot fight the ship without a fighting crew.

Lord Ormidale.—Then you cannot seize the ship till the crew is on board.

Mr. Cook.—The Crown must show that there was an intention

on my part that the equipment should be completed in the port, —that before the vessel left the port she should be completely equipped and manned,—the intention and the crime must exist in my mind. That is what constitutes the essence of the offence. The seizure may be made before the whole thing is done, provided the equipper be in the course of doing that which after it is fully completed, is a complete and proper equipment. Therefore, it is not necessary to warrant a seizure that I should actually have engaged a crew, or that I should have any cannon on board; but it is necessary in order to warrant a seizure that I, the equipper, have an intent and purpose that before the ship leaves the port in Her Majesty's dominions where the equiping is now going on, she shall be completely furnished and equipped?

Lord Ormidale.—That would fall under the count of attempting and procuring.

Mr. Cook.—Provided there is an intention that the equipment shall be complete, I quite grant that; but if the engagement is of this description, I am to equip and fit out only up to a point which leaves the vessel still quite unfit to cruise or commit hostilities;—if all that I am to do is to frame the hull of such construction as to be capable of receiving an armament of cannon or with fittings for working cannon, or some equipment towards fitting the vessel in a condition to commit hostilities, but still equipment short of the point of a complete equipment,—if that is all I am to do, and it is understood that I have an intent to do no more, then that is not an offence under the Statute, however far I may have gone in bringing up the vessel to that incomplete state of equipment. The Crown is not entitled to seize the vessel however far I have gone in my equipment of the vessel, if the equipment were to stop short of a final and complete equipment. If anything remained to be done which was only to be done not in a port of the United Kingdom, but in some port beyond Her Majesty's dominions,—if she was to receive no armament, and was not to be put in a state to commit hostilities till she reached one of the Confederate ports, then the seizure was unwarrantable. That is what the Crown have charged here. They *ex consulto* omit the word 'arm,' and, therefore, I am entitled to suppose that in using only the words equip, furnish, and fit out, they are using them in a sense which stops short of arming; but that is not an equipment with intent to cruise and commit hostilities; it cannot be an equipment with that intent, because your intent is to equip the ship, and to part with her in a state unfit to commit hostilities. Therefore, there is no such intent on our part. I believe I am entitled to maintain that argument on the structure of this Information, and therefore I submit that all these counts, taking into view the Crown's peculiar construction of the word 'equip,' fail to describe the offence made criminal by the 7th section. But was it admitted on all hands in the 'Alexandra' case, that this would not do? It was not. I shall read the words in which Sir Hugh Cairns states his objection to the Court in the course of the trial. It begins at p. 150 [p. 141 of other Report]: 'But now I come to another view 'of this section'—(*Reads to*)—'under your Lordship's sanction.' No judgment was pronounced on these objections of Sir Hugh Cairns, because the Jury found a verdict for the defendants on the whole 98 counts; and looking at the directions of the Lord Chief Baron, they could hardly have done anything else. The Chief Baron made it a very easy case for the Jury, because he directed them in express terms, that if they were satisfied that there was no evidence to the effect that it was intended there should be a complete equipment in the port of Liverpool, they must find for the defendant. He says in his charge:—'The offence against which 'this Information is directed is the equipping, furnishing, fitting 'out or arming. I have looked at Webster's American *Diction- 'ary*, and it appears there that "to equip" is "to furnish with 'arms," in the case of a ship especially. It is to furnish and com- 'plete with arms. That is what is meant by equipping. "Fur- 'nish" is given in every dictionary as the same thing as "equip." 'To "fit out" is "to furnish, supply," as to fit out a privateer; 'and I own that my opinion is that "equip," "furnish," "fit out," 'or "arm," all mean precisely the same thing.'

Lord Ormidale.—Do you think any two officers in any navy in the world would agree as to what is a perfect and complete equipment?

Mr. Cook.—I am putting it to your Lordship, not as an officer of the navy, but as a Judge. We must construe it according to the legal meaning of the phrase. No doubt there may be a difference of opinion as to what is complete equipment, but I am safe in saying that no officer of the navy would hold that a ship was equipped in a state fit for committing hostilities, unless she had some armour on board, and a crew to use it. He gave that direction to the Jury, and the Jury found the case consequently a very easy one, because there was not only no evidence, but scarcely an allegation that the ship either was in the port of Liverpool completely fitted, or that there was any intention completely to fit her and equip her in the port of Liverpool; the Jury found a verdict for the defendants, and Sir Hugh Cairns did not find it necessary to move in arrest of judgment. The only question which came to receive a judicial decision afterwards was, whether the direction of the Chief Baron to the Jury was right or wrong. The points which Sir Hugh Cairns would have raised in arrest of judgment did not require to be determined; there is some allusion to them in the judgment of the Chief Baron and some of the other judgments, but they were not determined. All that was determined was that the directions of the Chief Baron were not wrong, and that therefore the verdict must stand. But that the Chief Baron entertained the opinion that the Statute must be read as we construe it, is I think perfectly plain from one passage of his judgment. In pointing out that the Statute charges equipment with two intents, he says, 'When two intents are men- 'tioned'—(*Reads* as quoted at p.   , *ante*). His opinion was that it was not necessary to have a judicial determination of that, because he adhered to the opinion that the equipment must be complete. But here you have his opinion that the obvious and grammatical construction and reading of the 7th section is to take the two things as alternative—that there must be either an equipment with an intent on the part of the equipper that the ship shall be used against the foreign state, or that the ship shall be equipped with intent to cruise and commit hostilities. These, he says, are the two alternatives: both these intents must be entertained by the equipper, and that is the grammatical and obvious reading of the Statute. The reading attempted to be put on it by the Crown is a more forced and unnatural construction. We are here in a proceeding which is in substance and spirit a criminal proceeding, and I put it to your Lordship whether I am not entitled to ask you to adopt the obvious and grammatical reading of the Statute rather than the one which is forced and unnatural, the obvious meaning of the Statute being one which sets me free, the more unnatural and strained construction being one which infers a crime.

Lord Ormidale.—The Chief Baron referred to the interpretation of some of these words in Webster's Dictionary. If it was competent for him to examine a dictionary for the purpose of ascertaining the true meaning of the expressions in the Statute, and if it was necessary to ascertain the true meaning of these expressions in order to arrive at the conclusion that they had all precisely the same meaning, and were synonymous, may it not be competent that we should know from the evidence at the trial, from men skilled in such matters, what they mean, before we can determine the question. I should fancy that naval men would be better than a dictionary in such a matter.

Mr. Cook.—But is the case to be sent to trial in order to enable the Court, by the light of the evidence given at the trial to construe an Act of Parliament.

Lord Ormidale.—I have seen at trials here English counsel brought down to give us the meaning of an Act of Parliament.

Mr. Gordon.—That was done in one case, and it was strongly commented on in the House of Lords, because the idea of bringing down an English barrister to instruct the Court as to the reading of a British Statute is monstrous.

Lord Ormidale.—But it is another thing whether men of skill may not be adduced to tell us the meaning of technical expressions, and then we can apply the law.

Mr. Cook.—Some other points were noticed by Mr. Clark, and in particular he objected to the Information being split down into so many counts. I by no means give up what my learned friend said on that point, but as Mr. Rutherfurd did not refer to it, I do not trouble your Lordship with any farther observations upon it. I submit that all our objections are well founded, and should be sustained.

Mr. Gordon.—I attend your Lordship on behalf of the builders, and after the very full reply by my friend Mr. Cook, it will not be necessary for me to detain your Lordship by commenting at any length upon the terms of the Statute. I wish, however, your Lordship's consideration now to be directed to the course of procedure in this case. It was at first proposed that all questions of relevancy should be reserved entire to the defenders for discussion at the trial. That course was not acceded to in the only way in which we could consent to its being done, viz., by a judicial minute being put in on the part of the Crown, or by the understanding being embodied in an interlocutor pronounced by your Lordship; and your Lordship came to be of opinion that the proper course was that we should be heard at this stage upon the questions of relevancy. We have come therefore, on your Lordship's invitation, to be heard now upon these.

Lord Ormidale.—I think you misunderstand what I suggested, —and it was only a suggestion, not meant to control you, or perhaps even to guide you,—that the case might be sent to trial, but that you were clearly entitled to be heard; but I gave no opinion as to the proper course, and it is not upon my invitation that you are being heard now.

Mr. Gordon.—Did your Lordship not suggest that we should be heard?

Lord Ormidale.—On the contrary, I suggested that the case should go to trial.

Mr. Gordon.—But without any assurance from your Lordship that it would be open to us at the trial to state our objections to relevancy.

Lord Ormidale.—I could give you no assurance.

Mr. Gordon.—Then, having no such assurance, and it being suggested that we should be heard on this question, we are now before your Lordship upon our objections to the relevancy, in order that your Lordship may dispose of them before we go to trial. And what I now ask your Lordship is to find that, as regards certain of the counts to which we have taken objection, these are irrelevant, and ought not to be sent to trial. That course is attended with no inconvenience, and it is the invariable practice in the criminal court. It appears that there has not been much practice in the Exchequer Court in the matter, but so far as any practice does exist, it is consistent with the course which I am now pressing on your Lordship.

Lord Ormidale.—There was a great deal of practice in the Exchequer Court before the recent Statute.

Solicitor-General.—The constant practice formerly, when any question of law was desired to be raised, was to do it by a special case or a special verdict.

Mr. Gordon.—Is it proposed now that we should adjust a special case here?

Solicitor-General.—Certainly not, because we are not agreed upon the facts.

Mr. Gordon.—The way in which we desire to take this discussion is this, admitting that every word in the Information was proved by the verdict of a jury, you cannot ask the forfeiture of the vessel; and if your Lordship is of opinion that we are right in that matter, I submit it would be useless to send the case to a jury upon these counts, and that your Lordship should dismiss them altogether.

I am quite aware that in the Court of Session the course is sometimes, though rarely, followed, of sending cases for investigation by a Jury before the Court have decided the relevancy, *i.e.*, the legal right of the party to demand a remedy in the event of his obtaining a verdict. The Court have the privilege of deciding either law or fact in the first instance, but at all events that is a course which is adopted only in the class of cases where the law is attended with such doubt, that in order to pronounce a satisfactory judgment upon it, you must have the facts clearly established by the verdict of a Jury. But whenever a party comes to the Civil Court, founding upon an Act of Parliament, or upon any other kind of right, and states his case in such a manner that upon his own showing it does not come up to the requirements of the Statute, or to what the law requires, the Court will certainly not send for the determination of a Jury the facts stated by him, when, even admitting these facts, it is clear that he cannot get judgment in his favour. Now is that not the expedient course in the present case? We have here what may be called a monster Indictment or Information, containing no less than 98 variations of the alleged crime or misdemeanour. I don't know whether a copy of this Information will be handed to the Jury, but if it is, I can imagine nothing more calculated to perplex their minds; if it is not given to them, probably they will have as much difficulty in following your Lordship's direction upon these 98 counts.

Lord Ormidale.—Probably when it comes the length of my direction, they will be narrowed to half a dozen.

Mr. Gordon.—Then why should that not be done now? We are put on our trial here as *quasi*-criminals, and why are we to be perplexed with 98 different statements of the case against us, to all of which we must direct our attention? I think it is the clearest case that ever came before the Court for now pruning away the various charges which are not consistent with the legal statement of the case, and with the requirements of the Act of Parliament. I submit, therefore, that the fair and proper course for your Lordship to adopt is to find that those charges which you are of opinion cannot be supported by the Statute should not be sent to the Jury, but should be struck out. My learned friend has shown that these objections were stated by Sir Hugh Cairns at the trial in England, and that they were reserved by the Judge, that being the usual and recognised course in the Courts of England. It is from no unwillingness to meet our opponents before a Jury that I am pressing this, because it is with great reluctance we have had this discussion upon the relevancy at all; if we could have got an assurance judicially entered upon the face of the proceedings that it would be competent for us to state these objections at the trial, we would have not maintained these objections now before your Lordship. But what we ask now is a judgment upon these objections. The state of the law is this, that it is competent for any of Her Majesty's subjects to sell articles which are contraband of war to parties carrying on war against each other. It is quite competent for any of Her Majesty's subjects to furnish either the Northern or the Southern States with cannon, powder, and all the other *materiel* of war. It is further competent for any man in this country to build a ship of war, if he has not done it under contract, and he is entitled to sell that ship in the same way that he could sell cannon or powder to either of the belligerent parties.

Lord Ormidale.—The intent must exist while he is in the course of equipping?

Mr. Gordon.—Yes. The object of the Statute is this: the Queen exercises general authority over all her subjects, and she prevents them from enlisting in a foreign state, even though they are out of the kingdom. As regards the soil within our kingdom, she is by authority of Parliament enabled to prevent any person from building a vessel with the intention of its taking its departure as a cruiser, or as a transport or store-ship, with the intent of its entering the service of one of the belligerent parties, and committing hostilities against the other. The object was to prevent our ports from being made stations from which a hostile expedition should set out against one of the belligerents. Keeping that in view, what is required is, that there shall be an offence committed within the United Kingdom, that it shall be an offence which is called in the Statute equipping, fitting out, furnishing, or arming, and that that shall be done with one of two intents. This part of the case has been so fully discussed by my friend Mr. Cook, that I don't need to make almost any observations upon it. I shall merely say that the system of construction adopted by the Crown appears to me to be inconsistent with any construction which has been recognised by the Court, even with reference to Statutes which might be called remedial, and therefore entitled to a most favourable consideration. We are dealing with a highly penal Statute,—one for the first time creating an offence, and therefore you are to read it in such a way as not to give effect to it unless the words fully convey the meaning sufficient to constitute the crime. My learned friend says you are to read the words equip, furnish, fit out, or arm as disjunctively used, and therefore he says he will not introduce the word 'arm' into the counts, because the word 'or' is used disjunctively, although in the preamble the words are all connected by the conjunction 'and.' But how are you four or five lines farther, either to miss it out altogether, or to read it as used conjunctively, viz., when you come to the words, 'or with intent to cruise,' &c.? Though in the Information he does not conjoin the two intents with the word 'and,' substantially he does so by putting them both in the charge. But how is it possible, on any principle of construction of any Statute, above all, of a penal Statute, to hold that the word 'or' is to receive its full meaning in one part of the clause, and is to be held as being used disjunctively, and that when you go a few lines farther down, you are either to dismiss it altogether, or to hold it as used in a conjunctive sense? That is a rule of construction which has never yet been propounded in reference to any Act of Parliament. There is no difficulty whatever in construing this clause. Observe what is said: 'You shall not equip a ship.' There is the overt act; but equipping a ship being a perfectly innocent proceeding, it is necessary that you add a criminal intent. The Statute says you shall not equip or arm a ship or vessel with the intent that such vessel shall be employed in the service of a foreign prince as a transport or store-ship, or with the intent to cruise and commit hostilities. You commit an offence by building a ship with intent to use it as a transport, or with intent to cruise or commit hostilities. Where is the difficulty in reading the Statute? I can see none. I can quite understand how the question was not raised in the Alexandra case in the discussion on the motion for a new trial on the ground of the verdict being contrary to evidence, or in respect of misdirection, because all that was mooted on that occasion was, whether, looking to the terms of the Statute, the verdict was contrary to law or contrary to evidence. The question was properly raised at the trial, acknowledged by the Attorney-General as a serious question, which required to be reserved, and the Court did reserve it, and it was not required to be mooted again, in respect of the Jury having found for the defendants.

Lord Ormidale.—Does it appear that there was an arrangement that if the Court took a different view of it they would enter the verdict for the other party?

Mr. Gordon.—It was quite understood that that might be done. A good deal is done in the English Courts upon understandings, and that seems to be the usual course.

Lord Ormidale.—The case of the Alexandra affords a very good illustration of the danger of mere understandings. The whole miscarriage in the case took place in consequence of a misunderstanding.

Mr. Gordon.—My own experience is, that though people understand one another well enough to-day, there may be some unfortunate misrecollection in a week which leads to misunderstandings which are very disagreeable. It was for that reason that I would not take any private understanding in this case, unless our rights were reserved judicially.

Lord Ormidale.—You were probably quite right; but I think the Court would have gone very far wrong if they had in anticipation given any undertaking on the subject.

Mr. Gordon.—I have no doubt the course your Lordship took was the correct one, and I only ask your Lordship now to act in consistency with what you then did. As to these 72 counts, I think if your Lordship were to hear evidence for a week or a month you would be in no better position to pronounce judgment than you will be at the close of this debate. It is a legal question, upon which no light can be thrown by any evidence, and I now ask you to throw out of view altogether these 72 counts, upon the ground that they are not consistent with the legal construction of the Statute, even admitting the whole of the facts stated in them. What expediency is there in adjourning the consideration of this matter? It will only tend to perplex the Jury, if we ever come before a Jury, if the whole of this discussion is again to be repeated at the trial; no farther light can be thrown upon it, and therefore I press, with great earnestness, on your Lordship the propriety and expediency and justice of now determining this question of relevancy.

The next point is, whether it is necessary that the word 'arm' should be introduced into the charges, or whether it is sufficient that you sanction a charge going to the Jury with the word 'equip' alone, or with the word 'furnish' alone, or with the word 'fit out?' The Lord Advocate reads the word 'or' as used in a disjunctive sense here, and he says that the word 'equip' means something different from 'arm.' Now I would say, that if they are used in a disjunctive sense, the word 'equip' does mean something different from 'arm;' but if 'equip' cannot be made to cover the word 'arm,' on what principle is it that you support the relevancy of this charge? If the word 'equip' does not mean any portion of the armament of the vessel, if 'fit out' does not mean any step towards the arming of the vessel, and the word 'furnishing' is something distinct from 'arming,' then it comes to this, that here is a charge made against us for fitting out or furnishing us something different and distinct from 'arming.' If so, why should that not now be determined? My learned friend says, that we can ask for a direction from the presiding Judge, and that if he does not sustain our objection, if it is well founded, we will get a new trial. Is that a very comfortable position for a party to be put in who is now discussing the legal meaning of the terms in the Statute?

Lord Ormidale.—There would be no new trial according to your contention. There would be an end of the case.

Mr. Gordon.—If your Lordship were to send us to trial without any reservation of the objection, I very much fear that we might find ourselves hampered by any verdict following upon it; and therefore if you send any portion of this case to be tried by a Jury, in regard to which your Lordship thinks that the case may be irrelevant, and that it ought to be open to your Lordship at the trial to consider the relevancy, I ask your Lordship to reserve the effect of that in sending the case to trial. Don't let it rest upon misunderstanding, let it rest on a judicial recognition of our right to insist on the objection, so that if as regards any part of the case you think the relevancy doubtful, we may not be foreclosed in any after discussion by its being said that the discussion on the relevancy was taken before the Judge ordered the case for trial, and that it could not be raised afterwards.

I submit further, with reference to the third point, that the Crown ought not to split up the charges, and that the word 'or' is to be regarded really as used in a conjunctive sense here; that is to say, that you cannot charge me merely with equipping, omitting altogether the other words. I think there has been an unnecessary multiplication of charges in this case, and that truly there ought only to have been two, viz., that we did equip, fit out, furnish, or arm, with the intention of using the vessel as a transport, or with the intention of committing hostilities against the Northern States. There truly you have two offences, and certainly in framing any indictment under such a Statute as this, the Court would require the prosecutor either to use all the statutory words, or to use such plain language as indicated acts which would come up to the full meaning of the statutory words. But they choose, as they themselves say, in ignorance of where the true merits of the case lie, to multiply the charges to 98, though I think they should have been stated simply as alternative charges under this section. Now I say they are not entitled to do that, and that the multiplication of charges makes this Information irrelevant. The form which I have suggested appears to be the proper form as regards the Exchequer Court, because Mr. Clark pointed out that in Schedule B. of the Exchequer Act, with reference to the very case of seizure, where several acts are stated, all the statutory words are used in one count. Why should we not follow that example specially given us by the framers of that Act for our guidance in seizure cases? Why adopt a system which has not been recognised, so far as I know, in this country, of splitting up in this way the words used in the Statute, multiplying to an enormous amount the number of charges against the defender, who certainly must be very much perplexed when brought up on no less than 98 charges?

Lord Ormidale.—He would perhaps be more perplexed if the 98 charges were in one count.

Mr. Gordon.—I think not; but the 98th count does that—(*Reads it*).

Lord Ormidale.—Are they conjunctive or disjunctive there?

Mr. Gordon.—They are conjunctive.

Lord Ormidale.—Then that is one charge.

Mr. Gordon.—The 98th count is bad on other grounds. We object to it on the ground that it has the two intents, but we object to it on another ground. Perhaps I was wrong in saying that there were only two statutory offences, because there is the statutory offence itself, and there is also the attempt to commit the statutory offence. Now, the 98th count is bad, because it embodies in the count both the offence itself and the attempt to commit the offence. That, according to our forms in the Criminal Court, would be an improper way of setting forth a minor charge; in that count you would set forth first the substantive charge—the crime itself; and then you would put it alternatively, 'or that he did attempt to 'commit the crime,' so that the verdict should be clearly applicable either to the crime or the attempt to commit it. I think the proper course would have been to frame the charge in terms of the 98th count, omitting the double intent, making it as regards the intent consistent with the 3d and 4th charges, and omitting the attempt to commit the offence, making that, if they thought proper, an alternative charge. That would try the whole case. I submit that that is consistent with the form given in the Exchequer Act, and I submit that we shall be exposed to great injustice if your Lordship does not repel or sustain the objections which have been taken by us to the relevancy. I ask your Lordship to take either of these courses. If you sustain them then the Crown may acquiesce in the judgment. If you repel them I am afraid I cannot hold out the promise that the defenders will do so, but we shall at least have this satisfaction, that we shall have it in our power, and I should hope, even before the month of April, to get the judgment of the Court upon the relevancy, and in that way to clear the case from those objectionable charges, if your Lordship should be inclined to sustain these charges as objectionable. I submit that we are entitled to have these objections sustained.

Adjourned.

Saturday, 20th February 1864.

Solicitor-General.—I attend your Lordship for the Crown. The case is the second which has ever arisen in a court of justice upon the 7th clause of the Foreign Enlistment Act,—the only other being that of the Alexandra in England. It is impossible to conceive two cases more identical in their nature and character. The particular facts and circumstances may be very different, but the cases in their nature and character are the same; so much so, that I find it impossible to distinguish between them with respect to any question that can be raised upon the Statute. The facts in the one case may be sufficient to entitle the Crown to a verdict, while the facts in the other are not so, and yet the two cases be precisely alike, so far as they are capable of presenting any legal questions upon the Statute. This identity induced the advisers of the Crown in this country to follow, as nearly as possible, the Information which was presented to the English Court in that case. The facts to be charged were the same; the misdemeanour to be charged as a ground for condemning the seized vessel was the same in the one case as in the other. It must therefore be quite intelligible to your Lordship, why the advisers of the Crown here took as their model, and followed closely, the Information which was presented to the Court in the Alexandra case. It is very long, but long as it is, it presents really one single and simple case; and the explanation of its length is given by Chief Baron Pollock at the commencement of his charge in that case. He says, 'The Information is exceedingly long, containing some 90 counts; and the way in which 'this arises is this: the 7th clause of the Act of Parliament speaks 'of its being unlawful to equip, furnish, to fit out, or arm a vessel. 'Then there are counts charging the defendants, first, with furnishing, then with equipping, then with fitting out, but not with arming. Then the various forms in which the endeavour, the attempt, 'the being concerned, and so on, can be put, are all repeated over 'again with every variety of the equipping, furnishing, fitting out, 'and so on. And in that way the counts are swelled out to the 'number of 90. But they all come at last to this question, Was 'this vessel, as then prepared, at the time of the seizure, an 'object of seizure under the Act in question?' The purpose of the Information, here as there, is to have a vessel which has been seized by the Crown, proceeding on that clause, condemned as forfeited to the Crown. Of course the seizure was only right, and condemnation can only follow, if a misdemeanour has been committed under clause 7th of the Statute, aud therefore it is that the Information must set out the misdemeanour. The plea which we have now to consider is that each and all of the counts are bad in law. The plea does not set forth the objections in respect of which it is maintained, but we have heard these objections stated, and I am not in the least to complain of the course which my learned friends have followed. It is sufficient to say that it is a course which they were entitled to take; but I am further disposed to concede that it is a course which it was quite reasonable to take, and which may be attended with certain advantages, not because I anticipate that your Lordship will be disposed to decide upon the plea, or upon any of the objections stated in support of it, but because there is advantage in having the views of the parties communicated to each other, to a certain extent at least, before the trial, so that the trial may be conducted with a view to the questions of law which may ultimately be raised, or which are in the view of the parties, and which it may be in their power and in their intention afterwards to raise and to press. But before I proceed to consider these objections, I think it is fitting that I should state to your Lordship at the outset that I mean to object to their being decided. I shall state the grounds on which I do so, and I wish it to be quite distinctly understood that I do not desire to prejudice the case of the defenders by asking that they should be repelled, even though your Lordship should be very clearly of opinion that they are not well founded in law. The motion with which I shall conclude is that, notwithstanding of that plea, and the argument stated in support of the particular objections upon which it is founded, your Lordship should direct the case to be tried. I think my learned friends were under some misapprehension as to the views of the Court on the subject of stating these objections, and urging them at this stage. It is always competent for a defender to maintain that the Information against him is bad in law, so that the affirmance of it in point of fact cannot lead to any judgment against him. It is nevertheless open to the Court to decide upon any such question before the trial or not, as it shall appear in the particular case to be expedient to take that course or not; and no Court can be in a position to exercise a discretion upon such a matter until the nature of the objections upon which the plea is founded has been disclosed. Accordingly, when my learned friends announced that they had such a plea, which they meant at some time or other seriously to insist in, but at the same time professed, quite candidly no one can doubt, that they did not desire to delay the trial, but only that they should be kept safe by having their right to bring forward the plea or the legal objection at a future stage of the cause guaranteed or secured to them, by a reservation in the interlocutor sending the case to trial, your Lordship at once declined to give any such guarantee or assurance, but suggested that the parties, if they thought they had a legal objection which was fitting to be decided before trial, and a decision of which might prevent a trial altogether, should disclose the nature of it, and that course the defenders accordingly resolved to take; and they came here to disclose the nature of their objection, in order that your Lordship might determine, in the exercise of that discretion which undoubtedly the Court possesses, whether the objection was of such a nature that it was fitting to determine it before trial or no. There can be no question as to the competency of determining a legal objection before trial, but I was much surprised to hear the competency of taking another course questioned, viz., just leaving the objection alone, neither sustaining nor repelling it, but sending the case to trial, so that the party might raise any legal question after the trial, which was properly raised by the Information.

Lord Ormidale.—Or at the trial.

Solicitor-General.—Or at the trial. But my learned friends were under the apprehension that an interlocutor sending this Information to trial would impliedly decide that the counts in it are each and all of them framed upon a sound construction of the Statute. If sending the Information to trial would imply a judgment by this Court, that each and all of the counts in the Information were framed upon a sound construction of the Statute, so that the defenders should not thereafter be at liberty to object to any count, or to a judgment being pronounced upon a verdict affirming any count, on the ground that it was framed upon an erroneous construction of the Statute, nothing could be more reasonable than that the question upon the Statute should be decided now,—nothing could be more unreasonable than to object to the motion of the defenders that their objections should be decided now. The defenders, however, it is only just to them to say, suggested that there should be no doubt left upon this, and that their fears would be removed by a reservation, in the interlocutor sending the case to trial, of their objections to the Information in point of law. This was opposed by the Crown upon the ground, that it was not intended to reserve any questions or any objections by expression which the law did not reserve by implication; and that to introduce reservations expressly into an interlocutor, which were of such a nature that they reserved themselves—were reserved by necessary implication—would be to introduce an element of confusion and uncertainty into the course of practice. I think my learned friends might have taken some assurance and confidence from the procedure in the Alexandra case. The Information here is a copy of the Information in that case; it is only different in dates and names. There the construction of the Act of Parliament, which is at the foundation of the objection urged by the defenders here, did not escape the acuteness of the learned counsel who represented the defendants in that case. That construction, which the defenders here maintain to be the right one, the counsel for the defendants in that case also maintained to be the right one; but they did not think of asking that the Information should be thrown out before trial. On the contrary, the case was allowed to go to trial without any objection. At the trial, and at the commencement of his opening speech, the leading counsel for the defendants stated that construction of the Statutes which he maintained to be the right one, and the result to which it led. What was the observation of the Lord Chief Baron upon that, with the complete approbation and assent of the bar? One or other of two courses may be followed, with perfect safety to the interests of the parties: either by arrangement, the verdict, assuming it to be for the Crown, may be entered for the defendants, if the Court should be of opinion that your construction of the Statute is the right one; or you may arrest judgment upon the ground that a verdict affirming any one of the counts does not affirm a misdemeanour against the Statute, and therefore does not justify the Information and the condemnation. The first course can only be followed by arrangement noted by the Judge at the trial, though, as I understand, the arrangement is a matter of course. But if such an arrangement is not come to, the remedy of the aggrieved party is equally simple, and quite as complete and satisfactory. If the verdict in favour of the Crown is bad, in respect that it affirms a proposition which does not in law assert a ground of action,—in respect that it affirms a count laid upon an erroneous construction of the Statute, and the affirmance of which, therefore, does not affirm that a misdemeanour against the Statute truly construed was committed,—the defendant moves, in arrest of judgment, that the thing affirmed is not a misdemeanour justifying a judgment of condemnation; and under that motion he raises his question upon the construction of the Statute upon which the Information is laid. The notion that sending the case to trial implied a judgment to the effect that the Information was laid upon a sound construction of the Act of Parliament does not appear to have occurred to anybody, nor the notion that the defender was in any danger of having his ship condemned in respect of a verdict affirming as true in fact a count in an Information which did not aver a misdemeanour against the Act of Parliament.

Lord Ormidale.—It was suggested on the other side, that whatever may be the practice in England, arresting a judgment after a verdict was unknown in practice here, and that therefore there might be a risk if that was their only remedy.

Solicitor-General.—I should recommend my learned friends if they have any doubts upon that score, even with respect to proper Court of Session procedure, to study the judgment of Lord Brougham in Kirkpatrick *v.* Irvine. I state it as a proposition which appears to me unanswerably sound, that no verdict can do more with respect to any count in this Information than affirm that it is true in point of fact. There may be a great deal of law raised at the trial. The Judge at the trial will have to direct the Jury as to the meaning of these words which have given rise to so much discussion, 'equip, furnish, and fit out;' but proceeding upon a correct direction in point of law, a Jury can do no more than affirm the truth of any count in the Information in point of fact; but if that count does not aver in point of fact what is a misdemeanour under the Act of Parliament properly construed, how the affirmance of it in point of fact can lead to a judgment of condemnation upon the footing of such a misdemeanour having been found by the Jury I cannot conceive. No doubt the trial may be a very idle proceeding, but that a defender should take any harm from a verdict affirming as true in fact a count which does not aver a misdemeanour under the Act of Parliament, justifying a condemnation of the ship, is a proposition which is not even intelligible to my mind; unless indeed the Crown could be heard to say this—the very announcement of which as a suggestion appears to me to be extravagant.

Lord Ormidale.—Is there anything in the trial of the Alexandra case to indicate that all these questions of construction of the Statute might not have been raised at the trial, and that the Judge might not have told the Jury that the whole of the counts were ill-laid under the Statute, and therefore that there could be no verdict for the Crown?

Solicitor-General.—I should think it clear that that course might have been taken; and if the Judge had given an erroneous direction, it would have led to an exception, the result of which might have been a new trial, and therefore the course which the Lord Chief Baron said would be taken was the more convenient and expedient course, because the verdict of the Jury exhausted the Information, and left the question of law quite open.

Lord Ormidale.—He did give some directions in law?

Solicitor-General.—A great deal, in order to enable the Jury to try the Information before them. But is it doubtful that if the Court here extract an issue from a record and send it to trial, and the Jury affirm it in point of fact, that would not lead to a judgment in favour of the pursuer, and against the defender, if the defender could satisfy the Court that in point of law the affirmance of that issue in point of fact did not entitle the pursuer to a judgment against him? If anybody doubts that, again I say let him read the opinion of Lord Brougham in Kirkpatrick *v.* Irvine.

Lord Ormidale.—Are you aware of any precedent for this course, that where, in an ordinary action in the Court of Session, there is a plea on record against the relevancy, an issue is prepared and sent to trial without that plea being disposed of, either in favour of the defender or against him? When a verdict is returned by a Jury on an issue sent to them, which issue is intended to exhaust the case, do you know of any instance of a plea on the relevancy then being taken up and given effect to, notwithstanding the verdict? It may be done in the House of Lords, but do you know any instance of it being done in this Court after the verdict?

Solicitor-General.—I cannot mention an instance one way or other. If there are any such, I should think they must be extremely few. But I am not aware of the competency of it ever having been questioned.

Lord Ormidale.—My object in putting the question was in reference to your argument generally, that it would lead one to think that the proper course would be to let the Jury return a verdict on the counts of the Information, without directing them as to which of these counts were or were not sustainable in point of law under the Statute.

Solicitor-General.—I don't mean even to make a suggestion on that point. All I can now say with propriety is, that I think it would be competent for the Court at the trial to take either of the two courses, and I think the Judge might very properly take the parties along with him as to which was the most expedient of the two courses; either to direct the Jury (and the direction might come to a very simple matter as the case may be conceivably narrowed by the evidence) as to the legal construction of the count to which attention came to be particularly directed, and leave the validity of that direction to be made the subject of future discussion upon a bill of exceptions; or ask the Jury to dispose of the count, in point of fact, on the assumption that it was laid upon a true construction of the Statute, leaving that question to be afterwards raised upon the application of the verdict. Either course would be competent, and the most expedient course would be for the consideration of the Judge at the trial, and it might be thought fitting to take the views of the parties with reference to that.

And now I shall call attention to the three objections on which your Lordship is asked by the defenders to decide now, that each and all of the counts in this Information are bad in law. Two of them are based upon what the defenders maintain to be the sound construction of clause 7 of the Act of Parliament; the 3d, viz., the objection which is stated to the 98th count, is not of that nature, but is more properly an objection upon a point of pleading, and I shall deal with it first. The objection to the 98th count is, that it is cumulative, not alternative; that whereas the Statute uses alternative words, 'equip, furnish, fit out, or arm,' or attempt to equip, etc., the disjunctive 'or' is not used in the charge in the 98th count, but the conjunctive 'and,' the charge being that the persons named did equip, furnish, and fit out, and did attempt and endeavour to equip, furnish, and fit out, and did procure, etc. The objection therefore is, that the language of the Statute in using the disjunctive 'or,' the proper language of alternative, is not followed, but that the conjunctive 'and,' the proper language of a cumulative charge, is used. I need not remind your Lordship that we are required by the Statute to proceed as in a revenue Information for the condemnation of goods seized under one of the Revenue Acts, nor need I say that, by the Exchequer Act under which your Lordship is sitting, the Crown need not, under any Information, prove the whole of it, but only so much as may be necessary in law to entitle the Crown to a judgment. That is expressly provided in the 7th section of the Act. If your Lordship will look at a note upon the style and form of charges in Informations, which you will find in Mr. Bateman's book, p. 70, you will find the law and the practice, and a very large reference to authorities upon this point. He says, 'And care should be 'taken not to state the offence in the alternative; as that the de-'fendant did sell beer or ale, that the defendant imported, or caused 'to be imported; or that casks were used, or intended to be used. 'The conjunctive must be used, although the Statute be in the dis-'junctive. Thus, when a Statute prohibits maltsters from "tread-'"ing, ramming, or otherwise forcing together," the best way will be 'to state in the Information, "that the defender did tread, ram, '"and force together," &c.; and thereby such Information will be 'as positive as if it had mentioned the offence to have been com-'mitted by only one of the said methods; for where the nature of 'the offence is such that it may in part be committed by two, three, 'or more several methods or means, it is as positive to say it was 'committed by each of those particular methods, as to say it was 'committed by any one of them only.' That is the rule of the law of England in stating offences of this description, and it is not immaterial to observe that we are here following an English form, —introduced into this Court of Exchequer by the 6th of Queen Anne, and kept up by the recent Exchequer Act, the Act transferring the powers and jurisdiction of the Court of Exchequer to the Court of Session. That Act 6 Anne, c. 26, it is very material to attend to, and particularly the 6th clause, which gives to the Court of Exchequer in Scotland the powers, and enables them to follow the practice of the Court of Exchequer in England.

Lord Ormidale.—You must keep in view that by the 9th section of the Exchequer Act, it is expressly provided that the procedure in all causes commenced by *subpœna* shall, etc.—(*Reads*).

Solicitor-General.—That is the course of the procedure, but I am speaking now of the style and form of the Information. There is no rule and practice in the Court of Session as to Informations at all. But apart from the matter of authority, is it possible to state any objection to the reasoning upon which that result is arrived at? A man may commit a misdemeanour under this Statute by doing either of two things, with either of two intents. What is to hinder the prosecutor to say he did both things with both intents? Is not that saying he did each of them with each of the intents? If a man shall do either this or that, he shall be guilty of an offence; the prosecutor says he did both this and that, and that is objected to. Why? A question may arise hereafter,—I think it can scarcely be made a question, but I say nothing against its arising hereafter,—whether the Crown can obtain a verdict without proving the whole; but that the Crown is entitled to charge both seems as clear a proposition as can be stated. That the Crown does charge both is the objection to the 98th count of the Information here. I rather think there could be no objection to the Crown stating cumulatively several matters in an indictment in the Court of Justiciary, and being entitled to a verdict and a judgment by proving only one, or so much of the whole as might be sufficient. Frequently the prosecutor in the Court of Justiciary does not prove the whole of his indictment. Provision for this is made by the clause beginning with the words, 'all which or part thereof,' which simply mean to express what the law would imply, without any expression at all, that the charges are separable; so that if the prosecutor charges the prisoner with murdering two men, and succeeds in proving that he murdered only one, he shall yet be entitled to a verdict. If he charges the prisoner with stealing two horses, which I suppose he never would do in the alternative, he may only succeed in proving that he stole one, that is to say, one-half of what he charges; but if he succeeds in proving that he stole one, he will be entitled to a verdict. And so here, the Crown charges a misdemeanour under this Statute, committed in many ways, not alternatively, but charges that the defenders violated the Statute in every one of the particulars enumerated. That it is competent to charge this, I submit to be a proposition beyond the possibility of reasonable question, whatever may be the result of the trial with reference to the evidence which may be adduced.

I now pass to the more material objections which are founded on the construction of clause 7 of the Act of Parliament, and in respect of which your Lordship is asked to find that the Information is bad in law, or at least that several counts of it are bad in law. The first objection is that the intent to cruise and commit hostilities must be an intent on the part of the person equipping, furnishing, or fitting out the ship, not that it shall be employed by a foreign people, or indeed by any person other than himself, to cruise or commit hostilities against persons with whom the Queen is not at war, but an intent to cruise or commit hostilities with the ship himself. It rather appears to me, that though that idea did at one time occur to the learned counsel in the Alexandra case, being raised by the awkward and, at first sight, embarrassing manner in which the words 'with intent' are introduced immediately before the words 'to cruise or commit hostilities,' it was ultimately seen to be totally untenable, and given up. But that is no reason why my learned friends here should not maintain it as tenable now, and satisfy your Lordship, if they can, that it is the true reading of the Act of Parliament, and that, as this Information proceeds upon another reading, it does not aver a misdemeanour against the Statute in this respect, and that it would therefore be idle to send it to trial.

Lord Ormidale.—Though there were nothing very special in regard to that point, in consequence of the verdict being for the defenders in the Alexandra case, does it not sufficiently appear in the opinions of the Barons, in giving judgment on the motion for a new trial, that they were really at one about it?

Solicitor-General.—And that the parties had come to be at one, and to see that it was utterly untenable. The Attorney-General stated how they had all come to see quite clearly that the Statute must be read as if these embarrassing words so awkwardly introduced, 'with intent,' had not been there at all. However, the proposition is maintained now, and maintained to be so clear that it would be idle to send this Information, which proceeds upon what I submit to be a more rational construction of the Statute, to trial. Well, the case of the defenders here is this,—if any person equip, furnish or fit out a vessel with intent that it shall be employed in the service of a foreign state as a transport or store-ship, he shall be guilty of a misdemeanour under the Statute; but if he equip, furnish, or fit out, and, I may add, 'and arm'—for I may take these words in, in dealing with this objection—the ship with intent that it shall be employed by such foreign state to cruise and commit hostilities against another state with which the Queen is not at war, he shall commit no offence under the Statute. That is the argument. There may be words in the Act to support it, but there is no reason to recommend it. It is impossible that it can have been intended. I don't mean to say that a Statute shall not be construed against what a reasonable man may think was the intent of the Legislature. The words may be too strong for the intent or too strong for good sense, and the Court may be compelled to yield to the words against the sense and reason of the thing, and in all probability against the intent of the Legislature. But the Court won't yield to that except under the severest compulsion. To recommend a construction by force of words against the force of sense requires an irresistibly strong argument upon the words. I need say no more, I suppose, in order to satisfy your Lordship that the construction here contended for has not sense or reason to recommend it, but quite the reverse. All the recommendation of the sense and the reason of the thing is the other way. Now, the only words, so far as I can see, that are founded upon as compelling a construction against what must be admitted to be the sense and the reason of the thing, are these words, 'with intent,' when repeated for the second time; but if these words have the meaning and effect which is contended for, then I think it is plain that the words which follow them are entirely disconnected from the words which precede,—I mean in this way, that whereas by the preceding words of the enactment it is made a misdemeanour to equip, furnish, or fit out a ship with intent that such ship shall be employed in the service of any foreign state, etc., as a transport-ship, that is an offence without reference to the words which follow 'or with intent to cruise,'—I mean these words, 'againt any prince, state, or potentate, or against 'the subjects or citizens of any prince, etc., with whom His Majesty 'shall not then be at war.' So that the construction contended for would lead further to this, that it was an offence by this Statute to equip, furnish, or fit out a ship, with intent that it should be used by a foreign nation as a transport or store-ship, although not against another state with which this country was not then at war, for these words, 'against another state or people with whom this country was 'not then at war,' are disconnected by the second words, 'or with 'intent,' and connected only with 'cruising and committing hos-'tilities.' That is mere extravagance. The Statute does not make it an offence to equip a ship, with intent that it shall be used by any foreign state, etc., as a transport or store-ship, unless the intent is that it shall be so used against a people with whom this country is not at war; and in order to introduce that qualification, you must read the words which follow 'with intent,' as connected with the employment of the ship by the foreign people; and if you do that, then what is the meaning of the whole provision? It is, if you equip a vessel with intent that it shall be employed by a foreign state either as a transport or store-ship, or to cruise or commit hostilities against a state with whom this country is not at war, then you commit the misdemeanour. The words 'to cruise, or commit 'hostilities,' in that way refer back to the word 'employed,' and the whole provision is thus reasonable, sensible, unobjectionable. If any person in this country shall equip a ship with intent that it shall be employed in the service of a foreign state as a transport or store-ship, or to cruise or commit hostilities, in either case against a nation with whom this country is not at war, a misdemeanour shall be committed.

Mr. Cook.—Employed by whom?

Solicitor-General.—Employed by the foreign state.

Mr. Cook.—With intent that it should be employed by the foreign state.

Solicitor-General.—With intent or in order that such vessel shall be employed in the service of any foreign state as a transport or store-ship, or to cruise or commit hostilities. In short, you get at the right reading by doing what I think all the learned Judges in the Alexandra case said ought to be done—deleting the words 'with intent' when they occur the second time.

Lord Ormidale.—It is not clearly brought out what the learned Judges exactly meant on that point.

Solicitor General.—At p. 350, Baron Channell said to the Attorney-General, 'I understand your argument'—(*Reads* as at p. 41, *ante*).

Lord Ormidale.—And at p. 278, in the judgment refusing a new trial, I see Baron Pigott is reported to say, 'It is agreed on 'all hands that the latter words "with intent" may be taken as 'omitted here.'

Solicitor-General.—And Baron Channell at p. 329: 'It has 'been assumed on the argument on both sides'—(*Reads* as quoted at page 42, *ante*). But the argument of my learned friends is this, you must disconnect the words which follow the second intent from the words which precede, back as far as the words 'equip, furnish, 'fit out,' etc., and read it in this way: If any person shall in this country equip a ship with intent to cruise and commit hostilities against any prince, state, etc. Now, this reading is impossible, because the words which follow 'to cruise and commit hostilities,' viz., 'against any prince, state, or potentate,' qualify the employment of the ship as a store-ship, and therefore the words 'to cruise or 'commit hostilities against any prince,' etc., have reference to the employment of the ship, and the intent on the part of the equipper is that the ship shall be employed by one foreign state for that purpose against another. You have the intent on the part of somebody else in both branches of the clause. The equipper intends that the ship shall be employed by somebody else for one or other of two purposes. These purposes are his intent,—I mean the intent of the other who is to employ the ship. The equipper intends that the ship shall be employed by a foreign state against another foreign state, either as a transport or store-ship, or as a cruiser to commit hostilities; but whether the employment is the one way or the other, whether as a transport or store-ship, or as a cruiser to commit hostilities, that, as Mr. Cook observed, is the affair of the person employing the ship, not of the person equipping it. The person equipping it has no concern with it after he has handed it over to the person who is to employ it, and the particular employment for which that person uses it is his affair, not the equipper's affair; but surely it is intelligible to say, if you equip a ship with intent that it shall be employed by another for a particular purpose, this purpose shall be considered with reference to your intent, and the guilt of your intent. I procure a pistol for the purpose of another man using it to shoot my enemy, or to shoot his own enemy; my guilt consists in procuring it with the intent that it should be so used, not by myself, but by another. A person equips a ship with intent that it shall be used, not by himself, but by a foreign nation against another foreign nation with whom the Queen is not at war, either as a storeship or as a cruiser; there is no difficulty about the intent in the one case more than the other. The person for whom the ship is equipped is the person to use it, and it is immaterial to the person furnishing him with the ship whether his use is to be as a storeship or as a cruiser, provided that the purpose for which he intends to use it is known to the person who equips it for him. I don't see the embarrassment about the double intent.

Lord Ormidale.—Except the peculiarity of the language.

Solicitor-General.—Yes, of the introduction of the second 'with 'intent;' and the absurdity of speaking about the intent of the second party being the intent of the first, just shows that these words are blunderingly used.

Lord Ormidale.—It may come to be that the Statute is inoperative altogether.

Solicitor-General.—I don't think that was suggested by anybody in the Alexandra case. So much for the first point, which I don't ask your Lordship to decide; far from it. I don't ask your Lordship to prejudice the case of the defenders by finding now that this Information is laid on a correct view of the Act. It may never be necessary to decide the question at all; but it certainly would be very inconvenient to have it decided now, and to go to the Court now upon it, and to the House of Lords thereafter upon it, and then come down and have a trial, at which all sorts of questions may with propriety be raised, and upon which the House of Lords may again be resorted to. That is not the way to keep the case together, and it is in reference to that consideration of convenience that I ask your Lordship to send the case to trial, notwithstanding these objections, leaving them to be raised hereafter at the proper time, and when all the objections can be disposed of together, and if necessary the whole case appealed at once.

Lord Ormidale.—That was very much the view expressed by the Lord President in the case of Wyllie Guild *v.* Orr Ewing,—the expediency of saving the cost of a double litigation.

Solicitor-General.—I now proceed to the second objection, which is that the word 'arm' is essential to a charge where the intent is that the vessel shall be employed to cruise or commit hostilities; that it is no offence by the Statute to equip, furnish, or fit out a vessel with the intent that it shall be used by a foreign state to cruise or commit hostilities against another foreign state; that these words, 'equip, furnish, and fit out,' are applicable to the case of an intent that the ship shall be employed as a transport or store-ship, the word 'arm' being the word applicable to the intent that it shall be employed to cruise or commit hostilities. I think it is sufficient in answer to this to say that the words are all equally applied to both employments and both uses of the ship. There are in one sense two intents, in another only one,—the intent that the ship shall be employed in one or other of two ways. Well, what is the thing which if done with that intent is a misdemeanour? To equip, furnish, fit out or arm a ship. The intent is applied to the whole of these things put alternatively, and if you have two intents, both intents are made applicable to the same things put alternatively. If you shall equip, furnish, fit out, or arm a ship, with intent that it shall be employed as a transport or store-ship, or to cruise or commit hostilities, you shall be guilty of a misdemeanour. There is no such separation, as the objection implies or assumes. It is impossible on any principle of construction, when you have the words in the collocation in which they occur here, to separate them and say they mean this: If you shall equip, furnish, or fit out a ship, with intent to use it as a transport or store-ship, you shall be guilty of a misdemeanour; or if you shall arm a ship with the intent that it shall be employed to cruise and commit hostilities, you shall be guilty of a misdemeanour. The Statute says nothing of the sort. If a ship was armed with intent that it should be employed as a transport or store-ship against a nation with which this country was not at war, according to this construction no misdemeanour would be committed, for the word 'arm' is confined to the intent that it shall be employed to cruise or commit hostilities; for this argument, if it separates the words 'equip, furnish, and fit out,' from the intent that the vessel shall be employed to cruise or commit hostilities, equally separates the intent that it shall be employed as a transport or store-ship from the word 'arm.'

The argument is, You are to read the words 'equip, furnish, or fit 'out,' with reference to the intent of employment as a store-ship, and the word 'arm' with reference to the intent to cruise or commit hostilities. But if that be so, then it is no offence to arm a ship with intent that it shall be used as a transport or store-ship against a foreign nation. If you separate the words 'equip, furnish, and fit out,' from the intent to cruise or commit hostilities, you must, by parity of reasoning, separate the word 'arm' from the intent that it shall be used as a transport or store-ship. The plain reading of the Statute is, if you equip, furnish, or fit out, or arm a ship with intent that it shall be employed as a transport or store-ship, or to cruise or commit hostilities, you are guilty of a statutory offence. What is the meaning of these words, equip, furnish, fit out, or arm, this Information does not undertake to say, nor was it necessary that it should. That is a question for the trial, and I am not going to say almost anything on the meaning of these words, because while general definitions are difficult and dangerous, it may be found very easy with reference to the evidence in the particular case to say whether it shows equipping, furnishing, or fitting out within the meaning of the Act. A general definition of the whole meaning of a word is one thing; an opinion that it includes a particular matter is another and a totally different thing. It humbly appears to me that the learned Judges in the Alexandra case dealt too much with generalities, and too little with particularities. I should not like to undertake to give a dictionary meaning which should exhaust the word 'equip,' or the word 'furnish,' or the expression, 'fit out,' as applied to a ship. But there may, and probably there will, be little difficulty in saying whether the particular thing proved in the particular case to have been done was equipping, furnishing, or fitting out according to the true sense and meaning of the Act; and therefore the propriety of delaying the consideration of the meaning of these words till you see the particular facts with reference to which it is to be determined whether these words include and apply to them or not. For my own part, I humbly think that in a good many of the observations which have been made upon this matter, there has been a confounding of two different things; the one the meaning of the words as used in the Act,—what they will extend to and comprehend, and the other what particular facts within the meaning of these words will at the same time afford evidence of the intent with which they were done. It would not have occurred to me, I must confess, that the words 'equip, furnish, and fit out,' were limited in their meaning to warlike equipment, furnishing, and fitting out. That they include warlike equipment, furnishing, and fitting out, nobody can doubt, because the words are general, and include all sorts of equipping, furnishing, and fitting out; at least, I should have thought so. If the equipment (just to use one of the words) is not such as to indicate any knowledge on the part of the equipper that the vessel was to be used for warlike purposes, which it would not be if the equipment was not of a warlike character, it might, and probably would be in vain to ask a Jury to find that that equipment had been made with the statutory intent; that is to say, it might be impossible to persuade a Jury that equipments not at all of a warlike character, but the proper and ordinary equipments for the merchant service, were made with the intent that the vessel should be employed as a cruiser to commit hostilities. But apart from the question of intent, which may be proved in a hundred ways,—it may be proved even by direct evidence,—it would not have appeared to me that the nature and character of the equipment was of any materiality. But at all events your Lordship cannot be asked to determine now what extent or kind of equipment, furnishing, or fitting out will be sufficient to amount to the statutory offence.

Lord Ormidale.—The argument on the other side, as I understood it, was this, and it is quite intelligible, that where the offence charged is not the furnishing or equipping of a ship as a store or transport ship, but for the purpose of committing warlike operations, your having omitted the word 'arm' destroys your Information, because a ship not armed is not fit for that purpose. Possibly in one view that it is a plea which could be sustained independent of evidence altogether, because you don't say there was armour here.

Solicitor-General.—I quite understand the argument, and I don't mean to dispute in the least that it is quite competent to sustain that argument now, if it is thought to be well founded; but it appears to me to be clearly ill founded. In the first place, surely it is not to be maintained that you may not have equipment, even of a warlike character, short of arming. Does the equipment of one of the Queen's frigates begin and end with the arming of her? Does the equipment, fitting, and furnishing of one of the Queen's frigates for warlike purposes, and for nothing but warlike purposes, because the ship is constructed to be used for nothing else,—does the equipment, furnishing, and fitting out to cruise and commit hostilities begin and end with the arming? Is not that nonsense upon the very face of it? Surely the equipment, furnishing, and fitting out of a frigate must or may have proceeded a great length before you put the guns on board.

Lord Ormidale.—The powder, I suspect, is the last thing.

Solicitor-General.—But I don't know whether putting the powder on board is arming.

Mr. Cook.—That is furnishing.

Lord Ormidale.—Is the cannon arms without the powder?

Solicitor-General.—No doubt about it,—unloaded arms.

Lord Ormidale.—Can you say a ship is armed without the powder?

Solicitor-General.—The guns will do little harm without the powder, just as the cutlasses will do little harm without the men. But, says my friend, and I think truly, the powder is furnishing. You furnish the vessel with powder to feed the guns, just as you furnish her with provisions to feed the fighting crew. She is furnished up to the point of putting the guns on board, and yet no offence would be committed under this Act of Parliament! She is built as a man-of-war, she is equipped, furnished, and fitted out as a man-of-war in every respect, including the powder and the shot, up to the point of putting the cannon on board, and no offence against the Act of Parliament, my friend says, has been committed, because she has not been armed, and the word 'arm' is the word alone employed where the offence charged is to cruise and commit hostilities! This is the merest extravagance, and I don't think it necessary to dwell on the point any further. But I think the equipping, furnishing, and fitting out, referred to in the Statute, even where the intent is to cruise and commit hostilities, may be not of a warlike character at all, but of a description common to ships of war and merchant ships. Would it be an unintelligible provision, would it be at all inconsistent with the spirit and meaning and object of the present Statute, if the enactment, descending to particulars, had made it a misdemeanour to store or furnish with provisions a vessel with intent that it should be employed to cruise and commit hostilities against a state with which the Queen was not at war? The words used are general and comprehensive; a variety of expression is used in order to insure the greatest comprehensiveness and generality,—'equip, furnish, fit out.' The offence consists not in what is done, as my learned friend Mr. Cook very well stated it, but in the intent with which it is done. The thing done is innocent apart from the intent. It is the intent that stamps the guilt of misdemeanour upon it. Nothing can be more innocent than to furnish a ship with provisions, with beef, and biscuits, and water; the act is innocent in itself, but it may be made guilty by the intent with which it is done. If you furnish a ship, having a fighting crew on board, with provisions and clothes and everything necessary, except armour, to go upon a hostile expedition, your intent being that she shall go upon that hostile expedition, the act, innocent in itself, may by virtue of the intent, become a misdemeanour. Now again, I say I think there has been very great confusion here, between the nature of the act as affording evidence of the intent and the nature of the act which with evidence of the intent would infer a misdemeanour under the Statute. Unless the furnishing is of such a warlike character that the party making it cannot have failed to know the purpose for which the vessel was to be used, you may in vain expect a conviction; but the Crown may be able to prove the intent by evidence other than that which is to be inferred from the mere nature of the equipment. The nature of the equipment, furnishing, or fitting out, as affording evidence of the intent may be most material, but it is not material if you prove the intent otherwise. Now, I think there has been great confusion here, but it is not necessary, and indeed is not competent to proceed on these matters now. But as the subject has been adverted to, I have thought it right to explain my own view, which is this, that anything which amounts to equipping, furnishing, or fitting out a ship falls within this Act. I don't care whether it has proceeded the length of equipment, furnishing, or fitting out peculiar to a ship of war, or only the length to which the equipment, furnishing, and fitting out of a ship of war is the same as the equipment, furnishing, and fitting out of a merchant ship or any other ship. I suppose it is undoubtedly true, at all events your Lordship could not consider this case at this stage upon any other notion, that up to a certain point a ship of war is equipped, furnished, and fitted out in the same way as a merchant ship. If a party has proceeded no farther than that, you may not be able to prove his intent that that ship should be employed to cruise and commit hostilities.

Lord Ormidale.—Would you hold the building of a ship enough?

Solicitor-General.—No; because that is not equipping, furnishing, or fitting out a ship. You must first have a ship before you can proceed to equip, furnish, and fit it out. You first make or otherwise procure a ship, and then as you intend to use it for mercantile or warlike purposes, you equip, furnish, and fit it out. But up to a certain point, the equipment, furnishing, and fitting out will be the same whether it is intended to be used for the one purpose or the other. If you have no evidence against a person whom you are charging with equipping, furnishing, and fitting out a ship, with an intent that the vessel shall be used for warlike purposes, except that which is afforded by the nature of the equipping, furnishing, and fitting out, then you will get no conviction against him, unless the equipment, furnishing, and fitting out be warlike; but if you have any equipment, furnishing, or fitting out put upon a ship which you can prove to have been made by the party making it, with the intent that that ship shall be employed for warlike purposes, I don't care what the character of the equipment is, in short, the character of the equipment may be everything as evidence of intention,—it is nothing if you have the intention proved otherwise. Take a ship of the line with iron plating, it may be with a ram at the bow in order to run down the enemy; she requires to be equipped, furnished, and fitted out: she has got nothing on board, and she is brought into port in order to be furnished and fitted out for a crew; you require the equipments, furnishings, and fittings-out which are necessary for the accommodation of such a crew as would fight that ship; well, these are furnished, clothes of such a description as sailors and marines wear in a fighting ship, provisions, biscuits, beef, rum, &c., all the equipments, furnishings, and fittings-out are complete, except that there are no guns or cutlasses on board; and it is possible,—it would not occur to any sane man to suppose,—but it is possible that that vessel might go away with her crew on a pleasure cruise. Well, but it is proved to demonstration, proved by the man's own confession, that he who so equipped, furnished, and fitted it out, did so with intent, not that it should go on a pleasure cruise, not that it should go upon a mercantile expedition, for which it was manifestly unfitted, but that it should go to commit hostilities against the United States of America,—have you not the statutory offence? Therefore I think that not only is the absence of the word 'arm' here no objection, but that in order to prove the statutory offence, it is not even necessary to prove that the equipment, furnishing, and fitting out were peculiar to warlike ships, provided it can be proved that they were made with the intent that she should go to cruise against a state with which this country was not at war. If you have no evidence of that intent except that which the nature of the furnishing afforded gives, then unless these furnishings be of a warlike nature, you may look in vain for a conviction, and in the generality of cases, the evidence of intent may consist chiefly, and perhaps entirely, of reasonable inferences from the nature of the thing done. But it is not necessarily so.

Lord Ormidale.—That was a view taken by one at least of the learned barons,—by Baron Pigott.

Solicitor-General.—Perhaps your Lordship is right. Now these are generally the grounds upon which I ask your Lordship to take the course which I indicated at the commencement as in my view the right one. I have been necessarily lead to consider the legal objections stated to the Information, because without regard to these you could not determine whether it was expedient or no to decide them now ; but I have done so, not with the view of asking your Lordship to sustain our answer to them upon the merits, however clear I may think that answer is, and however ill-founded I may think the objections are, but to induce you, without regard to these objections, to send this case to trial.

Lord Ormidale.—Supposing I were to give effect to your motion, I think it rather appears, from Section 6 of the Exchequer Act, that I must appoint a day for the trial.

Solicitor-General.—In short, your Lordship would dispose of the case, as I have suggested, by appointing a day.

Lord Ormidale.—If that should be the view I take after considering the argument on both sides,—an argument which certainly, as the Solicitor-General has observed, will not be thrown away, whatever may be the result of it now, because both parties have communicated to each other their views on very important questions, which sooner or later will require to be determined,—but if that is the view that I take, I shall be happy to fix any day that I possibly can that will be convenient for both parties. If you are ready now to allow me to name the 5th of April, I shall do so. On the other hand, if you desire it, in place of making avizandum now, I will let the case stand on the roll till Tuesday morning by which time I shall probably have made up my mind as to the course that I shall take ; and then if that should be my view, we can fix the day. I would suggest, at the same time, that with a view to the trial going on, if that is the course to be followed, as early a day should be fixed after the ordinary sittings as you think convenient. I suppose you could not be very well prepared before the sittings ?

Solicitor-General.—I am not sure of that. We have a diligence here, which I cannot ask your Lordship to dispose of by any interlocutor at this moment, but if the trial is to go on, is there any objection to it ?

Mr. Gordon.—Yes.

Solicitor-General.—Then as we are all here, and the motion for diligence is on the roll, perhaps that discussion might be taken now; it is very advisable that the trial should not be postponed for the execution of a diligence.

Mr. Gordon.—Mr. Clark is instructed, I understand, to oppose it, and it was the distinct understanding that it was not to be taken up till this question was disposed of; the usual course being not to allow a diligence till an issue is adjusted, or till there is an order for trial.

Lord Ormidale.—Of course, they must be separate orders, but they may be done on Tuesday.

Mr. Gordon.—We are anxious to have the question of relevancy disposed of before the other question is entered upon.

Lord Ormidale.—Suppose I were of opinion that a day should be fixed for trial, and that I fix a day on Tuesday, and then by a separate interlocutor following that, grant the diligence in whole or in part, that would be no reason why you should not take the first or both interlocutors to review, if you are advised to do so. I don't suppose it would interfere with that in the least degree, if that is what you are aiming at; and, so far as I am concerned, I shall be very glad that you get a review of my judgment.

Mr. Gordon.—The usual course is to give notice for diligence after the issues have been adjusted, and I don't see why we should depart in this case from the usual course. I don't see why in this Exchequer penal or criminal procedure at the instance of the Crown, greater indulgence should be given to the Crown than to an ordinary litigant.

Solicitor-General.—The Crown is not asking any indulgence, and it surely would be no great indulgence that my friend should tell us on Tuesday what the objection to the diligence is.

Lord Ormidale.—The diligence having been intimated some time ago, I think it would be no indulgence to take it up on Tuesday. If we do that, I don't think it would be doing anything but what is done in any case. Certainly I will not do anything in this case that I would not do in any other case.

Solicitor-General.—The diligence has been on the roll, and with a notice for many days; and with the prospect of a speedy trial, all I suggested was that it might be discussed on Tuesday, so as not to lead to the postponement of the trial.

Adjourned.

Tuesday, 23d February.

Lord Ormidale.—I have made up my mind to appoint this case to be tried, and I have stated in a note to my Interlocutor the considerations which have influenced me in coming to that conclusion, and which I hope, whatever may be the fate of my judgment, may at least relieve the defenders from the apparent anxiety under which they are about their right afterwards to make available, to the full extent to which they ought to be made available, all their pleas in law and of relevancy. Now the question is what day shall I fix for the trial?

Mr. Clark.—Perhaps your Lordship will tell us what your interlocutor is?

Lord Ormidale.—It is in the statutory words, simply appointing a day for trying the matters put in issue by the Information.

Mr. Clark.—Does your Lordship in your Note express any opinion to the effect that all these questions are to be held as open?

Lord Ormidale.—Yes, I do; but there is no reason why the defenders, if they are under any anxiety about this, should not get the opinion of the Court upon it.

Mr. Gifford.—We are anxious to have the trial on the earliest day possible, but a good deal may depend on the defenders' objections to our diligence. We suggested the 5th of April, on the footing that we would get our preliminary investigations made, documents recovered under our diligence, and our evidence all ready by that time; but as the defenders may go to the Inner House, perhaps it is not absolutely necessary now to fix a day.

Lord Ormidale.—The Statute is very precise as to naming a day, and what I would suggest is, that we should fix the day just now; and if it is found that the trial cannot go on upon that day, it could be altered of consent afterwards.

Mr. Gifford.—Subject to the right of either party to get it postponed, if, by reclaiming note or otherwise, preparations for the trial are impeded, I have no objection to the 5th of April being fixed.

Lord Ormidale.—Then I shall insert the 5th of April. I have added this to my Note: 'On the assumption that the Lord Ordinary is right in appointing the case to be tried before disposing of any questions of law and relevancy, parties were agreed on the day fixed by the Lord Ordinary for the trial.'

Mr. Clark.—As we are going to reclaim, we can hardly say that we agree to the 5th of April.

Lord Ormidale.—Then I shall add, that in the event of going to the Inner House, as stated by the defenders, circumstances may require some other day to be fixed. I am very glad to think you are going to the Inner House, because you may be able to elicit from the Judges, even if they adhere to the Interlocutor, such observations as may keep you perfectly safe.

Mr. Gifford.—The only other motion that can be made to-day is the motion for a diligence at the instance of the Crown for the recovery of certain writings relating to this vessel. My friends have intimated that they are to reclaim against your Lordship's Interlocutor fixing the day for trial, and in that view it is desirable that we should have brought under the review of the Inner House at the same time this question of diligence.

Mr. Clark.—You may never succeed in getting a trial, and what right have you to be using diligence to recover documents before you ascertain if you have issues to go to trial with? Until issues are adjusted in ordinary practice, diligences are not granted. I think the Crown must be put in the same position as a subject in this respect, and is therefore not entitled to obtain a diligence to recover writings until the issues for trial are settled. The Crown pretend to be under great hardship, but, in point of fact, they are, to my great surprise, using diligence at this moment for the recovery of writings and documents, and fittings and other articles connected with the Pampero, under what warrant I am sure I don't know; but we have found out that the Procurator-fiscal is citing persons to appear before the Sheriff of Lanarkshire to be examined as witnesses in the case of the Pampero.

Mr. Gifford.—I apprehend we have now got your Lordship's Interlocutor adjusting the issues.

Lord Ormidale.—I think the proper course is to have this question of diligence settled at once, in order that if any dispute arises between the parties on the subject, it may be brought under the consideration of the Court at the same time as the Interlocutor appointing the day of trial, so as to save a double journey to the Inner House. If the Court recal the other interlocutor, they will, of course, recal this.

Mr. Gifford.—Then I move your Lordship for diligence, in terms of the specification.

Mr. Clark.—I have no objection to the first seven articles of the specification, and my friends may take a diligence for recovery of them. But I have an objection to the eighth, which is, 'all models, 'drawings, sketches, or plans of the said ship or vessel, or of any 'of her equipments, fittings, or furnishings, or intended fittings or 'furnishings.' Now, as to these models, drawings, etc., it is not said by whom they were made; they are not in any way connected with the parties whom I represent; and while I have that general objection to the whole article, I specially object to the recovery of models of what are called intended fittings or furnishings. If there are any equipments on the vessel which will bring the vessel within the Act, these equipments have been seized; they are on the vessel now, and that is all I think they are entitled to. It is out of the question to ask for models of intended fittings and furnishings. As regards Article 9: 'All orders or memoranda, or copies 'of orders or memoranda, in regard to the said ship or vessel, or 'the construction thereof, or of any of her equipments, fittings, or 'furnishings,'—it is not said by whom these orders or memoranda have been given; nothing is said to lead to any connexion between the defenders and these orders and memoranda, and therefore I object entirely to that article as it stands. The 10th Article is for the purpose of obtaining copies of documents which are already called for, and I don't object to that. The 11th Article stands thus: 'The whole equipments, furnishings of the said ship or 'vessel Canton or Pampero, in so far as not already seized for the 'use of Her Majesty.' They may seize whatever they like, but they are not entitled to get a diligence for the purpose of asking me to complete the seizure for them. Their right under the Statute is to seize the unlawful article. What they want a diligence for is to put the parties respectively upon oath, for the purpose of making them exhibit the article to be seized, and then seizing it. I object entirely to that article, and to the addition which they propose to make to it, 'as also for recovery of all drafts or copies 'of the writs mentioned in the first six heads of the specification.' That can only be obtained, of course, failing principals; and if that is added, I don't object, and the same qualification should be made as to Article 10.

Mr. Gifford.—I think I am entitled to get the drafts and copies without the limitation of failing principals, because I am here seeking to prove the intent of the parties who fitted out the Pampero. To Art. 8 my friend has two objections; 1st, That it does not say by whom the drawings or models were made, or for whose behoof they were made or used. He forgets that the present Information is not an Information against persons at all. I don't require to connect the drawings and models with any person; it is sufficient if I connect them with the thing. The allegation in the Information is that the ship has been furnished and fitted out for an unlawful purpose. No doubt I have mentioned certain persons whom I believed to have been concerned in that unlawful act, but I also say others or numbers of persons unknown; and it is not necessary for the success of the Crown in the present examination that they shall bring home guilt to any one person. It is sufficient for the purpose of the Crown if they prove that this vessel was fitted and furnished contrary to the Statute, in order to justify its seizure and forfeiture under the Statute. And accordingly in this action, which is an action *in rem*, all that the Crown require to do is to prove that the intent with which the ship was furnished, fitted out, and equipped, was contrary to the Statute; and surely a very unexceptionable way of proving that, is to prove by the models, drawings, sketches, and plans what the intention was.

Lord Ormidale.—The intention of whom?

Mr. Gifford.—The intention of those who built the Pampero; I don't care who they were. The Pampero is the thing I am attacking. I don't care who did it. I am not asking for a penalty against any individual. That I might have done, and I might then have been required to connect the individual with the act.

Lord Ormidale.—The intention of whom?

Mr. Gifford.—The intention of those who built the Pampero; I don't care who they were. The Pampero is the thing I am attacking. I don't care who did it. I am not asking for a penalty against any individual. That I might have done, and I might then have been required to connect the individual with the act. Even suppose it had been an accusation against individuals, surely I would be entitled to get models by whomsoever made, leaving me to prove at the trial the connexion of the parties with these models. It is not necessary in requiring notes, or documents, or bludgeons in a Crown trial, that before I get them I shall connect them with the panel. I must do that at the trial, or they will go for nothing. So here, if I get the models, I must prove at the trial that the vessel is fitted up according to these models. Suppose I were to find a model with the name Pampero or Canton upon it, with guns out at its port-holes, with all the equipments of a man-of-war, and the Confederate flag at the mast-head, would that not be good evidence in this case, because I cannot tell who made it? I may recover it in the hands of one of the defenders; I may recover it in the hands of the shipwright or the foreman, or the parties engaged in making it; and is it any objection to my recovering it that I don't say in the specification who made the model? Surely not. I must connect it in some way at the trial with the ship, but I undertake to do that; and I submit that nothing in this specification is more relevant or pertinent to the purpose for which the specification is asked than the models, and drawings, and sketches, and plans of the vessel in question. My friend's second objection is as to the 'intended' fittings and furnishings. My answer to that is, that the question to be proved at the trial is intent, and if I prove that these are her intended fittings, I go a great way to prove the intent with which she is fitted out.

Lord Ormidale.—According to a certain view that may be taken of the Statute.

Mr. Gifford.—Yes. Suppose one of her fittings were guns, and I find them marked with the word Pampero, is not that a piece of evidence with reference to the intent with which the ship was fitted out? Suppose I prove that she has port-holes, I may get in somebody's yard in Glasgow the ropes by which the guns are to be attached to the ring-bolts? I connect these with the vessel, and the warlike character of her is made out, looking at the port-hole in the ship, the ring-bolt in the deck, and the rope to be attached to them to keep the cannon in its place. Surely these are of the essence of the case so far as intent is concerned. As to the objection to Art. 9, I have answered that already. I don't think we have anything to do in this action *in rem* with the question by whom. It is not necessary for the Crown to bring home guilt to any individual. There is no conclusion for punishment or a penalty against any individual. It is an action against the ship, and against the ship alone; and accordingly the objection as to by whom, or to whom, or how they were used, is not *hujus loci*.

Mr. Clark.—Would you object to put it, 'All orders, memoranda,

'or correspondence, or copies of all orders, memoranda, or corre-
'spondence in regard to the said ship or vessel, or the construction
'thereof, or of any of her equipments, fittings, or furnishings?' and I will take a joint diligence with you to recover these.

Mr. Gifford.—I think we had better not have a joint diligence. But I don't object to my friend moving for the correspondence in the largest way; I don't think I will object to that. Art. 10 my friend has no objection to, except that it should be failing principals, and that I have already spoken to. As to Art. 11, if I have been successful in showing that I am entitled to get the drawings of intended equipments, I am surely entitled to get equipments already prepared and intended for the vessel, so far as not already seized. Of course the demand is limited to the equipments and furnishings of this particular vessel. I cannot get the equipments of any other vessel, and it will be a complete answer to any demand for equipments, fittings, or furnishings, that they don't belong to this ship. But if I am entitled to show the intent with which the ship is fitted out, I am surely entitled to get, it may be in some adjoining yard, or in some other place, her fittings and furnishings.

Lord Ormidale.—All these Arts., 8, 9, 10, and 11, bear express reference to the ship in question, and whether they may be evidence at the trial is another matter altogether; probably a good deal will be necessary on the part of the prosecution to make them evidence at the trial; but in this matter of diligence to recover writings, I don't see that there is any such clear objection to these articles as can be maintained at present.

Mr. Clark.—Then your Lordship will grant us a joint diligence as regards Art. 9.

Lord Ormidale.—I suppose there is no objection to that.

Mr. Gifford.—We don't, of course, consent.

Lord Ormidale.—On both sides all questions of confidentiality are of course reserved if anything of that kind should arise. I suppose models made on the order of professional gentlemen for the purposes of this trial will not fall under the diligence on either side.

Mr. Clark.—I will not press any motion for a joint diligence now.

The Lord Ordinary pronounced interlocutors fixing the day of trial, and granting the diligence, against both of which the defenders reclaimed.

The Interlocutors, Specification, and Reclaiming Note will be found in the Appendix.

Adjourned.

INNER HOUSE—FIRST DIVISION.

Wednesday, 2d March 1864.

Mr. Clark.—I appear for the reclaimers, the owners of the ship 'Pampero.' The present proceedings commenced by the seizure of that vessel under the 7th clause of the Foreign Enlistment Act, and that was followed by an Information filed on the part of the Lord Advocate, for the purpose of obtaining a decree to the effect that the ship had been forfeited under the 7th section of that Act. A claim was then lodged by Messrs. Fleming and others, maintaining that no forfeiture had been incurred, and that the facts stated in the several counts of the Information were not so stated as to set forth the offences under the Statute by reason of which a forfeiture had been incurred. The defenders maintained, at considerable length, before the Lord Ordinary, that the counts were not relevant or well laid under the Statute, and we asked his Lordship to determine that question as one which ought to be determined before any inquiry took place, and as a question which could not be raised, so far as we knew, in any form except in the form in which it is now raised before the trial. His Lordship pronounced an interlocutor appointing a certain day 'for trying the matters put in issue by said Information.' In short, his Lordship has held the different counts as issues raised for trial. We are all the more surprised at the course which his Lordship has taken, because he does not say that the pleas which we have raised are bad in themselves; and I think your Lordships will notice, with some surprise, that the Lord Ordinary says:—'So 'far as the Lord Ordinary can judge at present, the defenders will 'not be precluded, merely by the case being appointed to be tried, 'from afterwards availing themselves of any plea in law and relevancy which is in itself well-founded; but as the Lord Ordinary 'cannot prejudge any matter whatever, so he can give no assurance 'on the subject.' It may therefore be that we have excellent pleas in relevancy and law against the sufficiency of the Information, and yet we may be cut out from stating these pleas at some future stage of the case. It is therefore all the more important that we should now, under this Reclaiming Note, bring distinctly under your Lordships' notice the pleas which we maintain against the relevancy of the different counts, and that we should have them definitively disposed of.

The Information consists of 98 counts; but from the Abstract of it you will see that, so far as the purposes of this argument are concerned, there are only ten counts which need be considered, viz., the first eight and the 97th and 98th. The counts, from the 9th to the 96th, both inclusive, are mere variations upon the first eight, and therefore the first eight may be taken as representing substantially all the others of the 96.

Before referring to these counts, I think it will conduce to clearness that I should bring under your Lordships' notice, in the first place, the terms of the Act under which these counts profess to be libelled,—I mean the Foreign Enlistment Act, 59 Geo. III. c. 69. The Act proceeds on the narrative—'Whereas the enlistment or 'engagement of his Majesty's subjects to serve in war in foreign 'service, without his Majesty's licence, and the fitting out and 'equipping and arming of vessels by his Majesty's subjects without 'his Majesty's licence, for warlike operations in and against the 'dominions or territories of any foreign prince, state, potentate, or 'person exercising, or assuming to exercise, the powers of govern- 'ment in or over any foreign country, colony, province, or part of 'any province, or against the ships, goods, or merchandise of any 'foreign prince, state, potentate, or persons as aforesaid, or their 'subjects, may be prejudicial to, and tend to endanger the peace 'and welfare of this kingdom,' &c. This is the preamble of the Statute, directed against the enlistment or engagement of his Majesty's subjects to serve in war in foreign service without his Majesty's licence, and directed against the fitting out and equipping and arming of vessels by his Majesty's subjects for the purpose of being used in war against a foreign state. The second section deals exclusively with enlistment. The third, fourth, fifth, and sixth regulate matters of procedure; and the seventh is the section on which this Information is founded—(*Reads seventh section*). The clause contains so many alternatives that I shall read part of it again, leaving out a number of the words which I think merely tend to confuse :—'If any person within any part of the United Kingdom shall, 'without the leave and licence of his Majesty for that purpose first had 'as aforesaid, equip any ship or vessel with intent or in order that 'such ship or vessel shall be employed in the service of any foreign 'prince as a transport or store-ship, or with intent to cruise or com- 'mit hostilities against any prince, state, or potentate, &c., such 'person shall be guilty of a misdemeanour.' The offence or offences under the Statute are contained in these words, the equipping of any 'ship or vessel with intent or in order that such ship shall be em- 'ployed in the service of any foreign prince as a transport or store- 'ship, or with intent to cruise or commit hostilities against any 'prince, state, or potentate;' and according to the reading which the owners of the ship put upon this Statute, there are two distinct offences under it, 1*st*, the equipping of any ship or vessel with intent that such ship or vessel shall be employed as a transport or store-ship against a foreign state; and, 2*d*, equipping any ship or vessel with intent to cruise or commit hostilities against any foreign state. These seem to me the two offences which the Statute creates, —the equipping with intent to employ as a transport ship, and the equipping with intent to cruise and commit hostilities against a foreign state; or in other words, I think the two expressions, 'with 'intent,' which occur twice in the clause, must both, according to ordinary construction, be referred to the words equip, furnish, fit out, or arm.

I shall now bring under your Lordships' notice the terms of the ten counts in the Information, which will disclose the character of all the rest—(*Reads* 1*st count*). Throwing out the language which is properly there, but which obscures the meaning of it, the charge is this, that Messrs. Fleming and others did equip the said ship or vessel with intent and in order that such ship or vessel should be employed in the service of the Confederate States of America, with intent to cruise and commit hostilities against the United States; and that charge consists not of libelling one intent, but of libelling cumulatively the two intents which are specified in the Statute. It is a charge that they did equip the vessel with intent that it should be employed in the service of the Confederate States, with intent to cruise and commit hostilities, and therefore, instead of the Information being so framed, on the footing that there are two crimes under the 7th clause of the Act, it is so libelled as to combine the two intents set forth in the Act, and by that combination to create one crime, which it seems to me perfectly incompetent for the Crown to do; because they are libelling under this count a crime or misdemeanour which is not within the Statute at all. The 2d count is exactly the same as the 1st, except that it is stated to be against the citizens of the Republic. The 3d count charges that the owners did equip the said ship or vessel with intent to cruise and commit hostilities against a foreign state, viz., the Republic of the United States of America; and so far as regards the objection that I am now stating, that seems to be a count which is well stated under the Statute. I shall consider whether there is any other objection to it subsequently, but as regards the objection which I am now making, it is well stated, because the words 'with intent to cruise' are made to refer to the equipment of the vessel. The 4th count is the same as the 3d, with the variation of citizens, and the 5th, 6th, 7th and 8th are the same as the 1st count, altering the name of the foreign state in whose employment the ship was to be, and the name of the foreign state against whom it was to be employed. In the whole of these eight counts, for the purposes of my present argument, I may say there are just two offences charged. In the first place, there is charged the equipment of the vessel with intent that it should be employed in the service of the Confederate States, with intent to cruise and commit hostilities against the United States; and, 2d, the equipping of the vessel with intent to cruise and commit hostilities against the United States. The first is a charge which libels cumulatively the two intents set forth under the Statute; the second is the equipping of the said ship or vessel with intent to cruise and commit hostilities,—the intent to cruise and commit hostilities being directly referred to the equipping of the vessel in the one case, but not in the other. It may be right to say, further, that the 9th to the 96th counts are all framed upon the same model as those eight to which I have already referred. There are 72 of these 96 counts which charge what I call the first offence charged under the Information, and there are 24 which charge the second offence. There are 72 which charge the two intents libelled in the 1st count, and there are 24 which charge, in the form of the 3d count, one intent only, namely, equipping with intent to cruise and commit hostilities against the United States—(*Reads 97th count*). That seems to be charged in the manner in which the first offence ought to be charged,—that they did attempt to fit out the vessel with intent that it should be employed as a transport or store-ship against a foreign state; and so the offence here consists not of the combination of the two intents, which are specified in the Act, but simply of a charge of intent that the ship should be employed in the service of a foreign state, as a transport or store-ship against another foreign state. The 98th count is very different, though making a charge with reference to a store or transport ship —(*Reads it*). This is certainly by much the most complicated of all the charges contained in this Information. It first charges the complete equipment, furnishing, and fitting out; second, the attempt and endeavour to equip, furnish, and fit out; third, the procuring to be equipped, furnished, and fitted out; and fourth, the knowingly aiding and assisting in the equipping, furnishing, and fitting out. In other words, it charges as an offence the complete equipment in the first place, and the attempt to equip in the second place. Then, with reference to the intents, it charges that the equipment was with intent and in order that such ship or vessel should be employed by the Confederate States as a transport or store-ship against and with intent to cruise and commit hostilities against a foreign state. The offence charged here, so far as regards the intent, is an intent to employ her as a store-ship against and with intent to cruise and commit hostilities against the foreign state.

These, I think, are all the charges contained in this Information, and they consist simply, I may say, of four. Of the first you have a specimen in the 1st count of the Information, the equipping with those two intents; of the second you have a specimen in the 3d count, equipping with intent to cruise and commit hostilities; of the third you have the only example in the 97th count, the equipping with intent to use as a transport or store-ship; and of the fourth you have the only example in the 98th count, the employment of the ship as a store-ship, and also with intent to cruise.

Lord President.—Is there any difference between the 5th count and the 1st count, except as to the parties who are to employ the ship?

Mr. Clark.—No; but the first count is a specimen of 72, with the variations mentioned; the 3d count is a specimen of 24 with variations; there is one constructed in the form of the 97th, being the 97th itself, and one constructed in the form of the 98th, viz., the 98th itself.

Lord Deas.—Does the 98th charge cumulatively all the intents charged in the others?

Mr. Clark.—I think so.

Lord Deas.—And describes all the characters described in the others? That appears to me to be the object of it, and I want to know if I am right.

Mr. Clark.—It combines both the intents.

Lord Deas.—Does it not give all the characters? If it was not meant for that purpose, Lord Advocate, what was it meant for?

Lord Advocate.—It was meant for the purpose which it sets out.

Mr. Clark.—With intent that its meaning should be concealed from those charged with this crime and misdemeanour! Now, taking the first charge in the Information, let me consider whether that is a charge which is relevantly laid under the Statute. And here I may inform your Lordships that we press for a judgment upon that question,—a question which we think it for the interest of the parties whom we represent to raise, and a question which we think must be disposed of before trial. The Lord Ordinary has said that he does not think proper to dispose of it before the trial, but it may turn out that though well-founded, we would not be entitled to raise it at or after the trial; because though that may be the Lord Ordinary's opinion, he says he can give no assurance on that matter. The very fact that the Lord Ordinary is in doubt upon the matter, and that I may possibly be prevented from raising this point at the trial, or subsequently to the trial, gives me the most absolute right to ask for your Lordships' judgment on the construction of this count. In short, we are trying here what I take to be little more or less in substance, whatever it may be in form, than a criminal charge or Information against these parties; and before we go to try whether the offence or misdemeanour has been committed, I am pleading, according to our Scotch form, against the relevancy of the indictment. And therefore supposing these persons had been tried at the bar of the Justiciary Court for the offence which they are said to have committed, and which leads, in consequence of their committing it, to the condemnation and forfeiture of the ship, the question just comes to be, whether, if the statement which is contained in the 1st count of the Information was contained in a criminal indictment under this Statute, directed against these individuals, your Lordships would or would not sustain the relevancy of that indictment? because nothing can lead to the condemnation and forfeiture of the ship, unless your Lordships should also affirm that the same thing being proved would lead to its being held that the owners, for whom I appear, were guilty of a misdemeanour under the Statute. Now, the Lord Ordinary has been led away, I think, by an extreme and unnecessary admiration for the course which was adopted in the case of the Alexandra, without considering whether or not we have the same remedies and the same opportunities in Scotland for raising the pleas which I now state. I am informed, as regards the case of the Alexandra, that while it might not have been competent to object to go to trial upon a demurrer without admitting the facts of the case, the right of the party is to move in arrest of judgment, assuming that a verdict is pronounced against him forfeiting the ship, or in a criminal information finding him guilty of the statutory offence. It is incompetent, I believe, without admitting the facts, to demur in the Court of Exchequer. It was so until the Procedure Act was applied to the Court of Exchequer, and it was not applied till the Alexandra case was tried. It may be now competent to demur without admitting the facts, but in England, prior to that Act being applied to procedure in the Court of Exchequer, it was incompetent to demur without admitting the facts; and if the party did not demur, but chose to go to trial, that is to say, to dispute the facts, or went to trial to ascertain whether or not the facts charged were true, he did so with this right reserved to him, that in the event of an adverse verdict being given, he was entitled to move in arrest of judgment in consequence of the counts not being well laid under the Statute on which the Information proceeded. And therefore it seems to me to be a very dangerous course indeed to follow blindly the procedure which took place in the sister kingdom under this Statute in the case of the Alexandra, and for that reason I have the extremest interest to have ascertained by the judgment of this Court, whether the Information relevantly charges a crime under the Statute, before I can be required to defend myself or my property against the accusation of the Crown. With these observations, let me ask your Lordships' attention to the 1st count, for the purpose of ascertaining whether it is or is not relevant; and I think it important, in aid of the construction, to consider what may be done in the way of equipping or arming vessels, without incurring the statutory penalty, or coming within the Statute at all. Upon that point we have certain American authorities, which were cited in the case of the Alexandra, and which were recognised as stating the law correctly under the English Act. I am considering this question for the purpose of ascertaining what is the meaning of the words 'with intent' under the Statute. It was held, in the cases to which I am about to refer, that it was no contravention of the American Act for a citizen of the United States to equip and arm a vessel of war, and send it to a foreign belligerent power for the purpose of selling it to that belligerent power.

Lord President.—That is, to send it to the territory of that power, for the purpose of selling it to that power if it is disposed to buy?

Mr. Clark.—Yes.

Lord Curriehill.—You say it was no contravention of the American Act?

Mr. Clark.—Yes; it was an American decision, and they, of course, had to decide it on the terms of the American Act, which is dated 20th April 1818, but that is simply a continuation of the Act of Congress of 1794. The clause of the American Statute under which this question arose was this:—'That if any persons 'shall, within the limits of the United States, fit out and arm, or 'attempt to fit out and arm, or procure to be fitted out and armed, 'or shall knowingly be concerned in the furnishing, fitting out, or 'arming of any ship or vessel, with intent that such ship or vessel 'shall be employed in the service of any foreign prince or state,' &c.

Lord President.—The word 'equip' does not occur there.

Mr. Clark.—No, it is 'fit out and arm, or shall knowingly be 'concerned in the fitting out or arming;' but no question turned on the equipment in the case to which I am to refer. The offence under that Statute was the fitting out and arming of a ship or vessel with intent that such ship or vessel should be employed in the service of a foreign state, to cruise and commit hostilities against the subjects of another foreign state, with whom the United States were then at peace. The question occurred whether it was a contravention of this Statute that a citizen of the United states should fit out and arm a ship of war, and send it for sale to a belligerent power at the port of that belligerent power, and sell it, and that it was used in committing hostilities thereafter in the service of that power; and it was held by the Court that that was not a contravention of the Statute, though, of course, the ship in its transit from the United States port to the port of the belligerent power—

Lord President.—To the market.

Mr. Clark.—Yes—was contraband, and subject to capture as contraband of war. The case is reported in 7 *Wheaton's Amer. Rep.*, p. 283. It is the case of the Santissima Trinidad, and the question arose in a somewhat odd way, viz., whether the captures made by the ship which was so armed and sent by the United States to certain Spanish colonies, were lawful captures as regarded the condemnation of the vessels which she had taken? It is shortly stated in the rubric: 'The sending of armed vessels or of munitions of war'—(*reads to*)—'by the other belligerent.'

Lord President.—That is, it is contraband of war.

Mr. Clark.—Yes, during transit. Mr. Justice Story's opinion is given at length at p. 340. It was maintained that the Independencia was not capable of making lawfully captures, in consequence of her being fitted out in contravention of the American Act; and Justice Story, in giving the opinion of the Court, used these words: 'The question as to the original illegal armament'—(*Reads as quoted at p. 12 ante*). So that, as regards what I may call the municipal law of the United States as fixed by their Act of Congress of 1794, which was the Act in force when the Independencia was sent to Buenos Ayres, it is fixed by this judgment that it is no violation of that Act of Congress if a citizen of the United States arms a ship of war and sends it to a belligerent power for the purpose of selling it to that belligerent power. It is quite true that the ship was sent from the neutral port to a port within the territory of the belligerent power, but the only illegality I may say which occurred in all that was this, that the person sending it from the neutral port was merely despatching to the belligerent power what was contraband of war, which, under international law, subjects the thing so sent to seizure in the course of the transit, but which was in no respect a violation of the Act of Congress.

Lord President.—It was a piece of merchandise.

Mr. Clark.—Yes; so that the fitting out a ship and arming a ship for the purpose of sending it to a foreign power, and no doubt for the purpose of that foreign power using it if it bought the ship, in fighting its battles with the power with which it was at war, was not an offence under the Statute at all; and I think, plainly for this reason, that there was no intention upon the part of the person who was equipping and arming the ship to employ that ship as a weapon of offence: the intent to use the ship as a ship of war was only an intent that the ship should be used as a ship of war by persons in the service of the foreign power to whom it was sold.

Lord President.—Who might buy it, or who might not buy it?

Mr. Clark.—I shall consider whether the matter of contract makes any difference, but I was giving your Lordship a note of the authorities. We have the same question decided in the case of the United States *v.* John D. Quincy, 6 Peters, 645; I quote from the appendix to the Alexandra trial, but it was substantially repeating the former decision—'The law does not prohibit armed 'vessels belonging to citizens of the United States from sailing out 'of our ports; it only requires the owners to give security that such 'vessels shall not be employed by them to commit hostilities against 'foreign powers at peace with the United States.' These are the words quoted from the judgment which was given in the Supreme Court of America with reference to a ship called the Bolivar, which was sent out as an armed ship.

Lord Deas.—Who does the word 'them' mean?

Mr. Clark.—The owners who had equipped it. They were the persons who had sent it out, and the question was, whether the ship was fitted out and armed contrary to the same Act of Congress to which I have referred. It was sent by them for the purpose of being sold at a foreign port, and the opinion of the Court is in the words which I have just read—'The law does not prohibit armed 'vessels belonging to citizens of the United States from sailing out 'of our ports; it only requires the owners [that is, the owners of 'the vessels who took these ships out of the ports of the United 'States] to give security that such vessels shall not be employed by 'them [that is, the owners taking the ship out to the foreign state] 'to commit hostilities against foreign powers at peace with the 'United States.'

Lord President.—That is the security it requires from the parties going out to sea with an armed vessel.

Mr. Clark.—It was a question whether it was illegal under this Act of Congress to send out a vessel of this description. The Court said it is not illegal to send out a vessel for the purpose of being sent to a belligerent power; but you shall give security that it shall not be employed by you against a foreign power.

Lord President.—But when you say, 'being sent to a belligerent 'power,' what do you mean by these words? Do you mean that it had already been contracted to be given to that belligerent power?

Mr. Clark.—I don't think any contract is specified.

Lord President.—But it is sent for sale?

Mr. Clark.—For sale it may be.

Lord President.—If they choose to buy it.

Mr. Clark.—Yes. I think, however, that, according to my reading of the Statute, that is immaterial. I don't say there was any contract in the one case or the other; my proposition was, that the mere fact of arming the vessel, and sending it out to the neutral country for the purpose of its going to the belligerent power, where it might be sold, or with the view and intent of selling it, created no offence under the American Act; and it was held to be no offence under the English Act, which is quite the same, because all the Judges who considered this question in the Alexandra case in the Court of Exchequer were of opinion that the cases which I have referred to were well decided. Now if the mere fact of arming a vessel and sending it from a neutral port to the port of a belligerent power with the intention that it should be purchased and used by that power to commit hostilities against another state, is not a contravention of the Act, will it be any contravention of the Act that it is preceded by a contract under which that is done? I think not.

Lord Curriehill.—A contract of sale do you mean?

Mr. Clark.—A contract for the equipment of the vessel. I may lawfully, under the Statute, build a ship as a mercantile speculation of my own, contemplating, however, that the armed vessel which I build shall be sold and used by a belligerent power as an armed ship against another belligerent power with which the British nation is at peace. That is a thing I may lawfully do, and I may lawfully do that as I think, because that vessel is not to be employed by me in the commission of any hostilities at all. If I may lawfully construct and arm a ship for the purpose, and with the intent that it should be so used, but after a purchase made by the foreign belligerent power, will it be unlawful if I enter into a contract with another person, by which he contracts with me for a certain sum of money to do that which I may do at my own risk?

Lord President.—Then is your proposition that the Statute means that the ship is to be employed by the equipper?

Mr. Clark.—Yes, that is the proposition which I am leading up to. My contention is, that if the first proposition, which I support by the authorities to which I have referred, is sound (and I don't think it will be disputed), it can only be sound in consequence of its being the case that the vessel is not to be employed by the person equipping; otherwise it seems to me that it would be necessarily a contravention of this Act. You are equipping a vessel to be employed in the service of another power, and your intent and purpose are, that it shall be so employed, because you construct it in order that it should be bought and employed in that way. Well, if the construction of an armed ship, and the sale of, it to a belligerent power, with intent that that belligerent power shall use the ship against the power with which it is at war, is not an offence under this Statute as regards the person who so equips and arms the ship, the only reason I can see why he is not contravening the Statute is this, that he is equipping it for the purpose not of using it himself, but of having it used by the foreign power to whom it is disposed to; and I think a little reference to the origin of this Statute will plainly show that I am right. It arose in consequence, I believe, of Sir Gregor M'Gregor, or a gentleman who assumed that name, having fitted out ships for the purpose of making war himself, upon his own account, in the service, no doubt, of a foreign power, or of persons assuming to exercise government in South America,—I mean persons exercising the government in certain Spanish colonies then in a state of revolt against Spain. He armed in this country a number of vessels of war, and sailed with them, for the purpose of himself engaging in the hostilities then going on between the Spanish colonies and the mother country, and his purpose was to use himself in the service of these colonies the warlike vessels which he so equipped in this country. And hence it is that we have the preamble of the Statute to which I have referred, and which seems to me to throw (in connexion with the decisions to which I have referred) the greatest possible light on the construction of the 7th section. Just see what the preamble of the Statute was, and what was the mischief which the Statute was intended to prevent. It is, 'Whereas the enlistment or engagement of His Majesty's subjects to serve in war in foreign service without His Majesty's license'—that is, the actual enlistment of His Majesty's subjects wherever they were, to serve in war; that was one of the mischiefs which this Statute was intended to remedy; and the other mischief is, 'the fitting out, equipping, and arming of vessels by His Majesty's subjects without His Majesty's license for warlike operations in or against the dominions or territories of any foreign prince,' &c. These were the two mischiefs which the Statute was intended to remedy; and it struck at the one mischief by the 2d section which forbade the enlistment of any subject of Her Majesty in the service of any foreign power whatever; and to remedy the other mischief the 7th section was passed, the mischief being the equipping with intent, and in order that the vessels should be employed against foreign states. No doubt that 7th section does not refer merely to Her Majesty's subjects; I don't say that it does; the purpose was to prevent any person who intended to use vessels of war against a state with which this country was at peace, from doing so in any part of Her Majesty's dominions. And, therefore, while the 2d section extends to all Her Majesty's subjects wherever they are, whether within this country or beyond our territories, the 7th section refers merely to the use of the ports of this kingdom for the purpose of the equipment within these ports, by any person whomsoever, of ships of war which he intends to use for the purpose of committing hostilities against a foreign power. It was to put down the use of the ports of this kingdom for the purpose of enabling a person to raise an armament, which he meant to use to the effect of committing hostilities.

Lord Deas.—Do you construe the enactment as being exclusively against a certain kind of privateering by Her Majesty's subjects?

Mr. Clark.—I think it comes very much to that. I think the Statute did not forbid the construction of vessels, however numerous these vessels, or however formidable they might be, as war vessels. I, as a British subject, may construct any number of vessels, and I may send them for sale to the Confederate States, or to the Federal States, and I may put them up to auction between these two powers if I please; but then I am sending them plainly with this intent and for this purpose, that the power which shall have the opportunity of buying (and I may give the opportunity only to one power and not to the other), shall use the ship which I have constructed within Her Majesty's dominions, as a ship of war against the United States, I shall say; I construct a ship with the intent that that ship shall be employed ; I may be delayed, to be sure, in having that purpose carried out, but the completion of my purpose is not the crime ; the crime is completed by the intent or the purpose which I have in view. I equip with the intent that the ship shall be sold to a foreign power, for the purpose of that foreign power using it as a ship of war. That is not an offence, though undoubtedly it will come within the very language of this Statute, unless you hold that the intent which is referred to in this Statute means, and exclusively means, the intent of the equipper. Let me now ask attention to the 1st count, for the purpose of considering whether it is a relevant count. The Statute says, 'it shall be unlawful to equip any vessel 'with intent or in order that such ship shall be employed in the ser-'vice of the foreign power as a transport ship, or with intent to 'cruise and commit hostilities.' The 1st count in the Information charges that the owners did equip the said vessel with intent and in order that such ship or vessel should be employed in the service of certain foreign states styling themselves the Confederate States, with intent to cruise and commit hostilities. Now, reading that count, would it not bring a person so charged within the Act, if this is a relevant count at all, who had done nothing more than the citizen of the United States had done who fitted out the Independencia ? He fitted that vessel out and armed her, with intent and in order that she should be employed in the service of a foreign state, for he was very anxious that the foreign state should buy the vessel, in order that it should so employ it. He sent it to be sold as an armed vessel, that is, he sent it to be sold to a belligerent power, that it might use it for the purpose for which it was sold. Then there comes the charge 'with 'intent to cruise and commit hostilities.' Now, what does that second intent refer to in the Information ? Is it the intent of the equipper, as specified, I think, in the Statute, or is it the intent of the Confederate States who buy the ship ? I think it is plain, under this count, that the intent which is libelled here (and I am construing merely the words of this Information, of course), is the intent of the Confederate States. And therefore the charge comes to be this, that the owners equipped this vessel with intent that she should be employed in the service of the Confederate States, who were to have the intent of themselves employing her and cruising against the United States. Now, is that, in any respect, under this Statute ? I submit that it is not, because it divorces the second words, 'with intent,' from the words with which they can alone be coupled under the Statute, viz., the words, 'did 'equip.' I don't care so much what the words, 'with intent,' which are here mentioned, really mean. I think they mean the intent of the Confederate States, who are employing the ship which may be sold to them, but, at all events, the intent which we have in the Statute is an intent which is referred not to the employing, but to the equipping,—I mean clearly as regards the second intent. The Statute creates two offences which are perfectly separate and distinct in their character. The first is the equipping of vessels to be employed in the service of a foreign state as store-ships or transport ships. Though the preamble referred to the commission of hostilities alone, the Statute went a little farther in its enactment, and said it shall be unlawful to fit out ships which are to be employed by British subjects, or by the persons who fit them out in British ports, in the service of foreign states as transport ships. That is one intent. Equipment with that one intent is undoubtedly an offence. But then the Statute went farther, and said that equipment with intent to cruise and commit hostilities was also an offence. The offence consists in the first place of equipment, with a certain intent or intents. Any person who shall equip any ship or vessel with intent or in order that such ship or vessel be employed in the service of any foreign state as a transport or store-ship,—there is the first form of the offence,—or with intent to cruise or commit hostilities against any state; the only question is, whether these words, 'with intent,' refer to the verb 'employed' in the immediately preceding part of this clause, or referred to the word 'equip' in an earlier part of the clause? Now, considering that your Lordships are dealing here with a Statute which, for the first time, made what is set forth in the Statute a crime, it must be read strictly, and as Statutes introduced for that purpose are generally read. I am entitled to take, and I am perfectly willing to accept, the fair, and, as I think, the only grammatical reading of the 7th section. I find that the Statute declares this to be an offence,—the equipping with intent that such ship shall be employed in the service of a foreign state as a transport or store-ship, or with intent to cruise or commit hostilities. The equipment of the unarmed vessel, the transport or store-ship, was to be an offence under this Statute, because the legislature thought it would be likely to endanger the peace of this realm if the ports of this country were used for fitting out transport-ships, which may be unarmed ships, and which might be used for carrying the stores of one belligerent to the injury of the other belligerent; and therefore they did not make the law strike against ships of war only, but introduced transport and store-ships, so as to prevent the equipment of ships within this kingdom to be used for that purpose. But there are two distinct intents, and the equipment with one intent is one offence, and the equipment with the other intent is another offence. To equip, to be employed as a transport-ship, is one offence, or one form of the offence; to equip, with intent to commit hostilities, is the other form of the offence. And if we are to consider this case as we would consider an indictment which was libelled under this Statute, would it be a relevant indictment under this Statute if Mr. John Fleming was charged in this way, —You are guilty of the offence specified in the 7th section of the Statute, in so far as on a particular day, mentioning the date, you did wickedly and feloniously equip a ship, with intent that it should be employed in the Confederate States of America, with intent to cruise and commit hostilities? I think the answer would be very clear, and it is the answer which I am now urging upon your Lordships; you may charge under the indictment the intent whatever it be, of employing that ship as a transport-ship,—that is one form of it; you may also charge, if you please, the equipping with the intent to cruise and commit hostilities—that is another form of it; but you cannot leave out that most important word in this Statute, 'or,' altogether, and accumulate these two intents so as to make that an offence, which I think is not set forth in the Statute at all as an offence, by making a part of the offence charged against the owners, an intent which they themselves may be said to possess, and an intent which the Confederate States may, upon the other hand, possess; because under that indictment, or under the Information, I think the deletion of the word 'or,' which occurs before the second words 'with intent,' and which word 'or' does not occur in the Information,—the deletion of that word 'or' has necessarily this meaning, that you refer the 'with intent' to the word 'employ,' instead of referring it to the word 'equip.'

Lord President.—It adopts that construction of the Statute, and the question is whether that is the right construction.

Mr. Clark.—That is the question; and I submit that the right construction plainly is, that the words, 'with intent,' necessarily refer to the words, 'did equip.' That is the only grammatical construction of them, and for this reason, I think, amongst others (though I don't require to put my case upon that), that it is the intent of the equipper which is struck at by the Statute.

Lord President.—As to its being grammatical, won't the question be, is this expression in the Information a grammatical one, because it is the grammar of that construction of the Statute?

Mr. Clark.—No doubt it is.

Lord President.—If it is a grammatical sentence in the Information, and consistent with that construction of the Statute, then you will hardly make out that the Statute is ungrammatical?

Mr. Clark.—I would say the Statute is quite grammatical.

Lord President.—I mean upon their construction. Upon their construction that is the way to read the Statute. Now, is the Information grammatical?

Mr. Clark.—I have not considered the question of their grammar, but it seems to be grammatical enough. The language which they use is perfectly grammatical, and if they did not use a single word which occurred in the Statute, it might be a perfectly grammatical charge. The question is not what is the grammar of the Information, but what is the grammar of the Statute, and if they can leave out the word 'or,' I quite admit that it is a perfectly grammatical construction, but it would be very bad grammar to use 'with intent, and in order that such ship or vessel should be 'employed in the service of the Confederate States, or with intent 'to cruise or commit hostilities,' if they intended that the second words, 'with intent,' should refer not to the word 'equip,' but to the word 'employ.'

Lord President.—Employed in the service as a transport, or with intent to cruise,—that is the way they read it. If the intent to cruise had been the first alternative, perhaps you would have had a better argument.

Mr. Clark.—I hope it would not be better than it is.

Lord President.—If it were less doubtful it would be better.

Mr. Clark.—Wherever there is doubt, I think the construction must be in my favour, because we are here dealing with a very penal Statute, and the Crown are pressing the Statute against us for the purpose of forfeiting the vessel. I am therefore entitled to have the strict reading of the Statute adopted to the effect of seeing what the offence is. Now I find the words in the Statute, 'equip with intent;' that is the first charging of an offence; then it goes on, 'equip with intent that it should be employed' (as I read it 'by the equippers') 'in the service of a foreign state as a transport-'ship against another foreign state.' That is a perfectly intelligible construction of the Statute, and I think it is the most natural construction, because then you have the other words, 'with intent,' plainly alternating not with the words, 'as a transport or store-'ship,' but with the words, 'with intent, or in order that.' To put it another way, the question comes simply to this, whether do the words 'with intent,' which occur second, alternate with the first words 'with intent,' or with the words, 'as a transport or 'store-ship?' Now when you are considering a Statute which makes the crime to consist of an act with certain intents, the natural construction, and, as it seems to me, the only proper grammatical construction, of the Statute is this, that you take the word 'equip' with the first intent libelled as the first form of the offence, and then you have the other alternative, 'with intent to commit hos-'tilities,' as the second form of the offence, or as a second crime. But when a Statute says, If you do a certain thing with an intent, or the same thing with another intent, the plain and ordinary construction of the Statute I think comes to be this, that the two intents are there stated alternatively and not cumulatively. That is the argument which I have to submit to your Lordships on that part of the Statute.

Lord President.—What is the meaning of an employment with intent to cruise? An employment in cruising I understand, but what is an employment with intent to cruise?

Mr. Clark.—That is just what I desiderate an explanation of.

Lord President.—I suppose there is an answer to it which has been given elsewhere already.

Mr. Clark.—Not yet. This question was stated, but not argued in the Alexandra case.

Lord Advocate.—It was stated, but it received no weight whatever from any quarter on the bench.

Mr. Clark.—It was never argued; it was merely stated by Sir Hugh Cairns, and the Lord Chief Baron ordered the trial to proceed, because it would be competent in the event of a verdict being found for the Crown, to move in arrest of judgment.—(*Reads observations of Sir Hugh Cairns and the Lord Chief Baron at foot of p. 143 of Alexandra trial*). So that this objection was raised by Sir Hugh Cairns, and the Court said that it was not convenient then to dispose of it, and that the proper course was to go on with the trial, and if there was a verdict in favour of the Crown, the defendants could then move in arrest of judgment, that is to say, the Crown would not be entitled to get decree of forfeiture, because if the objection was good, the count was not well charged under the Statute. Now we have no motions in arrest of judgment; and I am now pressing the same objection before the trial, for the purpose of ascertaining whether the count or Information is relevantly laid; that is to say, we are following our practice instead of following the practice of England, which is not similar to ours. We ask a judgment of the Court on the relevancy. Of course, in the Alexandra case the defendants did not require to make any motion in arrest of judgment, because the verdict was in their favour.

Lord Advocate.—But that would have been an answer to nine-tenths of the argument on the rule.

Mr. Clark.—The Lord Chief Baron says on this point—(*Weekly Reporter*, p. 266)—' When two intents are mentioned'—(*Reads*).

Lord President.—What does he mean by the intent of the party committing the act? Which act?

Mr. Clark.—The equipment.

Lord President.—According to all the rules of pleading it must mean that; and you say that according to all the rules of grammar it means otherwise, and that this Information charges the Confederate States with the intent.

Mr. Clark.—That is to say according to the rules of pleading, the only intent which can be competently libelled is the intent of the person who is accused.

Lord President.—Whereas here?

Mr. Clark.—Whereas here the intent is the intent of some other than the person accused. And applying that to the Statute, unless you give force to the word 'or' as making the two expressions 'with intent' to alternate with each other, you necessarily introduce into this count an intent which is not the intent of the person committing the act at all, but the intent of the person immediately before mentioned, viz., the Confederate States of America. Now I think these are all the observations which I have to make on that part of the Statute; and what I have said consists simply in applying the decisions to which I have referred to the Information before us, for the purpose of showing that the intent in the Statute was the intent of the person equipping the ship, and that it was the intent of him to employ that ship in the service of the foreign state as a transport-ship, or the intent of him to use that vessel as a cruiser. Now if your Lordships will only sustain the plea which I am now urging, you will get rid at once of 72 counts.

Another objection which appears on the face of the Information is this, and this applies to the first 96 counts; the Statute charges the equipping, furnishing, fitting out, and arming, and with those four acts it connects intents. The Information here uses throughout the words equip, furnish, and fit out, but there is no count which contains the word 'arm.' The first 8 use the word equip, as descriptive of the act which, coupled with the intents, comes within the meaning of the Statute; the other counts use the words furnish or fit out, or procure to be equipped, furnished, and fitted out, &c., but there is no count which charges arming, and therefore I think it is pretty plain that the Crown do not mean to charge that there has been any act upon the part of the owners of this ship which amounts to an arming of the ship, otherwise they would not have contented themselves with charging equipping, fitting out, and furnishing. Now we have under the Statute which regulates procedure in the Court of Exchequer, forms given for the libelling of counts of this kind, where you have alternative words, or words which are separated, I should rather say, by the word 'or.'

Lord Deas.—Counts of this kind, did you say?

Mr. Clark.—Counts in a Statute which, like this, contain words separated by the word 'or.' The way in which the Exchequer Act, 19 & 20 Vict. c. 56, specifies the manner of libelling Information of this kind in cases of seizure is, in the eighth head of Schedule B,—'I, the Right Hon. A. B., Her Majesty's Advocate, 'inform the Court, &c., 1st count, that the said malt was fraudu-'lently deposited, concealed, or conveyed away from the sight of 'the officers of excise, contrary to the Statute, &c., whereby the 'said malt became forfeited.' If the form adopted in the Alexandra case were there used, each of these three words would have a separate count to itself. Now, here we have an Information which excludes in all the counts the word 'arm,' and therefore I read the Information as meaning that the Crown don't intend to charge the offence of arming. They mean to charge something short of arming; and the question comes to be, whether anything short of arming is an offence under the Statute?

Lord Ardmillan.—The charge is that you did equip.

Mr. Clark.—We don't get the meaning of equip as it occurs alongside of other words in the Statute, but we get the meaning of it as it occurs in this Information. If, for instance, we were tried on an indictment under this Statute, the public prosecutor would draw it thus, 'that you did, upon such and such a day, wickedly and 'feloniously equip, fit out, furnish, or arm, and all which or part 'thereof being found proven,' &c. But the Crown don't put the words equip, fit out, and furnish alongside of the word 'arm,' but they divorce the word 'arm' from the rest, and all we have in this indictment is a count charging equipment short of arming.

Lord President.—If it were an indictment, the indictment would, according to our form, first set forth the clause in the Statute, and then it would charge that the party equipped. Now, would that not be good?

Mr. Clark.—I think our style would be— did equip, fit out, furnish, or arm the said ships.

Lord President.—What would be the objection if it only alleged one of them, if one of them would be a contravention of the Statute?

Mr. Clark.—If the Crown had charged equipment, and were to tell us that they did not mean to charge arming the vessel, then I should say that it would not be a relevant count or indictment under this Statute, because the equipment must be a warlike equipment,—an armed equipment,—before an offence can be committed and if that is so, and if the Crown mean to tell me they don't mean to charge warlike or armed equipment, then I am not bound to go to trial with them, because I am prepared to show that it must be a warlike or armed equipment in order to be an equipment within the meaning of the Statute.

Lord President.—It must be an equipment within the meaning of the Statute, and if the Statute is set forth, and then it is said that in contravention of the Statute, you equipped the ship, the charge must be interpreted by the Statute.

Mr. Clark.—It is an equipment to cruise or commit hostilities.

Lord President.—'Contrary to the Statute.'

Mr. Clark.—I put it in this way, that I think we gather from the Information, which excludes the charge of arming, that the Crown don't mean to say there was a warlike or armed equipment.

Lord Ardmillan.—I don't know that you can take it in that way.

Lord Deas.—Are you taking it that the words 'furnish, equip, 'fit out, and arm,' are used in the Statute as synonymous?

Mr. Clark.—Substantially I am, in this view, and that the Crown, if they show that they don't mean to charge arming, don't mean to charge the only thing which will make an offence under the Statute, viz., an armed or warlike equipment. I am aware that that may be said not to arise so plainly upon the face of the Information as the other objection which I have stated, and I don't want to press this objection unnecessarily. The question perhaps will arise in the future, what is the meaning of equipment under the Statute. At the same time I do gather from the fact that the Crown have carefully kept out in these 96 counts the charge of arming, that they have no intention of charging the owners with having armed this ship. It would have been very easy to have added other 8 counts, which would have made the thing *totus teres atque rotundus* in this matter, and they have the power still to do that. There is another view of the Statute which I ought to have stated first as to the meaning of the words, equip, furnish, fit out, and arm. I think there is another construction, and I am bound to bring under your Lordships' notice all the constructions of which this Act is susceptible as regards these words. There is, in the first place, a transport ship mentioned; and, second, a cruiser. Now, the transport, or store-ship, is the unarmed vessel, and the cruiser is the armed vessel; and I think it not an unfair reading of this penal Statute to say that the meaning to be put upon this clause is, that you must refer the words, 'equip, fit out, and furnish,' to the transport ship, and the word 'arm' to the cruiser. The word 'arm' has no meaning with reference to a transport ship at all; and if it is absurd to speak of arming a transport ship, and if the Statute is enacted for the purpose of preventing cruising by any person from the ports of this kingdom, I think the fair meaning of it is, that it is an offence to fit out, equip, or furnish a ship to be employed as a transport ship against any foreign power; and second, that it is an offence to arm or fit out a ship with intent to commit hostilities against a foreign power. In short, you cannot use the word 'arm' with any degree of sense or propriety as regards the transport ship, nor can you use the words, 'equip, fit out, or furnish, with any degree of propriety as regards a cruiser, using them short of the word arming; and therefore if the arming is all the offence, and if it is necessary, in order that the ship, if not a transport ship, shall be armed in order that it shall be within the Statute, then I say the reading of it is this,—the words, equip, fit out, and furnish, do not include arming, and therefore are not applicable to a ship intended to commit hostilities, but refer to a transport ship, while the ship intended to commit hostilities, being a ship which must be armed, the word 'arm' applies to that ship, and to that ship only.

Lord Ardmillan.—Then, if that is correct, you don't now insist on equipping, fitting-out, and arming as being synonymous?

Mr. Clark.—I take it alternatively. If the Crown say that they don't mean to charge arming under this indictment, then I am prepared to show that nothing short of a warlike equipment is an offence within the Statute. On the other hand, I read the Statute as a Statute which creates two kinds of the same offence—splits up the offence in this way, that while a transport ship used in the service of the foreign power is an unarmed ship, yet it shall be unlawful to fit out, equip, and furnish a transport-ship, if it is to be used as a transport-ship in the service of one power against another, and that is an offence under the Statute, though no arming whatever took place; on the other hand, it is an offence against the Statute if you allow a ship to be used as a cruiser; and therefore I read the words, furnish, equip, and fit out as referring to the transport-ship, and the word arm as referring to the cruiser, because you cannot refer all these words to both, according to any natural construction, and therefore you must make a separation between the two.

Lord President.—With reference to that observation, may not all of them refer to a cruiser, and some of them only to a transport?

Mr. Clark.—That may be, but the Statute was intended to put down warlike proceedings. When you come to a cruiser, the only offence, I think, must be the arming of the cruiser; and, I think, the natural construction of the word arming is applicable to the cruiser.

Lord President.—Then the practical deduction from that, I suppose, is, that there is here no good charge as regards the cruiser?

Mr. Clark.—That is so.

Lord President.—And that all those parts of the counts which relate to vessels must be read as applicable to transport ships?

Mr. Clark.—Yes.

Lord President.—Then you take out all the counts applicable to cruisers?

Mr. Clark.—Yes; and that gets rid of 24 counts.

Lord President.—That is the practical result?

Mr. Clark.—Yes. That is what I intended to state as my second objection, which I hope will enable your Lordships to get rid of this cumbrous Information. I pass over the 97th count, which seems to me to be well enough laid under the Statute. It seems to be a charge of equipping a transport ship with intent that it should be employed in the service of certain persons as a transport or store-ship against the United States; and I think that the 97th count brings out very clearly the objection as to the 1st and other counts framed on that principle. The 98th count seems to me to be the most remarkable of all. It combines the two intents, it combines the transport ship and the cruiser, and it combines the completed offence with the attempted offence; in short, it attempts to combine everything which can be charged, or which can be made an offence under this Statute. It charges the equipping and the attempting to equip, and the procuring to be equipped, and the assisting to be equipped. Now, I think that, according to our style, is not a style of indictment which would be permitted at all. It would never be permitted to charge in one count the completed equipment, the attempted equipment, the procuring to be equipped, and the aiding to be equipped.

Lord President.—As a transport or as a cruiser?

Mr. Clark.—As a transport and as a cruiser, and with the two intents.

Lord President.—And that you did all these things at once.

Mr. Clark.—Every one of them, and though I completed the equipment, I never got beyond the knowingly aiding and assisting in equipping the vessel which I am charged with equipping!

Lord President.—Is that the order they put them in?—because they might begin by aiding and assisting, and then come to completed equipment.

Mr. Clark.—That is the order they put it in. I could have understood if they had said we assisted and attempted, and ultimately did equip, but they don't put it in that way. They begin by stating, You equipped, and then you attempted to equip, then you aided in equipping, and then it comes down till you don't know what it is they mean to charge under this incongruous charge, which charges the completed equipment alongside of the attempt to equip, contrary to all our forms of pleading.

Lord President.—It does not say all, or each, or one, or more of them?

Mr. Clark.—No, nor does it make any alternative at all. It is all cumulative. Then they say they charge it with intent that the ship should be employed as a transport ship, and with intent to cruise and commit hostilities.

Lord Deas.—You say it is contrary to our style of information?

Mr. Clark.—I meant to say indictment.

Lord Deas.—Surely it is an information, and not an indictment.

Mr. Clark.—I think substantially it is a criminal indictment under the Statute. The only form of information we have is to be found in the Exchequer Act, which provides the procedure to be followed in these matters.

Lord Deas.—And which does not, except by the most distant analogy, provide a form for an Information of this kind.

Mr. Clark.—On the contrary, it by very express enactment provides forms of this kind. It gives you the very form in a seizure.

Is there any difference between seizing tobacco or spirits, and seizing a ship?

Lord Deas.—When you say according to the form prescribed in the Statute, you mean that part applicable to the case of a seizure?

Mr. Clark.—The Statute says so.

Lord Deas.—What is it you say in this Information is inconsistent with that part of the Schedule?

Mr. Clark.—I said one thing was that it did not set forth all the words of the Statute, and next, I say it gives no warrant for charging a person cumulatively in one count with the completed act, with the attempt to commit that completed act, and with aiding and assisting in that completed act, or in that attempt. We are left to a great extent to gather from our other forms of procedure what shall be applicable to cases of this kind. We have certain specimens given in the Exchequer Act, but there is no specimen of an Information which combines a charge of this kind, that you did do a thing, and a statement that you attempted to do a thing, a statement that you procured a thing to be done, and another statement that you aided and assisted in procuring that thing to be done, or in attempting to procure that thing to be done. Now, what is the authority in our law for an Information of this kind? Certainly we have no authority for it under the Exchequer Act, and we have no authority for it in any of the rest of our procedure in Scotland, because I don't think that this count makes a charge which is in the least degree like a charge which would be made under an indictment; and I cannot see why there should be any difference whatever.

Lord Deas.—I confess I have great difficulty in seeing how, if you had been framing this Information, you could have got much assistance from the part of the schedule appended to the Exchequer Act which relates to seizures. I don't think that could have been of any use to you at all.

Mr. Clark.—It gives the style, I think, and it tells you how to charge the offence, for that on a particular day, A. B., a maltster, did fraudulently deposit, conceal, or convey away certain malt within certain premises, contrary to the Statute in that case made and provided, whereby the said malt became forfeited. Is that not what we are dealing with here?—for that on a particular day, you did equip a certain vessel with intent to commit hostilities, contrary to the Statute made in that case and provided, whereby the said vessel became forfeited. There is precisely the same charge, only I think the proper charge following that provision of the Statute would be, that you did equip, furnish, fit out, or arm the said vessel, in order to cruise or commit hostilities, contrary to the Statute made and provided, whereby the said vessel became forfeited.

Lord Deas.—All I say is, that I don't see that your observation has any more force in consequence of this schedule about seizure being here than if it were not here at all.

Lord Ardmillan.—But have you any interest, on behalf of the defenders, to object to the extraordinary accumulation of these charges in the 98th count, because if you are correct in saying that there is no alternative here at all, then the prosecutor must prove all these accumulated charges before he could get a conviction on this count? And if that be so, it occurs to me that it is the interest of the defenders to let such a charge stand.

Mr. Clark.—I don't know what might take place at the trial. There is a power which is given the Crown down to the verdict of amending, and the amount of cobble that might take place between the commencement of the trial and verdict which is asked, of course I don't know. If I were to go to trial with this as the issue in a case between subject and subject, I think there would be a great deal in your Lordship's observation; but as I cannot go to trial with these as the adjusted issues, but must go to trial on them with a power in the Crown to amend to any extent they please before the verdict, I think it right to object to their going to trial at all. And I object therefore to that accumulation, which I think is against all our practice; and I object also to the other accumulation, which comes within the scope of my former argument.

Mr. Shand.—On behalf of the builders, Messrs. J. & G. Thomson, who are also here as claimants, I adopt the argument of my friend Mr. Clark.

Solicitor-General.—The Lord Ordinary, who heard all these objections urged in support of the plea that the Information in all its counts is bad in law, thought fit to send the case to trial, notwithstanding of that plea and these objections, not thinking it fitting to decide upon all or any of them before trial; and before stating the argument of the Crown in answer to these objections, I think it right to state that I am going to ask your Lordships to take the same course, viz., to ask you not to sustain these objections, but to send the case to trial; for I am not going to ask your Lordships, however clearly I may think that the objections are ill founded, and the answers to them conclusive, to prejudice the case of the defenders by a substantive finding that the Information in all or any of its counts is relevant; that is to say, laid upon the true construction of the Act. The first and second objections, as my learned friend stated them, are drawn from the construction of the Act, which the owners and the other parties who are here resisting the Information contend to be the true one. They come to this, that upon a sound construction of the Statute, the Information here does not in any of its counts disclose a misdemeanour under it. The last objection to which my friend Mr. Clark referred is of a different order, and applies only to the 98th count, and if I understand it aright, it is, that the charges in that count are not in the alternative, but are cumulatively stated. The Statute uses the language of alternatives, 'if any person shall, without leave and license, equip, 'furnish, fit out, or arm, or attempt or endeavour to equip, furnish, 'fit out, or arm, or procure to be equipped,' &c., 'or knowingly aid 'or assist to be concerned in the equipping, furnishing,' &c. You have there the proper language of alternative, and I don't know any exception to this in statutory enactments upon similar subjects. Statutes are always in the alternative. Where it is provided by Statute that any one, by doing one or other of a variety of things, shall be guilty of an offence, and shall be punished in a particular way, it always uses, just as this Statute does, the language of alternative. The 98th count, which is meant to exhaust in itself every way under which a misdemeanour under section 7 may be committed, is not in that language of alternative, but substitutes the conjunctive 'and' for the alternative 'or' wherever it occurs in the Act. Now this form of proceeding by Information, I need not tell your Lordships, we derive from England, and it was quite familiar to us in the Court of Exchequer long before the passing of the recent Exchequer Act. It is also unnecessary to remind your Lordships that by the Statute of Queen Anne, under which the Court of Exchequer was established in Scotland after the Union, we were referred to the English practice and procedure in all matters whatsoever; and this Information is prepared upon a model so closely followed, that it is as exact a copy as we could make it of the Information in the Alexandra case. Now, in English pleading there is an abhorrence of the language of alternative, and the reason of that is manifest enough to those who consider the matter. The shortest and most comprehensive and intelligible account of it which I find anywhere, is in a note to Mr. Bateman's book on the Excise Laws, p. 7, in which he states the rule and refers to the authorities. He is treating of the mode of stating the offence in Informations, and he says this, 'Care should be taken—(*Reads to*)—any one of 'them only.'

Lord President.—That is the difference between each and any one. The question is, whether it was not committed by them all. He does not mean that it was committed by all of them.

Solicitor-General.—No, certainly not; he only means a charge that it was committed by each. Now, I may notice that the 7th clause of the Exchequer Act says, 'And provided further, that, not'withstanding the terms of any such Information, it shall not be 'incumbent,' &c.—(*Reads*). But if any such plea were open to the defenders, there is nothing sought to be done to prejudice that now. The Statute provides, that if any person shall do this thing or that thing, he shall be guilty of an offence. The Information charges he did both this and that, and that is objected to. Now I don't discover the reason of the objection, I must confess. If he does either, he shall commit the offence. The Crown, in the Information, say he committed both; he did this and he did that; they may prove both if they are consistent.

Lord President.—As I understand Mr. Clark's objection, it is that they were not consistent.

Solicitor-General.—I am not going to overlook that. He may prove both if they are consistent; he can only prove one if they are inconsistent, but it is sufficient if he proves enough to warrant the seizure or the condemnation. I don't trouble your Lordships with any further observations on this, the only objection founded on by the defenders on the construction of the Act of Parliament, but I proceed now to consider the objections which are founded upon the construction of the Act, and which are well founded if the construction of the Act urged by the defenders is the right one.

Lord Deas.—There is one thing I would like to be more clear about before you go farther. You say that the form of the Information is necessarily taken from the English form.

Solicitor-General.—I said it was taken.

Lord Deas.—I understood you to say it was rightly and necessarily taken.

Solicitor-General.—Rightly taken.

Lord Deas.—Is it quite clear, that under this Statute we have anything to do with the English form of information, I mean under the Exchequer Act? That Act provides, that the Lord Advocate may commence his proceedings by a *subpœna* of which the form is given, and that *subpœna* is to be followed by an information; and section 7 says, 'every information lodged in terms of this Act 'shall be in the form, as nearly as may be, of Schedule B hereunto 'annexed;' and section 9 says, 'that the procedure in all cases 'commenced by *subpœna*, &c., shall, in so far as not specially pro- 'vided for in this Act, be regulated by the Lord Ordinary, or if 'not so regulated by the Lord Ordinary, shall be conducted as 'nearly as may be in conformity with the procedure before the 'Court of Session in ordinary actions.' I want to know whether the result of that be not this, that, except in so far as the form of Information given in the Schedule is applicable, we are now to follow in these Informations, as nearly as may be, our own forms?

Solicitor-General.—The form of procedure to be followed in the Court of Session, unless the learned person referred to in the Statute should otherwise direct.

Lord Deas.—I am speaking of the form of Information.

Solicitor-General.—I must ask your Lordship to excuse me from entering on that discussion at present.

Lord Deas.—I should be much obliged if, before answering it, you would consider it, because, when we come to consider the argument, that will be an embarrassment we shall have to get out of at the very outset.

Solicitor-General.—No such objection has been referred to by my learned friend Mr. Clark, and no such objection was taken in the Outer House. If my learned friends on the other side think, in consequence of the objection which your Lordship has now thrown out, that they can object to this Information on any such ground, probably the more regular course will be for my learned friend Mr. Cook or Mr. Gordon to take it, and then my learned friend the Lord Advocate will have an opportunity of answering it.

Lord Deas.—I am not suggesting it as an objection to the Information. I am only suggesting it as a matter which seems to me requires to be considered and understood before we can know on what principles or how we are to construe the Information. When we come to consider the Information, we must consider whether we are to construe it as we would do a Scotch instrument, or whether we are to construe it as an English instrument; that meets us at the very outset.

Solicitor-General.—It will probably be found that the procedure referred to in that clause of the Statute is the procedure of the Court in the conduct of the cause following on that Information; but, in the meantime, I shall proceed to consider the construction of the Statute, with which this question don't interfere.

Lord President.—You are now done with that last count. I suppose it contains nothing that is not to be found in one or other of the remaining counts.

Solicitor-General.—No.

Lord President.—It is just a summing up of the whole thing.

Solicitor-General.—The objection is a matter of importance, but this count is in this case of no manner of importance.

Mr. Clark.—I said it was inconsistent on the ground of accumulation.

Lord President.—Saying that a thing is both black and white.

Mr. Clark.—Yes.

Adjourned.

Thursday, 3d March.

Solicitor-General.—I was proceeding to consider the objection stated by the defenders to this Information, founded on the construction of the Act of Parliament which they contend for.

Lord President.—As I understand the argument according to the contention of the defenders, there would be in this Statute no prohibition against parties fitting out a vessel with the intention that she should be used by one foreign state to commit hostilities against another.

Solicitor-General.—No; they say the intent must be by the equipper himself.

Lord President.—On the other hand, on your reading of the Statute, there is no prohibition against British subjects fitting out a ship with intent themselves to cruise. There may be other laws against that, and there is a subsequent part of the clause of some importance, which we have not yet heard about.

Solicitor-General.—It is proper to notice that the Information is not an indictment for a misdemeanour against clause 7 of the Act, but is for a condemnation of the ship seized, as forfeited in consequence of a misdemeanour having been committed under that clause. It is therefore necessary, I quite admit, that this Information, which seeks condemnation of the vessel as duly forfeited, should well aver the misdemeanour under the Statute, in respect of which alone the forfeiture is contended for. Before I proceed farther, I should like to read a single sentence from the charge of the Lord Chief Baron in the Alexandra case, explanatory of the multitude of counts in the Information. He says at p. 227, 'The Infor- 'mation is exceedingly long'—(*Reads, as quoted at p.* 66, *ante*). Now, the Information here charges equipping, furnishing, and fitting out, but not arming. It also charges the intent that the vessel should be employed as a transport or store-ship, and the intent that it should be employed to cruise and commit hostilities, in both cases in the service of one foreign state against another. There is only one count, viz., the 97th, which charges the attempt to fit out the ship with intent that she should be employed as a transport or store-ship. I am not quite certain whether this count was intended to be objected to.

Mr. Cook.—It is not intended to be objected to.

Solicitor-General.—Then I need not further refer to it. There are, besides the 98th count, which I have already spoken to, 96 counts, and these my learned friend Mr. Clark very properly divided into two classes, the one class consisting of 72, and the other of 24. 72 charge the intent that the vessel should be employed to cruise and commit hostilities as an intent that she should be so employed in the service of one foreign state against another, without charging that it was the intent of the persons equipping, or attempting to equip, &c., themselves to cruise with the vessel; and the 24 counts charge those who equipped or attempted to equip the vessel with having done so with the intent themselves to cruise and commit hostilities with her, or some of them. Now there are two objections to these 96 counts, one of them applying to the whole 96, and one of them only to 72. The objection which applies to the whole 96, is that none of these counts charge that the vessel was armed or attempted to be armed; the objection which applies only to 72 of the 96, is that the intent that the vessel should be employed to cruise is not charged as an intent that those who equipped or attempted or aided in equipping it, themselves intended to cruise with the vessel. There are 24 founded upon the model of the 3d count.

Lord Deas.—What is the objection to them?

Solicitor-General.—The only objection to them is that which is stated to them in common with the whole 96, viz., that arming, or attempting to arm, is not charged. The objection to 72 counts, viz., the 1st, and the 71 founded on the model of it, is that the equippers of the ship are not charged with themselves intending to cruise with her. Now, I think it will be convenient to take the objection which applies to the whole 96 counts first.

Lord Deas.—Then there are just two sets of objections.

Lord President.—Yes; the want of the arming, and the not intending themselves to cruise.

Solicitor-General.—There are 98 counts. I have said all I intend to say about the 98th, and the 97th is not objected to; 96 remain, and there is only one objection which applies to the whole 96, which is, that arming is not charged; another objection applies to 72 of them, which is that the equippers of the ship are not charged with themselves intending to cruise.

Lord Deas.—These two classes of objections are quite beside the objection to the 98th count.

Solicitor-General.—Yes. The objections I now come to are founded on the construction of clause 7 of the Act of Parliament. The first question—that upon which the objection applicable to the whole 96 counts depends — is whether clause 7 of the Statute requires, in order to a misdemeanour under it, where the intent is that the vessel shall be employed to cruise or commit hostilities, that the vessel shall be armed. Now, substantially the clause comes to this, that if any person within any port of the United Kingdom shall, without the leave and licence of her Majesty, equip, furnish, fit out, or arm any ship with intent or in order that such ship shall be employed in the service of any foreign state as a transport or store-ship, or with intent to cruise or commit hostilities against any foreign state with whom her Majesty shall not then be at war, or shall within the United Kingdom issue or deliver any commission with the intent that such ship shall be employed as aforesaid, every person so offending shall be guilty of a misdemeanour. In terms, therefore, this clause of the Statute makes it a misdemeanour to equip, furnish, fit out, or arm any ship with the statutory intent. Now, in dealing with this question I of course assume the statutory intent, and that the statutory intent is well charged. Whether the statutory intent is well charged or no forms the subject of another objection; but if the statutory intent is well charged, then I submit it to be quite clear, upon the plain words of the Act of Parliament, that if, with that statutory intent, any person within the kingdom shall equip, furnish, fit out, or arm any ship, he shall be guilty of a misdemeanour. The argument which is maintained in support of the objection here is twofold; in the first place, that all these four expressions, viz., equip, furnish, fit out, or arm, are synonymous, but that the Crown, by dropping one of them, 'arm,' indicate that they do not use the others in the proper statutory sense; and a second argument appears to be this, that these expressions, viz., equip, furnish, fit out, and arm are not synonymous, but that, applying the rule of construction *applicando singula singulis*, the intent that the vessel should be employed as a store-ship is referable to the words equip, furnish, or fit out, and the intent that it shall be employed to cruise or commit hostilities is referable to the word 'arm.' I think these were the two arguments on which this objection was rested, and I shall deal with them in their order. The two arguments are stated alternatively; 1st, the words are synonymous, but you indicate that you don't use them as synonymous by dropping one of them; 2d, they are not synonymous, but, according to a well-known rule of construction, certain of them are to be applied to one subject, and certain of them are to be applied to another. Now, I don't admit,—far from it,—that 'equip, furnish, fit out, and arm,' are synonymous. I think it is very clear that they are not; but assuming that they are, it is an offence to equip, or to attempt or endeavour to equip, any vessel with the statutory intent. Now this Information charges that, and of course the word in the Information must be held to have the same meaning there which it has in the Statute. What the meaning is which it has in the Statute, which must be the same as that which it has in the Information, is not for your Lordships now to determine, and for this plain reason, you could not determine it now except by means of a general and exhaustive definition. Now that is a duty upon which Courts of Justice never unnecessarily enter, and it is fortunately rarely necessary for them to enter. A general and exhaustive definition of the meaning of a word, or of four words, is a very different thing from determining upon the facts in a particular case, whether you have the meaning of that word satisfied by these facts. At the trial the question will arise, whether the equipment, which the Crown allege to have been made, or attempted, or assisted in, is an equipment within the meaning of the Statute. To determine that is a very different thing from laying down an exhaustive definition of the word 'equip.' And there is perfect safety to the parties here. The Crown must be held to have used each of the statutory expressions which is used in the Information, in the statutory sense; and at the trial, with reference to the facts proved, the question will arise in such circumstances that it may with safety be determined, and without entering upon the generalities, whether the facts are sufficient to satisfy the words, or any of the words, in the statutory sense. And therefore, upon this view, that the words are synonymous, while I think it is quite clear that they are not so, I submit that, even upon the assumption that they are, there is no validity in this objection,—for any one or more of the words used in the Information must, upon that assumption, be taken to be used in the statutory sense,—and that there is no foundation for the suggestion, such as I never remember to have heard made before, that one, two, three, or four expressions are not to be held as used in the statutory sense, because a fifth or sixth, which the Statute uses in the same sense, is not also to be found in the Information. But it is sufficient for me here to refer to the plain language of the Act itself, which is, that if any person shall equip, or attempt to equip, a ship, with the statutory intent, he shall be guilty of a misdemeanour. If he shall equip or attempt to equip, if he shall furnish or attempt to furnish, if he shall fit out or attempt to fit out, or if he shall arm or attempt to arm, a ship with the statutory intent, he shall be guilty of a misdemeanour. I say you equipped or attempted to equip it, and so on, and it is said he is not to be held guilty of the statutory misdemeanour, although that be true, because we have not also charged the last alternative mode in which the Statute might be contravened, viz., armed or attempted to arm.

Lord President.—If the use of the word 'arm' in the Statute gives a certain character or significance to the words equip, furnish, or fit out, then that must be their statutory meaning, and when they are used in the Information, they must receive that statutory meaning at the trial by reference to the Statute. That will be the key for construing them at the trial.

Solicitor-General.—Surely. Not only the word 'arm' which occurs in this clause, shall be used as a glossary in order to determine their meaning, and as throwing light upon the sense in which they are used in the Statute; but other words occurring in the Statute shall be used for the same purpose; nay, other words occurring in other clauses of the Statute may be used for the same purpose. According to all the principles of construction, you may refer to anything within the four corners of the Statute, in order to determine the meaning of any word or expression which you find in any one of the clauses; and in order to determine the meaning of equip, furnish, fit out, or arm, you may refer to the collocation of these words in the clause; you may refer to each of them as illustrating the sense, or the intent or probable intent of the Legislature in using the others. I say nothing against that; I say nothing of the argument or of the force of the argument which I can very well anticipate may be used in that way at the trial before the Jury or before the Judge, and there is nothing in this Information which can prejudice it. I use the expressions 'equip, furnish, and fit out' in the Information in the statutory sense, as that shall be legitimately determined by reference to the Statute.

Lord Deas.—The argument upon the other side is that by leaving out the word 'arming' you reject the glossary which that word would have afforded.

Solicitor-General.—I so stated the argument which I was attempting to meet. I cannot reject the statutory glossary or the statutory interpretation of the word.

Lord Deas.—Can't you go wrong?

Solicitor-General.—I can go right, and I am going right. I cannot reject a reference to this clause of the Statute, to any word or any clause in the Statute, to any expression in any part of the Statute, or, if it be legitimate, in any other Statute, in order to determine the meaning of the words in question. It is a matter in which you cannot go wrong; you cannot use a statutory word in other than the statutory sense in charging the statutory misdemeanour. The Court will necessarily fix that meaning in the Information; if the Statute says, 'if any person shall equip or attempt to equip a ship with a certain intent,' and I in the Information say, You did equip it, or attempt to equip it with that intent, I cannot be heard to say, Oh, I did not use the word 'equip' in the statutory sense; the statutory sense of the word is so and so, but that is not the meaning of it in the Information. That is an impossibility, and so clear do I feel on that, that I will not dwell on it a moment longer. I now proceed to the other argument, which is, that the words are not synonymous, but that according to the rule of construction which I have referred to, some of them must be referred to one employment of the ship, and some of them to another. Now, this rule of construction is very plainly inapplicable, because all of the words are sensible and intelligible with reference to each use of the ship. Whether the ship is to be used as a transport or store-ship, or whether it is to be used to cruise or commit hostilities, these words are all intelligible and sensible. A vessel may be equipped, furnished, or fitted out with intent to be employed as a cruiser, to commit hostilities, although the armour has not yet been put on board. Upon this subject I would refer to a single sentence in the opinion of Mr. Baron Bramwell. I rather think the Chief Baron had throughout a notion which he could never free his mind completely from, that the words were all used as synonymous, but all the other learned Judges were quite clearly of a contrary opinion, and I am not sure that the Chief Baron ultimately adhered to the view which he originally had, at all events he did not rest upon it. But the other Judges were clearly of another opinion, and Baron Bramwell says on this point (*Weekly Reporter*, p. 269):— 'I am satisfied that equip, furnish, and fit out are not limited to 'transport and store-ships. The rule which interprets *reddenda* '*singula singulis* does not apply, because all the words, "equip, '"furnish, and fit out" are sensible in reference to vessels intended 'to cruise or commit hostilities.' I had marked some other passages, but it is sufficient to say that all the learned Judges were of opinion that these words cannot be taken as used synonymously.

Lord Deas.—If they are not synonymous, has each of them a different meaning?

Solicitor-General.—That may be or may not be. I cannot say that your Lordships are at present in a position to say what will amount to equipment as distinguished from furnishing, and what will amount to furnishing as distinguished from fitting out, because that may depend upon the evidence.

Lord Deas.—It will not depend on the evidence whether each of them has a different meaning.

Solicitor-General.—I think that may depend on the evidence, because it relates to a matter of which your Lordships cannot take judicial cognizance. Can any of your Lordships tell me what equipping a ship, what furnishing a ship, what fitting out a ship may mean, without reference to evidence?

Lord Deas.—That is quite a different question from what I was putting.

Solicitor-General.—But till you have information on these subjects, you cannot tell whether they are all the same thing or not. If there should be a unanimity of evidence to this effect,—the words equip, furnish, and fit out, are always used as signifying precisely the same thing, and no seaman, and nobody engaged in the trade of furnishing and fitting out vessels, ever means anything else when he uses them,—surely that would be most material. If, on the other hand, the evidence is clear to this different effect, that to equip a vessel means something quite different from to furnish her, —if naval men and tradesmen engaged in that department say,— when you speak of equipping a vessel, you mean so-and-so; when you speak of furnishing her, you mean so-and-so different; when you speak of fitting her out, you mean this different thing,—is not that most material in the interpretation of the Act of Parliament?

Lord Deas.—I understand your observation perfectly, if you mean to say that, before we can judge whether the words are used synonymously or not, we require evidence; but if you once assume that we don't require evidence to hold that they are not synonymous, then I don't well understand it.

Solicitor-General.—Your Lordship will keep in view what I said at the very outset of my observations on this case, that I don't ask your Lordship to determine anything without evidence. On the contrary, I deprecate your determining anything without evidence. I think you cannot do it with safety, and farther, I think it is not in your power to do it, from ignorance as to the meaning of these words without evidence; for the Court cannot take judicial cognizance of what words which relate to a particular department of trade or business really mean.

Lord Deas.—Then do you mean that, without evidence, we cannot determine or know whether these words are all used synonymously?

Solicitor-General.—Clearly.

Lord Deas.—Then I understand that.

Solicitor-General.—I think you cannot determine one thing as to the meaning of these words without evidence.

Lord Deas.—No,—that we cannot determine without evidence whether the words are all used synonymously or no.

Solicitor-General.—If you cannot determine without evidence what any one of them means, of course you cannot determine whether or not they all mean the same thing.

Lord Deas.—That is a consistent proposition, which I understand.

Solicitor-General.—I wish it quite distinctly understood that I desire the Court to determine no question as to the meaning of any one of these words. I think that will be properly left for determination, and must of necessity be left for determination, because it cannot otherwise be intelligently or safely determined till after the evidence is submitted to the Jury, with reference to which the prosecutor shall contend, if at the conclusion of his case he shall contend, that he has established that you fitted out, furnished, or equipped a vessel contrary to the Act of Parliament; for, as I said before, it is one thing to give a general definition of any one term, and another thing to determine whether certain facts are covered by a term, and are sufficient to satisfy its meaning or no. Your Lordships are asked to throw out this Information, 1*st*, upon the ground which you are to reach without evidence, that these expressions are synonymous; and, 2*d*, upon the other ground, inconsistent with it, which you are also to reach without evidence, that they are not synonymous; and then upon that alternative view, to apply the rule of *applicando singula singulis*, and to say that certain of the expressions are referable to one thing, and certain of them to another. What I say in answer to all that is, that the Statute uses the words in the alternative, and in reference to both employments of the ship alike. The words are used in the alternative whether the intent is to employ the ship as a transport or as a cruiser, and the Information which charges one of the things done with the statutory intent, must be read as charging that thing in the statutory language used in the statutory sense, leaving it for determination at the trial whether the evidence satisfies that act under the statutory language or no. Questions may or may not arise according to the evidence, as to the meaning of these words, requiring direction at the trial. There was, in the case of the Alexandra, a very serious contest between the parties, both as to the matter of fact and the matter of law: as to the matter of fact, whether the equipment established was of a warlike character,—I mean, such equipment as is put upon a vessel intended for war, as distinguished from the equipment of a peace vessel,—without reference to the extent to which it had been carried, but looking to the nature of it merely; and an important question of law, whether the nature of the equipment was at all material, except as indicating the intent with which it was made; that is to say, whether anything that satisfied the meaning of the word equip, as applied to any ship, was not sufficient to constitute the statutory offence, provided the statutory intent was proved. It was upon that latter question that the great discussion took place in the Court of Exchequer, after the verdict in the Alexandra case. Now, we may or may not have a discussion of that kind here, according to the facts. The facts here may prove complete equipment of this vessel of the most warlike character,—the equipment of a war-vessel as distinguished from the equipment of a merchant ship,—everything equipped for war, furnished and fitted out up to the point of arming. Now, I ask your Lordships to determine nothing which will prejudice the case of the defenders with reference to these questions; and without dwelling further upon this matter, I pass now to the objection which I understood to be chiefly relied upon by Mr. Clark,—I mean the objection that the intent to cruise is not charged as an intent by the equipper to cruise. That argument was founded upon the repetition of the words 'with intent,' before the words 'to cruise or commit hostilities;' and it was this, that that intent to cruise or commit hostilities was referable not to the employment of the ship, but to the act of equipping, furnishing, fitting out, or arming the ship, and my learned friend Mr. Clark seemed to think that by expressing it in this way, that the intent to cruise or commit hostilities is referable to the act of equipping, &c., he demonstrated that that intent had not reference to the employment of the ship. Either use of the ship is the intent with which it is equipped, but the intent with which the ship is equipped is an intent which has reference to the use of the ship, and to nothing else. There are two uses, the intending of either of which satisfies the requirements of the Statute. These two uses are, as a transport ship, or to cruise or commit hostilities, and whether the intent with which you equip is an intent that she shall be employed in the one way or the other, you have the statutory intent which constitutes the act otherwise innocent a misdemeanour. But just consider for a moment the sense of the thing, without reference to the cogency of the words, particularly the repetition of the words 'with intent,' somewhat awkwardly, I must confess, before the words 'to cruise or commit hostilities.' Consider the sense and the reason of the thing for a single moment, because it is always important to attend to that, for if the construction which it is maintained the words bear is not a sensible or reasonable construction in itself, it is not too much to say that the words will require to be all the more forcible, and will only under the severest compulsion of the language bear a construction which is contrary to all sense and reason. Now, it is conceded to me, and indeed could not be disputed, that to equip a ship with the intent that it shall be employed in the service of one foreign state against another as a transport or store-ship, is an offence against the Statute, although there is no intent on the part of the equipper himself to employ it as a transport or store-ship.

Mr. Cook.—We never said that.

Solicitor-General.—Then you object to the 97th count. Does my learned friend mean to say that the statutory offence is not committed by a person who equips a vessel, or, without reference to the meaning of the word equip, using all the statutory expressions you like, with intent that it shall be employed by one foreign state against another as a transport or store-ship?

Mr. Cook.—Employed by the equipper in the service of a foreign state.

Solicitor-General.—I am speaking of a transport or store-ship just now. There is no charge in the 97th count, or in any count, that the equipper of the vessel intended himself to use it as a transport or store-ship. But whether it is conceded or not, it is too clear for one moment's argument that the Statute makes it a misdemeanour to equip a vessel with the intent that it shall be employed in the service of one foreign state against another with whom the Queen is not at war, as a transport or store-ship. Well, that being clear, and past the necessity of being argued on this side at least, the proposition which I am going to consider is, that although you cannot do the one thing without the statutory misdemeanour being committed, you may arm a ship to the teeth with the intent that it shall be used as a cruiser to commit hostilities by one foreign state against another with whom the Queen is not at war, provided only you don't yourself mean to use it as a privateer for your own behoof! That is the result to which the argument leads; and I say further that it is not reasonable or sensible in itself that a misdemeanour shall be committed by fitting out a vessel as a transport or store-ship to be used by one foreign state against another, but shall not be committed by arming a ship to be used as a cruiser to commit hostilities by one state against another, the meaning of the Statute there being, that no offence shall be committed unless the party arming intends himself to cruise with the ship. Now, the argument leading to this construction of the Statute to an irrational effect, is founded, and founded I think exclusively, upon the repetition of the words 'with intent' before the words 'to cruise or 'commit hostilities.' Now, cannot I satisfy these words unhappily introduced, without the necessity of resorting to that irrational construction of the Act of Parliament; for if I can, then that irrational construction is not one to which the Court is by these words driven. I cannot forbear here calling your Lordships' attention to the way in which this matter was ultimately dealt with in the Court of Exchequer in the Alexandra case. It had occurred to Sir Hugh Cairns, representing the interests of the defendants there, that the Statute was capable of that construction, and he had suggested it at the trial; but in the argument before the Court after the verdict, I don't understand that he again resorted to it, or even suggested that the Statute was capable of that construction; and I find, in a very full report of the discussion before the Exchequer Chamber, this passage between one of the learned Judges and the Attorney-General (p. 350)—(*Reads remarks of Baron Channell and Attorney-General, as quoted at p. 41, ante*). And when they come to give judgment, all the learned Barons deal with the clause so, except the Lord Chief Baron, in the passage read by Mr. Clark, and I think in a subsequent passage he reads it so also. But Mr. Baron Channell adverts to it most pointedly. He says (and I read the passage only in order to show that the counsel on both sides came to be quite satisfied that no argument could be founded on these words):—'It has been assumed in the argument 'on both sides that this may be read as if the words "with intent" 'were there omitted, as they are in the American Act. Whether 'this is right or not, their insertion certainly causes great confusion. 'In the first place, it provokes comparison with the other clause 'commencing "with intent," causing one, at first sight, to read 'them as showing alternative intents, either of which would, with 'the requisite act, constitute the offence. This, on looking into 'it, is agreed on all sides not to be the right construction;'—and it would be very strange indeed if it were the right construction, leading, as it does, to such a monstrously absurd interpretation of the Statute as I have just pointed out. But are not these words very clearly satisfied, without resorting to a nonsense meaning by the Legislature in order to satisfy them? Can't you satisfy them, and still attribute only good sense and consistency to the Legislature in this matter? which I take leave to say your Lordships will not only be inclined to do, but are bound to do. Is it not a sensible construction, if any person shall equip a ship, with intent or in order that such ship shall be employed as a transport or store-ship, or to cruise and commit hostilities, or if he shall equip a ship with intent that such ship shall be employed in the service of any foreign state with intent to cruise or commit hostilities,—what would you understand these words to mean now, taking the argument as it appears to have been taken at one stage of it in England,—just leave out the one use, in which we are not interested, in considering the meaning of the Legislature as to the other use, viz., to cruise and commit hostilities,—put the words 'as a transport or 'store-ship or' within parenthesis, and you have the words of the enactment then as to the only use with which we are now concerned, with intent or in order that such ship shall be employed in the service of any foreign state with intent to cruise or commit hostilities. These are the words of the Information, and they are objected to because they proceed upon a false construction of the Act. How so? The counts of the Information in which they occur have no reference to a contemplated use of the ship as a transport or store-ship. Therefore, the words applicable to that use are properly omitted, and only the words applicable to the other retained. But are any words in the Statute omitted except those which are exclusively applicable to that use with which the counts of the Information are not dealing? They omit no other words except these, 'as a transport or store-ship or,' and necessarily, because that is the connecting word, with the use to which the Information does relate. Now, how can an Information which uses the language of the Statute in regard to the matter with which alone it deals, be said to proceed on an erroneous construction of it?

Lord President.—Does the word 'or' make an alternative to the uses, or an alternative to the intents? That is the question.

Solicitor-General.—It just depends upon that. I say it makes an alternative to the uses, the intent having reference to the uses. There is no offence committed by equipping a ship without an intent; but whether that intent is as to one use or another use don't signify; either use, if intended by you, shall make your act, otherwise innocent, a misdemeanour.

Lord Deas.—You observe that in the first part of the clause the words are, 'with intent or in order that the ship or vessel shall 'be employed in the service of any foreign prince,' &c., and in the second part of the clause the words are 'with intent' simply, without the words 'or in order.' Now, if you leave out 'with intent' in the second branch of the clause, the effect is the same as if you were to introduce there the words 'or in order.' That makes an important difference, because the words 'or in order' to the employment of the ship in the foreign service seem to point very directly to the use in the foreign service, whether by the individual who fitted it out or no.

Solicitor-General.—The meaning of the words 'or in order' was the subject of consideration by all the learned Judges in the Alexandra case, and I think they all came to the conclusion which I am sure your Lordships must arrive at too, that they are put there merely as explanatory of the intent.

Lord Deas.—Clearly; that is the view in which I am referring to them.

Solicitor-General.—I am not sure that I have quite followed your Lordship's view there.

Lord Deas.—It appears to me that the words 'or in order' in the first part of the clause materially aid the construction you are contending for in regard to a transport or store-ship, and if they are to be held as repeated in the second branch of the clause, they materially aid your construction that it is enough to be employed in the service of the foreign power though not by the fitter-out; and therefore it comes to be very important whether the words 'in order' are to be held to be repeated, or what would come to the same thing, whether the words 'with intent' in the second branch are to be left out, in which case the words 'or in order' are applicable to the second branch as well as the first.

Solicitor-General.—I am not sure.

Lord Deas.—Do you take no aid from the words 'in order' in construing that first branch.

Solicitor-General.—I don't think it. I think it would be precisely the same without them. I should submit exactly the same argument to your Lordship without them.

Lord Deas.—But not quite with equal force to my mind.

Solicitor-General.—I think the words 'or in order' are exegetical. It would be the same whether you had both of them with the disjunctive 'or,' or only one of them, and it would not signify which of them. If you equip a ship in order that it shall be employed, that is to say, you having the intent that it shall be employed, or with the intent that it shall be employed, that is, you equip in order that it shall be employed. I think it would come to the same thing, but it was very proper in the Legislature, in case there should be any doubt as to the meaning of the one expression, to use the other also as synonymous with it, as exegetical, for in this matter your Lordships can without evidence, and must without evidence, determine the meaning of the words 'with intent and in order that' as occurring in the Statute. Evidence can have no bearing here as in the case of equipping, furnishing, &c., and I should think the judicial interpretation of either expression would be the same, and the judicial interpretation of both together, separated by the word 'or,' in such manner as to show that each is used as exegetical of the other, must be the same as if you had either of them. But the second intent is a little different according to the interpretation which I put upon it. I think it would have conduced to clearness of expression if the words had been omitted, although the awkward introduction of words don't always, and don't here affect the meaning. You may have the same meaning clearly enough expressed in different words, but more distinctly and with greater propriety in the one set of words than in the other. And so here, I think the same meaning would have been expressed with greater propriety without these words 'with intent,' but still the introduction of them, although awkward, don't affect the sense according to my reading. But I read these words 'with intent' in connexion with the word 'employed.' The first intent, 'with intent and in order 'that,' is the intent which is required to be predicated of the act of equipping in order to constitute the misdemeanour. If you shall equip with intent and in order that the ship shall be employed, how? In the service of a 'foreign state with intent to cruise or 'commit hostilities.' Put it otherwise,—If your intent in equipping the ship shall be the employment of it by a foreign state with intent to cruise, or with intent to commit hostilities, the second intent is there predicable of the employment of the ship. The first intent which overrides it no doubt is, however, the expression which is referable to the act of equipping. If you shall equip with intent, or in order that the ship shall be employed in a certain manner, you shall be guilty of a misdemeanour. Employed in what manner? Employed by one state against another, either as a store-ship or with intent to commit hostilities. That is the intent of the employment, or the purpose of the employment. Suppose it had been in the service of any foreign state as a transport or store-ship, intended to carry transports or stores for warlike purposes against another state with whom the Queen was not at war,—there again you might have the complaint of awkwardness of expression, but there could be no dubiety about the meaning. Now, observe, my purpose is to satisfy the meaning of the words 'with intent' as they occur before the words 'to cruise,' consistently with sensible and rational legislation,—not to defend them as elegantly used, but to satisfy their meaning without the necessity of imputing nonsense to the Legislature. Now, don't I do so by reading them as I have done? If you shall equip a ship with intent that it shall be employed by one foreign state with intent to commit hostilities against another, then you shall be guilty of a misdemeanour. Now, substantially this amounts to the same thing as leaving out these words 'with intent' altogether, as an unnecessary and clumsy expression of what would be implied without them. I am afraid that in Acts of Parliament, as well as in other documents, we have frequently words awkwardly employed to express a meaning which would more plainly have appeared without the use of them at all, and I think that is the case with these words here, but still they are so used as not to change the meaning, but merely unnecessarily to express what without them would have been implied. If you read the provision without them altogether, it would be with intent that such ship shall be employed in the service of any foreign state to cruise or commit hostilities against any state with whom Her Majesty is not at war. That is quite a sensible construction, and that is the language of the American Act. But with the words I think you satisfy the meaning completely, by referring them to the employment of a ship by the foreign state in whose service it is employed. Now, I was somewhat surprised, I confess, at the reference made by Mr. Clark to the American cases, because in the American Act, the words upon which alone this whole argument is rested don't occur, and therefore this argument could not arise in America, and never did arise in America. The cases which my learned friend referred to were cited in the case of the Alexandra, but for a totally different purpose. My learned friend Mr. Clark said, that these American cases had been approved of by all the learned judges in the Court of Exchequer, even for the purpose for which they were cited. Now, I don't find that any one approves, and I find that one of the learned Barons, at least, who concurred with the Lord Chief Baron, pretty strongly censures the reference to these cases. The first case my friend referred to was the case of the 'Independencia,' and Mr. Baron Bramwell, at p. 270, thus refers to it:—'The case of the "Independencia" has not 'the slightest bearing on the present. The "Independencia" was 'an armed vessel.' The next case Mr. Clark cited was the case of the United States *v.* Quincy, and Baron Bramwell says, with respect to it: 'The next case is the United States *v.* Quincy. I say, with all respect, that the case was wrongly decided. The learned

Attorney-General confessed it. It supposes that a person can assist in doing what nobody is doing or trying to do. It applies a pleading test,—very little use in discussing a Statute,—and doubly misapples it; and he criticises that case, arriving at the result, that it is quite erroneously decided, and has no application to the case in hand. But lest your Lordships should think it necessary to refer to these American cases, I shall very briefly notice them. The first is the case of the 'Independencia.' It was not an Information for a condemnation of the ship, nor was it an indictment for a misdemeanour under the Statute. The question was, whether a capturing ship having come into one of the ports of the United States with goods which she had captured at sea from her enemy, the enemy could claim restoration of their goods upon the ground that they had been captured contrary to the neutrality of the United States. It was maintained that they had been captured contrary to the neutrality of the United States by the Spanish owner, first in respect of a treaty between the United States and Spain. That of course could have no bearing on the present case, or upon any case, because it was found that the treaty had nothing to do with it. In the second place, it was maintained that these goods had been captured in violation of that neutrality, because the ship had originally been equipped as a cruiser, contrary to a clause of the United States' Act corresponding to this one. It is not necessary to say more upon that than that it was attempted to be proved that the vessel had been equipped in the United States, with the statutory intent of being used as a cruiser, to commit hostilities against a nation with whom the United States was not at war, and there were witnesses examined in order to show that, of whom Mr. Justice Story says, that they were altogether unworthy of credit, and he says, p. 54—'We adhere to the rule which 'has been already adopted by this Court, that restitution ought not 'to be decreed upon the ground of capture in violation of our neu'trality, unless the fact be established beyond all reasonable doubt.' Now the fact alleged that the vessel had been equipped with intent to cruise and commit hostilities against Spain, the Court was of opinion was not proved. It was proved, however, to the satisfaction of the Court—and it is the observation of Justice Story here that Mr. Clark referred to the case for—that the vessel had been equipped in a United States' port, not with intent to be used as a cruiser to commit hostilities against Spain, but with intent, after it was equipped, to take it out and offer it for sale to the Buenos Ayres Government; and Mr. Justice Story was of opinion,—and I don't find that that was contested by anybody there,—that if you had the intent merely to sell if you could find a customer, that was not the statutory intent that the vessel should be employed as a cruiser, or to commit hostilities. We are contending for nothing of that sort here. The observation of Justice Story is at p. 55:—'There 'is nothing in our laws'—(*Reads as quoted, p.* 16, *ante*). That observation might have been referred to for what it is worth, and it may be worth a great deal, if the Information here had charged not an intent that the vessel should be employed to cruise and commit hostilities against the United States, but an intent to sell her to the Confederates, if the Confederates could be induced to buy her. I think if that intent had been charged, the argument might very well have been used which that observation of Justice Story's would have gone to support. But that is not the intent charged. The intent charged is not the intent to sell; it is an intent that the vessel shall be employed to cruise and commit hostilities. Now there is abundance of authority in America,—and I suppose the authority is right,—that the intent which the Statute requires, is a distinct, positive, existing intent, not contingent, or dependent upon circumstances or events; your intent in equipping that vessel, or procuring it to be equipped, or aiding and assisting in equipping it, must be that she shall be so employed. An intent to take her into the market, and a belief that she will be so employed by the purchaser, if you succeed in selling her to a particular purchaser, whom you have in view, will not be the statutory intent; at least, that is Justice Story's opinion. But no such question arises here. I charge the statutory intent in the statutory language, but how does that go to support the only contention in support of which it was cited, that let the intent to use the vessel as a cruiser to commit hostilities be never so clear, unless it is the intent of you yourselves to cruise in her and commit hostilities with her, that won't satisfy the Statute. Justice Story says nothing about that, nor could he well do so; for the American Statute don't use the words in respect of which it is contended that that is the meaning of our Statute. I really don't understand what is suggested as the true meaning of the American Act, if it be not that the offence shall be committed if the vessel is intended to be employed in the service of a foreign state, to cruise or commit hostilities. The American Statute is in the very words of this Information. I pray my learned friend to consider it in that light; and I think it is a sound test and criterion, because it disposes at once of the whole reference to the American cases. The American cases were of course determined with reference to the American Statute. Well, they are cited to show, that even according to American law this Information proceeds on an erroneous construction of the Statute. Suppose that this Information proceeded upon the American Statute, would that not have been right? Here are the words of the American Statute: 'If any person shall, within 'the limits'—(*Reads as quoted at p. 17, ante*). These are the very words of the present Information,—I don't mean in every respect, but they are the very words in the respect with reference to which the objection which I am now considering is stated,—the intent that the vessel shall be employed in the service of a foreign state to cruise or commit hostilities against another foreign state. These are the words of the Act.

Mr. Cook.—Of the American Act.

Solicitor-General.—I am saying so; but I am considering the application of the American authorities. Well, an Information under the American Act, in the very terms of the Information here, would have been a good Information, because the American authorities don't establish any such proposition as that which is contended for.

Lord Deas.—They say that is because the American Act is better framed than ours.

Solicitor-General.—But the point is this, whether the American Act requires that the intent to employ the ship as a cruiser must be the intent of the equipper himself to cruise in it. That is said to be the law of America.

Lord President.—No.

Lord Deas.—No; there must be some misapprehension about that.

Solicitor-General.—Then I profess my total ignorance of the reason for which the American cases were cited.

Lord Ardmillan.—I understood Mr. Clark to state expressly that the decision in the American Courts proceeded on this view of their own law, that in order to constitute the offence in America, it was necessary for the equipper or the fitter-out to cruise in the vessel.

Solicitor-General.—I so understood.

Lord Ardmillan.—It may not be a correct construction, but I understood that to be the construction.

Mr. Clark.—My argument was that the intent libelled was the intent of the equipper.

Lord Deas.—Do you mean the intent libelled in America?

Mr. Clark.—I maintain both. I said that they held in America distinctly on these authorities, that the intent must be the intent of the equipper.

Lord President.—The intent of the equipper that what thing should follow?

Mr. Clark.—The intent of the equipper that he should cruise and commit hostilities.

Solicitor-General.—It is rather that the employment should be the employment of the equipper. It must be that. There is no doubt it is the intent of the equipper. The Statute deals only with the intent of the equipper, as qualifying the act which constitutes a misdemeanour, if so qualified. It is his intent, therefore, necessarily. But the employment intended must be the employment of the equipper. That is what I understand to be the subject of contention. Well, is the American law the same as the British law, or is it not?

Lord Deas.—I confess I should like to have known whether the doctrine which Mr. Clark says was held in America, was held, because it appears to me more difficult to hold it on the American Act than to hold it on our own. It is very difficult to suppose that that should have been held in America.

Solicitor-General.—I think the American cases have nothing to do with this case at all.

Lord Deas.—They would have to do with it, if Mr. Clark was stating the matter rightly, that though the American Act is not subject to the objection taken by the other side here, they still held that it must be the intent of the party fitting out himself to cruise. If they held that, it would be a sort of *a fortiori* authority here. If they did not hold that, and I can hardly imagine they ever could have held it, then it has no application.

Solicitor-General.—I think clearly not; but the proposition which I have stated to the Court is unanswerably sound, that unless the American law is the same as ours in this respect, the American decisions upon the point have no application. The first question therefore is, whether the American law is the same; and upon that question I take my learned friends as saying that it is, because otherwise they cannot justify their reference to American cases. Now what do they say in this view? The American Act, which speaks of the intent that such ships shall be employed in the service of any foreign state to cruise or commit hostilities against another foreign state, must mean that the equipper shall intend himself to cruise and commit hostilities with the ship in the service of the one foreign state against the other; and that that is the meaning put upon it in the passage I have read from Justice Story, in a case in which that question was not presented, and not one word was said about it on the one side or the other! But suppose that to be the meaning of the American Act, which my learned friends say it is, in order to enable them to argue that it is the meaning of our Act also,—what I ask is this, suppose our Act had been in the same terms as the American Act, would not this Information *quoad* the charge of the intent be irresistibly relevant, being in the very words of the American Act, which they say has the same meaning? The objection to the relevancy here is to the way in which the intent is charged. It is charged thus:—Your intent was that the vessel shall be employed by one foreign state with intent to cruise and commit hostilities against another. They say that is the same in effect as if you had just said in words, 'with intent that the vessel 'shall be employed by one foreign state to cruise or commit hos-'tilities against another;' and that shows that you proceed on an erroneous construction of the Statute, because you drop or let fall the meaning of these words 'with intent,' used before 'to cruise.' But how is that objection consistent with their reference to the American cases? They refer to the American Act, in which the words 'with intent' don't occur before 'to cruise,' and yet they say the Statute has the same meaning without the words which our Statute has with them. But if you have the same meaning without the words, where is the objection to the Information, whether these words are in it or not? The words 'with intent' don't, in the American Act, occur before 'to cruise;' and yet the American Act, say my learned friends, has the same meaning with ours, in which they do. Our Information don't use these words before 'to cruise,' or it uses them in such a way as to show, they say, that no meaning is attached to them; the Statute reads as if they did not occur. Well, if the Statute has the same meaning with or without them, the Information must have the same meaning with or without them, and I don't understand the logic of the objection. But all that Justice Story says, in the passage quoted from his opinion, is this: You have not the statutory intent that the vessel shall be employed to cruise or commit hostilities against a foreign state, if you have no intent except that it shall be taken into the market for the chance of a sale. Now that has nothing to do with whether the cruising is to be by one person or by another person. I scarcely think it necessary to notice the case of Quincy, except just to observe that almost all the propositions in it are entirely consistent with, and not one of them inconsistent with the argument which I am maintaining. It was an indictment for a misdemeanour, and it was objected to as bad in law; the United States maintained that it was good in law, and asked a direction to that effect, and that was the judgment of the Court. Here is the Information held to be good in law under a Statute with precisely the same meaning as ours (for that is the argument on the other side), in a case referred to as an authority on the other side:—'The jurors on their oath 'do present that the said John D. Quincy, &c., was knowingly 'concerned in the fitting out a certain vessel called "The Bolivar," 'with intent that the said vessel should be employed in the service 'of a foreign people; that is to say, in the service of the United 'Provinces of Rio de la Plata, to cruise and commit hostilities 'against the subjects and property of a foreign prince,' &c. Is not that the very intent libelled here?—intent to be employed in the service of one foreign state to commit hostilities against another? That was a good Information in point of law under the American Act, which my learned friends say was the same as ours, notwithstanding the repetition of the words 'with intent' before 'to cruise' in ours. In that case also, the United States asked this direction, which was granted:—'2. That if the Jury find from the evidence 'that the traverser was, within the district of Maryland, knowingly 'concerned in the fitting out of the privateer "Bolivar," with intent 'that such vessel should be employed in the service of the United 'Provinces of Rio de la Plata, to commit hostilities, or to cruise and 'commit hostilities against the subjects, &c., of the Emperor of 'Brazil, with whom the United States then were at peace, then the 'traverser has been guilty of a violation of the 3d section of the Act 'of Congress of 1818, although the Jury should further find that 'the intention so to employ the said vessel was liable to be defeated 'by a failure to procure funds in the West Indies, where further 'equipments were intended and required to be made before actually 'commencing the contemplated cruise.' And this was further granted, 'That if the Jury find from the evidence that the tra-'verser was, &c., knowingly concerned in the fitting out of the pri-'vateer "Bolivar," with intent that such vessel should be employed 'in the service of the United Provinces of Rio de la Plata, to com-'mit hostilities, or to cruise and commit hostilities against the 'subjects, &c., of the Emperor of Brazil, &c., then the traverser has 'been guilty of a violation of the 3d section of the Act, &c., although 'the Jury should further find that the fulfilment of the intention 'so to employ the said vessel would have been defeated, if further 'funds had not been obtained in the West Indies, where further 'equipments were intended and required to be made before com- 'mencing the contemplated cruise.' On the other hand, the accused party maintained, and was found entitled to the direction, that if he had no fixed intention that the vessel should be so employed, but an indefinite and contingent intention, liable to be defeated or only to take effect in a certain contingency, in the event of his being able to procure funds in a foreign country, then the statutory intent was not established. There is great nicety certainly in saying that if you had the intention distinct and positive that the vessel shall be so employed you shall be guilty, although your intention is completely defeated before the vessel is seized, or before you are prosecuted, and has become impossible of being carried out; and, on the other hand, to say that if your intent is as clear as possible to take the vessel and expose it in a market, the purchaser in which will, in all probability, if you find one, use it in a particular way, that then you have not the statutory intent. The moral guilt in the one case may be as great as in the other, if there be moral guilt at all. The danger to the peace of the country may be as great in the one case as in the other. With all that we have no question at present. The question is this, Have I not charged in the Information here an intent that the vessel shall be employed in the way, the intention to have it employed in which qualifies the act charged so as to make it a misdemeanour? Now I think the true meaning of the Statute is that which I have submitted to your Lordships; and, therefore, having now adverted to all the objections put forward by my learned friends—

Lord Curriehill.—I suppose you say that the party whose intent the Statute deals with is the equipper?

Solicitor-General.—In one passage. The intent that the vessel shall be employed in a certain way must be his.

Lord Curriehill.—The party whose intent the Statute deals with is in that passage the equipper.

Solicitor-General.—Yes.

Lord Curriehill.—Does the Statute deal with the question who is to be the employer?

Solicitor-General.—I think it does not; and therefore I should have said that while I maintain this Information, and that I shall, when the time comes, if it shall be necessary, maintain that it is sufficiently established by evidence that those who equipped or attempted or were concerned in the equipping of the vessel had no intention themselves to cruise, but that the vessel, being equipped under a contract, should go into the service of a foreign state, or of others in the service of that foreign state, to be by them employed as a cruiser, I shall nevertheless at the same time maintain,—and this has reference to a question put by your Lordship at the outset, —that if the evidence should show that all or any one of those who are mentioned in the Information, and they are not all represented here,—one of them is a citizen, I believe, of the Confederate States, mentioned in the Information, and who is not represented here, but who is in this country,—I say if it should be proved that all or any of them intended themselves or himself to cruise in the vessel, and commit hostilities in the service of the one foreign state against the other.

Lord President.—But in the service.

Solicitor-General.—Yes; and I suppose that would not be objected to; indeed, that is the principle on which the 3d and other counts are framed.

Lord President.—My question went to not in the service.

Solicitor-General.—There might be a difficulty there about the evidence, because in one sense a privateer is in the service of one belligerent against the other, because, though it acts for its own ends and purposes and advantages, yet it is to promote the ends and purposes of the one state in its war against the other.

Lord President.—That point which you last argued as to the construction of the Statute with reference to the word 'intent' is the great subject of contention. That is the question upon the construction of the Statute, irrespective of the evidence. Now then, you say we are not to decide anything.

Solicitor-General.—If your Lordships are satisfied to decide that now, I do not much care.

Lord President.—You ask us not to decide; the defenders ask us to decide.

Solicitor-General.—I am quite content that on that last point, not involving the interpretation of the words equip, furnish, &c., your Lordships shall deal with that matter as you shall see fit. What occurred to me as to the convenience of not deciding it now was this. Of course if your Lordships should decide it one way, that would stop the trial under certain counts of this Information; but it would just lead to this, that we would have a course of litigation upon that decision, it may be going to the House of Lords, —indeed I may say almost with certainty going to the House of Lords,—and the result of that might be, that after running that course of litigation, with our hands on the seized ship all the time, we would come down here again to the trial. Now there is inconvenience in that. On the other hand, if your Lordships should repel the objections, and find the Information relevant, there is no immediate advantage gained by it, unless you are to allow the other party to go elsewhere too, and that would be attended with the same inconvenience. What I thought was that a question of law must of necessity arise at the trial,—of necessity, I mean looking to the course of the Alexandra case,—for we shall have questions as to equipping, furnishing, and fitting out, —it is better to keep all the questions of law together, and to try the question of fact, the verdict upon which in our way may anticipate all the questions together, and make them of no importance, and to leave all the questions of law to be raised at the same time.

Lord President.—But suppose, in the first place, we were to pronounce a judgment upon this matter, in what form would that judgment be? Would it be a judgment repelling or sustaining certain objections? Would that be the form of the judgment?

Solicitor-General.—If your Lordships were either to repel or to sustain, I suppose you would find in the one case that the counts objected to were not bad in law; and in the other, that the counts objected to were bad in law. If you think the more expedient course is not to determine these at all just now, and, not being clearly satisfied that any of them are bad in law, to send the case to trial, I suppose the judgment would be a simple adherence.

Lord President.—Suppose we abstained from deciding anything about it, is the matter open to the party afterwards?

Solicitor-General.—I never entertained the slightest doubt of that.

Lord President.—The Lord Ordinary says that he can give no assurance as to that.

Solicitor-General.—I think that the Lord Ordinary is right in saying so.

Lord President.—I am not saying that the Lord Ordinary is wrong in not giving an assurance, but it points at this, that he at least is not satisfied that the party would be safe.

Solicitor-General.—His Lordship expressed a decided opinion that there could be no question about the competency of raising this afterwards, but his Lordship thought that it was not proper to put an assurance in the shape of a reservation or otherwise into his interlocutor.

Lord President.—I am not finding fault with his not doing it; but he has intimated to us and to the parties in his Note, something which points at this, that in his own view he is not certain whether it may be open after all.

Solicitor-General.—That is not what was meant.

Lord Curriehill.—Mr. Clark says there is reason to fear that that would be the case, because in England there is a well-known remedy by arrest of judgment, and in Scotland we have hitherto been unaccustomed to such a remedy. So Mr. Clark explained, as giving importance to that remark of the Lord Ordinary.

Solicitor-General.—That is a reason why my learned friend urged very properly that your Lordships should decide the question of law now. I think it would be a reason, if it were sound in itself, but I think it is very clearly not sound in itself, and that there is no room whatever for the application.

Lord President.—How would it arise at the trial?

Solicitor-General.—In the first place, we would have the construction of the Judge at the trial. He must direct the Jury as to what amounts to a contravention of the Statute, and what does not; and if he is of opinion that the Information does not aver a contravention of the Statute, he may give effect to that opinion at the trial in the shape of a direction, or in the way of withdrawing it from the Jury, when his mind is more matured by the facts of the particular case. I do not think that that would be a reasonable or a convenient course, because it would lead to a bill of exceptions, which would be a more inconvenient and expensive way of raising the question than this. Your Lordships are not adjusting an issue, or approving of an issue. A verdict upon any one of these counts can do no more than affirm its truth in point of fact. Well, what would the Crown do with a verdict affirming, say the first count in point of fact? The Crown would come with that first count and the verdict affirming it, and, reading that as an affirmative proposition, it would ask judgment condemning the ship. What is the meaning of arrest of judgment *non obstante veredicto?* In England, judgment follows upon the verdict without resort to the Court, unless a motion to arrest the judgment is made to the Court. The judgment following on the verdict is below the Bench; it is in the Court offices; and so, if a party says this verdict does not affirm anything in fact which in law entitles you to a judgment, he interposes with a motion to the Court to arrest that judgment, which otherwise in the Court offices would follow. Here it is not so; the party with his verdict comes to the Court to apply it, and to pronounce judgment in his favour; and then a question would arise, not as in England by a motion in arrest of judgment, but by showing to the Court why judgment in favour of the Crown should not follow upon that verdict. Can anything be more clear than that a verdict affirming in point of fact a proposition which does not aver a misdemeanour in point of law, will not justify the condemnation of the ship?

Lord President.—Would the affirmance of the count affirm that the thing was done contrary to the form of the Statute in such case made and provided?

Solicitor-General.—I think not, unless the language used was language applicable to a thing done contrary to the form of the Statute, in that case made and provided.

Lord President—How?

Solicitor-General.—I mean if the Information does not aver a thing done which is contrary to the Statute, the mere application of the words that it was contrary to the Statute won't make it so, and would have no effect on the question. Suppose the statutory intent were omitted altogether,—you did equip that ship,—or suppose the words were, you put provisions on board that ship contrary to the form of the Statute in that case made and provided, and the Jury affirm that, they affirm nothing but the matter of fact; and if the matter of fact is not a contravention of the Statute, the suggestion, for it is no more, that it is contrary to the Statute would not make it so. I think there can be no doubt about the remedy of the party. Now, just a single word as to another course which was suggested as a course frequently taken in England, viz., an arrangement that the verdict should be entered the other way if the Court should be of a certain opinion in point of law. We have made such arrangements frequently in the Jury Court here, and there can be no doubt about their validity. But the legal remedy in England is a motion for arrest of judgment, if the thing affirmed by the verdict is not, as the prosecutor alleges, a contravention of the Act, and it will not become a contravention of the Act, if it is not so in itself, merely because the Jury have affirmed a certain count.

Lord President.—It is done in contravention of the Act according to one construction of the Act, but not according to the other.

Solicitor-General.—I take it that an Act is capable of only one construction.

Lord President.—But you are contending as to two constructions of it.

Solicitor-General.—What I am considering now is the possibility of raising the question of the true construction after the verdict.

Lord President.—Well, can that be done? Would it not require a bill of exceptions?

Solicitor-General.—I think very clearly not. The Lord Ordinary would have a great deal of law to deal with,—all the law that was involved in the Alexandra case as to the meaning of the words, what would satisfy the meaning of equip, furnish, &c., which is really the only law in the case of the least importance, or creating any difficulty. But I think there is no room for dubiety about this matter. If, taking the 1st count, the things which are there averred to have been done, with the intent there averred within the sense of the words used, may be proved to have been done contrary to the Act, there is an end to the objection as to the sufficiency in law of the charge, for a charge in such terms that a thing done contrary to the Act may be proved within it, is a good charge in law. The objection which your Lordships are asked now to sustain is that the things alleged in the 1st count cannot be shown to have been done contrary to the Act properly construed. We say that they may be done contrary to the Act properly construed. Well, after the fact that the things had been done has been affirmed, the same question would be presented. If these things could be done, as charged, contrary to the Act, there is no objection to the Information now, and there is no objection to the Information with the verdict. But if there is an objection now, there is equally an objection then. The thing could not be done contrary to the Act properly construed. If so, the verdict affirming that it was would be of no use.

Lord President.—But if, after argument here, we send this Information to trial, is not that equivalent to a construction of it?

Solicitor-General.—I should not have thought so, but I have no objection to your Lordships taking that point and deciding it, on the understanding, or in the hope and belief that if your Lordships should sustain the Information, we are not to have an appeal interposed between us and a trial of the facts.

Lord President.—Do you raise any doubt at all as to the competency of a bill of exceptions in the case?

Solicitor-General.—None whatever.

Lord President.—Or a motion for a new trial?

Solicitor-General.—None whatever. I was making these observations in answer to what Mr. Clark suggested, that we had no remedy here corresponding to the English remedy of motion in arrest of judgment. We have not that exact remedy, for this reason, that here the judgment is pronounced by the Court upon an application to it by the party holding the verdict, and the motion is not in arrest of judgment, but on cause shown why judgment should not be pronounced.

Lord President.—Then your answer to my question is that the party will have his remedy in any of several ways. He may except to the direction, or he may, without excepting to the direction, move for a new trial without following out the bill of exceptions; he may move for a new trial as against law, or on any other ground, or without doing that, he may raise the question on the attempt of the Crown to have the verdict applied. That is your view. All these are open to him.

Solicitor-General.—All these are open to him. See how plainly it is open to him on a bill of exceptions, which, I think, is the most ordinary, and probably the most convenient remedy. What is his law? This Statute is not contravened unless—

Lord President.—I am not raising a doubt about it; but I can conceive the party being a little nervous and apprehensive on the subject, after that intimation by the Lord Ordinary that he does not say but that the party may be finally excluded.

Lord Advocate.—We had no wish to have an argument at all. We were quite clear that the relevancy was reserved.

Solicitor-General.—It is right, in justice to the Lord Ordinary, that your Lordships should distinctly note that the Lord Ordinary, without any hesitation, and we on the part of the Crown with as little, intimated the clear opinion that this matter was open to the party in all these varieties of ways that have now been spoken of.

Lord Deas.—Do you hold it open to him both to take a bill of exceptions, and likewise to raise the whole law on the application of the verdict.

Solicitor-General.—Certainly.

Lord Deas.—Both?

Solicitor-General.—Certainly. I think that is open to every party, even in the Court of Session.

Lord Deas.—If it depends upon that, it depends upon a very doubtful matter.

Solicitor-General.—The Lord Ordinary meant to indicate, no doubt, upon that point, and the passage in his Note, to which attention has been called, was introduced in answer to the suggestion of the defenders, that an express reservation of this should be put in the Interlocutor. That his Lordship refused on what I think the Court will hold the very proper ground, that it would be introducing confusion and uncertainty into the practice,—that if you reserved by expression in some cases what is reserved by implication, you would just raise questions in other cases as to whether it was reserved.

Lord President.—The Lord Ordinary does say that according to his view the matter is open, but he says he can give no assurance. If he had not added that—

Lord Deas.—Do I understand you to say that the statutory intent may be proved although there is no arming?

Solicitor-General.—Yes.

Lord Deas.—Then suppose the proper officer of the United States Government were to write to Mr. Fleming saying, 'we commission 'you to build, equip, and furnish for us a vessel in all respects the 'same as the Great Eastern, in order that we may arm her, and 'employ her against the Confederate States,' would that be a statutory offence.

Solicitor-General.—I don't know. I would like to have the evidence as to the manner in which the 'Great Eastern' is equipped, furnished, and fitted out.

Lord Deas.—I am supposing equipment without arming.

Lord President.—In order that the United States may arm her and use her.

Solicitor-General.—A very important question may arise at the trial, or may not, according to the evidence. The evidence may be that the equipment, furnishing, and fitting out,—short of arming, but up to the very point of putting cannon on board,—were the equipment, furnishings, and fittings-out of a ship of war as distinguished from a merchant ship, in all respects in which the one is distinguished from the other. In that case, of course, the Jury, if satisfied with that evidence, would be of opinion that the equipments, furnishing, and fitting out were of a warlike character,—such as distinguished the equipments of a war-ship from the equipments of a merchant ship in those respects in which they don't correspond. In that case the question would not arise at all. Again, the evidence might be that the equipments which had been attempted or completed, in so far as completed at the time of the seizure, were only of such a character as were common to all ships, whether intended for purposes of peace or for purposes of war. Of course, upon such evidence as that, there would be nothing in the nature of the equipments to show the intent with which they were made; but although there is room for serious question there, we should contend that the character of the equipments was altogether immaterial, except as affording evidence of the intent with which they were made, and that if the intent with which they were made was proved otherwise, neither the character nor the extent of the equipments was of any materiality. The question probably won't arise here at all, but I am indicating to your Lordships now what we should probably contend for. I may just add that the numerous expressions used by the Statute are, we think, intended to make the provision of the most general description, applying to anything which comes within the meaning of equipment, anything which comes within the meaning of furnish, anything which comes within the meaning of fit out. It don't descend to particulars, preferring a generality of expression, which may be applied to anything according to the evidence in each particular case. But I think the general provision includes this particular provision, which, if it had been expressed, would not have been unintelligible to my mind,—If any person shall furnish with provisions a ship, with the intent that it shall be employed by a foreign state to cruise and commit hostilities against a nation with which the Queen is not at war, that innocent act shall, in consequence of the intent, be a misdemeanour. I am not saying that that is the meaning of the Act. I am merely saying that it is open to me to contend, and is quite rational in itself, that the equipment, furnishing, and fitting out is not confined to equipment, furnishings, and fittings of a warlike as distinguished from a peaceful character, but extends to all sorts, the stamp of misdemeanour being fixed upon any sort of equipment or furnishing with the statutory intent. In the general case, unless the equipments, furnishings, and fittings are of such a character as to indicate the use which it must have been intended to make of the ship, the Crown will look in vain for a conviction or for a condemnation. But if the Crown can, as it is possible they may, prove the intent, irrespective of its being indicated by the nature of the thing done, then I think the nature of the thing done is immaterial, provided it be equipment, furnishing, or fitting out,—words applicable to merchant ships as well as to war ships, although there is a point at which the equipments or furnishings of the one begin to differ from those of the other.

Lord Deas.—The case that I supposed, was an order for a vessel which has nothing warlike about her, but in which it appears upon the face of the writings by which she is contracted for, that both the parties intend and understand that she is to be armed by one foreign state, and employed against another,—that is the case I supposed, and my question was whether you maintained that that would be a statutory offence. I rather infer that you do.

Lord Advocate.—We should maintain that, but it will be time enough to consider it when the fact comes out.

Mr. Cook.—I attend your Lordships for the owners, and before speaking to the questions arising on the construction of the 7th section of the Foreign Enlistment Act, I desire to say a word or two in regard to the form of procedure. We ask your Lordships to decide the questions of relevancy now. The Solicitor-General asks your Lordships to reserve them, or, at all events, to refrain from pronouncing judgment upon them now, and to send the case to trial, it being understood that in some way or other we shall be at liberty, at an after stage of the case, to state our objections. We wish, however, to state them now, and to get a judgment on them now; and with reference to the question whether your Lordships ought to accede to our motion, I think it of some importance to observe that we are here in a process, in a Scotch Court, with reference no doubt to a class of cases in which the procedure is regulated by special Statute to a certain extent, but in which, so far as the procedure is not regulated by the provisions of that Statute, I apprehend it will be perfectly competent for us to betake ourselves to the usual remedies and the usual modes of raising any question in the course of a process which we may think it material to raise. The Solicitor-General says these questions may be raised in a variety of ways hereafter, and that it is inexpedient to raise them now, because the effect of that would probably be that the case would run a double course of litigation. Now, even supposing that should be so, the consequent hardship will chiefly fall on my clients; but apart from that, it is by no means clear that the other modes, suggested as modes by which these questions might be raised hereafter, would by any means save a double course of litigation. My learned friend suggested that we might have a bill of exceptions to the charge of the Judge, or a motion for a new trial on the ground that the case was decided contrary to law. Supposing either of these modes were resorted to, and suppose, which I think is doubtful, that it were competent for us to raise then the precise questions we wish to raise now, if we raise them by a bill of exceptions or a motion for a new trial, that would not have the effect of saving a double course of litigation, because, suppose I succeeded in my motion for a new trial, or prevailed in my objection, the result would just be a new trial. My learned friend also says, that though a motion in arrest of judgment may not be known here, we have a more direct remedy by stating an objection to the application of the verdict. Now, I am not aware of a single case in which that course has been resorted to in ordinary processes in this Court. The counts in this Information may not be precisely analogous to issues adjusted to try a cause, but they are very like it. They put the question whether such and such things have not been done, and whether in consequence the vessel is not forfeited, and if that is sent to trial, and the Jury find that such and such things have been done, and the vessel is forfeited, it is at least doubtful whether we would have any remedy. I don't know that the Crown would require to make any motion in this Court for the application of the verdict. I don't see that they would; they have got their judgment to the effect that the vessel is forfeited, and they require to do nothing more. But even supposing I am wrong in that, is there any incompetency in my resorting to the well known and usual form of objecting to the relevancy of the process before it is sent to the Jury at all? There is nothing in the Exchequer Statute to the effect that, as matter of course and of necessity, your Lordships shall at once send every Information to trial, reserving all questions of law for ultimate discussion. On the contrary, when the Information is lodged, the Lord Ordinary may either appoint parties to be heard, or appoint a trial to go on, as he may think best. The course which his Lordship saw fit to take here, was to appoint parties to be heard on the Information. On that point we stated our objections, and is it incompetent or inexpedient now to decide them? It is not necessary in order to their decision that a proof should have been led. The objection being, that upon the construction of the Statute, the counts aver nothing which is made criminal by the Statute, I cannot see that your Lordships would be in a better situation for determining that question after the trial than you are at present. The question arises on the contruction of the Statute, and proof never can be necessary to enable your Lordships to come to a conclusion upon the meaning of a Statute. The principal objection which we take, viz., that to the 1st count, and the other 71 framed upon the same plan, arises exclusively upon the wording of the 7th section of the Statute; and I submit that no light whatever on that question would be got from the result of a trial. I do not see therefore why we should be sent to trial on these 72 counts, while there is an objection which your Lordships can determine now, and which would supersede the necessity of a trial altogether, because it is quite possible that the Crown might be in a situation to prove the facts in those counts which are irrelevant, but that after these have been struck out of the Information as irrelevant, they may find themselves not in a situation to prove the truth of the facts averred in those counts which are relevant, and which remain in the Information. I therefore submit that we are entitled to ask your Lordship to decide these objections now; and I do not think I require any other argument in support of what we ask, than the intimation given by the Lord Ordinary, which makes it plain enough that whatever may be the opinion of the Solicitor-General, the Lord Ordinary was not so clear that we would have an opportunity afterwards of raising our objections, and that he might find himself in a situation of great difficulty at the trial, unless we came here and asked your Lordships to tell us whether the objections shall be decided now or reserved till a future period.

Lord Deas.—The Lord Ordinary at a trial cannot decide the relevancy of a summons.

Mr. Cook.—No. Suppose our first move at the trial was to ask the Lord Ordinary to withdraw 72 counts from the Jury.

Lord Advocate.—Surely there is nothing more common than to send a case to trial without deciding relevancy. That has been laid down as the proper course.

Lord Deas.—That is quite true, but the relevancy of the action remains with the Court.

Lord Advocate.—The case goes to trial, the relevancy being reserved.

Lord Deas.—It goes to trial on the issues, and the Judge who tries it has nothing to do with the relevancy of the action in that case. It remains with the Court. But would that apply here, where it is the Information or, in other words, the summons which is sent to trial?

Lord Advocate.—In the case of Grant and Galloway (20th June 1857), a complaint was made by your Lordship in the chair, and by Lord Deas, that Lords Ordinary in the Outer-House had got into a very bad habit of deciding points of relevancy before the trial.

Lord Deas.—The practical embarrassment I was pointing at was quite different from that. It was this, that whereas the Lord Ordinary in an ordinary case has nothing to do with the relevancy of the summons, and cannot decide it at the trial, though that remains with the Court, in this case if we send the Information to trial on the footing that is asked, it is very like putting before him the relevancy of the Information which comes in place of the summons.

Lord Advocate.—But in an Information there is no issue extracted at all. The Information is the issue. Therefore the question of fact under the Information may be affirmed, but it must remain to be considered whether any offence under the Statute is alleged or proved.

Mr. Cook.—The case of Galloway and Grant has no bearing in a case like the present. The question there was whether a person to whom money had been paid was the accredited agent of Dr. Grant; it depended on the extent to which Dr. Grant had authorized the party to act for him, whether he was his agent or not; and before deciding on the relevancy, your Lordships sent to the Jury not the general question, whether he was agent for Dr. Grant to a greater or less extent, but whether he was the accredited agent of Dr. Grant in doing the act which he had done; and the Jury having affirmed that, though our objection to the relevancy of the record remained the same as before, we found that it would have been in vain to state any objection to the application of the verdict. But here we have a definite statement in these counts, to which the Solicitor-General has told us he attaches a certain meaning, viz., the meaning the words have in the Statute. I submit, therefore, that the most expedient and fair course for the defenders is to decide our objections to the relevancy now. Before leaving the point of form, I may notice our objection to the 98th count as being bad in consequence of its singular accumulation of inconsistent acts said to have been done by us at the same time and with reference to the same ship. It may be true that the same count occurred in the Alexandra case, but it does not follow that it is right here. But the 7th section of the Court of Exchequer (Scotland) Act provides that 'every Information to be lodged in terms of this Act shall be in 'the form, as nearly as may be, of Schedule B, hereto annexed;' this is an Information following on a seizure, and I find the style of such an Information, No. 8 of Schedule B. On looking over the different examples of counts given there, I confess I see nothing of that abhorrence of alternative charges which my learned friend said was characteristic of English procedure. Every one of the examples in Schedule B of an Information, following on a seizure, contains alternative charges, whereas this 98th count accumulates a great number of inconsistent charges. I submit, therefore, that this count is not framed according to the direction of the Exchequer (Scotland) Act.

Lord President.—I asked the Solicitor-General what was the use of that count, and he said it was of no use at all.

Mr. Cook.—Then why encumber the Information with it? I object to it as accumulating a number of inconsistent charges.

Lord Deas.—That is to say, it would be inconsistent to give a verdict upon them all in favour of the Crown.

Mr. Cook.—Quite so.

Lord Deas.—In connexion with that, allow me to call your attention to the concluding portion of that section 7th, and 'provided 'further,' etc. Is not the object of that to entitle them to do as they do in England, viz., to prove any one of the things in that cumulative count, and then to get a verdict?

Mr. Cook.—But that does not affect the question whether the count is properly framed.

Lord Deas.—You were going on the footing, as I understood, that if the Crown got a verdict on that count, the verdict must affirm the whole of it, and that that would be inconsistent. Now it is not necessary, according to that section, that the verdict should affirm the whole of it; the verdict may affirm any limited portion of it.

Mr. Cook.—No doubt the Crown are not bound to prove the whole matters averred in any count, but they are bound to make their counts consistent. It may be true that the English practice is to charge a number of things cumulatively, and that the charge of all means a charge of each ; but that is not the mode in Scotch procedure, of charging each of a number of inconsistent acts. It must be done alternatively, and I submit it ought to be so done here. I now come to our more material objection, viz., that to the 1st count, and the others framed on the same plan ; and before adverting to the special words of the 7th section of the Act, I may say that in the view we take of the general meaning and purpose of this Foreign Enlistment Act, its object was to prohibit and prevent the commission of hostilities, or the engaging in warlike operations on the part of any of Her Majesty's subjects against a foreign power—(*Reads Preamble*). The Statute creates an offence out of the act of enlistment by a party to serve as a soldier in the army of a foreign power, and it also makes it an offence to equip a ship or vessel for warlike operations. The statutory offence, of course, may be committed by a subject without any overt act of war ; the mere enlistment with intent to serve in the army of the foreign power makes the offence on the part of the soldier, without any actual carrying of arms, or doing any overt service in the army of that foreign power. In the same way, the equipping of a ship, with the intent on the part of the equipper to carry on warlike operations with the ship, to cruise and commit hostilities with the ship, is an offence, although it has not actually gone to sea and committed any overt act of naval warfare. But according to our construction of the Statute, you must, in order to the statutory offence, have present in the mind of the party at the time he does the act prohibited, the intent either to serve as a soldier in his own person, or to cruise and commit warlike operations in his own person.

Lord Curriehill.—In dealing with this construction keep this in view, that the persons against whom the 7th section of the Statute is directed, are not limited to Her Majesty's subjects.

Mr. Cook.—I quite admit that the 7th section rather goes beyond the preamble, and prohibits the doing of any act by any person, whether Her Majesty's subjects or not.

Lord Ardmillan.—It not only goes beyond the preamble, but beyond the 2d section, which is expressly limited to natural-born subjects of Her Majesty.

Mr. Cook.—With reference to the case of the soldier, I don't understand that it is disputed by the Crown that at the time that he enlists he must have the intent of serving in his own person.

Lord Advocate.—Under the 2d section, procuring enlistment is an offence, and that is not limited to natural-born subjects. That is clear by the last part of the section.

Mr. Cook.—But in regard to the equipping of a vessel, I understand the Crown to say that the intent to employ the vessel in warlike operations need not be the intent of the equipper. The Solicitor-General says it is enough if it is said that the party equips the vessel with the intent that it shall be employed by another party, over whom he has no control, with the intent to commit hostilities. Our reading of the 7th section, and the Crown's reading of it, are, I think, correctly embodied in the 3d count of the

Information, and in the 1st. We say that the charge in the 3d count proceeds on a correct reading of the Statute, though we have an objection to it on another ground. The charge there is, that the parties did equip the ship or vessel with intent to cruise or commit hostilities, the intent there intended to be charged being beyond all doubt the intent of the equipper himself. But the first count charges that the party did equip the ship with intent and in order that such ship should be employed in the service of the Confederates, with intent to cruise and commit hostilities, the intent there being *ex concessis* not the intent of the equipper, but the intent of the Confederates. We maintain that, in order to constitute the offence, the intent must be the intent of the party charged with equipping, whereas the Crown say that it may be the intent of another party, over whom the equipper has no control at all, and to whom he is to hand over the vessel.

Lord Curriehill.—That is to say, the latter intent may be the intent of the party employing the vessel.

Mr. Cook.—Yes, who may be another party than the equipper. Now I submit that the construction for which we contend is that which is most agreeable to the general analogy of the law in matters of this description, and to the fair and natural reading of the terms of section 7. It is admitted, I think, that it is quite competent for a merchant or shipbuilder to build a ship or vessel of war, and to sell it to any party he chooses. It is not said that that is illegal, and a party may sell any other munitions of war to a foreign belligerent power, without incurring any offence at common law or under the Statute. If he may do that, it is surely a very fine distinction to say, You may equip a ship for general sale, and, after you have equipped it, you may sell it to a belligerent power at war with a friendly country, without committing any offence under the Act; but if you equip to the order of a belligerent power a ship or vessel, and furnish it to him, without any intent on your part, then you commit an offence under the Statute. That is what the Crown contend for, but is that a reasonable construction? I submit that it is an unreasonable construction, because the amount of the accommodation that you give to the belligerent power is precisely the same in the one case as in the other. I don't see that when you equip a ship on the order of a belligerent power, you give that belligerent power any greater amount of accommodation or assistance than when you sell the ship already built and fitted out for warlike purposes. You may do the one, the Solicitor-General says, without committing any offence, but the other is prohibited by the Statute. We say that is not what is prohibited. We say that by general law it is perfectly competent for any party, without committing any offence, to sell a ship of war already built and equipped to the best merchant, be he whom he may—a belligerent power or not; and this Statute never meant to prohibit parties from building and equipping ships of war on the order of belligerent powers, to be employed by belligerent powers with intent to commit hostilities against powers that they are at war with, but what it meant to prohibit was the equipment of vessels for the purpose of carrying on hostilities by the equipper, whether a subject of Her Majesty or not, if the act be done within the ports of the United Kingdom. We say that is the more reasonable and natural meaning of the words of the section. But the Solicitor-General says that when you read the 7th section, it is beyond all doubt that, with reference to the case of a transport equipped for the purpose of being used as a transport in the service of a foreign power, the intent to use the vessel there need not be the intent of the equipper at all, but may be the intent of the party in whose service she is to be employed, and he seemed to think that, in admitting the relevancy of the 97th count, we had conceded that. Now we have not conceded that, and I disputed my learned friend's construction of the 7th section, which relates to the fitting out of transports, and which he seemed to think showed that the intent may be the intent of any one.

Lord Ardmillan.—Not the intent of any one, but the doing of any one. It must be the intent of the equipper, but it may be the doing of the party who procures the vessel from the equipper.

Mr. Cook.—But with intent and in order that such ship or vessel shall be employed in the service of any foreign prince, as a transport or store-ship.

Lord President.—Though not by the equipper.

Mr. Cook.—Yes, it may be by anybody. He says that is the true construction of that part of the section relative to the transport.

Lord Curriehill.—What do you maintain as to that?

Mr. Cook.—I maintain that the employment and use of the ship must be by the equipper.

Lord President.—Even as a transport.

Mr. Cook.—Yes, as much as in the other case; and I illustrate that by referring to the case of Quincy, in which that part of the American Foreign Enlistment Act, which refers to fitting out and arming vessels with intent to cruise, is expressed in almost precisely the same terms as section 7 of our Act is as regards the use of the transport. Section 3 of the Act of Congress enacts, 'That if any 'person shall, within the limits of the United States, fit out and 'arm, or attempt to fit out and arm, or procure to be fitted out and 'armed, or shall knowingly be concerned in the furnishing, fitting 'out, or arming of any ship or vessel, with intent that such ship or 'vessel shall be employed,'—by whom? The Solicitor-General says by anybody, and that the party who was to employ these need not be the equipper, just as in the case of our Foreign Enlistment Act, the party to employ the transport need not be the equipper, but any one. But is that consistent with the construction that the American Courts have put upon that section of their Statute as applicable to cruisers? In the case of the United States *v.* Quincy, the defender was charged with a contravention of that section of the Statute, in respect that he had equipped and cruised with a vessel; and he asked the Judge at the trial for certain directions in point of law, the second direction which he asked being, that if the owner or equipper had no present intention of using or employing the vessel, but intended to go to the West

Indies to endeavour to raise funds to prepare her for a cruise, he was entitled to be assoilzied. He also asked for a direction, that if when the vessel 'was equipped at Baltimore, and when she left 'the United States, the equipper had no fixed intention to employ 'her as a privateer, but had a wish so to employ her, the fulfilment 'of which wish depended on his ability to obtain funds in the West 'Indies for the purpose of arming her and preparing for war,'— then he was not guilty. The employment and use of the vessel in both cases was by the owner and equipper himself.

Lord Ardmillan.—Did he, in point of fact, go with the vessel?

Mr. Cook—That does not appear from the Report. And what does the Judge say? He says: 'We think these instructions 'ought to be given. The offence consists principally in the inten- 'tion with which the preparations were made. These preparations, 'according to the very terms of the Act, must be made within the 'limits of the United States; and it is equally necessary that the 'intention with respect to the employment of the vessel should be 'formed before she leaves the United States. And this must be a 'fixed intention, not conditional or contingent, depending on some 'future arrangements. This intention is a question belonging 'exclusively to the Jury to decide. It is the material point on 'which the legality or criminality of the Act must turn, and 'decides whether the adventure is of a commercial or warlike cha- 'racter. The law does not prohibit armed vessels belonging to 'citizens of the United States from sailing out of our ports, it only 'requires the owners to give security (as was done in the present 'case) that such vessels shall not be employed by them to commit 'hostilities against foreign powers at peace with the United States.' That is the construction which the American Courts put upon the terms of their Foreign Enlistment Act, with reference to employing a vessel to cruise.

Lord Ardmillan.—Then that is an offence which could never be perpetrated by any man who did not go to sea? According to your reading, going to sea in the vessel is necessary to the commission of that offence?

Mr. Cook.—No; the intent to go to sea must be the intent of the party.

Lord Ardmillan.—That is, the intent to go to sea himself in the vessel, otherwise there is no offence.

Mr. Cook.—He may cruise in his own person, or by employing others to do that for him, but the control of the vessel in the warlike operations must be by the party. That is the construction they put on that clause of their Act. The Solicitor-General said that the construction which I venture to put on the words of the 7th section, as to the use of a transport, was so absurd that it did not require refutation; but your Lordships will see that though the American Statute, with reference to the use of a ship employed for cruising, is expressly in the same terms, they held that the employment and use of the ship must be by the owner and equipper.

Lord President.—Was the point which they were so disposing of, the question whether the intent must be the intent of the equipper, or does it only come out incidentally in expressing their opinion on another point? The questions raised did not involve that question.

Mr. Cook.—He asked directions on the whole points in the case.

Solicitor-General.—He was the owner of the ship, and he commanded it.

Lord Curriehill.—I think what was said on that point was *obiter.*

Mr. Cook.—There is another view of the construction of the 7th section, viz., what is it that the 7th section makes the alternatives? Is it the two intents, or is it the use of the vessel as a transport or store-ship, or the use of the vessel with intent to cruise or commit hostilities? We say it is two intents that are made the alternative, and not the use of the ship as a transport, or to cruise and commit hostilities; and the question is, whether the one is the alternative of the Statute or the other?

Lord Deas.—In that view of it, you don't found on the change of phraseology?

Mr. Cook.—We say that the alternatives are the intents. Equipping with intent to use the ship as a transport is the one intent prohibited; and the other intent prohibited is equipping the ship to use it for the purpose of cruising or committing hostilities. On my learned friend's reading of it, it is the employment of a vessel as a cruiser in the service of any foreign power that is prohibited, no matter who the employer may be. That construction would infer that although the main and leading purpose of the Statute is to prevent the commission of hostilities by Her Majesty's subjects, what is prohibited here is not the fitting out of a vessel for the purpose of the equipper or fitter out using it himself for the purpose of committing hostilities, but it is the fitting out of a vessel in order that it may be employed by another party to commit hostilities.

Lord Curriehill.—To be employed by any party.

Mr. Cook.—It comes to this, that what is prohibited, is the employment in the service of any foreign prince, &c.? The employer must be not the equipper, because it is in the service of any foreign state.

Lord Curriehill.—Why should he not be in the service of the foreign state?

Mr. Cook.—He may not be the party.

Lord Curriehill.—But he may; you don't exclude him.

Mr. Cook.—I think he is excluded. Another very fair way of testing whether the one reading of the Statute or the other is more likely to be correct, is to compare the proposition stated in the one count and in the other, and to say which is the more intelligible and reasonable of the two. There is no doubt about the meaning of the 3d count; no one can mistake what it means; it is an intelligible proposition, and it is a construction at which you arrive without omitting or interpolating a single word.

Lord President.—It does not involve the element of cruising and committing hostilities being in the service of a foreign state.

Mr. Cook.—It is that you did equip the vessel with intent to cruise and commit hostilities against a certain foreign state.

Lord President.—Although not to be used in the service of any state.

Mr. Cook.—Yes, or although to be used; he might use it himself; he might have the intent of cruising in the ship either in the service of a foreign state or not.

Lord President.—According to this count, but that was not the Solicitor-General's construction of the Statute.

Mr. Cook.—According to this view of the meaning of the Statute, what is prohibited is the equipping of the vessel with the intent on the part of the equipper himself to cruise and commit hostilities, whether in the service of the foreign state or at his own hand as a privateer, is immaterial. But that is what is prohibited; it is the commission of hostilities by one of Her Majesty's subjects, or any person equipping a vessel in one of the ports of the United Kingdom, with a view on the part of the equipper to cruise and commit hostilities against a foreign state. That was certainly a construction of which the words of the Statute are quite susceptible, or why have you got it in this Information at all? It is a most intelligible proposition; it involves no violation whatever of the rules of grammar, and you arrive at it without omitting a single word used in the section, and without interpolating or adding a single word, and there is no difficulty in understanding it. But what is to be said with reference to the 1st count? To my mind it states something as an offence, the meaning of which I have great difficulty in understanding at all. It prohibits the equipping of a vessel with intent and in order that such vessel shall be employed in the service of the Confederate States with intent. It is declared to be illegal, according to this reading, to equip with intent that the vessel shall be employed with a certain intent. Now, who does the second intent refer to? My learned friends say it refers to any party, and that it need not be the intent of the equipper. But in order to arrive at that meaning, or to make it reasonable, you require to miss out the second intent. They say it should be read like the American Statute, which does not contain the second intent at all.

Solicitor-General.—That is what you say.

Mr. Cook.—No. I submit that whether you look at the words of the Statute itself, or at the general analogy of the law, the construction for which we contend is the more reasonable one, and that there is no offence charged in the 1st count, and the 71 framed on the same plan, on the ground that they charge as criminal an intent which the Statute don't make criminal at all.

Lord Deas.—How would it have stood in the 1st count, if the words 'with intent,' occurring for the second time, had been left out?

Mr. Cook.—I object to taking these words out.

Lord Deas.—What difference do they make upon the meaning?

Mr. Cook.—It makes us responsible for the intentions of the Confederate States.

Lord President.—Are you talking now of the Statute or of the Information?

Mr. Cook.—Of the Information. The first count deletes all

about the use of a ship as a transport, and the word 'or' following on that, so that it destroys the alternative meaning of the Statute altogether.

Lord Deas.—If these words 'with intent,' occurring the second time, had been 'in order,' would there have been any such objection as you are now taking?

Mr. Cook.—In that case the first part of the Information would have been relevant, because it would have been an offence to equip the vessel with intent and in order that such vessel should be employed in the service of certain foreign states.

Lord Deas.—The question is whether the words 'with intent,' occurring the second time, mean more than the words 'in order' would have done.

Lord President.—I think they make very little difference on the Information, and I think the construction the Crown contend for on the Statute is that there is no substantial difference between them; but Mr. Cook says that the introduction of the word 'or' makes a substantial difference between them, that word not being introduced into the Information.

Mr. Cook.—What was intended to be prohibited, was the use of the vessel as a transport, or the equipping of the vessel with intent to cruise; but that is not what is charged in the first count. Now our second objection is founded on the omission, in the first 96 counts, of the word 'arm.' We say there can be no proper equipment of a vessel for cruising in order to commit hostilities without arming the vessel for that purpose; and we say that according to the reading of the 7th section, the words equip, furnish, and fit out, used in reference to a vessel employed to cruise and commit hostilities, are synonymous with the word 'arm.' But the Crown have interpreted the meaning of the word 'equip' as being something short of arming; because, having the word 'arm' alternating with equip, furnish, and fit out in the Statute, they use in all the counts only the words equip, furnish, and fit out, and they omit 'arm.' Therefore they charge as an offence the equipping of a vessel to cruise and commit hostilities without arming. They don't intend to prove that the vessel was armed, and they maintain that they are entitled to ask a verdict from the jury that the vessel is forfeited, even though they fall short of proving that she was armed. I submit there can be no intent to equip a vessel with a view to cruise and commit hostilities without arming. The vessel is not fit to cruise and commit hostilities without being armed. Therefore, if the intent be to charge here as an offence any kind of equipment which is short of arming, as an equipment to cruise and commit hostilities, the thing is an absurdity. No man can have the intent to equip a vessel to cruise and commit hostilities without arming her. But these counts are framed on the footing that the Crown may get a verdict without proving arming. I submit that that cannot be, and on this point I refer to the opinions of the Lord Chief Baron and Baron Bramwell in the Alexandra Case, both of whom laid it down as their construction of the Statute, that the equipment in the 7th section, when used with reference to a vessel employed to cruise and commit hostilities, was a complete equipment, including arming.

Lord Deas.—Did the ultimate decision hold it to be so?

Mr. Cook.—Yes. Baron Bramwell at p. 269, and the Chief Baron throughout his charge, and most emphatically at the conclusion of it, lays it down that the ship is not employed to cruise and commit hostilities unless it is armed.

Lord President.—Is not intended to be employed. She is not equipped with intent to cruise unless she is armed; and equipped means completely equipped; he put it that way.

Mr. Cook.—When you talk of a vessel being equipped for cruising and committing hostilities, you mean an armed vessel. Everything that can properly be described as an intention to equip a ship to cruise and commit hostilities must be an intention to equip her up to the point of arming her. That is the only meaning of equip in the case of an armed vessel. Therefore they both held that if the facts proved before the Jury showed that there was no intent on the part of the defenders to equip the vessel up to the point of arming her,—if there was no intention to arm her completely before she left the port where she was seized, there was no offence under the Act, and on that the verdict went.

Lord President.—Intention to arm her?

Mr. Cook.—Intention to equip, including arming.

Lord President.—May there not be an attempt to equip without the complete equipment?

Mr. Cook.—No; they said there was no equipment unless the vessel was armed; the principal offence of equipping is not committed unless the vessel is armed; no attempt to do something that does not constitute a criminal offence is prohibited.

Lord President.—But suppose arming is a portion of the equipment of the vessel,—a necessary portion we shall say, but still only a portion, and there are other things that constitute a portion of the equipment of a vessel to cruise, if the other things are the first in order, and if you are in progress towards equipment, is a person who aids in that a person attempting to equip?

Mr. Cook.—I say not, unless he has the intention in his own mind to carry it farther, and to arm the vessel before she leaves the port.

Lord President.—It may be another man that supplies that other portion of the equipment,—the arming.

Mr. Cook.—Then I am not criminal if all I do is to attempt to equip the vessel up to a certain point.

Lord President.—With intent that she shall be fully equipped and sent out.

Lord Deas.—You seem to admit that your intention to arm would do.

Mr. Cook.—No; there must be acts done. The point I wish to make is this,—if the result of the proof were to show that if it was the intention of the parties that the vessel should leave a port in this country still unarmed, then nothing that they do in furtherance of that purpose is an offence under the Statute.

Lord President.—If there was no intention in anybody that she should be armed.

Mr. Cook.—That she should be armed before leaving the port.

Lord President.—I mean so.

Mr. Cook.—Under this count, the Crown are quite entitled, if there was an intent anywhere, to say—If you were cognizant of the intent that she should be armed elsewhere, it is of no consequence that she was to leave the port unarmed, you are guilty of the statutory offence. I submit that is not an offence under the Statute.

Lord Deas.—Do you mean that it would be a statutory offence if you had fully equipped her in other respects, and you intend or know that she is afterwards to be armed elsewhere? Are you admitting that that would be the statutory offence?

Mr. Cook.—Certainly not. If she is to be armed elsewhere, I deny that it is the statutory offence. She must be armed in a port of the United Kingdom in order to make the statutory offence.

Mr. Gordon.—I attend your Lordships on the part of the builders, and I shall only supplement the observations of Mr. Cook, without going at any length into the general argument. But the procedure in this case is a very important matter, and there is naturally some anxiety on the part of the defenders with reference to the course to be followed, so that they may not be shut out from pleading at the proper time an objection which goes to the very substance of the charge. In considering this case, we must not be led away too much by the precedent of the Alexandra case, because that proceeding took place in accordance with the old rules of pleading in England, one of which rules was, that if any defendant intended to object to the relevancy of an Information, he could not do so without admitting the facts. It was, I believe, in the power of the plaintiff or of the Crown, to move the Court to dispose of the question of law before the question of fact was sent to the Jury; but in the Alexandra case, the Crown did not avail themselves of that privilege, and it was not competent for the defendants to do so. Now that is a proceeding in England which, in all other cases except Exchequer cases, has been altered by the Common-Law Procedure Act of 1854. Therefore, you must not suppose that the rule which prevails in the Court of Session is opposed to the general practice of the English Courts. On the contrary, in remodelling the forms of procedure so late as 1854, the Legislature was of opinion that the proper course was to give the Court an opportunity of deciding upon questions of law, where they thought such a course expedient. But the defendants in the Alexandra case could not avail themselves of that, because they were not under the forms of procedure enacted in 1854; and such difficulty was found in working out even the Alexandra case, that when the verdict was returned, it was found necessary for the Court to make a new set of rules applicable to the discussion which should take place on the verdict, these rules enabling the question to be raised by way of a motion for a new trial. Unfortunately, however,—and that is one of the hardships which we may have to complain of in this case,—when the case came to be submitted to a Court of Error, the Judges were equally divided as to whether an appeal was competent from the Court of Exchequer. So that your Lordships see how carefully and warily we must proceed in this case, when we find that in England such difficulties have occurred. Now, the general rule in our criminal court—and this is a case analogous to a criminal charge—is, that before you send a case to trial, you shall decide whether the charge is relevant or not. I know of no case in the criminal courts in which that course has not been followed. With reference to a claim which is made in the civil court, there is a direction given to the Lord Ordinary when the case comes before him to consider whether the summons is in such a shape as will entitle the party to proceed with his action, and a defender is entitled to avail himself of that opportunity, and to state that it has not been relevantly charged, and the case may be thrown out at that stage, or the question may be reserved till the record is made up; and the Court, when they have seen a full statement of the case for the pursuer, will then take up the question of relevancy. As a general rule, I think I am right in saying that the practice of the Court is to dispose of questions of law, where they are of such a character that they can be disposed of without any investigation in fact, and where, therefore, it would be a useless waste of time to have investigation into the fact. When issues are appointed to be tried, these issues constitute the test of the rights of the party as they shall be negatived or affirmed by the jury. Now, there are a few cases of late where your Lordships, without deciding questions of relevancy, have sent them to trial, and it is of importance to observe what is the course in the civil court, because the Exchequer Act says we are to follow the practice in the civil court where there is no special direction. There is one very marked case, Guild *v.* Orr Ewing and Co., January 1858, 20 Dunlop, 392. The interlocutor which your Lordships pronounced in that case was: 'The Lords, having 'heard counsel for the parties on the questions of law and relevancy, 'which they maintained ought to be disposed of by the Court 'before trial, find it unnecessary and inexpedient in this cause to 'dispose of any questions of law or relevancy before trial.' There was there a recognition of the right of the party to have at some time or other the question of law or relevancy raised. We asked the Lord Ordinary in this case if he would not sustain our objections, at all events, to put in the interlocutor remitting the case for trial, something which would show that we had made the application, and that it was the opinion of the Court that this was not the proper stage, indicating clearly that we had not lost the time for stating them, and that we would have it in our power at an after period to state them. His Lordship, however, from excessive caution, it appears to me, refused to follow the precedent of that case.

Lord Advocate.—Will you take judgment in these terms now?

Mr. Gordon.—I ask judgment on the relevancy, but if I don't get that, I ask for this as an alternative demand. The Lord Advocate referred to the case of Dr. Grant, but I appeal to the experience of the Lord Advocate whether the course followed in that case was advantageous for the defender. It was thought that Dr. Grant would have an opportunity of raising all possible questions after the verdict, but a verdict was pronounced adverse to his claim, and he had no opportunity of raising the question on the application of the verdict.

Lord Deas.—What we held in Dr. Grant's case, I think, was that the words in the Record might bear a meaning that was relevant, and that it depended on the proof whether they bore the meaning that was relevant, or the meaning that was not relevant.

Mr. Gordon.—I think the question was as to the sufficiency of the averment. It was said the words were somewhat ambiguous, and it was a question whether you could construe them in such a way as to hold that they would imply direct authority. Now, let us see what is the course of procedure suggested by the Crown. We have made this application that the question of relevancy shall be disposed of at a period of the proceedings when it is admittedly competent. I am brought by the Lord Advocate to answer to 72 counts, which I say are absolutely inconsistent with the terms of the Act of Parliament, and also with 24 other charges framed upon the same Act of Parliament, because you cannot read the Statute in the two ways contended for by the Lord Advocate, viz., that it is sufficient if it be the intention of the equipper in the one case, and the intent of the hostile state on the other. Now, is it not important to get rid of 72 or 24 or 96 counts, as we submit. I don't know if the Information will be put into the hands of the Jury.

Solicitor-General.—No.

Mr. Gordon.—Then it will be still more embarrassing to them to have to dispose of 96 or 98 counts, if they have not the advantage of seeing them in print. Is it not therefore most convenient now to get rid of 72 charges or of 24? But we are told that it is not expedient to do that now, and that it may be done hereafter. When? We have never yet received a distinct answer to that question from the Crown or from the Bench. We certainly have not received it from the Lord Ordinary. All he says is, that his present opinion is that at some future time—when we are not told—we may raise it; but he qualifies that, and though he is the Judge that must preside at the trial, and no other Judge, I believe, he says, I am of that opinion just now, but I don't know what opinion I may have when the case comes on for trial, or at any other stage of it. It is suggested that we may state our objections at the trial. That course was tried in the Alexandra case, but was not followed, for this reason, that in England a party has it in his power, after the verdict, to come forward and say that the claim or charge made against the defendants was one not consistent with law, and which therefore could not support the verdict. But I know of no case in our practice where a motion has been made to resist the application of a verdict. It is said, however, that we can do it by way of exception at the trial; but I infinitely prefer to state it now, for I know nothing more perplexing and difficult than for counsel to frame, in the hurry of a jury trial, exceptions to the law laid down by the Judge, or to prepare propositions which he asks the

Court to give effect to, because if you make a slip in expressing the law which you ask the Judge to lay down, that exception will be thrown aside, though the substance of it be obvious to every one. In the same way as to the direction which you ask, you have difficulty often in adjusting the terms of it; and I prefer infinitely, instead of raising these questions during the hurry and excitement of a jury trial, to raise them now before your Lordships on an abstract proposition, which don't require any proof for its elucidation, but which is a mere question of the construction of a British Statute, and where you have an opportunity of consulting with one another upon the true construction, instead of having it submitted to a single Judge at the trial. I infinitely prefer, therefore, having this matter disposed of now, and not by way of exception. But, it is said, you can move for a new trial on the ground of misdirection on the part of the judge, if he don't give effect to what you claim in law. There is no doubt that there has been a vague impression that it is competent to take an exception to the law as laid down by the Lord Ordinary, and bring it before your Lordships on appeal, and to take an exception to any decision of the Court refusing a motion for a new trial in so far as it proceeds upon erroneous law.

Solicitor-General.—That is quite settled the other way.

Lord President.—That is a mere motion to set aside a verdict on the ground of misdirection, without following out a bill of exceptions.

Mr. Gordon —I don't think that is a course which has been followed in our Courts.

Lord President.—Very little; because when you embody it in a bill of exceptions, you have the power of carrying it to appeal, and therefore it is generally preferred to take that course.

Mr. Gordon.—It has been tried in some cases where you move for a new trial, upon the ground of the verdict being contrary to law, in consequence of misdirection.

Lord President.—Even without misdirection, contrary to the law laid down by the Judge.

Mr. Gordon.—The rule there is, that you have no remedy by appeal. Therefore, I object to that course of moving for a new trial, because, in the event of the judgment being against me, I shall be deprived of the remedy of an appeal to the House of Lords.

Lord President.—Yes; but the difficulty in that course of procedure is this: Suppose the Judge lays down right law at the trial, and the Jury go against that law, you move to have the verdict set aside as against law.

Mr. Gordon.—If the evidence does not come up to what is sufficient to constitute the legal right, then you have it in your power to say it is contrary to evidence, because they have not proved the facts which are sufficient to bring them within the rule of law.

Lord President.—Upon the Judge's view of the law.

Mr. Gordon.—Yes; and there have been several cases where effect has been given to that view, and I think it has always been in the view that it is contrary to evidence.

Lord President.—Well, it is the same result. You would still be landed without an appeal, though the Judge laid down right law.

Mr. Gordon.—But I would not then be complaining of the Judge, and my case rests upon the facts alone.

Lord Deas.—You would always have the difficulty of being able to show in that case what the law was which the Judge laid down, because we have no record of that.

Mr. Gordon.—Except by way of a bill of exceptions.

Lord President.—Therefore it is an embarrassing kind of remedy.

Mr. Gordon.—It is embarrassing; and we have felt it in practice. We tried to get the benefit of an appeal where the Court laid down law in disposing of the motion for a new trial,—we excepted to that law, but I am sorry to say we could not prevail on the Court to sign the exception. I refer to the case of Cuthbertson *v.* Young, 27th January 1852. Therefore we are in this position, that we are not told when is the proper time for stating this objection, which I must assume in this discussion is well founded.

Adjourned.

Friday, 4th March.

The Lord Advocate, on the part of the Crown, moved the Court to grant commission to examine the Hon. Robert Walker, at present in Paris.

Mr. Watson.—We object to this, first, because it is not said that the witness cannot attend at the trial; but a stronger ground of objection is that from the interrogatories which the Crown propose to put to the witness, we find that the whole matter relates to certain documents, correspondence, and letters which are not in process, and which, so far as we can see, are not proposed to be put in process, for they are proposed to be exhibited to the witness in the hands of Mr. Dudley, United States' consul in Liverpool. The whole interrogatories are with reference to the handwriting and signature of these documents. It appears to the claimants that this examination should not be permitted unless these documents are within the control of the Court, or unless the claimants shall have access to them in order to use them as part of the deposition. Otherwise, if the Crown should not avail themselves of the deposition, it would be quite impossible for the claimants to do so, because they have no access to the documents, and they cannot ask your Lordships to enforce access to them; they are dependent entirely on the will of the Crown, or of the American consul in Liverpool, for their production. In this case copies cannot be held as sufficient, because the question is the authenticity or genuineness of particular documents. Unless, therefore, it is proposed to produce these documents to the Commissioner, and place them within the control of the Court, we submit that this inquiry should not be allowed.

Lord-President.—Are the interrogatories entirely with reference to the genuineness of the subscription and handwriting?

Mr. Watson.—Entirely.

Lord Advocate.—As to the witness not being able to attend the trial, we have produced an affidavit, which is quite sufficient. He has gone abroad for his health. He is to be in Paris till Monday night, and thence he goes to Nice, and his intention is to make a long journey abroad, so that the difficulty and expense of taking his evidence will be increased by every day's delay. In regard to the objection that he is to be examined to authenticate documents not in process, this is not the time to inquire into the admissibility of the documents if they be authenticated. We take our risk of that, and all objection will be open. They are not produced in process because they are not within our power. The American consul at Liverpool has hitherto declined to produce them in process, but that is no reason why we should be deprived of the evidence of their authenticity. We may have great difficulty in recovering them, or making them evidence, but that is no reason why Mr. Walker's testimony should not be taken. I will do all I can to induce Mr. Dudley on this examination to leave the documents in the hands of the Crown, and even to produce them in process. I shall either do that, or take a diligence to recover them from Mr. Dudley.

Mr. Clark.—Take your diligence first.

Lord Advocate.—No. These documents are not within the power of the Crown, and it is necessary, in order to prevent the loss of evidence, that Mr. Walker's deposition should be taken.

Lord Deas.—I understand the objection to be rested on that very thing that the documents are not within the power of the Crown. The other party says what I take to be correct enough, that by the Act of Sederunt they are entitled to use that deposition if you don't use it; and if you don't recover the documents and put them in process, the other party can't use it; so that if it is all in their favour, you may not use it, and they cannot use it.

Lord Advocate.—The question is in whose handwriting are these documents. I am about to lose evidence, in consequence of Mr. Walker's absence, in regard to that matter. I think I am entitled to be protected from that loss.

Lord President.—Are these documents to be transmitted to Paris, in order to be shown to this gentleman?

Lord Advocate.—Yes, Mr. Dudley is willing to go to Paris with them.

Mr. Clark.—It seems to me that the Lord Advocate has not taken the proper course here. The first thing he ought to do is to apply for a diligence to recover these documents, so that they may become part of the process; and when they become part of the process, so as to be used at the trial,—for they cannot be used at the trial unless they form part of the process,—then he is entitled to take a commission to show documents which either party may use at the trial, to a witness for the purpose of identifying handwriting and signature. But what he proposes is to take a commission which may be useful to him, but which, if unfavourable to him, never can be useful to me, for we don't know whether the examination is to refer to documents which may be produced or not.

Lord President.—If matters were taking the ordinary course, it would be this: that the documents would be produced eight days before the trial, and that when the trial came on, the witness would be put in the box to identify the documents. The other party would have no access to them till eight days before the trial, and they would have no deposition as to their authenticity till the day of trial. Now the question we have to consider is whether the defenders are put to any disadvantage by what is proposed. It is an examination of a witness to identify documents. The defenders are present at that examination, and they see the document that is proposed to be identified. I suppose there will be no objection to their obtaining copies of the document at that time, and that is a considerable time before the trial. That, so far as it goes, is an advantage to the defenders. Suppose the Lord Advocate does not use these documents at the trial, this deposition which is proposed now to be taken would be of no use to anybody. Whether the witness says I do identify that as such a person's handwriting, or I do not identify it, would be of no consequence, if the documents are not produced. If they are produced, then you know that this is a witness to their identification; but if in the meantime you get copies of them, you have seen them, and you can make inquiry and have evidence against their authenticity, just as you would have if they were produced eight days before the trial. Is there anything more than that in it, Mr. Clark?

Mr. Clark.—No; I think not.

Lord President.—They may not be able to use the documents, but how does the identification of these now put you in a worse position than in the case of an ordinary trial? But I would like it to be understood that the defenders are to be at liberty to take copies of the documents, because that may enable them to make inquiries as to their authenticity, which they would not otherwise be able to make.

Mr. Clark.—Of course we cannot show the documents to other parties.

Lord President.—Neither could you till the trial. It will be another question whether, when the trial comes on, they have been lodged in due time; and if they are lodged in due time, you will have all the benefit that you would have had if this deposition had not been taken. If they are not lodged in due time, the question may arise whether the prosecutor was entitled to produce documents, though not lodged in due time, if he gives a good reason for not having produced them? But that does not prejudice the course he is taking now. I don't see the prejudice that the defender undergoes if copies are given.

Lord Advocate.—Copies will be given.

Lord Deas.—The only possible disadvantage to the defender would be in case he himself, after seeing the documents, thought they were favourable to him and wanted to use them; but even in that case he may take means to get them, and if the law cannot give them to him, it would not give them to the Crown either.

Mr. Clark.—The Crown may have more power than the defenders in that matter.

Lord Advocate suggested that Mr. John Hunter should be appointed Commissioner.

Lord President.—Then copies will be given?

Lord Advocate.—I cannot say absolutely, because they are not absolutely in our power, but I expect to be able to get from Mr. Dudley an authenticated copy.

Lord President.—We will grant commission to Mr. Hunter to take the examination of the witness, and to take copies of the documents.

Lord Deas.—The Commissioner can authenticate them.

Commission to be reported in ten days.

Mr. Gordon.—I have now to call your Lordships' attention to one or two passages in the Exchequer Act, 19 and 20 Vict. c. 56, and first, I refer to section 6—(*Reads it*). The Act, therefore, contemplates that parties were to be heard on the Information. Then it says that on the verdict being given, 'the Lord Ordinary presiding at the trial shall pronounce decree in conformity therewith.' These words introduce considerable difficulty with reference to the finality of the verdict. As I understand it, the Lord Ordinary presiding at the trial is then and there to pronounce decree in conformity with the verdict given by the Jury, 'and as may be just and according to law.' It is not 'or as may be just,' &c., but 'and.' It appears to me, therefore, that there is very great risk that, in the event of a verdict being returned against my clients, they would be held as foreclosed from raising any question interfering with the verdict as returned by the Jury. Then there is a provision in section 9, that in so far as not regulated by this Statute, the procedure shall be conducted, as nearly as may be, in conformity with the procedure before the Court of Session in ordinary actions. So that we have here incorporated all the rules with reference to the finality of verdicts, as existing under the Jury system established for the trial of civil causes, except in so far as it may be affected by the special provisions of this Statute. I have already pointed out the great danger there is of miscarriage in the way of taking exceptions at the trial, because, if we take our remedy to be an appeal to the Court for a new trial and to quash the verdict and set it aside, we may not only be met with the 6th section, that the verdict is final, and that judgment must be given in accordance with it; but even if it were to be held that that is not the meaning of the 6th section, our only remedy would be to apply for a new trial, and if we did not succeed in establishing our right to a new trial, we would lose our right of appeal. That is one of the risks which the Crown have encountered in the Alexandra case, on the motion for a new trial. The Court of Error were equally divided on the point, and I suppose the matter goes to the House of Lords on the competency of the appeal, as well as upon the merits.

Lord President.—Does not that about the Lord Ordinary giving decree, taken along with the other section, mean, if no notice of motion is given for a new trial within the time fixed for that in the ordinary course of procedure, just as in a Jury case the Lord Ordinary gives decree, but not till after the time for a motion for new trial has expired. Still that only puts it back, as you have said, to the insufficiency of the remedy.

Mr. Gordon.—Now, it is not for the prosecutor in this case to say that I may be very well content with the remedy open to me, if I am deprived of that which litigants in ordinary cases enjoy as a privilege, viz. that of appeal. That of itself is a good reason why your Lordships should now determine this question. The Lord Ordinary invited us to discuss it, and we did so. Is all that discussion to go for nothing? It is said that the result will be to cause delay, but there are worse evils than delay. Injustice, and depriving a party of privileges which he is otherwise entitled to, are worse than delay. But why should there be delay? If we succeed, the Crown need not appeal. The Crown can go to trial with the other counts, which they say are perfectly good; or if they think those counts to which we object are essential to their case, what litigant can complain less of the evils of a judgment which leads to an appeal than the Crown, because they have only to enter an appeal, and they are entitled to precedence in the House of Lords as in this Court, and they will have the case taken up along with or immediately after the Alexandra case. There is therefore no reason why there should be any great delay arising from a judgment adverse to the Crown. Then your Lordships will observe, that if the verdict of the Jury is in conformity with the Information that we have acted in contravention of the Statute, we shall probably have great difficulty in getting redress against that finding. It is a question of fact and law mixed up together, sent to the Jury, and the Jury are the masters of the answer to be given to the proposition raised by the Information. It is not a mere question of fact, but they are asked, whether what we have done is not a contravention of the Statute? Judgment is to be given in conformity with their verdict, and great difficulty, I can conceive, may arise in getting the better of a judgment of that kind. For just observe what is the effect of it. At present the *onus* lies upon the Lord Advocate to show that he has stated a relevant charge against us; the moment the verdict of the Jury is returned, the *onus* is thrown upon us of showing that the Jury have returned a verdict which cannot be supported. At present he is the prosecutor, bound to establish that his proposition is right in point of law, and with reference to the facts alleged; but the moment the verdict of the Jury is pronounced, we are the parties obliged to impugn that verdict, so that we are put in quite a different and a much more unfavourable position after verdict in taking objections than we are now stating our objections to the relevancy of the charge. Now, why should we not have this matter, which has already occupied the Court so much, disposed of? I hope nothing will occur to prevent the Lord Ordinary, who has heard the discussion in the cause, from presiding at the trial; but supposing he is unable to preside at the trial, and some other Judge is appointed to try the case, all this discussion, which occupied three days in the Outer House, would have to be gone over again in the course of the trial. I therefore submit to your Lordships that the expedient course, and admittedly the competent course, is that which is in consistency with the invariable practice in the Criminal Court, and with the almost invariable practice in the Civil Court, and which, I think, is in consistency with the only practice which we have had in the Exchequer Court; because the present Lord Ordinary has, after hearing parties upon an Information in the Exchequer Court, thrown out one count as irrelevant, and only sent one for trial; I forget the name of that case, but his Lordship recollected the case; and the Crown will admit that I have correctly stated the import of the judgment. And your Lordships need not be alarmed that you would be running counter to what was done in the Alexandra case, because in that case they could not have adopted this course under the form of procedure under which they were acting; and the English courts have now borrowed from our system, and allowed the defenders to demur in the common law courts, as well as to plead in denial of the charge. I submit that the course suggested is the expedient course, and the only fair and just course to the defenders, who will be exposed to serious risks, while the Crown will encounter none of these risks, in the event of your Lordships resolving to reserve these questions to a time which we have not yet heard exactly specified, whether at the trial or after the trial. I submit, therefore, that your Lordships should now dispose of these questions of relevancy. With reference to the charges in the Information, after the observations submitted by my learned friends, I shall not go critically into any examination of the Statute; but there are a few general observations which I would submit as entitled to some consideration in construing it. We have 98 counts, and we say they are not only bad in law, but inconsistent with one another; 72 of them, at least, are inconsistent with 24. The Statute is undoubtedly a Statute of difficult construction, and it is very hard that tradesmen, such as my clients, should find it so difficult to know whether they are committing a crime or not, though they believed they were not committing a crime. But one would think that all dubiety would be at an end when the Statute came to be enforced by the head of the criminal department in this country; one would think that the representative of the Government insisting in this prosecution would be able to tell us when there was a breach of the Foreign Enlistment Act committed, and when there was not. But that is not the principle upon which this Information has been framed, for 72 counts are inconsistent with 24.

Lord President.—On their construction of the Statute, you mean; not as to the facts alleged.

Mr. Gordon.—Not as to the facts alleged. I could imagine them taking alternative charges as to the facts alleged, because they are entitled to do so; but if you state the same facts, and make out that they must be referred to different constructions of the Statute, I say then that the Lord Advocate appears in the most extraordinary position of a public prosecutor founding upon a Statute, without saying whether the defenders have committed a crime of the character charged in the 72 counts, or of the character charged in the 24 counts. It is the misfortune sometimes of a public prosecutor to be wrong in his construction of a Statute, but it is certainly not his duty to be inconsistent in the nature of the charges which he makes. The Statute may be expressed in confused terms, and I may have committed a breach of it without knowing that I was doing so; but certainly the public prosecutor should know when a breach of it has been committed. But what he is now asking your Lordships to do is to send to trial an alternative charge against my client on different views of the Statute, founded on the same facts. My learned friend says we will be better able to construe the Statute when we have had the benefit of the evidence. My client was bound to construe the Statute without the benefit of any evidence.

Lord President.—Without any evidence of his own acts?

Mr. Gordon.—Well, he must take care what he is about; but the Statute is certainly not written in such terms that he who runs may read, and I must say that it is calculated very much to perplex the defender to have these alternative views submitted to him, without knowing the precise issue to which his evidence must be directed. One class of charges is founded upon the intent of the Confederate Government to employ this ship; another is founded upon the intent of the equippers themselves to cruise and carry on hostilities. It is very perplexing to the defender not to know to which of these points he is to direct his evidence; although all difficulty will be removed if your Lordships now determine the questions of relevancy.

Lord President.—The Solicitor-General said the Statute would meet either case.

Mr. Gordon.—He was obliged to say so to a certain extent, but I think it is very difficult to support that proposition. It seems to me that the Crown are very much in the position of saying that at the trial something may turn up, and that then they will be able to tell the Court which proposition they mean to insist in. But I say it is only reasonable to ask them to tell us now what is the proposition which they are going to insist in. This question was not pleaded in the Alexandra case on the motion for a new trial, because there was a verdict there for the defenders on the whole 96 counts. Therefore the point to which the attention of the counsel and the Court was chiefly directed, was this, whether the equipment was an equipment in contravention of the Statute; for, assuming that the 72 counts with the double intent were not well founded, the Crown still had the 24 counts with the single intent, and these are not liable to this objection, and therefore if the Judge had given a wrong direction, or the verdict was contrary to evidence in so far as regarded the matter of equipment, a new trial might have been ordered with reference to these 24 counts. Therefore the question did not require to be raised before the Court of Exchequer on the motion for the new trial, and your Lordships therefore cannot look on this as a question which was argued before the Court. Great difficulty was expressed by some of the Judges as to the construction of some of these counts, but they said that the matter had not been argued, neither party having been inclined to go into the question. Now let us see what was the state of the law before the Foreign Enlistment Act was passed. Before that Act was passed any merchant or shipbuilder might sell or contract to sell munitions of war of every kind to a belligerent, and not only might he sell munitions of war, that is, arms, powder, shot, but he might sell a ship, and he might also sell an armed ship, and he might contract to sell an armed ship.

Lord-President.—There is nothing in this Statute against sale of any kind.

Mr. Gordon.—No. He might sell or contract to sell a ship, or a ship fully armed with the equipments of war of that day. The Foreign Enlistment Act has made certain things criminal which it was formerly lawful for Her Majesty's subjects to do. It could not be intended to operate any change upon international law; the only operation of the Act is to change the municipal law, and the intention was to make that a crime which was not previously a crime. I say not only was it not a crime, but it was not immoral. There was nothing immoral in the act of selling an armed ship before the passing of the Act. So much is that recognised, that in this very Act it is allowable for the subjects of the Queen to sell an armed vessel, or to contract to sell an armed vessel, or to furnish an armed vessel to a belligerent at peace with the Queen. We have an example of that in the ships of war sold to the Chinese Government, or rather attempted to be sold, because I believe the Chinese have lately repudiated the transaction; and that was done, according to my recollection, by leave of Her Majesty, in order to prevent any infringement of this Act. Therefore what the Act does is to declare, that that which was previously lawful shall now be criminal, and to subject any person committing the act to a penalty, and to confiscation of the ship. Now, let us see the admitted state of the law since the passing of the Act, for it will go very far to help us to construe the Act, to see what was the mischief intended to be remedied. I say that they may still sell guns, powder, and shot to the belligerents.

Lord President.—They may sell anything; that is to say, this Act does not strike against sale.

Mr. Gordon.—Quite so. If I was a dealer in these articles I might freight a vessel, and send out 100 cannon, and so many casks of gunpowder and tons of shot, all invoiced, and addressed to Jefferson Davis, President of the Confederate States, or to Abraham Lincoln, President of the United States,—I might have them all invoiced and passed at the custom-house, and no one could challenge the transaction. Surely, then, it was not to prevent this country getting into hostilities with a belligerent that this Act was passed, because I suppose the Confederate Government have felt very strongly to see the arms that their opponents are furnished with coming from a State with which they are on terms of amity. No doubt these articles might be seized on their way as contraband.

Lord President.—That is by the law of nations.

Mr. Gordon.—Yes. But not only may these things be sold, but it is admitted that my clients might build the 'Pampero,' and not only build her with some fittings suited for warlike purposes, but arm her with cannon, and if that was not done under contract,—if they sailed her out of the Clyde, and were able to conduct her in safety to Charleston, or any other port in the Confederate States, they might sell her, and they would have committed no infringement of the Foreign Enlistment Act. Your Lordships see, therefore, how much liberty is admittedly left to the subjects of Great Britain to trade with belligerents even in the matter of arms or armed ships.

Lord President.—How imperfectly the Act infringes on the liberty of the people!

Mr. Gordon.—It has always been an object to our Government to cherish as much as possible the building of ships, not only for our own use but for foreign nations; and I daresay if it had been proposed to infringe too much on the right to build for foreign countries even in a state of war, the Act might have met with opposition, and it might not have passed in its present shape. However, it does not affect these matters. My friend would relieve me very much if he would admit that I have stated correctly the law as to the right to sell an armed ship.

Lord Advocate.—I am not aware of any law on the subject.

Lord President.—This Act is not directed against sale.

Lord Advocate.—Certainly not; but my friend is assuming a great deal of international law which I am by no means disposed to admit in the terms in which he states it.

Mr. Gordon.—At p. 261 of the *Weekly Reporter*, I find that the question was put by Mr. Baron Bramwell to the Attorney-General:—'May those neutral subjects fit out a vessel so as to be 'ready for war, and start from the neutral port without a breach of 'international law?' and the Attorney-General says, 'I think so, 'but the authorities differ. It is clear a vessel may be sold by a 'neutral fully armed.' Baron Bramwell adds:—'But then it is 'without a fighting crew, and therefore harmless, but if a crew is 'also on board, it would make the neutral port a station of hostilities.' And the Attorney-General says, 'I find no such distinction 'laid down. There is no authority for the assertion, that taking a 'ship fully prepared for war from a neutral port is a proximate act 'of war, though it is no doubt very injurious to the belligerent.' The Chief Baron at p. 268 says:—'A shipbuilder may build a ship 'altogether of a warlike character, and may arm it completely to 'the latest and most mischievous invention for the destruction of 'human beings, and may then sell it to one of two belligerents with 'a perfect fitness for immediate cruising, and ready to commit 'hostilities the instant it is out of neutral territory, provided there 'was no contract or agreement for it. But if there be any contract, 'it cannot be made to order with the slightest warlike character 'about it, though this be part of the accustomed and usual trade 'of this country, and though the ship leaves our shores a mere hull, 'utterly incapable of cruising or committing hostilities, and, as far 'as war is concerned, as innocent and harmless as the mere timber 'of which it is built, the means of evasion which this furnishes is 'obvious—a signal, a word, a gesture may convey an order wholly 'incapable of being proved. It is unnecessary to dwell upon this; 'it is at once perfectly obvious, and the real difference between a 'crime and an act of commerce almost disappears.' Baron Channell at p. 276 says: 'I agree with the Lord Chief Baron and Mr. 'Baron Bramwell that what this Statute forbids is an equipment 'for war.' He also says: 'Again, the Lord Chief Baron having 'stated that a man may sell an armed ship to a belligerent if he 'has it ready, which is, I think, correct, proceeds to draw from that 'a conclusion that he may make one to order.' I apprehend, therefore, that it was conceded in the Alexandra case on the part of the Crown, and that we have the authority of all the Judges, that you may sell an armed vessel. The point where they diverge was whether, if there was a contract, the party was not committing an infringement of the Statute. It is of importance, therefore, to keep fully before you, in construing this Statute, what may be done apart from the provisions of the Statute. It is said that the mischief intended to be remedied was that the ports of this country were not to be made stations of departure for hostile armaments to be used against countries with which we are at peace; and I believe it was chiefly with reference to the probability of disturbances within this kingdom in the event of permission being given for the departure of such hostile armaments from the ports of this country that the Act was passed. I think I may say this at all events, that it was not passed to prevent belligerents from getting munitions of war from this country, because there is nothing against that in it, and it is still perfectly lawful to furnish a belligerent with munitions of war.

Lord President.—There is no other Act against it.

Mr. Gordon.—There is no other Act against it. What then is the principle of construction to be applied to this Act? There is first what may be called strict construction; second, there may be the literal or grammatical construction; and third, there may be a liberal and free construction. The Crown find it necessary to maintain the last of these.

Lord President.—There is a construction we have heard talked of a good deal, viz., the reasonable construction.

Mr. Gordon.—The Crown have always said you must give effect to their construction, because you must look to what was the mischief intended to be prevented. Well, the mischief more immediately intended to be prevented, and probably that was what the Legislature had chiefly in view, was the departure of Sir Gregor M'Gregor from this country in 1818, with ships fully commissioned and armed. That was probably the mischief which was sought to be remedied by the Act; but certainly it was not to prevent our furnishing munitions of war to belligerents. Now, I submit that we are entitled to a strict construction of a penal Statute,—a Statute infringing on the liberties of Her Majesty's subjects, and constituting an act previously lawful a crime. But that is not necessary for my case, because I think I may with safety put my case in this way, that the words used in the Statute, according to their grammatical meaning, admit of two readings, both of which are equally reasonable, and that therefore you will give effect to that reading which will prevent the mischief sought to be remedied by the Statute.

Lord President.—You must first take your fixed proposition of what is the evil to be remedied. You say it was to prevent Sir Gregor M'Gregor.

Mr. Gordon.—No doubt parties were all agreed that he was the cause, if he was not the mischief; but what I submitted was, that it was not to prevent munitions of war being sent from this country to belligerents.

Lord President.—It does not do that, and it does not profess to do it.

Mr. Gordon.—Therefore that was not the mischief sought to be remedied, but it was something else which we will see when we consider the clauses of the Statute. But I think it is a fair way of putting it, that if your Lordships find that the Statute admits of two readings equally grammatical, you will construe it in such a way as to remedy the mischief, if you can discover what the mischief intended to be remedied was.

Lord Deas.—If you could make us sure about that, you would help us very much.

Mr. Gordon.—Perhaps it is not my interest to make you sure of it.

Lord President.—No doubt you have stated a good canon, but it implies the ascertainment and previous fixing of the mischief to be remedied.

Mr. Gordon.—I have stated what I consider to be the mischief sought to be remedied, and I cannot suggest any other, looking to what the Statute has left undone.

Lord Curriehill.—The mischief, as I understand it, which you say was intended to be prevented or remedied, was the making of the ports of this country stations of hostilities against other countries at peace with Great Britain.

Mr. Gordon.—Yes, for the departure of hostile expeditions against these countries. I submit therefore that you must first be satisfied that the Lord Advocate's reading of the Statute is in consistency with the grammatical construction of it, and gives effect to all the words used, and you must further find that the act which he is seeking to indict my clients for having committed, is an act of the nature of the mischief which the Statute was intended to remedy. I think I am entitled to have the Statute construed very much like an entail. I think I am entitled to do everything which I am not prevented from doing by direct words in the Act.

Lord Deas.—Would you construe the Statute in England according to Scotch entail law?

Mr. Gordon.—The principle, as laid down in Anstruther *v.* Anstruther, 1842, is this, that if you have two constructions equally grammatical and equally reasonable, you will adopt that which is favourable to freedom from the fetters. That is the construction to which I refer. Now I submit that the Lord Advocate cannot read the 7th section of this Statute without deleting some words, or adding some other words. It is said that the words 'transport 'or store-ship or' occur very awkwardly, and that they would have been much better out. No doubt about it; but is that the way to construct a penal Statute? You are not construing a will, although even in that case you must try to put a meaning on every word.

Lord Deas.—You must put a meaning on every word that you can.

Mr. Gordon.—Yes; if there are two readings, one which gives effect to the whole words, and the other which does not, you must adopt the former. Now section 8 of the Statute affords another very peculiar illustration of the way in which this Act was framed. Section 8 is, that if any person, in any part of the United Kingdom, without leave and license, &c., shall, by adding to the number of the guns of such vessel, or by changing those on board for other guns, or by the addition of any equipment for war, increase and augment the warlike force of any ship or vessel of war in the service of any foreign prince, &c. This section does not require that the vessel be a vessel belonging to a belligerent at all. Suppose that a French vessel were to come into one of our ports imperfectly armed, and requiring some extra guns, and the captain applied for guns from a certain manufacturer, and he contracts to sell and put cannon on board, though we are at peace with France, and France is not at war with any nation in Europe, that would be an infringement of the Foreign Enlistment Act. And yet if the Emperor Napoleon was to ask any manufacturer in this country for 1000 cannon, he might ship them all by any vessel sailing from a port of this country to France. I point this out as showing how difficult it is to arrive at what was the true evil sought to be remedied by this Act, and that you are not to be deterred from adopting the grammatical and reasonable construction, by considering that it may lead to anomalies. The Statute is full of anomalies.

Lord Deas.—With reference to the character or uses of the vessel mentioned in section 8, do the words 'such vessel,' which occur near the outset of that section, refer back to section 7?

Mr. Gordon.—I don't think it.

Lord Deas.—What does 'such vessel' mean there?

Mr. Gordon.—It is very difficult to say.

Lord Curriehill.—Is there any antecedent to it?

Mr. Gordon.—It cannot refer back to ships merely which were built within this kingdom. It applies to all ships of war in the service of a foreign power.

Lord Curriehill.—What is the aid you derive from section 8?

Mr. Gordon.—What I point at is this, that it is very difficult to ascertain from the provisions of the Statute what were truly the evils sought to be remedied by the different sections.

Lord Deas.—You found, as I understand it, on the dark or imperfect phraseology in other sections, as showing that you are not to take them literally, but are to get at their real meaning.

Mr. Gordon.—It is a peculiar argument that because other sections are obscure, therefore you are to adopt their reading of an obscure section.

Lord President.—What is the inference you deduce from the obscurity of the evil to be remedied?

Mr. Gordon.—The inference I deduce is, that as you may sell an armed vessel, so you may contract to sell an armed vessel. I say that is not struck at by the terms of the Act.

Lord President.—Does the obscurity of the evil to be remedied help you to that result?

Lord Deas.—I thought you were arguing that we were proceeding on the footing that you had found out the evil to be remedied?

Mr. Gordon.—And I think that is the evil to be remedied; but I am meeting the view that there is some other evil which I cannot understand.

Lord President.—Then is the legitimate result of that reasoning that we must guess at the meaning of this Statute as we best can?

Mr. Gordon.—I have given your Lordship the proper meaning.

Lord President.—You have given us your meaning, and the more you can make out that clearly to be the meaning the stronger your argument.

Mr. Gordon.—I think the enactments are in consistency with what I have said to be the mischief sought to be remedied. Now, in reference to the 7th clause itself, I may give your Lordships one or two passages from the opinions of the Judges in the Alexandra case, with reference to the construction of such Statutes. At p. 264, the Chief Baron says:—'If I were asked whether there be any difference left between a criminal Statute and any other Statute not creating any offence, I should say that in a criminal Statute you must be quite sure that the offence charged is within the letter of the law; in some other cases the Statute is to be applied unless you are sure that the case is not within the law. As to this particular Statute having for its object prevention, not punishment, which was pressed on our notice more than once, that is not a matter peculiar to this Statute. I apprehend that it has that object in common with all other criminal statutes that were ever passed, which are all intended, not to punish guilt, but to prevent crime; and as to the recital that the existing law was not sufficient, to which our opinion was particularly called, I presume that recital really belongs to every Statute, whether mentioned in it or not, for if the law be sufficient, the Statute is a piece of superfluous legislation.' Then, at p. 270, Baron Bramwell says:—'It may be said this is a lawyer's mode of dealing with this question—merely looking at the words. It is, and I think it right. A judge discussing the meaning of a Statute in a court of law should deal with it as a lawyer, and look at its words. If he disregards them, and decides according to its maker's supposed intent, he may be substituting his for theirs, and so legislating. As has been excellently said,

'" Better far be accused of a narrow prejudice for the letter of the '" law, than set up or sanction vague claims to discard it in favour '" of some light interpretation more consonant with the supposed '" intentions of the framers, or the spirit which ought to have ani- '" mated them."' And at p. 276, Baron Channell has a passage to the same effect. Let me now shortly direct your Lordships' attention to the terms of the Act itself. *Prima facie* your Lordships can have no doubt that any person reading the Statute without paying any very great attention to its terms, but reading it fairly, would understand that there are two offences referred to in the 7th section, put alternatively both as regards the use to be made of the vessel, and the intent with which that use is made.

Lord President.—The intent with which the use is made, but the intent that the use should be made.

Mr. Gordon.—The first crime is equipping a vessel with the intent or in order that she should be employed in the service of a foreign state as a transport or store-ship, and then it goes on, 'or ' with intent to cruise or commit hostilities against a foreign power ' with which this country is at peace.' Now, any person reading these words would, I think, at first be inclined to say, that here were two different kinds of crime. Both the use and the intent are different, and if you are to say that there is any virtue in the words, 'in order that,' it more clearly makes out my proposition; because, while you have the intent repeated with reference to the second alternative, you have not the words 'or in order that.' I say, therefore, that the fair grammatical and reasonable construction of this Statute is in accordance with what I have stated, that there are two separate alternative offences here which may be committed. The expression 'employed by' in the first alternative has been combined with reference to the same words in the American Statute, as meaning that the use of the vessel shall be by the equipper and not by the hostile State. The Solicitor-General read one or two passages, in answer to Mr. Clark, from the opinion of Baron Bramwell, where he said that American cases were not to be relied on with reference to some points; but there is no doubt that the American law is as I have stated it, because, in the case of Quincy, Judge Thompson says: 'The law does not prohibit armed vessels ' belonging to the citizens of the United States from sailing out of ' our ports, it only requires the owner to give security, as was done ' in the present case, that such vessel shall not be employed by ' them to commit hostilities against foreign powers at peace with the ' United States.' This was the case of a person who carried out his vessel in order to find his market at a belligerent port. And Justice Story says: 'But there is nothing in our laws (*Reads as quoted at p.* 16 *ante*). At page 267 of the *Weekly Reporter*, the Chief Baron says: 'So with respect to the law and the construc- ' tion of the American Act of Congress, the judgment delivered by ' Mr. Justice Thompson in the United States *v.* Quincy gives to the ' citizens of the United States a right to send armed vessels out of ' their ports, it aims at preventing the citizens themselves from ' committing hostilities against foreign powers at peace with the

'United States, but leaves them at perfect liberty to sell the vessel
'to one of the belligerents, and provided hostilities are not committed by the citizens of the States, there is no breach of the law.'

Lord President.—You say the words of the Statute are the same. Let us understand exactly what the words of the American Statute are. The syntax of the section in the American Statute is not dislocated by the introduction of the words, 'as a transport or store-ship, or with intent.' These words are not in it, and these are the words which create the difficulty here.

Mr. Gordon.—I am speaking on the words 'employed by.'

Lord President.—Do you say that, according to the American authorities, the party fitting out must be the party who is to act with the cruiser?

Mr. Gordon.—Yes.

Lord President.—And that fitting her out for other persons to employ her in the service of a foreign prince will not be a contravention of the Act?

Mr. Gordon.—That is the construction which the American lawyers have put on their own Statute.

Lord President.—Therefore, if these words were left out, 'as a transport or store-ship, or with intent,' you would say that in that case the Statute would have the limited meaning which you seek to give to this last branch of it?

Mr. Gordon.—Yes.

Lord President.—Then has the first branch of it here a different meaning from that last branch?

Mr. Gordon.—I think if you construe the first branch in accordance with the principle of the decisions in the American cases, there is not a difference between them.

Lord President.—There is a vast difference in the expression.

Mr. Gordon.—There is a difference in the expression, but I am quite ready to meet the case upon that view. I say you are to construe the first branch as the American courts have construed it.

Lord President.—That would be, that in the case of a transport, the parties fitting must themselves intend to use the transport?

Mr. Gordon.—Yes. Our construction of the second alternative is *a fortiori* of the American; but I am speaking just now to the first alternative; and I say that if you construe it as the Americans have construed it, you reconcile the two. But assume that they are different; assume that if it is a transport or store-ship, it is sufficient if it is employed in the service of the Federal Government, but that if it is an armed vessel, it must be employed by the equipper. It may be said there is an inconsistency there. It is not the necessary construction; but suppose you take that construction, there is an inconsistency. But is not this Act full of inconsistencies? and because there is an inconsistency here, are you to put on it a different meaning from that which the word will grammatically bear. My reference to the 8th section was to point out how inconsistent that section is with what might be held to be the spirit of the Act, and my reference to the right to sell munitions of war, and to sell a ship, if I don't contract for it, goes to this, that the Act is full of inconsistencies; and you are not, because you find an inconsistency between the two alternatives of this 7th section to say, We shall put a meaning upon that which the words won't admit of, unless you strike out the word 'or,' or unless you insert some other words. I say therefore that we must construe the first alternative in accordance with the American judgments. If you don't so construe it, you cannot ignore the word 'or,' which is a very important word in my friend's argument with reference to equip, fit out, furnish, or arm; for what has the whole structure of their Information been founded upon except this, that you are to construe the word 'or' there as disjunctive, creating an alternative charge, and yet when you come a little farther down where the matter is far clearer, where the two intents and uses are put into opposition, the word 'or' is to be left out as utterly unimportant. Is that adopting a principle of construction which is consistent or rational? I submit therefore that there is no reasonable construction of this Statute which you can adopt, except that which is contended for on the part of my clients. I do not think it necessary to add to the argument already submitted to your Lordships on the other branch of the case.

Lord President.—In what case is the passage which puts the construction you say on the American Statute?

Mr. Gordon.—The 'Independencia.'

Lord President.—Was that a case which raised the question?

Mr. Gordon.—I think so; it had reference to a vessel which was sent out from an American port armed to a certain extent; it was to be used in South America, and it was to be sold to belligerents.

Lord President.—But it was sold after it went there?

Mr. Gordon.—Undoubtedly.

Lord President.—But where is the doctrine distinctly laid down that the employment of the vessel contemplated by the Statute is an employment by the equippers?

Lord Advocate.—There is no such thing. The facts in neither of the cases admitted of raising that.

Mr. Gordon.—I think it is at p. 79.

Lord President.—Well, I have looked at that passage, but I don't find it there. There is the expression which Mr. Cook referred to, about not detaining them unless there was some evidence that the vessels were intended to be employed by the owners to commit hostilities. That was a general observation in reference to the matter, but it was not the point before the Court. I don't see any distinct laying down of that doctrine; nor do I see very well how it could be, consistently with the words of the Statute, because it says: 'If any person shall, within the limits of the United States, fit 'out and arm, or attempt to fit out and arm, or procure to be fitted 'out and armed, or shall knowingly be concerned in the furnishing, 'fitting out, or arming of the ship with intent;' nor does it require that the person who shall be knowingly concerned in doing any one of these things shall himself go away with the vessel, or be an employer of her.

Mr. Gordon.—That is the construction which has been put upon it.

Lord President.—Where?

Mr. Gordon.—At p. 79: 'The collectors are not authorized to 'detain vessels,' &c.

Lord President.—I see that passage, but that was not the point before the Court. The words, 'by the owners,' are introduced there, but that was not the point before the Court, and so we cannot take that as a doctrine limiting the application of the Statute.

Lord Advocate.—I shall now very shortly resume and sum up what has been very fully stated on this side, because I don't think your Lordships will find it necessary to decide those questions at present, but will rather follow the course of the Lord Ordinary, and allow the case to be tried.

Lord President.—That is a point, however, on which the Court would like to hear you.

Lord Advocate.—The first question is whether your Lordships are to pronounce a judgment on the objections which my learned friends have taken to the relevancy of this Information; and I am by no means sure that, on the part of the Crown, I have much interest to contend that your Lordships should not take up these points; but the grounds of my learned friend's argument would lead to this, that if your Lordships think the objections ill founded, you shall now decide them to be so, the result being that we go to trial with these objections repelled. That has not generally been considered an advisable course; it is in that view only that we have resisted those questions being raised, and in the course of the argument your Lordships have had many shades and differences of fact put which might have a most material bearing upon the effect of the interpretation of the Statute and of the Information. We are not here, it is true, in an ordinary summons and record, but that, I think, instead of being in favour of deciding the points of relevancy at this stage, is all the other way. But if we were here on a summons and record, I think your Lordships have in the cases referred to laid down very distinctly what the general rule in such cases ought to be. I don't deny the competency of raising the question of relevancy at this stage, supposing we were now in a closed record. I admit its competency, if your Lordships think it right to do so; but I find that in the case of Galloway *v.* Grant, 20th June 1857, 19 Dunlop, 875, Lord Deas says—'A practice has 'been recently creeping in'—(*Reads.*) The same thing was laid down by your Lordship in the chair with great fulness in the case of Guild *v.* Orr Ewing. I do not say that it is not competent for your Lordships now to decide these points if you think that the ends of justice will be better served by doing so. I only say that in the general case such a course is the exception, and not the rule. But my learned friends say: 'How do we know 'that these objections will be reserved to us afterwards, and when 'are we to raise them?' Now that might very strongly and fairly be put in the case of an ordinary action with a Closed Record, and an Issue approved of by the Court. But in an Information, which goes to trial at once, it is plain the Court don't interfere in the slightest degree to fix the issue. That is fixed by the prosecutor in the suit; and therefore, in going to trial, nothing is tried but the facts alleged. My learned friend has pleaded that the Information is bad in law. That plea remains undisposed of. It seems to me perfectly certain that if, after a verdict on an Information, on the motion to apply the judgment, the objection is taken that the facts don't come up to anything which, under the Statute, the Crown is entitled to prosecute for, it is impossible that the defenders would not be entitled to do so then.

Lord President.—Like a proof before answer?

Lord Advocate.—That is the nature of it. My learned friend says such a thing has never been done. Has a case not gone to trial on an Information before? Did my learned friend ever hear of a question of relevancy being discussed and decided in the way he wishes this to be discussed and decided? It does not follow that it is not competent. In the Exchequer Court, the Information is a copy of the Statute, and the real question arises at the trial. We don't require to set out the matters as we do in ordinary Records, so as to extract issues. The practice in the Court of Exchequer is to make the counts truly an echo of the Statute on which the case is founded, and in that way relevancy can scarcely arise.

Lord President.—But to know whether it is an echo, you must hear the sound!

Lord Advocate.—Precisely. So that on the whole of this first matter, while I have nothing to say against your Lordships entertaining it, if you think the justice of the case will be forwarded thereby; on the other hand, it is perfectly obvious that my learned friend's objection to the whole scope of this information is as entire as it possible to be. I think nothing that your Lordships could do in sending the case to trial could possibly prejudge that.

Lord Deas.—Do you mean that those questions which they are raising now would be open, and would be raised before the Lord Ordinary before he pronounced that decree that the Exchequer Act speaks of?

Lord Advocate.—I think the proper stage for stating the objections would be probably on the motion to apply the verdict, supposing we got a verdict, but many of them might be raised by way of exception.

Lord Deas.—You mean that every question of law would be open to be raised before the Lord Ordinary before pronouncing the decree mentioned in section 6 of the Exchequer Act?

Lord Advocate.—Certainly.

Lord Deas.—Is that judgment subject to review?

Lord Advocate.—I have no doubt it is. The Lord Ordinary in Exchequer is subject to your Lordships' review, and there is nothing to exclude it. I don't at this moment appreciate the difficulty.

Lord Deas.—The clause says that the Lord Ordinary shall pronounce decree.

Lord Advocate.—As may be just and according to law.

Lord Deas.—What discretion he has or what he is to hear does not appear.

Lord Advocate.—The section gives him power to pronounce such a decree as the verdict warrants. If the verdict does not warrant the decree, he cannot give it. The object evidently is to give the Lord Ordinary a power to give effect to the verdict of the jury.

Lord Deas.—Is that very reconcilable with the notion which, I suppose, you adhere to, that all the law and relevancy may be heard at the trial, and, of course, if it may be argued at the trial, it may be decided by the Lord Ordinary in the course of the trial, —is it very consistent that after he has pronounced his decision, he is to hear it all over again, and perhaps come to a different result?

Lord Advocate.—I cannot conceive where there can be any inconsistency.

Lord Deas.—He can review his own judgment.

Lord Advocate.—Not the least. I have not stated anything like that. At the trial, the question of fact is for the Jury. It will be in the power of the party to say that that question of fact does not warrant conviction upon the count as it stands. That is clearly law for the Judge to lay down. The party may go further, and say not only that the facts do not warrant a conviction on the count, but that the count is not reconcilable with the Act of Parliament, and therefore should be withdrawn from the Jury. Well, the presiding Judge may withdraw it; or he may take the course which probably he would take, and say: 'That is a matter which I would not withdraw from the Jury, but I shall leave you to raise it when the verdict is applied, because it relates not to a fact which the Jury are to find, but relates to how far the count in the Information is founded on the Statute.' In either of these ways the question may be raised. Probably the more regular way would be to raise it in the latter of these ways, the Judge not deciding it at the trial, but leaving it open to be decided when the verdict is applied. There are many ways of trying these questions. You may try them under a bill of exceptions, or under a motion for a new trial. These remedies are all open. My own opinion is, that the questions mainly raised here are properly questions of law to be disposed of on the application of the verdict; but I by no means say that my learned friend would be prevented from raising them at the trial. Let me put a case. Lord Deas, the other day said, suppose the Great Eastern were to be prepared for the service of the Confederates, and were equipped so far as was necessary, would that be arming? That is obviously a question depending upon the facts. If warlike armament is proved, and equipment means equipment in a warlike manner, that is sufficient to sustain the Information. If, on the other hand, warlike armament is not proved at the trial, the question will arise, and will only then arise, whether warlike armament is included in the term equipment. It is a question which your Lordships cannot decide on the relevancy: it does not relate to the relevancy. The Statute uses the word 'equip.' The meaning of that word must be considered when you see what proof is brought that equipment is taking place. I use that as an illustration to show how closely the question that we have been discussing here is bound up with the merits. We have heard a great deal about the right of selling a vessel; but between selling a vessel and contracting for it, there may be a very obvious line of demarcation; it may depend very much on the facts to be proved at the trial. It does not seem to me that there is any inconsistency in saying that the Lord Ordinary may, on the application of the verdict, consider whether it is just and according to law that the verdict should be applied, so as to give decree. There is nothing inconsistent in saying that, and in saying that at the trial he shall consider any questions of law that may be raised.

Lord President.—In what form would it arise? It would not be a motion for a new trial when argued before the Lord Ordinary?

Lord Advocate.—No; it would be a motion for decree.

Lord President.—And he gives his decree. Then you think it might be brought here by Reclaiming Note, and might be appealed to the House of Lords?

Lord Advocate.—I think so. I see nothing to exclude that.

Lord President.—I don't know that there is, but it is different from our existing forms. The Exchequer process just now is a sort of amphibious thing.

Lord Advocate.—No doubt about it. There are a good many things not yet regulated, but I don't think the Statute excludes that review. Nor is there anything new in it, for I apprehend that the right to object to the application of the verdict has existed all along. It was necessary all along under the old Court of Exchequer to apply the verdict, and I don't doubt that there was an appeal from the old Court of Exchequer judgments to the House of Lords, and that there is no novelty except in this, that the Lord Ordinary comes in place of the Court of Exchequer, and may do what it could have done, subject to Reclaiming Note. That is the view which I take of the first part of this case.

Lord President.—The issue raised in any one of these counts is a different thing altogether, I suppose, from an adjusted issue, in its import. From the way you put it, it must be, because the issue asks the question, whether these things were done contrary to the Statute in such case made and provided. Now it is quite a usual issue with us, whether such a thing were contrary to the Bankruptcy Act, for instance; and the verdict by the Jury is a verdict finding that it was contrary to the Statute, and that can only be got over in our known forms. That is part of the fact put to the Jury. Therefore these words must in this Information have a different effect from what they would have in an issue. If we put the question, whether certain proceedings were contrary to the Act '96, and the Jury find they are, we could not get over that, except by a motion for a new trial.

Lord Advocate.—I don't mean to say that the form of process is the same. It is not the same. It could only be got over by a motion for a new trial, which would not be appealable to the House of Lords; but I don't think in Exchequer processes there is any such restrictions, unless the Court of Session form is followed, which it may be.

Lord Deas.—Must it not be followed? The words of the Act are: 'In so far as not so regulated, shall be conducted as nearly as 'may be in conformity with the procedure before the Court of 'Session in ordinary actions.'

Lord Advocate.—That is where we begin by Information, but I rather think under the Statute it could have been done by summons. It is quite clear it cannot be given full effect to, because the Lord Ordinary in Exchequer is to pronounce decree; and that is the whole point. I have no doubt if you were to proceed by a Bill of Exceptions, or a motion for a new trial, you must follow the ordinary course in the Court of Session.

Lord President.—The Lord Ordinary could give the time that in ordinary practice would be allowed for moving for a new trial in a case tried before the Lord Ordinary on issues, and he could pronounce decree, if no motion for a new trial was made within the time.

Lord Advocate.—And what does all this tend to? Only to this, that at the worst they are in the same position as if there had been an action in the Court of Session, to which there were objections on relevancy, which had not been sustained.

Lord Deas.—That is not the worst of it; at least what puzzles me is the difficulty of knowing what would be competent.

Lord Advocate.—I cannot tell what would be competent except what I find in the Act: but it would certainly be an entirely novel view of the Statute to say that there could be no Bill of Exceptions or motion for new trial.

Lord Deas.—But it may be one reason in favour of deciding something beforehand which we would not otherwise decide, that it is exceedingly dark and doubtful whether it could be decided afterwards.

Lord Advocate.—I by no means see the darkness or obscurity.

Lord Deas.—Then I want you to help me to dispel it.

Lord Advocate.—My learned friends, with all their ingenuity, did not discover that these concluding words prevented them from having a new trial or a Bill of Exceptions. Of course, if your Lordships are prepared to decide this matter I have nothing more to say, excepting that it appears to me to be a great pity to forestal questions of relevancy before the facts are ascertained, and that exactly on the views which Lord Deas stated in the case of Grant *v.* Galloway.

Lord Deas.—If there be any real difficulty as to the competency of what might follow, both parties are equally interested to avoid that difficulty.

Lord Advocate.—On the part of the Crown, I certainly don't think it right even to imagine that that could be the ground on which your Lordship could proceed, because this is not the only Exchequer case that may possibly be tried. There have been as many as fifty or sixty cases tried under this Statute, and if your Lordships are to decide this on the ground of obscurity in the Exchequer Act, I trust that it shall be decided so that we shall at least know what that obscurity is. I do not think it is doubtful that by exception at the trial the defenders might ask the Judge to lay down that the things proved were not against the Statute in that case made and provided, and if the Judge did not lay that down, they might then except to his ruling, and if the Judge did, and the Jury returned a different verdict, they might proceed by motion for a new trial. The question whether there would be an appeal in that last case or not, is a different question.

Lord President.—Have any questions arisen under the Act by arrest of judgment.

Lord Advocate.—No, I don't think so, either under this or the previous Act.

Lord President.—Or under a Bill of Exceptions since the Exchequer Act.

Lord Advocate.—I think not.

Lord President.—Have there been any motions for new trial?

Lord Advocate.—No, I think not.

Lord Ardmillan.—I think I remember a case where the defenders objected to the Information, and it was argued before the case went to the Jury; the case was tried before Lord Cunninghame, and that was called demurring. It was a hopeless attempt to demur, and the defender failed in it.

Lord President.—It used to be a very common way in Exchequer to take a special case or a special verdict.

Lord Advocate.—And in this case I don't know that that might not come to be in the view of both parties; but that will be matter for after consideration. But it would be a serious matter to lay down that wherever the relevancy of an Information is objected to, that must be decided beforehand.

Lord Deas.—Nobody says that.

Lord Advocate.—On the whole matter I think your Lordships, in considering the objections, will see how desirable it is to have the facts ascertained before judgment is given on the relevancy. The objections, as I understand them, are two, first, that it is necessary under the 7th section of the Statute to aver and put in issue the intention of the parties themselves to make use of the vessel in the way prohibited by the Statute, and that even although they should not be vessels of war, but should be transports or store-ships.

Lord President.—The latter not so confidently.

Lord Advocate.—The latter not so confidently. The second objection is that we have not alleged arming along with the equipping, furnishing, and fitting ont. I don't think my learned friend, Mr. Gordon, said anything about that last point, and therefore what I have truly to meet in substance is the first, and that raises the construction of the 7th section of the Statute. My learned friend said a good deal, following the argument in the case of the Alexandra, on what he called the mischief which the Statute was intended to prevent. I think that there is a good deal of fallacy in a great many of the observations which were made on that matter. It seems to be thought that Sir Gregor M'Gregor was the sole cause of the Foreign Enlistment Act; but surely Sir Gregor M'Gregor was not the cause of the American Act of 1818, and still less was he the cause of the American Act of 1794. History shows us plainly enough that the evil intended to be prevented was that set out in the preamble of the Statute,—the danger of war with belligerents if neutrals did the particular things, or things of the same kind, that are set forth in the Foreign Enlistment Act. My learned friend said that, before the passing of this Act, these things were lawful by the law of nations. I am not prepared to admit that as a general proposition. On the contrary, I think the Foreign Enlistment Act was passed for the purpose of giving effect to the law of nations, and to give power by the strong hand at once to prevent things being done that might be reasonably complained of as a breach of neutrality by other nations. In 1794, the Foreign Enlistment Act of the United States took its rise in a complaint on the part of our own Government of a breach of neutrality in permitting vessels to be built by French agents in ports of the United States, and then again after the peace in 1814, they passed in 1818 their second Foreign Enlistment Act for the purpose of preventing precisely the same thing. At that time Spain and France were at war, and their interest to prevent war between these two nations was as great as it had been before. Our Foreign Enlistment Act was passed in 1819, and the object of it I think was obviously to prevent those things being done in this country which could be reasonably said to be a breach of neutrality. It was not absolutely necessary to make that unlawful which had previously been lawful. I don't think it could be said that it was lawful by the law of nations, though it may not have been prohibited by the municipal law of this country, so as to enable the Government to take action as under the Foreign Enlistment Act. My learned friend says that according to the law of nations it is lawful to sell a vessel however armed, and he quotes Justice Story and the case of Quincy for the purpose of showing that. Now I don't think that is very material to the present discussion, because the thing pointed at in the Foreign Enlistment Act is not sale, and we have not accused the defenders of selling a vessel. And therefore I don't see that that affects this argument even if my learned friend were well founded in it. But it is in vain to disguise that if that doctrine were pushed to its legitimate extent, it would strike at that which he himself admits to be the thing which the Foreign Enlistment Act was intended to prevent. Suppose Mr. Fleming were to keep a store of warlike vessels in the Clyde, and to advertise to the world that he has a set of the most eligible war-vessels ready at the shortest notice for anybody who chooses to buy, and the Confederates buy, and they come here with their crew, and put them on board to take away the vessel, I rather think the danger of a collision with the Federals in the Firth of Clyde would be fully as great as anything contemplated in the Foreign Enlistment Act. So that if the purchase and sale is to be carried into effect in the territory of Great Britain, I am not disposed to make any admission to my learned friend as to how far that would or would not be legal. The *dictum* of Justice Story in the particular case is sound enough, for there he went solely on this, that the war-vessel had not been constructed with the intent of being used by a belligerent, but for the open market, and that he had gone for the purpose of selling it in the open market. He did not know whether the belligerent would buy or not, and therefore there was not the intent of the Statute. But I think all these matters are beside this case. If it ever came to be considered as an abstract proposition whether according to the law of nations you might carry the traffic in war-ships to any extent without a breach of neutrality, I think a great deal more would require to be said on that question before your Lordships could come to a decision upon it. With these observations, let us see what this Act does. The general ground that I am combating is this: It is said it contemplates solely and entirely the actings of the party against whom the infringement is alleged. I say it is not the case that in any of its provisions it contemplates acts being done for the purpose of assisting belligerents, though the party himself does not intend to take part in the proceedings contemplated. Under the 2d section, where the enlistment of subjects of this country in foreign service is prohibited, it was supposed that there the Act entirely related to things done by the parties against whom it was directed in their own persons, but my learned friend omitted to observe that there is a prohibition in the clause against parties procuring enlistment, and there it is not contemplated that they shall do anything but get another man to serve the foreign potentate. But passing over that in the meantime, the 8th section surely does not relate to taking service in a foreign state. It relates clearly to the fitting out in ports of this country, of vessels which are in the service of and belonging to some foreign potentate. It may be that there was a defect in the structure of the clause in order to connect it with a belligerent, but it is quite clear that whatever is intended to be prohibited by the 8th clause, it is the doing of something by parties in this country who are not and never mean to be in the service of a belligerent power. So that my learned friend can gain nothing from the general complexion of the Statute. And now we come to the construction of the 7th section, and I must fairly own that if it were not for the able criticism that has been made on it, the difficulty could not have occurred to me on reading it grammatically. On the contrary, I don't think there is more than one reading of the section that is possible. I am supported in this, because though this point was started by Sir Hugh Cairns at the commencement of the trial in the Alexandra case, it was subsequently abandoned on the motion for a rule. It would have been a most material element in the motion for a rule if it could have been shown to be well founded; but both Baron Channell and the Attorney-General treated the matter as one on which in the end they had all come to be agreed. I apprehend the grammar of the clause to be this, if they shall equip a vessel with intent or in order that such vessel shall be employed in the service of any foreign prince, as a transport or store-ship, or that it shall be employed with intent to cruise or commit hostilities. It goes to the employment of the vessel in either case, and it would be a very strong reading on the mere matter of grammar to cut out from the sentence applicable to cruising and commiting hostilities, all the words after 'vessel,' that is to say, some eight lines, and then to make it run, 'or with intent to cruise or 'commit hostilities against any state,' &c. The intent in the second case is not the intent in the same sense as in the former. To employ a vessel with intent to cruise means to employ it with the intent that it shall cruise and commit hostilities,—to send it out on a voyage of which that shall be the object,—that it shall have for its purpose in sailing not merely to cruise but to commit hostilities; in other words, it is a bad periphrasis, for a warlike cruiser, or a hostile cruiser, or a cruiser against the enemy. The only difficulty arises from 'intent' being there. Suppose it had been 'for 'the purpose of cruising,' or in order to cruise, or with the intention of cruising, what then? So that, after all, it comes to be the most minute criticism on the words as they stand. But I want to know how my learned friends are to finish this section in their way of reading it, because I think it is impossible to read it in their sense at all. 'Or with intent to cruise or commit hostilities against 'any prince, state, or potentate,'—are these words confined to cruising or committing hostilities? What is to become of the transport or store-ship. They read it in this way: 'With intent or in 'order that such vessel shall be employed as a transport or store-'ship, or with intent to cruise and commit hostilities against any 'prince, state, or potentate;' but in that case, 'against any prince, 'state, or potentate,' would not apply to the transport or store-ship, and it would prohibit the making of any transport or store-ship, whatever it was to be employed in.

Lord President.—That is, if it was to be employed in the service of a foreign state, though not to be used against a prince, state, or potentate.

Lord Advocate.—Yes; but that is not all, because when you come to the issuing of commissions there is a prohibition against issuing or delivering any commission for any ship or vessel with the intent that such ship or vessel shall be employed as aforesaid. How employed? As a transport or store-ship? A commission for a transport or store-ship! That is the only employment mentioned before. Is it not quite clear that the section presupposes and assumes that the employment of the ship is really of the substance of the whole transgression against which this is directed, and that a commission to serve in a ship as aforesaid means not a transport or store-ship, but specially a ship that is going to commit hostilities. But the words are used evidently to imply that under the employment expressly provided for in the former part of the clause, has been included not only the transport or store-ship, but the vessel that is to cruise and commit hostilities also. So that, on the first reading of it, I don't see where the ambiguity lies. If any synonym had been used for the word intent, it never would have occurred to anybody to raise the objection. My friend says that they are to get a liberal construction. Well, this is a penal Statute, I admit, and you are not to assume that a penalty has been incurred unless the Statute says so, but it is also a Statute of the greatest possible moment and importance to the whole Empire. You are to give it the construction that its words manifestly import. You are not to endeavour, by some mode of construction which puts the words together according to a way which is not their ordinary collocation, to defeat the manifest object of the Statute. You are not to torture the words in order to give it a construction which no common sense would ever have suggested. And what is the construction? Why, it is this; that if you make a transport or a store-ship and intend it to be used by a belligerent power against a power at peace with her Majesty, that is prohibited; but if you make a cruiser or a ship of war, unless you mean to sail in her yourself, that is not prohibited. They must either come to that, or they must maintain that in the case of a transport or store-ship it requires the acting of the party, which I think your Lordships will find without the slightest ground or authority. That absurdity was clearly pointed out by the Solicitor-General. But what of the 8th section? According to their view, you may arm a vessel to the teeth without being touched by the 7th. You may build it in your yard, arm it, and send it out for the purpose of being used by the Confederates against the Federals, but if that vessel returns within a fortnight, and if you put a single gun in it, you commit an offence under the 8th section. I think the object was to prevent the so dealing with one of the two belligerent parties as to give reasonable ground of offence to the other. That is obviously struck at just as much as the taking of actual service.

Lord President.—'With intent to cruise or commit hostilities' cannot be an intent in the ship. She can have no intent; she cannot cruise or commit hostilities, though she may be cruised with. If you read it this way—'with intent that such ship or 'vessel shall be employed to cruise,' then that is an intent in the equipper; but if you read it this way—'with intent that such 'vessel shall be employed in the service of a foreign state as a 'transport, or with intent to cruise,' that is an intent in the employer. Now, whether is this intent here an intent in the equipper or in the employer?

Lord Advocate.—The second intent is an intent on the part of the employer. It is a qualification of the employment.

Lord President.—Then you don't read the Statute 'with the 'intent that such ship shall be employed,' because that would be intent in the equipper.

Lord Advocate.—I read the cruising clause in this way: 'With 'intent or in order that such ship or vessel shall be employed in 'the service of any foreign prince, with intent to cruise or commit 'hostilities.'

Lord President.—That is an intent in the equipper. It is the last intent that is the difficulty.

Lord Advocate.—I say the intent is a qualification of the employment.

Lord President.—But you gave us two readings, one of which would have made it the intent of the equipper, and the other the intent of the employer, and yet each of these would have supported your view of the case.

Lord Advocate.—I cannot possibly say that that second intent, reading it as I do, is an intent on the part of the equipper, because I read it in this way, 'with intent or in order that it shall be em-'ployed with a particular intent.' It is a qualification of the employment. I would read it as if it had been this, 'with intent 'or in order that such ship should be employed with intent to be 'used as a transport or store-ship, or as a cruiser.'

Lord President.—Then the intent is the intent of the employer.

Lord Advocate.—Yes.

Lord President.—And you hold that that part of the Statute covers the case of the cruising or committing hostilities, being either by the equipper or by anybody else in the service of the foreign state.

Lord Advocate.—Just so.

Lord President.—And, therefore, that it sustains both classes of counts, according as the evidence shall show that the equippers were themselves to be the cruisers, or that the equippers were not to be the cruisers themselves, but were to give the vessel to others, who were to be the cruisers.

Lord Advocate.—That is precisely the answer that I give to my learned friend's argument; nor is there anything to be said about it being the intent of the employer and not of the equipper, because the using as a transport or store-ship is an intent. It is not merely the things it does, but the object and motive with which it does them; and though the vessel may never have taken a prize or fired a gun, if it has the intent of cruising or committing hostilities on the part of the employer, that gives it its character.

Lord President.—A third party, not a foreign state, but a party wishing to assist a foreign state, might have a cruiser and a transport or store-ship.

Lord Deas.—It looks a little like as if a store-ship meant a store-ship of the Government.

Lord Advocate.—It is to be used against the foreign prince.

Lord President.—In the service.

Lord Advocate.—In the service of one foreign prince against another.

Lord President.—Do you hold that the first part of the section means with intent that the ship shall be employed as a store-ship, though not in the service of a foreign prince?

Lord Advocate.—Oh, no!

Lord President.—Of course not; and the cruising also must be in the service of the foreign prince.

Lord Advocate.—Yes.

Lord President.—Whoever be the party manning the vessel?

Lord Advocate.—Yes; and that suggests another objection to their reading, because that quality of being employed in the service of any foreign prince would, according to their reading, be entirely cut out of the paragraph.

Lord Ardmillan.—That is the greatest difficulty about it.

Lord Deas.—On that part of the argument they found something on the first words of the preamble.

Lord Advocate.—I already gave the answer to that, because I showed that procuring enlistment was as much prohibited as enlistment itself; and I think, also, the subsequent words, 'may 'be prejudicial to, and tend to endanger the peace and welfare 'of this kingdom,' cannot by possibility be held as limited to the chance of collision in British waters between the two belligerent powers. Now, I don't intend to trouble your Lordships with farther remarks on the syntax of that section. As to the American cases, it is clear that neither one nor other have much bearing upon this case. The case of the 'Independencia' could not possibly affect this case; and in the other case all that was determined was not in the least that it was necessary under the Foreign Enlistment Act in America, that the party equipping should also be the party committing the hostilities, or intending to commit hostilities; but it was held that you must have a present intention, and that that was prohibited by the law,—that the law prohibited the equipping with an intent, and that that intent had not been formed at the date when the vessel was equipped;—a fine enough question, no doubt, and a question that might give rise to difficulty, but still not this question, or anything like it. It is quite true that in that case the equipper did sail with the vessel, and was the captain of the vessel. At p. 67 you will find the direction which was ultimately held to be right. The first was, that if the Jury should find that the traverser was knowingly concerned in the fitting out of the privateer with intent that such vessel should be employed in the service of the United Provinces, they were to find against him; and in the ultimate ruling at p. 78, you will find that in relation to the first of the instructions maintained for Quincy, the Court say:—'We are accordingly of opinion that it is not necessary that the 'Jury should believe or find that the "Bolivar," when she left 'Baltimore, and when she arrived at St. Thomas, and during the 'voyage from Baltimore to St. Thomas, was armed, or in a condi-'tion to commit hostilities, in order to find the defendant guilty of 'the offence charged in the indictment.' So that that ruled two points material in this case: *1st*, That it was not necessary that the ship should be in a position to commit hostilities at the time the offence was committed; and *2d*, That it was enough, for the conviction of the party, that he should knowingly have fitted out the vessel as a privateer, with intent that she should be employed by any one in the service of a foreign prince. So much for the first objection. The second objection relates to the question whether arming must be put into the Information. That depends on whether the words are synonymous, or whether they mean something different in the Statute. If they are synonymous, and equip means arming, I charge the defender with arming when I charge him with equipping. If they are not synonymous, but mean a different thing, I charge him with that different thing, for I have used 'equip,' and not 'arm.' They don't say that 'arm' is necessary to give 'equip' a meaning in the Information; because 'equip' in the Information can mean nothing but what it means in the Statute. Therefore, if it rested on that, I think the answer is conclusive. But, 2*d*, I say that 'equip' does not mean 'arm.' There may be equipment under the Statute that does not go the length of armament, and yet it may be equipment with that intent. There is a question, and that question may arise or may not arise in the case on the trial, whether to equip with a clear intent that the equipment shall result in armament, if it be not in itself of a hostile nature, shall be sufficient to bring them within the clause. That may give rise to some difficulty; it may depend on what is proved of the nature of the equipment. If the equipment is of an ambiguous nature, and the intent is clearly proved otherwise, that intent will throw a light on the object and intent of the equipment. But it would be idle to go into that at present, because we may prove the clearest hostile equipment, though not amounting to that which may be technically called armament. Gun-carriages without a gun may not be arming, but it is very like an equipment with the intent in question. Port-holes of themselves are not arms, but they are very necessary parts of the equipment of a ship of war. A great many other illustrations might be put. We shall see about that when we come to the evidence. Meantime, I say that, according to my reading of the Statute, equipment means something different from arming; and therefore it is no objection, if it be prohibited by the Statute, to say that we are not charging something else which is also prohibited, but which we don't allege.

Lord President.—Supposing their construction of the Statute to be right, that there can be no equipment of the cruiser without arming; that the Statute means arming of the cruiser, and that you don't charge arming; won't that strike against the relevancy of some of the counts?

Lord Advocate.—That depends on the way it is put. If they mean to say that the Statute must be read as if it were equip and arm, that might be so.

Lord Deas.—Or equip by arming.

Lord Advocate.—But the Statute cannot be so read, and it would not be reasonable so to read it, because what was intended to be prevented was allowing belligerents to make use of the building-yards of this neutral country for the purpose of equipping war-ships already built. If the equipment has not gone the length of arming, but the intention is manifest and obvious, is that not within the spirit of the section? If your Lordships were to hold that nothing short of arming would be an offence under the Statute, there might be a great deal to say; but the Statute gives no colour to that. You must take the words as you find them in the Statute. The words used are equip, furnish, fit out, or arm. Surely I am entitled to say that each of those things is an offence under the Statute, if proved, and that it is not necessary that all the words shall be used if they don't mean the same thing. If it was meant equip by arming, I say that the Statute cannot bear that interpretation on any reasonable reading of it; but if that were the state of it, the question would be, what do you mean by arming? I need not consider that, because I have not alleged arming. If your Lordships are prepared to hold that it is no offence under the Statute, if the equipment has not reached the point of arming, that is a different matter altogether.

Lord President.—They said that the first three things, viz., equip, furnish, and fit out, are applicable to store-ships or transports, and that the last thing prohibited, viz. arming, is applicable to cruisers.

Lord Advocate.—There is ingenuity in that, but there is no foundation for it in the Statute. It is clear that a transport or store-ship might not require armament, but it would require equipment. On the other hand, is there anything in the Statute leading you to suppose that it is to be read *applicando singula singulis?* I see nothing of that kind. How inconsistent that notion is with the idea that it all means war,—that it is equipment by arming. It cannot be equipping and furnishing and fitting out by arming, if 'equipping, furnishing, and fitting out' relate to the transport, and 'arming' to the other vessel.

Lord President.—Mr. Cook put it in another way. He said to equip means to equip fully, and he says you cannot equip fully a cruiser without arming her, and you have purposely abstained from charging arming, because there was no arming.

Lord Advocate.—My answer to that would be that the attempt is sufficient. If equip means full equipment, I may prove full equipment, and that will satisfy the counts of my Information.

Lord President.—He assumed that you were not going to prove arming, from your not having charged it.

Lord Advocate.—He must read the Statute and the Information for himself. I put him on one or other of the horns of a dilemma. If equipment in the Statute means equipment to the point of arming, I have alleged it.

Lord President.—I think this dilemma is like most others, where the parties are tossed from horn to horn by each other.

Lord Advocate.—I don't at present see that I am fixed on either horn. On the contrary, I think the meaning of the Statute is plain, and that equipping and furnishing and fitting-out may be short of arming. That is the way I read it; but on the matter of relevancy, where your Lordships have nothing to do with the facts, it is not in my learned friend's mouth first to say that equipment means arming, and second, to say you have not alleged arming against me.

Lord President.—In the Alexandra case, what became of that hydra-headed count, the 98th.

Mr. Gordon.—The 97th and 98th counts were abandoned by the Attorney-General.

Lord Deas.—The defenders also found on the preamble in this part of their argument, because they say the word is 'and' armed, not 'or' armed.

Lord Advocate.—I don't think that, in the construction of a Statute, it is sound to refer to the preamble, but I don't think it would have made the slightest difference if it had been 'and' armed in the clause.

Lord Deas.—Do you hold that any sort of equipment of a ship would do, provided you can prove clearly what was the intent of the party.

Lord Advocate.—I have already said that that cannot arise on the relevancy. It is a question which may, though I don't think that it will, in this case, come to be a serious one, whether equipment, with the clear intent prohibited in the Statute, will be sufficient to bring a party under it, though the equipment have no warlike character in it. That question may arise, but I decline to argue it now, because we don't know what may be proved under the word 'equip;' and it never will arise, if we prove not merely a peaceful equipment, such as a merchant-ship may have, but warlike equipment, such as a merchant-ship would not have.

Lord Deas.—It is very difficult to apply one's mind to the construction of the Statute, without considering that.

Lord Advocate.—It is not now in question as to peaceful equipment with warlike intent. Your Lordships cannot decide that at this stage, because it is not here, and may never be in this case at all. I may prove the clearest warlike equipment; I may prove that this vessel was built from the beginning as a war-vessel, and that all her fittings had a warlike character; and therefore what is the use now of going into the question suggested by your Lordship.

Lord President.—You undertake to prove all the equipping that the Statute requires.

Lord Advocate.—Yes.

Lord Deas.—But have you enough on the face of your Information to show that it is relevant?

Lord Advocate.—Surely if I allege the statutory offence, it is relevant.

Lord Deas.—But the question they are contesting is whether you have alleged the statutory offence.

Lord Advocate.—In the view your Lordship is now taking, I have alleged equipment, and they don't deny that to be a statutory offence, if I have alleged the intent. But putting aside their argument, that it must be intent to use it themselves, how can they deny that it is sufficient under the Statute? They cannot say it is not sufficient, because a peaceful equipment would not do. I have not alleged peaceful equipment.

Lord Ardmillan.—I suppose the Lord Advocate is not bound to add any quality to the equipment he charges, unless that quality be in the Statute?

Lord Advocate.—The presumption is, that I will prove up to the statutory limit.

Lord Ardmillan.—That leaves it of course open to contend that the equipment under the Statute is not peaceful.

Lord President.—What is the present state of the Alexandra case? I understand it is trying to find its way to the House of Lords, but that it has not got there.

Lord Advocate.—I believe so.

Lord President.—Could we not open a shorter way, if the great object is to get the judgment of the House of Lords ?

Lord Advocate.—I think it is very undesirable on both sides to do that, because it is quite plain that the loss necessarily incurred in a proceeding of this kind will be greater the longer the delay that takes place. I think, therefore, that we should have a proof of the facts in the first instance, and there are obvious reasons why that course should be taken.

Lord President.—The defenders say they don't value that inconvenience much.

Mr. Gordon.—The Government is good security for damages!

Lord President.—Then it is their interest to get on.

Avizandum.

Friday, 18*th March* 1864.

Lord President.—This Reclaiming Note brings under review an Interlocutor pronounced by Lord Ormidale, sitting as Lord Ordinary in Exchequer Causes, under the powers conferred by the Act 19 and 20 Vict., chap. 56. The proceedings originated in an Information of seizure of a ship or vessel called the 'Pampero.' That Information is laid on the Act 59 Geo. III., cap. 69, commonly called the Foreign Enlistment Act. It is directed against John Fleming and certain other persons. It contains ninety-eight counts, in which the defenders are charged, or are intended to be charged, with contraventions of the seventh section of the Statute. The first count sets forth that certain persons, to wit, John Fleming and others, on a certain occasion stated, 'without any leave or 'licence of Her Majesty, for that purpose first had and obtained, did 'equip the said ship or vessel with intent and in order that such 'ship or vessel should be employed in the service of certain foreign 'States styling themselves the Confederate States of America, with 'intent to cruise and commit hostilities against a certain foreign 'State with which Her Majesty was not then at war, to wit, the 'Republic of the United States of America, contrary to the form of 'the Statute in such case made and provided, whereby and by force 'of the Statute in that case made and provided, the said ship or 'vessel, together with the said tackle, apparel, and furniture, became 'and was forfeited.' Other seventy-one counts are substantially the same as the first, only substituting for the word 'equip' the words 'furnish' or 'fit out' or 'attempt to equip,' &c.

The 3d count sets forth that the defenders 'did equip the said 'ship or vessel with intent to cruise and commit hostilities against 'a certain foreign state,' &c. Twenty-three other counts are substantially the same as the 3d, only varying the expression from 'equip' to 'furnish' and 'fit out.'

The 97th count sets forth that the defenders 'did attempt to fit 'out the said ship or vessel with intent and in order that such ship 'or vessel should be employed in the service, &c., as a transport or 'storeship against a certain foreign state,' &c. The only other count is the 98th, which the Solicitor-General told us was of no use. It appears to be a compound of the essence of all the preceding counts, irrespective of concord or consistency.

Fleming and Others, against whom the Information is directed, have claimed the vessel as owners. Certain other parties, viz., Messrs. J. & G. Thomson of Glasgow, the builders of the vessel, have also claimed as for a right of lien or retention over the vessel for a sum of £16,000 due to them as builders. The pleas put in by the owners are to the effect—*1st*, That the vessel had not become forfeited for the several supposed causes in the Information mentioned, or for any of them, as by the Information charged; *2d*, That each and all of the counts in the Information are bad in law; *3d*, That each and all of the counts are unfounded in fact. The pleas put in by the builders are to the same effect as the pleas for the owners. A motion in the cause having been made before the Lord Ordinary in Exchequer Causes, an argument took place as to the relevancy of the Information. The defenders contended that the greater number of the counts were irrelevant, and could not be sent to trial. The substance of the objection was that the matters alleged on the face of the Information as regards the greater number of the counts were not contraventions of the Statute according to the true reading and construction of it, and that the defenders were not bound to go to trial upon allegations which, even if proved, would not be contraventions of the Statute or grounds of forfeiture. The Lord Ordinary did not think it necessary or expedient to decide before trial the questions of law and relevancy so raised by the defenders, and he pronounced an interlocutor by which he appoints Tuesday the 5th April for trying the issues in said Information. That judgment has been brought under review by the present reclaiming note, in which the defenders pray your Lordships to recal the interlocutor of the Lord Ordinary and to dismiss the Information.

In the very full and able argument with which we were favoured from the bar, it was contended, on the part of the defenders, that the case involved questions of law and relevancy which ought to be disposed of at this stage, and which, if now decided in their favour, would cast the greater number of the many counts in this voluminous Information. No objection on the part of the Crown was stated to the competency of the reclaiming note, or to the competency of deciding at this stage the questions of law and relevancy raised by the defenders, or at least some of those questions; but it was contended that the more convenient and expedient course would be to abstain from deciding any of these questions at this stage, and to leave them to be raised by bill of exceptions in the course of the trial, or by motion in arrest of judgment.

The Court has come to the conclusion that some of the questions raised by the defenders ought to be decided at this stage. It is unnecessary to go at large into the reasons which have influenced the Court in coming to that conclusion. The considerations which in ordinary cases generally influence the Court in determining whether questions of law or relevancy raised before trial ought to be then decided, or ought to be left for a later stage, when a decision may be facilitated or perhaps obviated by the light reflected from the evidence, were explained in the cases of Galloway *v.* Grant, June 20, 1857, 19 D., and Guild *v.* Orr Ewing, January 16, 1858, 20 D. But it is obvious that much must depend on the character of the case, and on the nature and effect of the questions raised. Here the case is of a penal character—an alleged contravention of a Statute, the consequences of such contravention being punishment by fine and imprisonment, and forfeiture of valuable property. The nature of some of the questions raised is as to whether the allegations in the Information are really allegations of any contravention whatever of the Statute. The effect of a decision favourable to the defenders on these questions would be to cast those counts of the Information to which the objection might be found to apply. The defenders would thereby be relieved from the burden of a trial as regards these counts. It is most consistent with our practice in prosecutions for punishment that such questions should be disposed of before going to trial; and although this prosecution is for the forfeiture only, and not for the fine and imprisonment, which the Statute attaches to the offence, there does not appear to be any sufficient reason why as regards this matter of procedure the same course should not be followed, which undoubtedly would have been followed if a prosecution founded on the same facts had had for its object fine and imprisonment, and not merely forfeiture. But other considerations also have weighed with the Court in coming to the conclusion that some of these questions should be disposed of by decision at this stage. There are points involved in them affecting the interpretation of the Statute 59 Geo. III. cap. 69, which may be of great importance to the parties as well as of general importance to the law, and it would be inexpedient to deal with this case in such a way as to expose parties to the risk of having these questions stifled by some miscarriage when that risk might be avoided by a decision on them now. We cannot disguise from ourselves that there may be risk of such mishap if the case is sent to trial without disposing of any of the questions that have been raised. This is an Exchequer cause, and our jurisdiction in regard to it is derived from the Statute 19 and 20 Vict. cap. 56. That Statute contains only general directions as to the course of procedure to be followed in Exchequer causes originating by information. It is almost silent as to the appropriate remedies for supposed wrongs or injustice done in the course of a trial. It gives a power to make regulations, but that power has not yet been exercised. In these circumstances, it might be perilous to trust to the efficacy of those remedies with which we are familiar in causes of a different kind, and in regard to which our jurisdiction is derived from a different source. That the remedies would not be in all respects the same is obvious, and was assumed, or rather maintained, on the part of the Crown when relying on the remedy that might be afforded by motion in arrest of judgment. The sufficiency or certainty of that remedy was not, however, made out to our satisfaction. But there is no doubt that a decision pronounced at this stage may be made the subject of appeal either now or at the end of the cause, and so may be carried to the Court of last resort.

Having stated thus generally the grounds on which the Court has come to the conclusion that some of the questions raised by the defenders should now be disposed of by decision, I shall next state very briefly the points which, in my opinion, ought to be so disposed of. They are proper objections to the relevancy of certain counts of the Information as not alleging any matters, that, if proved, would amount to a contravention of the Statute. The first of these objections was directed against the 1st count and seventy-one other counts. It was contended for the defenders that the allegation set forth in the 1st count (which may be regarded as a specimen of the other seventy-one), was not one of the things against which the Statute was directed. This objection was founded upon the manner in which in that 1st count, and in the others similar to it, the intent was set forth in reference to the parties concerned, and it came in substance to this, that in the Information the parties were not charged with having had the intent which the Statute requires they should have, in order to constitute a contravention of it. The words of the Statute are, that if 'any person 'shall, without the leave of His Majesty first had and obtained 'as aforesaid, equip, furnish, fit out, or arm, or attempt or 'endeavour to equip, furnish, fit out, or arm, or procure to 'be equipped, furnished, fitted out, or armed, or shall knowingly 'aid, assist, or be concerned in the equipping, furnishing, fitting 'out, or arming of any ship or vessel, with intent or in order that 'such ship or vessel shall be employed in the service of any foreign 'prince,' &c., 'as a transport or store-ship, or with intent to cruise 'or commit hostilities against any prince, state, or potentate, or 'against the subjects or citizens of any prince,' &c., certain consequences shall follow. Now the 1st count in the Information does not set forth that the defenders or any of them acted with the intent to cruise or commit hostilities; and it was contended on the part of the defenders, that as regards a vessel that is to cruise or commit hostilities, the Statute requires that the intent to cruise or commit hostilities should be an intent on the part of those who are charged with the offence—who are alleged to have equipped and fitted out the vessel. This question has undergone a great deal of discussion, both historical and critical. Many nice criticisms upon the terms of the Statute, and ingenious suggestions as to various modes of reading it have been made both here and elsewhere. The 7th section in particular has been subjected to every possible test and trial, by punctuation, deletion, insertion, transposition—I believe that no clause ever was more thoroughly dissected and discussed. It seems to be generally agreed that the dubiety (for where there is so much difference of opinion among learned persons, I cannot say there is not dubiety) is owing to the introduction into the Statute of the words 'as a transport or 'store-ship, or with intent;' and it has been suggested, and I believe the suggestion has been considered a correct one, that these words were inserted in committee, after the bill had been introduced without such words, and that thereby the continuity of the clause as originally framed had been disturbed, and the clause in a manner dislocated. That may be a correct account of the manner in which the difficulty has been created, but it does not assist us in the solution of it. The words are there, and we must read the Act as we find it. I do not propose now to occupy time in canvassing the relative merits of the several criticisms that have been made upon it, I merely refer to them, and confine myself to saying that in my opinion the reading of the Statute contended for by the defenders is not a correct reading. It appears to me that the Statute is directed against the equipping, furnishing, and fitting out of a ship, with intent or in order that it shall be employed in the service of a foreign state with intent to cruise or commit hostilities, whether the persons engaged in such employment be the equippers or persons under their control, or others in the service of a foreign state. This, in my opinion, is the fair and reasonable construction. Any other reading of the Statute would imply, that the Legislature was much more careful in its prevention of fitting out store-ships than in its prevention of fitting out vessels to commit hostilities. On this part of the case I adopt the reading contended for by the Crown as being in my opinion the fair and reasonable reading, as well as the legitimate reading of the Statute. I therefore think that the objections founded on the construction contended for by the defenders, and directed against the 1st and other seventy-one counts, ought not to be sustained.

The second objection was directed against all the counts in the Information, except the 97th and 98th. That objection was of this nature, that the Information does not contain any allegation that the vessel was armed or was intended to be armed. In support of this objection it was said, in the first place, that the words 'equip, 'fit out, and furnish' were not meant to apply to a cruiser or vessel to commit hostilities; that, according to the true reading of the Statute, these words were meant to apply to the case of a transport or store-ship, and that the word 'arm' was meant to apply to the case of a cruiser, or vessel to commit hostilities, upon the principle of the rule *applicando singula singulis*. I think that is a very strained interpretation, and I cannot adopt it.

Another view contended for by the defenders in support of this objection was, that in the case of a vessel intended to cruise or commit hostilities, arming to a greater or less extent is necessary, and that being so, the word 'arm' would have been introduced *in terminis* into the allegation if it had been intended to prove arming; but that word not having been introduced, it must be presumed that it is not intended to prove arming; and there being no intention to prove arming, the Information must be held to imply that there was no arming, or intent to arm, and consequently is defective in allegation. I cannot adopt that view. I think that the words 'equip, furnish, and fit out' are sufficient, and that they would cover a case of arming; whether a greater or smaller amount of arming. I think that to fit out a cruiser, or to fit out a privateer, are expressions that would cover the case of fitting her out in an armed state; so also of the word 'equip.' The words in the Information are, in my opinion, sufficient to cover a case of arming, and I cannot at this stage assume that arming or intent to arm will not be proved if that is necessary. I am therefore for repelling that objection also. I am thus of opinion that both of the objections should be repelled, and that this should be done by express decision, which may be made the subject of appeal at a future stage.

In the course of the discussion other questions were raised by the defenders as to the construction of the Statute—questions of great importance; and it is not improbable that the case may eventually depend on the solution that may be given of these questions, or some of them. But they are not *hujus loci;* they are not objections to the relevancy of the Information, and whatever might be the opinion of the Court in regard to them, they could not at this stage be so dealt with as to have the effect of casting or excluding any one of the counts in the Information. It may depend on the nature of the evidence whether these questions, or any of them, will ever arise for decision. If the course of the evidence shall be such as to raise them, the ruling or direction of the Judge in regard to them may be made the subject of exception. But I am not disposed to deal with them prospectively, either by decision, if that were permissible, or even by the expression of opinion. In my judgment, it is not necessary, and would be inexpedient to do so. The questions I allude to are such questions as the progress that must be made in order to bring the vessel within the operation of the Statute, the condition in which she must be before she can be held to be equipped as a cruiser, and involving in that also what must have been the condition in which she was intended to be put by the parties aiding in or attempting to fit her out, because all that goes to the intent to accomplish what the Statute was intended to prevent. All these are questions which I think we cannot deal with practically at present, and I purposely abstain from indicating any opinion on conjectural cases. It would be in vain to endeavour to define or enumerate the particulars which would suffice to bring a vessel within the operation of the Statute, or the cases which would not be within the operation of the Statute. When the actual case is presented for the consideration of the Court and the Jury, it may not be difficult to say whether that particular case comes within the operation of the Statute; but to attempt to define beforehand all the cases that would be within the operation of the Statute, and those that would fall short of the operation of the Statute, and leave no case unprovided for, would be a task which, I think, we ought not to undertake. It would settle nothing decisively, and it might hamper the Judge who is to try the case in regard to the direction he should give when the facts are disclosed. What I would suggest is, that the two objections I have alluded to, the one as to the intent, and the other as to the omission of the word arming, should now be repelled by decision, and that the case should go to trial with these findings, which the party against whom they are pronounced may appeal afterwards, if they think it expedient to do so. But I think that at this stage we cannot decide, and ought not to prejudge any other matter.

Lord Currichill.—The Information, under which this case comes before us, sets forth, that, on 10th December last, the defenders, without Her Majesty's license, did at Glasgow perform certain operations, with certain intents, on a ship or vessel called the 'Pampero,' and that these proceedings were in contravention of the 7th section of the Statute 59 Geo. III. c. 69 (commonly called the Foreign Enlistment Act), and that in consequence the ship, with her tackle, apparel, and furniture, has been forfeited. The acts, and the intents, so charged against the defenders are set forth in a great variety of forms in 98 counts. The defenders, besides denying these allegations, maintain that they are not matters which are prohibited by the Act. To enable us to decide the question thus raised, we must ascertain what is the true import of these allegations in the Information? And then we must inquire whether, or how far, such matter fall under the enactments in the Statute?

The general import of the counts, when stripped of the technical verbiage in which they are clothed, is, that at Glasgow, on 10th December 1863, the defenders did, in contravention of the Statute, equip (or did one or other of various things set forth as equivalent to or in reference to equipping) the ship in question, with an intent, and in order, that she should be employed as therein set forth against the Republic of the United States of America, with which this country was not at war. And, in the first place, *what are the acts* which are set forth in the Information?

The *act*, charged in the first count, is that the defenders did *equip* the ship with the intent therein set forth. In the other counts the act is described by other denominations,—such as, 'did 'fit out,' 'did attempt and endeavour to equip,' 'did attempt and 'endeavour to furnish,' 'did procure to be equipped,' &c. But it is not necessary, at the present stage of the proceedings, to consider the meaning and effect of these varieties in the description of the act; because all and each of them appear to be specially prohibited by the Statute. But all and each of these descriptions of the act are maintained by the defenders to be insufficient and irrelevant, because *arming* is not also set forth as part of that description. We shall therefore have to consider whether or not it is essential that the Statutory offence be described in the Information as consisting of *arming* in addition to equipping? This objection applies to all (excepting perhaps the last two) of the 98 counts.

The *intents*, again, with which the defenders are accused of committing these acts, are different in different counts. In 72 of them the defenders are alleged to have committed these acts, 'with intent 'and in order that the ship or vessel should be employed in *the 'service of certain foreign states styling themselves the Confederate 'States of America*, with intent to cruise and commit hostilities' against the Republic of the United States of America. The phraseology of this charge requires attention. It sets forth two intents of two different parties. The first is the intent of the defenders themselves in equipping the ship; and the intent imputed to them is, that she was to be employed in the service of the Confederate States; so that if the intent of the defenders had been that the ship should be employed in the service, not of these States, but of themselves, or of any other private individuals, that would have been a different offence from what is thus charged. The other intent set forth in these counts, is that of the Confederate States; and what they are said to have intended is that the service in which they were to employ the ship should be in cruising and committing hostilities against the Federal States. Thus the meaning of this charge is, that the employers of the ship in that service was to be the Confederate States,—or in other words, that it was not as a private ship in the service of the defenders themselves or of other private individuals, but as a *public ship* of the Confederate States, she was intended both by the defenders, and by these States, to be so employed.

The relevancy of all the 72 counts which are so charged is objected to by the defenders, on the ground that, as they maintain, what the Statute forbids is only the equipping of ships with the intent of their being employed *by the equippers themselves* in cruising and committing hostilities against a state with which this country is not at war. And in order to judge of this objection, we shall have to inquire whether or not that is the sound construction of the Statute?

The Public Prosecutor himself raises this question, inasmuch as 24 of the counts of the Information are charged on the footing of this being the true reading of the enactment. Thus the 3d count charges the defenders themselves with equipping the ship, at the time and place before specified, '*with intent to cruise and commit hostilities against a certain foreign state,*' viz., the Federal States, with which Her Majesty was not at war. And in other 23 of the counts the same charge is repeated, with variations similar to those I have already noticed. The difference between these 24 charges and the other 72 charges already noticed, consists in *the different services* in which the ship is said to have been intended to be employed. In the first set, as already mentioned, the intention charged is, that she was to be employed as a public ship in *the service of the Confederate States*, and in cruising and committing hostilities against the Federal States. In the latter set the intention charged is, that she should be employed *by the defenders themselves, individually*, in cruising and committing hostilities against the Federal States,—or in other words, that she was to be employed, not as a public ship, but as a privateer. And the defenders, while they deny that allegation in point of fact, do not dispute that their equipping of the ship with such an intent would be the statutory offence.

In addition to the 96 counts to which I have adverted, the Information contains other two counts. By the 97th the defenders are charged with *fitting out* the ship with intent and in order that she should be employed 'in the service of diverse and very many persons exercising the powers of government over part of a certain foreign people, to wit, part of the people of the United States of America, *as a transport or store-ship*,' against the Republic of the United States. The defenders, as I understand their argument, deny the truth, but don't dispute the relevancy of that count.

By the 98th, and the last, count the defenders are charged with equipping, fitting out, and furnishing the ship, or attempting, &c., to do so, with intent and in order that she should be employed in the service of the Confederate States as a transport or store-ship, and with intent to cruise and commit hostilities against the Federal States. I do not understand this accumulation of the inconsistent alternatives in the other counts, and it was stated that it was not meant to be insisted in.

Thus the questions of relevancy, which alone we are called upon to decide at present, are only, *first*, whether or not the *act* which is charged against the defenders in each of the first 96 counts of the Information is such an act as is prohibited by the Statute in respect that it is not expressly described in the Information as including *arming?* and *secondly*, whether it is that *intent* which is imputed to them in the 72 counts first mentioned (that the ship should be employed in the service of the Confederate States or as a public one), or that other intent which is imputed to them in the other 24 counts (that she should be employed by themselves as a privateer), which is prohibited by the Statute? The solution of these questions depends upon the meaning of the 7th section of the Foreign Enlistment Act; and therefore I now proceed to inquire what is the true interpretation of that enactment, so far as it bears upon these questions.

This inquiry is not free from difficulty, because that enactment appears to me to be so constructed as to be capable of either of the disputed readings; and the rules of grammar are not alone sufficient for solving the questions. It therefore becomes necessary to inquire which of these readings of the ambiguous expressions is most conformable to the objects of the Legislature in passing the Act?

Its general object is to facilitate the Government of the country in maintaining its neutrality between foreign states, which are at peace with us, but at war with each other. According to one established international law, neutrals are not entitled to allow their ports to be used by either of two belligerents, with whom the neutrals are not also at war, as stations for fitting out armaments to commit hostilities upon the other. But according to another of these laws it is lawful for neutrals to allow vessels to be *built*, and also to be equipped, and even armed as ships of war in their ports, provided these operations are merely trading or commercial speculations, and the ships are merely constructed as articles for sale in the market to any parties who may choose to become purchasers, even although these purchasers should be the belligerents, or either of them. Both of these rules are universally recognised in the law of nations. But there is plainly much risk of the latter of these rules being abused by being made a pretext for violating the former,—by the belligerents under the disguise of merely *building* ships of war at neutral ports, or of *buying* them there ready built and armed,—getting them there also fitted out and sent to sea as armaments *against each other*, and of thus contriving to make the neutral ports serve the purpose of arsenals for carrying on such hostilities. Such dishonest pretexts might be resorted to, not only by the belligerent States themselves, but likewise by the owners of privateers, to whom the governments of the belligerents, or either of them, might issue letters of marque; and although the barbarous system of privateering has, in a great measure, if not entirely, been abolished from the public law of Europe by the declaration of the Congress of Paris in 1856, yet, at the era of the Foreign Enlistment Act, privateering was an institution in general observance, and in conformity with the law of nations. And as the United States of America did not think it consistent with their position to accede to the Declaration of Paris, privateering still remains one of their institutions; and now both the Northern and the Southern States, since they have unfortunately come into the position of being belligerents, may lawfully commission privateers against each other.

It is matter of history, that in the early part of the present century, when the general revolt of the Spanish colonies in South America took place, and they came to be at war with the mother country, and were recognised as belligerents, other maritime states, and particularly Britain and her Colonies, and the United States of America, experienced difficulties in maintaining their neutrality in consequence of disingenuous practices, such as I have referred to. This led the Legislatures in both countries to strengthen the hands of their respective Governments by passing their Acts known as the Foreign Enlistment Acts. The American Congress led the way; its Act, which was passed in 1818, having among other things enacted, that if any person within the limits of the States should *fit out and arm* any ship, with intent that she should be employed in the service of any foreign state, or of any colony, district, or people, to cruise or commit hostilities against the subjects, citizens, or property of any foreign prince or state with which the United States are at peace, such person should be guilty of a misdemeanour, and the ship should be forfeited, as therein set forth. That Act empowered the Executive Government of the United States to protect its ports from being made stations where such armaments might be fitted out by, or for, one belligerent state against another with which they were at peace. That remedy, important as it was, did not reach to the full extent of the evil. In particular, it did not extend either to vessels which might be so fitted out in American ports, with the intent of being employed as transports or store-ships in the service of one belligerent against another. Nor did it extend to privateers which might be fitted out under letters of marque issued by the Governments of either of the belligerents, with the intent of being employed only in the service of the owners, and for their own emolument, against the other belligerent. Whether or not these omissions were intentional, does not appear.

In the following year, 1819, the British Foreign Enlistment Act was passed; and some of its enactments, and even some of the phraseology in which these are expressed, are the same as those in the American Act. But in other respects, the phraseology and the enactments are different. I mention this for two reasons. One is, that these differences between the two Acts render some judgments, which have been pronounced in American Courts, of much less service to us than they would have been, if there had not been such differences between the Acts. The other is, that when, in the British Act, the phraseology which had been used in the American Act is changed, there is fair ground for inferring that the change was made *purposely*, and that the substituted language is to be used in its strictly literal meaning. The enactment, in the 7th section of the British Act (which differs in some important respects from the corresponding section of the American Act), is, 'that if any person within any part of the United Kingdom, or in 'any part of His Majesty's dominions beyond the seas, shall, without 'the leave and licence of his Majesty for that purpose first had and 'obtained as aforesaid, equip, furnish, fit out, or arm' any ship or vessel, or attempt, &c., to do so, 'with intent or in order that such 'ship or vessel shall be employed in the service of any foreign 'prince, state, &c., as a transport or store-ship, or with intent to 'cruise or commit hostilities against any prince, state, &c., with 'whom His Majesty shall not then be at war,' such person shall be deemed guilty of a misdemeanour, and be liable to be fined and imprisoned, and the ship shall be forfeited. And now we come to the question whether or not *those acts* and *those intents* with which the defenders are charged in the first 96 counts of the Information, are the acts and the intents described in this enactment?

The Statute describes *the act* which constitutes the offence as equipping, &c., *or arming* with the intent therein mentioned. But the act imputed to the defenders in the indictment is described as equipping the ship, without the word *arming* being added to that description; and is the act so described the statutory offence? In the American Statute, the act is described by the words 'fit out '*and* arm.' But in the British Statute the phraseology is changed, the description being 'equip, furnish, fit out, *or* arm.' As the word '*or*' thus appears to have been substituted purposely for '*and*,' there is reason to infer that the Legislature truly did not intend that '*or*' should be here used conjunctively, and that it should be expressly charged in addition to equipping. Nor perhaps could it reasonably be held that the word 'or' was used as describing *arming* as an *alternative* act, so that the offence might consist in arming a ship without also equipping, fitting out, and furnishing her. But even if that were its meaning, then the want of the word *arming* in the indictment would have no effect; because in that case it would be sufficient that the other alternative of equipping is charged in this Information. It appears to me, however, that all the words *equip*, *furnish*, *fit out*, *or arm*, are used in the Statute as synonymous with or as exegetical of each other; so that *equip* is used with such a meaning as is conformable with these expletives. Moreover, 'equip' is to be read in such a sense as will harmonize with the *intents* set forth in the context; that is to say, the equipment referred to in the Statute is to be of such a kind, as well as to such an extent, as would render the ship fit for a transport or store-ship, or for cruising to commit hostilities, according to the purpose for which she should be intended. If she had been intended to be used only as a transport or store-ship, and had been fully equipped, without being armed, so as to serve that purpose, I think the act intended to be prohibited would have been fully and correctly described by the expression *equipping*, without adding the words '*and arming*.' There are several cases in which they might have been intended even to commit hostilities, without being armed in the usual meaning of that expression. For example, a fire-ship, or a ram, or a tender of a ship of war, might be in that predicament. And I think that, in such cases, the statutory offence might be committed without there being any intention to arm such vessel otherways. I am, therefore, of opinion that the objection, that *arming* is not expressly added to *equipping*, in describing the offence in the first 96 counts of the indictment, is not well founded.

The next question then is whether *the intent*, which is imputed to the defenders in 72 of these counts, namely,—the intent that it was in *the service of the Confederate States* the ship should be employed to cruise and commit hostilities against the Republic of the United States,—is such an intent as is struck at by this enactment? Or whether the statutory intent is that which is imputed to the defenders in other 24 counts, namely,—the intent that they themselves should cruise and commit hostilities against that Republic? The enactment appears to me to admit of either of these two readings, and therefore we must endeavour to ascertain which of them is in conformity with what the Legislature intended. The ambiguity arises from the Legislature having used the expression '*with intent*' in two places in the same sentence, without making it clear whether it was to the intent of the same or of different parties it referred in the two places. The sentence contains *some alternative*, to the words 'or with intent to cruise or commit hostilities;' and the question is, what does that alternative consist of? According to the one reading the alternative would be that the offence would be committed by persons who should equip, &c., a ship *either with the intent* that she should be employed in the service of a foreign state, and as a transport or store-ship, against any other foreign state, &c., with which this country is not at war, *or with the intent* that such persons should themselves cruise or commit hostilities against such foreign state. If so read, the words 'with intent' would be applied in both alternatives to the same parties, viz., the equippers. According to the other reading, the alternative would be that the offence would be committed by such persons if they should equip, &c., the ship with the intent that she should be employed in the service of a foreign state, &c., either as a transport or store-ship, or to cruise or commit hostilities against such a friendly belligerent. According to that reading the words 'with intent' would be applied in the former part of the sentence to *the equippers*, and in the latter part to the *state* in whose service she is intended to be employed.

I have felt considerable difficulty in adopting the latter of these readings. In the first place, when the same expression is twice used in the same sentence, it is presumable that it is used as having the same meaning in both places, where there is nothing in the sentence to indicate the contrary. Nor is it easy to see why the expression '*with intent*' was repeated in this enactment, if the meaning of the Legislature was merely to state that the offence would be committed by the vessel being employed in the service of a foreign state in either of two ways,—either as a transport or store-ship, or as a cruiser to commit hostilities. That meaning would be expressed as well without the use of the words 'with intent' being prefixed to the latter alternative. Indeed in that case these words tend to obscure the meaning; because what they require the equippers to intend is,—not that the foreign state in whose service the ship is to be employed shall cruise and commit hostilities,—but only that they shall have an *intent* on their part to do so; and I do not very clearly understand how an offence can consist in one party having *an intent* that some other party *should have an intent*, that an article in his service should be employed for some purpose. But my chief difficulty in adopting this reading is,—not that it is exposed to such literary criticism,—but that it leads to a result which would render the Statute insufficient to a great extent to effect the avowed object for which it was passed. What I mean is that I do not see how it would prevent owners of ships, having letters of marque from either of two belligerents, from fitting them out as privateers in British ports, and putting them to sea from thence to cruise and commit hostilites against the other belligerents. It must always be kept in mind in construing this Statute, that it was passed in the early part of the present century, when privateering was recognised as a lawful institution among belligerents according to the law of nations; that it was then resorted to extensively by some of the belligerents in the wars between Spain and her revolted provinces in South America; and that such privateers, if they were to be left at liberty, notwithstanding the Statute, to use the ports belonging to the British Crown at home and abroad for fitting out armed cruisers to commit hostilities on countries at peace with this country, the object of providing to Government the means of preserving its neutrality by such proceedings would have been but very inadequately attained. And although the American Act of the preceding year left matters in that state in America; yet, as the British Act expressly provided to our Government against another defect which was in the American one,—by preventing transports or store-ships from so being fitted out with such intent from our ports,—it might be reasonable to construe that Act as likewise prohibiting privateers from being fitted out and despatched from these ports as cruisers to commit hostilities against friendly belligerents, since that Act is fairly susceptible of such a reading, as appears to me to be the case.

For these reasons, I have experienced considerable difficulty in rejecting that reading of this enactment. And yet I feel myself compelled to do so; because, according to that reading, the risks to which the neutrality of the country would have continued to be exposed, would have been still more direct and far more formidable. In that case, either or both of foreign belligerent states themselves would have continued to be at liberty to come to our ports at home or in our colonies, and there to have fully equipped public ships of war, and to have despatched them from thence to cruise and commit hostilities against foreign states at peace with this country. The Act, according to that reading, while it would enable our Government both to prevent the owners of privateers to whom letters of marque are granted by one of the belligerent states, from equipping, &c., their ships in our ports to cruise and commit hostilities against the other,—and also to prevent either belligerent state itself from so equipping, &c., ships in our ports from being employed as transports or store-ships merely in its own public service against the other,—would nevertheless leave Government as powerless as ever to prevent either belligerent state itself from availing itself of our ports as arsenals from which to despatch armed fleets to cruise and commit hostilities against the other. I cannot impute to the Legislature a meaning so extravagant and so irreconcilable with the object of the Statute; and therefore I feel myself compelled to reject that construction of the enactment, and to hold that the intent imputed to the defender in the 72 counts of the Information is the statutory intent.

I am confirmed in this construction of the 7th section of the Act by the enactment in the 8th section, which forbids, under heavy penalties, any persons from *increasing or augmenting the warlike force* of any ship of war, or cruiser, or other armed vessel of any foreign state, in any of the ways therein mentioned, in any of the British dominions. And, consistently with this prohibition, in the Act against the warlike force of public ships of foreign states being increased to any extent whatever in ports belonging to Britain, I cannot construe that other part of the same Act,—which prohibits the *original equipping*, with such warlike force, ships which are intended to be employed in the service of such states,—as not also applicable to the public ships of such states. It appears to me that, in 1819, our Legislature, in this respect, left our Government in the same predicament as that in which, in 1818, the executive of the American Government was left by the Congress of that country.

I therefore think that the objection stated by the defenders to 72 counts of the Information, on the ground that *the intent* therein charged is not the statutory intent, ought to be repelled.

It also follows that, in my opinion, the other 24 counts ought not to be sustained; because the intent therein charged, namely, the intent that *the defenders* did equip, &c., the ship, with intent to cruise and commit hostilities, is not the statutory intent. According to my reading of the *Information*, it means, by these counts, to charge the defenders with an intent to employ the ship as a privateer; and according to my reading of *the Statute*, it does not forbid such an employment of her.

In the argument addressed to us by the parties, and chiefly by the defenders, there was a good deal of discussion as to what proceedings would amount to equipping in the meaning of the Information and of the Statute. I purposely abstain from indicating any opinion whatever on these points. These are matters which will arise on the trial, and will be dealt with by the Jury under the direction of the presiding Judge; and should any errors be committed as to such matters, I have no doubt that the usual remedies will be available to either party. I would probably have been of opinion, that even the question of relevancy, upon which the defenders have pressed for our judgment, should also have been reserved for the trial, if I had been quite certain that the rights of the parties to take such questions ultimately by appeal to the House of Lords would have remained entire. But as, according to the practice of Scotland, it is in the discretion of the Court to decide such questions of relevancy before trial; and, as in consequence of the mixture of English and Scottish rules of procedure in Exchequer cases in this Court, serious doubts, to which your Lordship has alluded, suggest themselves,—whether or not the parties might not ultimately be deprived of the privilege of appealing these questions of relevancy, I think that, in the exercise of a sound discretion, we should now pronounce a judgment, which will ultimately be appealable, on these questions of relevancy. And, accordingly, I have stated what, in my opinion, that judgment ought to be.

Lord Deas.—If I felt unusually impressed with the importance of this case, the first thing I should do would be to endeavour to free my mind from that disturbing element. Statutes are best construed, and law is best decided, when the Judge feels no greater anxiety than that which is inherent in every properly constituted judicial mind,—to decide the law rightly, whatever the consequences may be, and whether the case be great or small. That is the spirit in which I desire to consider this case.

The Information is laid on the 7th section of the Statute 59 Geo. III. cap. 69, commonly called the Foreign Enlistment Act, which makes it a criminal offence, punishable by fine or imprisonment, or both, and forfeiture of the ship and her appurtenances, to equip, furnish, fit out, or arm any ship or vessel with the intent therein specified, or to attempt to do so, or to procure it to be done, or knowingly to aid, assist, or be concerned in doing so. The Information, which is in the English form, extends to 65 printed quarto pages. It contains 98 counts; and it charges the offences (which, after all, do not seem to be intended to be more than two) with every possible variation of language, but without giving any narrative of the particular facts relied on as would have been given, in a comparatively brief form, in a Scotch summons or Scotch indictment. The Information, taken as a whole, amounts, as the Lord Advocate expressed it, to a mere echo (certainly a prolific echo) of the section of the Statute. Not much embarrassment, however, arises from its prolixity, at least not at the present stage of the proceedings. The 98th count embodies, cumulatively, all or most of the charges, consistent and inconsistent, embraced in the previous counts. This might have been objectionable in a Scotch summons, and certainly would not have been allowed in a Scotch indictment. But the Act transferring the Exchequer jurisdiction to the Court of Session authorizes the Lord Advocate to proceed in this Court either by Summons or Information, and does not say that the form of Information previously in use in Exchequer shall be changed or discontinued. On the contrary, the Act seems to assume that the old cumulative mode, in which Exchequer offences were not unfrequently charged, may still be followed, for it provides, section 7, 'that notwithstanding the terms of any such Information, 'it shall not be incumbent to prove against the defender in order 'to recover under such Information, any matters stated therein, 'except only such matters as are by law required to be proved in 'order to the forfeiture of the penalty, or the recovery of the duty 'or debt, or the condemnation of the seizure sought for.'

There are two objections to the relevancy of the Information anxiously pressed upon us for decision by the defenders:—1. It is said that the first count and certain other counts in the Information, to the number of 72 in all, are irrelevant, because they do not charge the defenders with the intent which, by the Statute, is essential to the crime. 2. It is said that these 72 counts and 24 others—96 in all—are irrelevant, in respect they do not allege that the vessel was either armed, or attempted to be armed, one or other of which allegations is, it is contended, essential to the statutory crime. The same objections are, of course, applicable to the 98th count, in so far as it repeats the others. A preliminary question has been agitated, whether we ought, at this stage, to decide these questions, or whether we ought to send the case to trial, as the Lord Ordinary proposes to do, without either deciding them, or expressly reserving them. Now, I adhere to my opinion in Galloway *v.* Grant (quoted by the Lord Advocate), that it is not generally expedient to decide *in limine*, points of law which, when the facts come to be ascertained, may be found not to arise in the case. But here, if the defenders be right in their first objection, there are 72, or rather, as it appears to me, 73 counts upon which, although the whole facts alleged were proved, the Crown could not obtain a verdict, because the statutory intent would still be awanting. And if the defenders be right in their second objection, although wrong in the first, the Crown could not obtain a verdict upon any of the counts except the 97th, let the facts proved be what they may. The 98th count is necessarily open to both sets of objections, because it is in substance an accumulation of all the others. If the argument of Mr. Cook (to which he adhered when I asked him the question) be sound, that, equally as regards a transport or store-ship and a cruiser, the intent must be the intent of the equipper to use the vessel himself, or by those acting for him, against one of the belligerents, it necessarily follows that the defenders' first objection, which was urged as applicable to 72 counts, applies also to the 97th count, which was not specially objected to. The result is, that if effect were given to the defenders' second objection, there could be no trial except upon the 97th count; and if effect were given to both objections, there could be no available trial at all, because, according to the defenders' argument, no facts which could be proved would entitle the Crown to a verdict.

Moreover, there is a difficulty, as the Lord Ordinary intimates in his Note, as to when or how the objections in question would be open to the defenders afterwards if not dealt with now. If the defenders had been indicted in the Justiciary Court the relevancy of the indictment must have been, as your Lordship has said, decided *in limine*, and this whether it was objected to by the accused parties or not. When a summons is brought in this Court, although we may refuse to pronounce any judgment before trial either on law or relevancy, there is usually an implied decision upon relevancy, in a certain sense, involved in the approval of the issues, and the relevancy, strictly so called, of the summons never comes before the Judge at the trial at all. But the Exchequer Act, as we call it, which transfers the Exchequer jurisdiction to this Court, enacts that when the Lord Advocate proceeds by Information there shall be no issues. And it, at the same time, enacts, that, so far as not otherwise provided (and, as your Lordship has observed, nothing has been as yet otherwise provided), the procedure upon the Information shall be the same as the procedure in ordinary Court of Session causes. In this state of matters (and further difficulties might be suggested) I can foresee that embarrassing questions of competency might arise connected with the future disposal of the objections to relevancy now insisted in if these objections were not dealt with at this stage of the case; and as no doubt has been, or can be, suggested of the competency of our dealing with them now, it appears to me that the safest course is the best, and I concur, therefore, in holding that they ought to be now disposed of.

The *first* objection raises this question:—Does the statutory intent apply only where the equipper intends, by himself or others under his control, to employ the ship or vessel in the service or in aid of one of two belligerent states with neither of which Her Majesty is at war, or does it apply also to the case where the equipper intends the ship or vessel to be employed in the service of one of those belligerents against the other after he has, by delivery of the vessel, parted with all control over it?

In proceeding to consider this question I derive no material light from what is called the history of the Statute, or the circumstances which are said to have led to it. It might very well be that an expedition fitted out, or in course of being so, by Sir Gregor Macgregor, directed attention to the subject, and yet that the Legislature dealt with the subject, when before it, upon other or broader grounds. This can only be safely gathered from the Statute itself.

It is more relevant to look to the preamble of the Statute, and to the enactments which precede and follow the section now in dispute. But after carefully doing so, I find little in these either to lead me to do otherwise than to trust mainly, for a sound construction of the section, to a minute consideration of the terms of the section itself.

To say that the intent of the equipper must be an intent himself to employ the vessel to commit hostilities, appears to me to be contrary to the very words used, so far as regards a transport or store-ship. The words are expressly directed against equipping, &c., any ship or vessel, 'with intent or in order that such ship or 'vessel shall be employed in the service of any foreign prince, 'state,' &c., 'as a transport or store-ship.' The words, if we were to stop here, would be too broad, because they would include every ship or vessel intended to be used in the service of a foreign prince or state as a transport or store-ship, whether against a state with which Her Majesty was at peace, or not. But as regards the intent of the equipper, the words are not with intent that the vessel shall be employed by him, but generally, that it 'shall be employed 'in the service of any foreign prince, state,' &c. The words thus comprehend both cases—the case of the equipper himself intending to employ the vessel as a transport or store-ship in the foreign service, and the case of his intending it to be employed in that service, without being himself the direct employer;—the last case being even more clearly comprehended under the words than the first.

There is more difficulty, or, at least, obscurity, as to the intent with regard to a cruiser. After the words already quoted with reference to a transport or store-ship, the section proceeds, 'or with 'intent to cruise or commit hostilities against any prince, state,' &c., 'with whom His Majesty is not at war.' There is here a dislocation of the sentence, by the repetition of the words 'with intent,' without repeating the words which follow them in the previous part of the sentence. If the words which follow the words 'with 'intent,' in the first part of the sentence, be not held or understood to be repeated after the words 'with intent,' when these words occur again, the natural reading may be said to be, if any person shall equip, &c., any ship or vessel, 'with intent to cruise or commit 'hostilities against any prince, state,' &c., 'with whom His 'Majesty is not at war.' These words, taken by themselves, might seem to refer to an intent on the part of the equipper himself to cruise or commit hostilities, and the plausible argument, I think, would be, that when the Legislature thus changed its language, it must be held to have changed its meaning. But this was not the argument submitted to us for the defenders. Their contention was, that equally as regards a transport or store-ship and a cruiser, the intent to employ the ship to commit hostilities, must be an intent on the part of the equipper so to employ the ship himself. I think that view is altogether untenable; and I think the other view which I have said might have been taken, although plausible, is not sound. It would disconnect altogether the words descriptive of the prince or state, &c., against whom the vessel is intended to be employed, with the words 'a transport or 'store-ship,' and lead to the extravagant result that the first part of the enactment was directed against the equipping, &c., of any ship or vessel with intent or in order to its being employed in the service of any foreign prince or state, &c., as a transport or store-ship, without reference to existing hostilities, or to whether Her Majesty stood towards that prince or state in a neutral position or not. That plainly is not what was meant, and as we must thus read what follows the words 'with intent to cruise or commit hos-'tilities,' in connexion with what goes before these words, in order to get the meaning of the enactment as to a transport or store-ship, so, I think, we must read what goes before the same words in connexion with what follows after them, in order to get the meaning of the enactment as to a cruiser; and the legitimate result appears to me to be that, in both cases, it is enough if the equipper's intent be that the ship or vessel shall be employed in the service of the one belligerent against the other, although the equipper may not intend, himself, so to employ it. This would have been the inevitable reading, if the words 'with intent,' which occur in the first part of the sentence, had not occurred again before the words 'to 'cruise,' &c., and although we cannot well deal with the words 'with intent,' thus repeated as if they had not been repeated, it is not, I think, inadmissible to hold that what follows the words 'with intent,' where they occur in the first part of what is substantially one sentence, is to be understood as repeated where the words 'with intent' next occur in the same sentence, the result of which is, that the meaning comes to be the same as if the words 'with intent' had not been repeated at all. The grammar is not good. But bad grammar does not necessarily prevent the ungrammatical clause, either in a deed or a Statute, from receiving effect, if its meaning satisfactorily appears. The words commented on are not the only instance of defective phraseology in the Statute. For instance, in the outset of this very section (7th), it is not said, although it is obviously meant, that the equipping, &c., must be within His Majesty's dominions, but only that the person equipping, &c., must be within these dominions. The phraseology is frequently loose and inaccurate throughout, and this makes a good deal of construction necessary in reference to both the objections pleaded to us. I agree in the observation, when rightly understood, that penal enactments are to be strictly construed. They are not to be extended by implication to anything not expressed. But that does not import that where their meaning is not at once apparent we are not to take the trouble to find it out. Besides, the degree of strictness legitimately applicable is not always the same. The evil arising from vessels being equipped, &c., by His Majesty's subjects for warlike operations is not said in the preamble of the Statute to have been experienced merely as regards vessels employed in such operations by the equippers themselves; and in dealing with a remedial Statute, some reference must be had to the promotion of the remedy, as qualifying the rule of strict construction even in a penal Statute. On the whole, my opinion, upon this first question, is in favour of the construction of the Statute contended for by the Crown, and, consequently, that the objections to the relevancy of the Information, so far as these proceed upon a different construction, are not well founded.

I have only to add, upon this part of the case, that the American decisions upon the construction of their Foreign Enlistment Act, which is differently expressed from ours, do not appear to me to be in point, otherwise I should have considered them of great value and importance; for I have always thought, and often said, that one of the most striking features in the history of America, as a new country, is the remarkable progress and advanced state of her jurisprudence, which commands the study and respect of the legal profession in Scotland, as well as in the sister kingdoms of England and Ireland,—not to speak of the jurists of other countries.

The *second* leading objection taken to the relevancy of the Information is, that it does not charge the defenders with arming or attempting to arm the vessel in dispute.

The defenders maintain, with considerable plausibility, that the words 'equip, furnish, fit out, or arm' are to be read (*applicando singuli singulis*), so that the three first expressions shall be applicable only to a transport or store-ship, and the last expression ('arm') only to a cruiser. They farther say that, by leaving out the word 'arm' in the Information, the prosecutor must be held to have precluded himself from proving arming, or attempting to arm, under the charge of equipping, furnishing, or fitting out, supposing it would otherwise have been competent for him to do so.

If this be a correct reading of the enactment and Information, all the counts, with the exception of the 97th and part of the 98th, are obviously irrelevant; for it is not, *in terminis*, averred in any of them that the defenders either armed or attempted to arm the vessel. But the reading thus contended for, although plausible, is, in my opinion, not sound. I think the words 'equip, furnish, 'fit out, or arm,' according to the natural reading of the clause, all connect themselves equally with a cruiser as with a transport or store-ship. I further think that, under a charge of equipping, furnishing, or fitting out the vessel with intent to cruise and commit hostilities, it is competent for the prosecutor to prove arming or attempting to arm, so far as arming, or attempting to arm, may be part of his case, and that he has not precluded himself from doing so by refraining from the use of the word 'arm' in the Information.

Assuming the words 'equip,' 'furnish,' or 'fit out' to comprehend arming, it does not follow that the addition of the word 'arm' in the Statute is to be held superfluous. Suppose A had, on mere speculation, built an ordinary ship of war in a British port, and provided her with everything except her armour, and B had then purchased her, and, with the statutory intent, added her armour in the port where she lay, B would be clearly liable to be convicted upon a charge of arming with the statutory intent, although the Information said nothing whatever of equipping, furnishing, or fitting out the vessel.

But, while I am thus of opinion that it is not essential that the Information should, *in terminis*, charge arming, I by no means mean to say that the use of the words 'or arm' in the Statute is not important, as throwing light on the sense in which the other words, which occur along with them, are used with relation to a cruiser.

Still less do I mean to indicate an opinion in favour of the argument submitted to us on the part of the Crown, that, if the statutory intent be proved, any and every step in the progress of building the vessel in the form of a ship of war, will infer the statutory crime, and expose the vessel to immediate seizure.

The word 'build' does not occur in the Statute, and it is inconceivable that that word would have been omitted, especially where enumerative words are used, if the mere building of a ship in the ordinary form of a ship of war, with the statutory intent, had been intended to be struck at by the Statute.

Neither can I take the view, alternatively suggested on the part of the Crown, that anything, of whatever sort, done with the statutory intent towards equipping, furnishing, or fitting out the vessel after she is built, will infer the statutory offence of equipping, or attempting to equip, furnish, or fit out the vessel.

It is requisite, however, in considering the argument for the Crown, to distinguish between what may be necessary to constitute equipping, furnishing, or fitting out the vessel, and what may be necessary to constitute *attempting* to equip, furnish, or fit out the vessel.

Now, to constitute the statutory offence of equipping, furnishing, or fitting out the vessel (apart from the question of attempt), it appears to me that two things must concur:—1*st*, The statutory intent,—the nature of which has been already sufficiently pointed out; 2*d*, The equipping, furnishing, or fitting out the vessel, either as a transport or store-ship, or as a cruiser for committing hostilities, as the case may be.

The nature of the equipment, furnishing, or fitting out may be such as to form an important element in the proof of the intent. But however clearly the intent may be proved *aliunde*,—say by written evidence under the hand of the equipper,—I hold that it must also be proved, not only that the vessel has been built, but that it has been equipped, furnished, or fitted out so as to be more or less fit for its purpose as a transport or store-ship, or as a cruiser to commit hostilities, as the case may be.

The words of the Statute are, if any person 'shall equip, furnish, fit out, or arm;' not if any person shall partially equip, furnish, fit out, or arm. The words thus used must receive their natural meaning. The word equip, for instance, cannot be held to mean to equip in part, occurring as it does in an enactment which makes an act a crime which was not a crime before. The question whether there has been equipment, must depend upon the use for which the vessel is intended. If intended for a transport or store-ship, the vessel cannot be said to be equipped unless she has been made less or more fit to be used as a transport or store-ship; and if intended for a cruiser to commit hostilities, the vessel cannot be said to be equipped, unless she has been made less or more fit to be used as a cruiser to commit hostilities. The same observations, of course, apply, *mutatis mutandis*, to the words 'furnish' or 'fit out,' whether these words be held to be used in the Statute as synonymous with the word equip or not.

A transport or store-ship may have fewer distinctive characteristics than a cruiser, and, consequently, less may require to be proved to warrant conviction or forfeiture in the case of a transport or store-ship than of a cruiser. But until these distinctive characteristics have been substantially added—I do not say literally completed—the vessel cannot be said to be equipped. If intended for a war-ship to commit hostilities, the vessel must be less or more fit to commit hostilities, otherwise it cannot be said, with the accuracy required in a criminal information, that the vessel has been equipped as a vessel of the class to which she belongs.

The views I have now expressed apply only to the charge of equipping, furnishing, or fitting out the vessel with the statutory intent. But the defenders are charged also with an attempt to equip, furnish, or fit out the vessel with the statutory intent. I think the counts applicable to that charge relevant, although they do not expressly charge an attempt to arm, for the same reasons that I think the other counts just spoken to relevant, although they do not expressly charge arming. But I feel that this opinion might be misunderstood if I did not explain that I arrive at it only upon the footing that the attempt must be to add or complete those distinctive characteristics which render the vessel fit to be used as a vessel of one or other of the classes described in the Statute,—that is to say as a transport or store-ship, or as a cruiser to commit hostilities, as the case may be. Here, again, I think two things must concur—the statutory intent, and the attempt to add or complete the distinctive characteristics already spoken to. Let the intent,—as I have said in the former case,—be proved *aliunde* ever so clearly, such as by evidence under the hand of the accused party, still the attempt itself must also be proved, and must be shown to be an attempt to do what I may call the ultimate thing or things which would constitute when accomplished the completed offence; for instance in the case of a cruiser the thing or things which would render the vessel less or more fit to commit hostilities.

I cannot hold that the mere building of the vessel, although in the ordinary form of a ship of war, and still less that, as the Lord Advocate contended, the laying even of a single plank in the course of her construction, with the statutory intent, would amount to the attempt struck at by the Statute. Neither can I hold that every act done with the statutory intent towards rendering the vessel fit to sail after she has been built, would amount to an attempt in the sense of the Statute. I think the attempt must be to do that which would give to the vessel her distinctive characteristic or characteristics, as belonging to one or other of the classes described in the Statute; and this, as I have already said, in the case of a cruiser, would be an attempt to do what would render her more or less fit to commit hostilities. To illustrate what I mean, suppose a vessel built as a ship of war, with the statutory intent, to have all her gun-carriages and everything else on board except her guns, which were lying upon the quay or in an adjoining warehouse ready to be shipped (at midnight it might be), it might be difficult to say that there was not here the statutory attempt, although the vessel had not a single offensive or defensive weapon on board. But I put this supposed case merely to illustrate the distinction which I point at. The question whether there has been the statutory attempt or not, must always be, to some extent, a question of circumstances. And the question whether the vessel has been equipped, furnished, or fitted out in the sense of the Statute, must also be, to some extent, a question of circumstances. Without forming and expressing an opinion upon both of these questions to the limited extent which I have now done, I could not, satisfactorily to my own mind, and consistently with what I think my duty to the parties and the public, have formed and expressed my opinion upon the relevancy of the charges in this Information, of equipping, furnishing, and fitting out, or attempting to equip, furnish, or fit out the vessel without expressly charging arming or attempting to arm. But I wish to express no opinion towards the formation of which material light may be got from the proof at the trial, and consequently I do not even express any opinion upon the meaning which may be attached to the word 'arm' in the Statute; nor as to whether, in these days of invention, a cruiser may be made fit to commit hostilities, although, in ordinary phraseology, she might not be said to be armed. Questions such as these may or may not arise at the trial, and I think it better to say nothing in regard to them.

I can easily see that the construction of the Statute upon which I base my opinion of the relevancy of the Information leaves considerable room for evasion. But I am not much moved by that consideration in dealing with a highly penal Statute directed against a mere *malum prohibitum*, and not calculated, in any view of it, to do more than diminish the evil or risk against which it professes, in the preamble, to be directed. For instance, it does not strike at the sale of a ship of war not previously contracted for, but already, with a view to some lawful purpose which has proved abortive, or on mere speculation, fully equipped, furnished, fitted out, and armed, although the purchase may be made for one of two belligerent states, with neither of which Her Majesty is at war, and although a collision may in consequence be naturally looked for even within sight of the British shores. Neither does it strike against furnishing arms and other articles contraband of war to one of the belligerents, although the other may seize them on their way, and misunderstandings and quarrels may arise in consequence. The Act is a mere municipal regulation for preventing to some extent what, as the preamble bears, 'may be prejudicial to and tend 'to endanger the peace and welfare of this kingdom.' But to what extent it is to have this effect can only be gathered from the enacting clauses of the Statute itself. We have no right to extend these clauses beyond their terms from policy or expediency. That would be assuming legislative in place of judicial functions,—which no Court on either side of the Atlantic will be found for a moment disposed to do.

Lord Ardmillan.—I need add nothing to what has been already said by your Lordships in regard to the importance of this case to the parties and to the public, or to the expediency of now disposing of these objections. Of the competency of our doing so, there is no doubt; and I think that the course we take is the best and safest for the interests of all parties. Certainly, if we were of opinion that, in regard to all or any of these counts, the objections to relevancy are well founded, I think it would be better for all parties so to decide at once, and not permit a trial to take place on counts which we think not relevant.

I am, however, of opinion that none of the objections to the relevancy of the Information are well founded.

As the Information professes to be, and must be, a transcript of the Statute, thrown into the form of counts or charges to meet a variety of possible contingencies in point of fact, the objections truly resolve into questions of construction of the Foreign Enlistment Act of 1819 (Statute 59 Geo. III. cap. 69, sect. 7); and, in proceeding to the task of construing the Statute, I wish to make a remark on the principles or canons of construction which have been founded on. On the one hand, this is a Statute of a penal character. It creates an offence, it imposes penalties, and it declares a forfeiture of property consequent on the commission of the offence. There can be no forfeiture of this ship, unless one or other of the offences created by the Act has been committed. It is a sound canon of construction, that a penal Statute must be strictly construed. But I think it is now quite understood, that the strict construction which is appropriate to a penal Statute, is not a strained, unnatural, and unreasonable construction, so as to withdraw from the reach of the Statute cases or persons plainly within its scope. While this is a penal Statute, it is also a remedial Statute; and it is a sound canon of construction, that a remedial Statute shall, if the words will bear it, be so construed as to abate the mischief and advance the remedy; but this must not be done by straining words, so as to extend the statutory provisions to cases not clearly within them. Taking both of these canons of construction as sound, they do not appear to me to be so inconsistent as has been represented at the bar. The end and aim of all construction is to reach the true import of the words. It is our duty to ascertain, if we can, the true meaning of the Statute, without, on the one hand, unduly extending its penal scope, or, on the other hand, unduly restricting its remedial provisions.

We have had some discussion on the historical origin of this Statute, and on the question, What is the mischief for remedy of which this Statute was enacted? This is to be found not in speculations from its origin, but in the preamble. Without dwelling minutely on this I may observe, that the mischief specially set forth as resulting from all the different proceedings enumerated in the preamble is, that these 'may be prejudicial to, and tend to 'endanger the peace and welfare of this Kingdom.' This is a peculiar form of expression; and I have some doubt if its meaning has been sufficiently appreciated. Many Acts of Parliament have been passed to repress proceedings tending to endanger 'the public 'peace,' or 'the peace of the lieges,'—of which the whole series of Acts known as the 'Riot Acts' are examples,—but by the expression 'the peace of this kingdom,' I rather understand a peace of a wider character than public order or internal tranquillity. I am disposed to think that the meaning is, the peaceful relations of this kingdom to foreign powers. This view is confirmed by the consideration, that some of the proceedings set forth as tending to endanger the peace of this kingdom are acts by British subjects which may be committed, not in this kingdom, but in any part of the world, while others are acts by any person whatever, whether a British subject or not, committed within the realm of England. This tends still further to show that the peace of the kingdom, in its widest sense, is what the Legislature sought to protect; and danger to that peace of the kingdom is the mischief for which the Legislature sought to provide a remedy. The act is accordingly penal, but it is also remedial, and as it seeks to suppress what may *tend* to endanger 'the peace of this kingdom,' it is *preventive* in order that it may the more effectually be remedial.

Proceeding to the construction of the seventh section, the first question is, What is the intent set forth in that section? The words, 'with intent,' are twice used in the earlier part of this section; and it has been argued to us that, on both occasions, the intent must be in the mind of the equipper, and that on both occasions the thing intended to be done must be intended to be done by the equipper himself and not by another. This was very broadly and strongly urged:—*First*, It was said that the intended employment of the ship in the service of a foreign prince, as a transport or store-ship, must be by the equipper himself, and cannot be by another; and *secondly*, That the intended cruising or commission of hostilities must be by the equipper himself and not by another. In my opinion this contention on the part of the defenders is not well founded. The clause is ill expressed; and it is not surprising that difficulties have arisen in regard to the use of these second words 'with intent;' but in regard to the first words 'with intent,' I have no difficulty. It appears to me to be quite clear that while the first intent must be the intent of the equipper, the employment as a transport or store-ship in the service of a foreign prince, &c., may be either by the equipper or by any one else. It must be within the equipper's intent that the ship be so employed; but it is not necessary that he shall intend to be himself the employer. This is, to my mind, too clear to admit of doubt; and no doubt of it was raised in the case of the 'Alexandra.' Nothing to the contrary was decided in the American cases which have been quoted, and I do not understand that any of your Lordships have difficulty on the point. In regard to the second use of the words 'with intent,' the objection is more plausible, but, in my opinion, is not sound. It is said that the two intents set forth must be read as alternative, so that the offence would consist in the equipping, &c. of any ship either with the first intent, viz., with intent or in order that she shall be employed in the service of any foreign prince, &c. as a transport or store-ship; or with the second intent, viz., with intent to cruise or commit hostilities against any prince, &c. with whom Her Majesty shall not be at war. This reading of the section is, I think, untenable. It dislocates the language of the section, so as to lead to results which it would be absurd to suppose were contemplated by the Legislature. If this were the true reading, then the description of the first intent would stop at the word 'store-ship,' and then it would be an offence to equip a ship with intent that she should be employed in the service of a foreign prince, &c., as a transport or store-ship, though not for belligerent purposes—not against any other prince, &c.,—which is absurd. But, again, it is argued that even if that view were not taken, the second intent must still be read as the intent of the equipper, and, being followed by the words, 'to cruise or commit hostilities,' must mean that the equipper intends himself to cruise or commit hostilities. I cannot adopt this construction. In the first place, the effect of it is to separate the intended employment of the ship in the service of any foreign prince, &c., from the intended cruising or committing of hostilities, a separation inconsistent with the subsequent words of the section—'or shall issue or deliver any commission for any ship or 'vessel to the intent that such ship or vessel shall be *employed as* '*aforesaid*,' these words, 'as aforesaid,' being plainly applicable both to the case of a 'transport or store-ship,' and to the case of cruising and committing hostilities. The employment in the service of a foreign prince, &c., is applicable to both alternatives; and a construction which separates that employment from the last alternative must be erroneous. Besides, I think that this Statute is not required to meet the case, and is certainly not intended to be limited to the case, of one who, without leave and license of Her Majesty, and without intending to employ the ship in the service of a foreign prince, shall equip a ship with intent, for himself and on his own account, to commit hostilities against a prince, state, &c., with whom Her Majesty is not at war. The commission of hostilities under such circumstances, without license, and without employment in the service of a foreign prince, would be an act of piracy, and the equipping of a ship with intent to cruise and commit such hostilities would be an attempt to commit piracy. But piracy is a great crime at common law. The pirate is *hostis humani generis;* and this Act is not required to reach him, and at least is not limited to that case. Still farther, if I am right in holding that, if the ship is intended to be employed in the service of a foreign prince, &c., as a transport or store-ship, that intended employment may be either by the equipper or by another, and if the construction for which the defenders contend is, that the intended cruising or commission of hostilities must be by the equipper himself, then this most absurd and unreasonable result is reached,—that the most hostile act, the act most dangerous to 'the peace of this kingdom,' is most favoured. If the Statute is to be read so as to permit a party to equip a ship with intent that another shall use her to commit hostilities, while it prohibits that party from equipping a ship to be employed by another as a transport-ship, that were truly to construe the Act so as to restrict its scope by a subtilty, and so as not to abate the mischief and advance the remedy, but to impair the remedy and promote the mischief. Rejecting, therefore, these constructions for which the defenders contend, I have arrived at the conclusion that this section must be read, as having substantially the same meaning as if the second words, 'with intent,' were not there, or as if the words were 'in 'order to.' So reading the section, the second intent is connected disjunctively with the words as a 'transport or store-ship,' and is within that employment in the service of a foreign prince, &c., which is the foundation of the whole sentence as the original intent of the equipper. This was the construction of the section adopted by the Admiralty Judge of the Bahamas in the case of the Oreto, who thus, with reference to the facts before him, explains the intent required by the Act: 'With intent that she should be employed 'in the service of the Confederate States, and that such service was 'to cruise and commit hostilities,' &c. It appears to me that this construction was right, and that it was adopted and approved of by the Judges in the Court of Exchequer in the case of the Alexandra.

I proceed now to consider the second objection by the defenders. That objection is, that the Information does not set forth the arming or attempting to arm the ship.

I concur with your Lordships in being clearly of opinion that it is not necessary that the Information shall allege arming. The words 'equip, furnish, fit out, or arm, or attempt or endeavour to 'equip, furnish, fit out, or arm,' are disjunctive in this section; any one of these things, if with the Statutory intent, is struck at by the Act; and it is not necessary that an Information under the Statute shall set forth all the acts which may alternatively or disjunctively amount to the Statutory offence. The first impression one has is, that the word in the Information must mean the same as in the Statute,—that if the four terms are synonymous (which I do not think they are), there would be no objection to the relevancy, for the one word would mean the same as the other in the Information, as well as in the Statute; but then 'equip' would mean 'arm,' and in that case it would be necessary to prove arming under a charge of equipping any ship, even a transport or store-ship. If, on the other hand, the words are not synonymous, but distinctive and disjunctive, then each one must be sufficient to express the Statutory offence in the Information as well as in the Statute. The plea urged by the defenders, that the Information is bad in law, because the arming of the ship is not alleged, received no countenance from any of the Judges in England in the case of the Alexandra. Some difference of opinion prevailed on a point to which I shall afterwards advert, but so far as I can perceive, no Judge, and indeed not even the learned counsel for the defendants, in England, maintained that the Information was defective because it did not charge arming. I shall not repeat what your Lordship in the chair has said of the construction which, *reddendo singula singulis*, applies the word 'arm' to cruisers, and the other words to 'trans-'ports or store-ships.' I am satisfied that this construction is not sound, and I think it was rejected by all the Judges in Exchequer. Baron Bramwell expresses himself decidedly on that point. I understand that, to-day, it is the unanimous opinion of the Court that this objection is not well founded.

As it has been thought, and very naturally thought, necessary to explain more particularly the grounds on which this objection is repelled, and as I concur in repelling the objection, but do not concur in some of the grounds which have been stated, I hope I may be excused if I proceed to explain in a few words what are the reasons which induce me to come to the same conclusion as your Lordships.

I am of opinion that it is not necessary to allege arming in the Information, 1st, Because the word 'equip' *may* cover arming to a greater or less extent; and, 2dly, because the offence under this Act, may, as I think, be committed without the ship being actually armed. In other words, the actual arming of the ship in the Queen's dominions, or the intention to arm her in the Queen's dominions, is not necessary to the constitution of this offence. It has been strongly urged that all muniments of war, including arms and armed ships, may be sold as articles of trade. I do not doubt it. We have no question here about selling,—about mercantile dealing in contraband of war. Whether, on the part of a neutral state, a trade in contraband—not being an accustomed trade, but opened only by the accident of war—is perfectly lawful according to international law, is a question which we need not discuss. Such trade is not struck at by this Statute; it is not forbidden by any positive law; it exposes to capture; and it cannot be favoured or approved by any state which duly appreciates and respects that *comitas gentium* which is the foundation of international law. But, for the purposes of this argument, we must hold that it is not unlawful.

Then it is pressed on us that building a ship, even a ship of war, with intent to sell her to a belligerent, is not struck at by this Act. In this I concur. As building is not here enumerated, I must conclude, 1st, That mere building of a ship, whatever be the intent, is not an offence under this Act; and, 2dly, That equipping is something done after building, or at least distinct and apart from mere building,—for the operation prohibited is, equipping a ship, which, in a clause that omits building, implies that there must be a ship built before it can be equipped within the meaning of the Act. I am unable to concur in the argument for the Crown, that the building of a mere hull, or, as it was expressed, the laying of the first planks, would, if the intent were proved, amount to the statutory offence. If that had been intended, the world 'build' would not have been omitted. But if, beyond the mere building, there is an operation of equipment which may or may not be of warlike character, then I am of opinion that the intent, if proved *aliunde*, must give its character to the operation. In pursuance of a peaceful intent, that equipment will be an equipment for peace; in pursuance of a warlike intent, that equipment will be an equipment for war. It cannot admit of doubt that proof of the intent, apart from inferences drawn from the operation itself, is admissible, and may be conclusive. It is not required that the equipment be such as to prove the intent by necessary inference. According to my view, the right construction is this,—that while, on the one hand, mere building is not sufficient, yet, on the other hand, any operation whatever in the way of equipment, tending to the fulfilment of the statutory intent, that intent being clearly proved, is an offence within this Act.

I think it important to observe that the words 'with intent to 'cruise or commit hostilities,' do not apply directly to the equipment, but to the employment, of the ship. If we are right in disposing of the first objection, then the offence consists, not in equipping with intent to cruise or commit hostilities, but in equipping with intent that the ship be employed to cruise or commit hostilities. The purpose of cruising and committing hostilities qualifies the employment, and fitness for that purpose is a quality of the ship when employed and not when equipped. It may thus be part of the intention, that her equipment may be carried on to completion by the foreign State, which is to use the ship to commit hostilities.

A case was put in illustration, both here and in the case of the Alexandra, to this effect. Suppose that, by arrangement, two ships leave the same port, the one with peaceful equipment only, the other laden with arms, and that as soon as they pass from neutral waters, the arms from the one ship are transferred to the other, and then the ship, no longer in peaceful equipment, pursues her way as a ship of war, to fulfil the intent proved to have existed from the beginning, that she should be employed to commit hostilities. This illustration was put by the defendants, who maintain that such a proceeding would not be an offence under this Statute. I cannot arrive at that conclusion. I think the illustration a good one, but fatal to the defendants' argument. Let me put another illustration. Suppose a man walks into a druggist's shop, and proposes to the druggist to purchase poison to destroy a person whom he names; the druggist, whose poverty and will alike consent, afraid of selling the poison, sells him two separate ingredients, neither of which is itself a deadly poison, but informs the purchaser, that, by a further process in combination of these ingredients, he will obtain the poison for his purpose. If the intent to use for murder of a particular person, and the sale with a view to that intent, be proved, can there be a doubt that that druggist would be guilty of accession to murder? The proved intent would, morally and legally, bind together the separate acts furnishing the separate elements whose combination would be fatal. So would it be, in the illustration put by the defenders; so it may be, in this case. The proved intent brings out the reality instead of the semblance of the proceeding. The truth may not always be discernible, it may be concealed by disguises, or escaped from by cunning evasions. But, if the truth is discovered, then, by the truth, and not by the fiction, the character of the transaction must be determined. Take the case of a transport or store-ship. How can that case be disposed of, except by referring to the intent? I do not know that there are any peculiar equipments exclusively suited to a transport or store-ship. A vessel fitted as an emigrant ship might probably serve as a transport ship, or fitted as a merchant ship might serve as a store-ship; but if the intent be proved, then the equipment for that intent is an equipment as a transport ship or as a store-ship. The intent explains the equipment.

In one word, my Lords, my view is, that, when the statutory

intent has been proved,—say by contract, letters, testimony, or confession,—that intent becomes a quality of the act of equipment, and gives to it its true character.

The intent, when clearly proved *quocunque modo*, is the discovering agent which rends away the mask and dispels the fictions, and brings forth the truth, by which the character of the operations on the ship must be determined; that proved intent is the cohesive agent which morally and legally combines 'the elements of arma- 'ment;' that proved intent is the premonitory agent, pointing to purposed wrong and coming danger, by aid of which this important Statute may be worked with justice and effect, as a remedial and preventive measure, to protect from peril the 'peace and welfare of 'this kingdom.'

Mr. Clark.—Before your Lordships pronounce any judgment, there is a matter which we think it right to bring under your Lordships' notice with reference to the 24 counts. As we understand the opinions delivered, interpreting the 7th section of the Act, your Lordships have held that the words 'with intent to cruise or com- 'mit hostilities against any prince,' &c., do not alternate with the words 'with intent or in order that such ship shall be employed,' but with the words 'as a transport-ship.' We contended that the alternation of the Statute was that the words commencing 'with 'intent or in order that such ship should be employed' created one offence, while the words commencing 'with intent to cruise or com- 'mit hostilities' constituted another and separate offence under the Statute; and therefore your Lordships in repelling that construction for which we contended, hold that the words 'as a transport 'or store-ship, or with intent to cruise or commit hostilities' formed the real alternative. If so, the charge in one form of it is the equipment of a vessel with intent that she shall be employed in the service of a foreign state as a transport-ship, and in the other form of it, with intent to cruise or commit hostilities; that is, that the employment of the ship in the service of a foreign state is part of the statutory offence—or the foundation of the statutory offence, as one of your Lordships expressed it. Of course I assume now that your Lordships' construction of the Statute is the correct one; and I wish to point out that the 3d count is not framed according to that construction of the Statute, because the charge in the 3d count, and in the other 23 formed on the same principle, is that the defenders did equip the said ship or vessel with intent to cruise and commit hostilities as against a certain foreign state; it leaves out the element of employment by the foreign state altogether, which your Lordships have said forms a necessary part of the offence, or the foundation of the statutory offence. And therefore it seems to us to follow from the judgment which your Lordships have pronounced, that while you sustain as relevant the 1st and other 71 counts, you must repel as irrelevant the 3d and others framed on the same model, because the pursuer might establish under the 3d count as a count laid upon the Statute, equipment with intent to cruise, though it was not to be in the service of any foreign state at all;

in other words, the act here charged seems to me not to be an act of privateering, but an act of piracy against which the Statute does not strike.

Lord Deas.—What are you asking us to do?

Mr. Clark.—I say it follows from your Lordships' judgment that the 3d count, and those framed on the model of it, must be held to be irrelevant; because the construction of your Lordships, repelling the objection to the 1st count, is inconsistent with the theory on which the 3d count is framed.

Lord Advocate.—My learned friend seems to say that the 3d count does not allege as a necessary element in the crime, the employment in the service of the foreign state. Whether that is necessary or not has not been argued yet, though I quite see that an argument might be raised upon it. It is obvious enough that some of these counts are not consistent with each other, and that is the reason why they are there. They are alternative views of the Statute, and that is the theory on which the Information is framed. But I don't think it is desirable that we should at this moment be put to say on which of these counts we stand. We may stand on one against one of the defenders, and on another against another. We may find, for instance, that the builders had no intention of cruising, but that Sinclair, one of the defenders, had an intention personally of cruising.

Lord President.—Of cruising not in the employment of a foreign state.

Lord Advocate.—The question is whether that is essential.

Lord Curriehill.—I expressed an opinion on the point which Mr. Clark has referred to, but none of the other Judges did so. [*His Lordship again read that passage from his opinion.*]

Lord President.—The question is whether in the service of the foreign state requires to be expressed, and whether it is inconsistent with the construction of the Statute. If the Statute requires that the vessel shall be used in the service of a foreign state, it would be inconsistent with that construction to hold that it might be used not in the service of a foreign state. That is the point. There is no inconsistency in holding that the Statute covers a case of equipping a vessel in order that she shall be employed as a cruiser either by the equippers or others under their control, or by any person, in the employment of a foreign state; but the question is, whether the being in the employment of a foreign state is necessary.

Lord Advocate.—If the counts are inconsistent, it would be a question for us on which of them we should stand. If the allegation is that we have omitted one of the elements of the particular statutory offence, we could supply that by amendment.

Lord President.—The view expressed by the Court to-day was that they should dispose of those questions of relevancy which, if sustained, were calculated to exclude the trial or to cast the counts. We have repelled objections that were calculated to cast 72 counts; we have done so upon a certain construction of the Statute; and the point now raised is whether that construction of the Statute does not necessarily lead to the casting of 24 counts, which are framed on a construction of the Statute, which is said to be inconsistent with that. That arises from not having introduced into the Information that it was to be in the service of a foreign state. If that can be obviated, by introducing it into the Information, that is one thing; but if that is not competent, the question would be whether the Lord Advocate intends to charge these parties with cruising at their own hand, as it has been called.

After the usual adjournment of the Court,

The Lord Advocate said—Your Lordships have now decided the construction of the 7th clause of the Statute. The 1st and similar counts are framed on that construction. The 3d and similar counts are framed on the footing of an opposite construction. I therefore propose to abandon the 3d count, and the other 23 framed on the same model.

Lord President.—That simplifies the matter. That is just what we thought you would do. You could hardly expect to prove that these gentlemen were to engage in privateering at their own hand.

Lord Curriehill.—What are you to do, Lord Advocate, with the 98th count?

Lord President.—In one reading of the 98th it has within it all those 24 counts that you are going to abandon.

Lord Advocate.—I must fairly say that I don't see the use of the 98th.

Lord President.—The Solicitor-General told us it was of no use.

Mr. Gordon.—And it was given up in the Alexandra case.

Lord Advocate.—Then it may go too.

Lord President.—The judgment which I had drawn up was this:—'Having heard counsel on the objections urged by the defenders against the relevancy of the Information, find as follows: 1*st*, as regards the objection urged against the relevancy of the 1st count, and certain other counts, on the ground that the matters therein set forth do not amount to a contravention of the Statute, inasmuch as it is not alleged against the defenders, or any of them, that they had the intent to cruise or commit hostilities, Find that the said objection is not well founded, and repel the same: 2*d*, as regards the objection urged against the relevancy of the 1st count, and certain other counts, on the ground that arming is not alleged *in terminis*, and that the terms "equip, furnish, and fit out," used in the Information, cannot be held to include arming, Find that said objection is not well founded, and repel the same.' Then we shall put at the commencement that the 3d and certain other counts are departed from.

[The Lord Advocate handed a note of the counts departed from to his Lordship.]

Mr. Clark.—The way we put our objection was this: we held that the Statute set forth two intents as each constituting what we thought a separate offence, that the first intent alternated with the other intent; and our objection to the charge was that it was framed upon the footing of combining the two intents, and that

that was not authorized by the Statute. Your Lordship puts it rather in the way of one of the illustrations which we used in support of our argument.

Lord President.—You contended for one construction of the Statute, and the Crown for another, these being opposite and inconsistent constructions. We have negatived your construction, and set up that contended for by the Crown.

Mr. Clark.—Perhaps your Lordships would make this the form of judgment,—to sustain, as well laid under the Statute, the 1st count, and all those framed like it.

Lord President.—I am not disposed to do that, because we might in that way be held as dealing with certain objections which have never been stated. We are deciding the construction of the Statute. The defenders contended that the counts were not well laid, because they were not laid according to their construction of the Statute, but according to an erroneous construction of the Statute. The objection was stated in various ways, and a great many illustrations of it were put. But some other objections may yet be found out, and I don't want to deal with these.

Mr. Gordon.—I move your Lordships for leave to appeal against this judgment.

Lord President.—That will require a petition.

Mr. Gordon.—I think not. The 15th section of the Act 48 Geo. III. c. 151 provides that leave is necessary in such a case. The general course undoubtedly has been to present a petition, but we have an interest in making the motion now, because the Session closes to-morrow.

Lord Deas.—Did you ever know leave granted without a petition?

Mr. Gordon.—I cannot say I have, because in general there is time to make the application; but in the other Division an opinion was expressed this week that it was a competent proceeding to make the motion. It is something like an application to the Lord Ordinary for leave to reclaim, and that is done by motion at the bar, very often when the judgment is pronounced. There is no direction that a petition shall necessarily be presented, but if your Lordships think it of importance we shall have the petition presented to-morrow.

Lord President.—I think there is something in the Judicature Act on the subject.

Mr. Gordon.—Not that I am aware of.

Lord Advocate.—The provision in the Judicature Act is this, 'And the determination of such previous question of law or relevancy shall not be open to appeal to the House of Lords without leave expressly granted, reserving the full effect of the objection to the decision in any appeal to be finally taken.'

Lord President.—I think it will be better that a petition should be presented.

Mr. Gordon.—We have one ready.

Lord President.—Then it can be put in, and you can move it to-morrow.

Lord Advocate.—I have no objection to my learned friend going on with it now.

Lord President.—Then we will hold the petition as lodged.

Mr. Gordon.—Then I submit that it is expedient that leave should be granted in the present case at this stage. Your Lordships have expressed an opinion that the questions raised on the construction of this Information, are questions of great public importance, as well as important to the interests of the defenders. It is therefore expedient that as soon as possible there should be an authoritative construction of the clauses of this Act, and particularly of the 7th clause. The only objection which I anticipate is, that the effect of an appeal will be to delay the trial. But as this is an Exchequer case, it will take precedence over other appeals, so that it can soon be brought before the House of Lords, and therefore the ultimate decision of the case will not be much retarded, because in the event of there being a judgment against us at the trial, I certainly cannot hold out any prospect that we shall acquiesce in your Lordships' judgment.

Lord Advocate.—I think that my learned friend has stated no ground for allowing leave to appeal just now, but quite the reverse. There are many questions which may be raised on the Statute at the trial, and the defenders will have their full remedy by taking the whole case to the House of Lords.

Lord President.—The opinion of the Court is, that leave to appeal should be refused, and that the case should go on; but we thought it very desirable to give the parties the benefit of our opinion upon those points which we have dealt with.

Lord Advocate.—Then there is a motion for a diligence, which the Lord Ordinary granted us by an Interlocutor of 23d February, but which my learned friends have reclaimed against.

Mr. Clark.—We don't object to the first seven articles of the specification. The 8th is, 'All models, drawings, sketches, or plans 'of the ship, or of any of her equipments, fittings, or furnishings, 'or intended fittings or furnishings;' and they ask for these without reference to the persons by whom these models were made, or the persons who intended to put the fittings or furnishings into the ship. We don't object to the 9th or 10th; but the 11th is, 'The 'whole equipments, fittings, and furnishings of the said ship, in so 'far as not already seized.' Now, I think a diligence cannot be granted for the purpose of enabling the Crown to complete a seizure. They can proceed to any extent which the Statute warrants, but they are not entitled, for the purpose of completing a seizure, to ask me to help them to recover these things. They propose, I suppose, to examine the defenders on oath for the purpose of making them state what were the equipments, fittings, and furnishings for the vessel, and producing them for seizure. Then as regards Article 12, I think it should be qualified in the usual terms, 'failing 'the recovery of principals.'

Lord President.—I suppose there is no objection to that.

Lord Advocate.—We want the drafts as well as the principals; because they may be very material. This is a proceeding *in rem;*

it is not a proceeding against certain defenders; it is against the vessel, and the parties to this suit have come in as claimants. As regards the objections to Article 8, surely nothing can be more pertinent to the question of the intent with which the ship was constructed. That may come out very clearly from the drawings. What does it signify who made them? If they are drawings relating to the ship, that is enough in this proceeding against the vessel itself. The drawings and plans may be made material evidence of the intent, as the letters may be very material as connecting the writers of them with the intent. The only serious objection however seems to be to the 11th article, which is the most important of all. This vessel has been seized; it may be said she was not intended for a war vessel; we believe there are fittings belonging to her in the hands of other parties, not yet delivered, but ordered by the owners or builders, and which would prove her warlike character beyond all question. Surely I am entitled to recover these by diligence. Seizure is a different matter; I may seize them or not, but supposing I could seize them, I am entitled to recover them as proving the intent.

Lord President.—It is the existence of the power of seizure which is stated as the objection.

Lord Advocate.—But that is no reason for our not having the same advantages as an ordinary litigant. The materiality of this in the present case must be sufficiently obvious, because we may find in the possession of other parties evidence which would be conclusive of the matter in dispute.

Lord Deas.—If you mean to prove the nature and construction of the ship without producing her, why can't you prove the nature of those other things without producing them?

Lord Advocate.—But this diligence may be necessary in order to ascertain what they are and where they are.

Lord Deas.—That would be a novel use of diligence.

Lord Advocate.—All I want is to get those appurtenances of the ship that go to prove her character.

Lord Deas.—The question is, whether you can get that under a diligence against havers.

Lord Advocate.—Why not, if they have them?

Lord Curriehill.—Are letters of diligence in our practice the appropriate remedy for recovering the *ipsa corpora* of moveables? Is the use of diligence not for the recovery of written evidence?

Lord Advocate.—My impression is that a diligence of this kind is not confined to writs, and that models, drawings, plans, and things of that kind are recovered in this way every day.

Lord President.—The cases in which you are most likely to find a precedent for this, if there be any, would probably be cases of infringement of patents.

Lord Deas.—I have a distinct impression that, as regards models and things of that sort, it has been done in patent cases, but that no objection was taken to it. So far as I know, it has never been determined that that is the proper use of a diligence against havers.

Lord Advocate.—I know no other mode of recovering them.

Lord Deas.—It may be a different question whether you could get a warrant to recover them.

Lord Ardmillan.—Suppose an action of damages for injury done by the fall of a bucket connected with machinery, and the party wants to exhibit the chain or rope to his own skilled witness to test its efficiency, has he not the means of obtaining from the Court a warrant, whether in the form of a diligence or not, to compel the other party to produce that rope?

Lord Advocate.—I should have thought there would have been no difficulty in including it in the diligence.

Lord President.—If the defenders have these things, and will undertake to exhibit them, that might facilitate the matter.

Mr. Clark.—We have a great many things falling under Article 11, and the Lord Advocate may see them if he likes. A great many things were exhibited to the Crown which they did not choose to take; we have no objections to their getting these, viz., all the fittings and furnishings of the Pampero, so far as they are in our hands.

Lord President.—Suppose you had put away the guns.

Mr. Clark.—We never had them; but if we had, arming would have been in the 72 counts.

Lord Deas.—This use of diligence, I think, would be a search-warrant of the most extraordinary description. If the Lord Advocate were to apply for a warrant to recover certain things, he would require to give some kind of specification as to what he wanted to recover; whereas if he is to get a diligence against havers, he may go over the whole kingdom with a search-warrant, and into every man's house or premises in a way which the law does not recognise.

Lord Advocate.—But I am limited to furnishings of this vessel. They may have been concealed, and I must have the means of tracing them, unless I am to be deprived of the ordinary privileges of a litigant.

Lord Ardmillan.—I would be very unwilling to grant the diligence here asked if it were to have the effect of subjecting all the recovered equipments to immediate seizure. I don't think the Lord Advocate is entitled to obtain opportunities of seizure by using a diligence against havers, but I think he is entitled to any form of warrant by which he can be aided in procuring the equipments of the Pampero, wherever they are, which he thinks may be evidence in the case.

Lord Advocate.—That is all I want. I have no intention of seizing them, and no wish to seize them.

Lord Curriehill.—I am for refusing this. I give no opinion upon the right of the Crown to get a warrant to find out these things, and either to seize them or to make use of them as evidence at the trial. My objection is that letters of diligence under the Signet are not the appropriate form of doing this, but that it is a use of that remedy which I never heard of in the practice of our Scotch Court, and I don't know what the consequences might be if we sanctioned such an innovation. The object of letters of diligence is to recover written evidence that can be used as such at the trial.

Lord Deas.—I am of the same opinion. I by no means say that the Lord Advocate might not get a warrant which would substantially serve his purpose; but he cannot get it in the form of a diligence against havers.

Lord Ardmillan.—Whether this is, the precise form of obtaining what the Lord Advocate asks may be matter of question. But, unless I am mistaken, a little search will discover that diligence against havers has been used for the recovery of what is not writings, and that once admitted it is not very easy to perceive the point at which you could stop. If a warrant can be granted by which the Lord Advocate can recover or discover these equipments, I have no objection,—it is of no consequence what it is called,—but I am against shutting the door against discovery of these pieces of evidence, and if there is no other mode of discovering them I am for granting this.

Lord Deas.—I don't say that diligence is confined to the recovery of writings; under it you may recover printed books, and things which are not writings.

Lord President.—I should like to know how the practice stands. I have an impression, with Lord Ardmillan, that diligence has been granted to recover articles that were not writings in cases of infringement of patent; to recover goods made by the alleged patent process. That might be inquired into by to-morrow. It is quite clear that some mode must be devised of getting access to these things, and if this is a mode that has been in use, I don't see why it should be withheld here.

Lord Advocate.—We shall look into the practice by tomorrow.

Mr. Clark gave notice that he would propose an alteration on Art. 9, with the view of obtaining a joint diligence for the recovery of the documents; the alteration being to insert 'letters' after 'orders,' and after 'construction,' the words 'sale or use.'

The Lord Advocate stated that it was proposed to fix the trial for 5th May; but this was also delayed till to-morrow, in order that the Lord Ordinary might be consulted as to whether that day would be convenient for him.

Saturday, 19*th March* 1864.

Lord President.—You had better put in a Minute withdrawing the counts, because we must found on that in our Interlocutor.

Lord Advocate.—We shall do so. As to the 11th Article of the specification, I have not been able to recal any case in which articles were recovered under diligence, but I have a strong impression that it has been done. I never knew an objection taken to it before; but I leave it in your Lordships' hands.

Lord President.—I am afraid it is too great a novelty; but if you want an order, or anything of that kind, it is another matter.

Lord Advocate.—We shall probably apply to the Lord Ordinary.

Lord Deas.—I think it is very clear that it cannot be done in this form, and I have looked back to the institutional writers and the Statutes and Acts of Sederunt, and I find no trace of such a thing. A diligence against havers is described by Stair at full length, and by Erskine, and in the Statute and in various Acts of Sederunt, and there is not a trace of anything being recoverable in that form except documents. It may have been done in patent cases, where no objection was stated, and the observation of the Lord Advocate to that effect is very important. The plea of confidentiality, and all the pleas that arise on diligences, are totally inapplicable to such articles; and this would just be a search-warrant in the shape of a diligence.

Lord President.—Then we strike out Article 11. We don't say the Crown is not entitled to get at these; all we say is, that we don't grant a diligence for their recovery.

Mr. Clark.—I submit that the 8th article should also be struck out, because it goes to intended fittings, and because this is not the proper form for recovering models.

Lord Deas.—The model may be pasteboard, with things written on it.

Lord President.—And all they can recover is the models of intended fittings, &c., for the 'Pampero.' The haver is asked to produce that; if he has a model of another ship, he won't produce it, but if he has a model of this ship, he will produce it.

Mr. Gordon.—The reason for allowing documents to be recovered, is that without the production of the document at the trial, you cannot prove its contents, unless it has been lost. It is different with reference to articles which you can get witnesses to speak to; and I think this is just an attempt by the Crown to commence their case by way of precognition on oath of havers, instead of bringing forward witnesses to speak to the existence of these articles.

Lord President.—I suspect it would be against the rule of our decision as to Article 11, to allow the recovery of models under a diligence. As to the intended fittings or furnishings, they propose to establish the intent by production of the drawings under which they say the vessel was to be completed. That, I think, may be very material, although the value of the thing recovered as evidence, and the admissibility of it at the trial, will, of course, not be disposed of by granting the diligence. It might be that a drawing of the vessel, fully equipped, with guns, &c., might be recovered, or the identification of the article with the vessel might be established otherwise.

Lord Ardmillan.—Suppose under one of the other articles, the prosecution recovers a letter referring to a sketch by number, colour, shape, or otherwise, and the letter is plainly connected with it, is the prosecution not entitled to recover the sketch which, by that letter, is so connected with the ship as to be, as he believes, proof of the intention with which it was equipped? The value of it afterwards is a very different question, but it would never do to exclude that evidence.

Lord Deas.—I have no doubt at all that with the exception of the models, they are entitled to article 8; but your Lordship has made an important observation, that in our practice the recovery of a document under diligence does not imply that it shall be admitted at the trial. It may be rejected. The whole question is, whether the party is to have such documents in their power, so as to use them if they can as evidence.

The 9th article was agreed to be altered as suggested by Mr. Clark yesterday.

Lord Advocate.—Then the diligence will apply to letters, &c. down to 10th December 1863, the date of the seizure.

Mr. Gordon.—There is some correspondence between us and the Government after that date which we wish to recover.

Lord President.—You can call on the pursuer to produce that. Then it will be down to 10th December. In reference to an observation made by Mr. Clark yesterday as to the finding on the objection to the 1st and other counts, I propose to make that finding a little fuller, so as perhaps to meet the view stated; we propose to make it, 'inasmuch as the allegation against the defenders set forth 'in these counts is not that they did equip or attempt to equip the 'vessel with intent to cruise or commit hostilities, but is that they 'did equip or attempt to equip the vessel with intent, or in order 'that such vessel should be employed in the service of certain foreign 'states with intent to cruise and commit hostilities.' Does that meet your view, Mr. Clark?

Mr. Clark.—Entirely.

The 5th of May was then fixed for the trial, it having been stated that the Lord Ordinary consented to that day.

The motion for leave to appeal was held as made to-day, in order to suit the date of the interlocutor.

Wednesday, March 30, 1864.

(*Before* Lord Ormidale.)

Mr. Watson.—I appear for both sets of claimants, and the questions for determination arise out of the execution of a joint commission and diligence granted by the First Division. (*Reads Art.* 9 *of Specification.*) Various havers were examined by the claimants, and I first ask attention to the depositions of Mr. Henry Miller, messenger-at-arms, Glasgow, and Mr. Adam Paterson, writer, Glasgow. (*Reads from Miller's deposition.*) So that the documents in possession of this haver are of four kinds; first, there are letters and memoranda relative to the 'Pampero,' and her construction and use, addressed by him to Mr. Paterson and to Mr. Underwood, the American consul at Glasgow; there are also communications made by him to Mr. Hart, the fiscal, and there is a note received by Miller from Mr. Underwood, and another note received by him from Mr. Hart. Now, Mr. Hart in his deposition is interrogated, 'Have you any such letters?'—(*Reads.*) The deposition of Mr. Hart is clearly to the effect that Miller was not employed by him at all on behalf of the Crown. Mr. Paterson in his deposition says, 'During the period from 23d October to 23d November last, I was professionally engaged'—(*Reads.*) On being called on to produce these documents, Mr. Paterson declines to do so on the ground of confidentiality, and of the duty which he owes to his client. The documents which he has are communications passing between the consul and himself, and communications addressed by Miller to the consul and to him in relation to the vessel,—just those documents, copies of which are held by the haver Miller, who declined also to produce, 'on the ground of con-'fidentiality, as I was employed by Mr. Paterson to assist him in 'making a private inquiry, and in precognoscing witnesses.' The haver, however, had no objection to the documents being sealed up, and they were produced to the Commissioner and sealed up, subject to your Lordship's determination. Now, it is plain that these documents are not confidential in this sense, that they are not documents passing between or prepared by or for the use of any of the parties to the investigation at present going on. The present question depends between the Crown on the one hand, and the owners and builders on the other, and it is not pretended that these documents were addressed to the agents of the parties, or to the parties on either of these sides. It is not pretended that Mr. Miller had employment from them. That is negatived by the Crown, and it will not be said that he was employed by me.

Lord Ormidale.—How is that negatived?

Mr. Watson.—Mr. Hart says so, and we have his own statement.

Mr. Rutherfurd.—He was not employed by the Crown.

Lord Ormidale.—But Mr. Paterson may have been employed by the Crown, and he may have been employed by Mr. Paterson.

Mr. Watson.—The haver's statement is distinct that his occupation was making a private inquiry, which I take it is in contradistinction to an inquiry at the instance of the public, and Mr. Paterson's statement is to the same effect. Now these documents fall within the specification which the Court has granted, and the only ground on which I can be deprived of them is that they are protected by confidentiality. But they are not protected by that rule, reading it in this sense, as excluding documents intimately connected with the present suit.

Lord Ormidale.—Or any suit. Confidentiality would be a plea perfectly available here, provided it was clear that these documents were got up with reference to any suit.

Mr. Watson.—Certainly, but that is not said. The forfeiture provided by the 7th section of the Act can only be enforced at the instance of the Crown, and any suggestion of a right to prosecute the owners on the ground of contract to give the Federals the vessel, is equally out of the question, because the accusation is that it was intended to be employed against the nation whose consul Mr. Underwood is. So that the employment of Mr. Paterson and of Mr. Miller seems to resolve itself into a sort of amateur employment, for the purpose of making inquiries into the construction and equipment of this vessel. It is for your Lordship to decide whether that is privileged on the ground of confidentiality. Now the principle upon which this plea rests is, that a party shall not damage his own cause by exposing all his private and confidential communications upon the subject-matter of the litigation; that he is quite as much entitled to have his communications with his agent, in regard to the subject-matter of the suit, protected, as he is to keep them within his own breast if he chooses. But every man who speaks to an agent, or employs an ex-captain of police, is not entitled to say, You shall not have the result of my investigations either from me or from this captain of police. It is not alleged that these investigations are kept up for fear of damaging any litigation at the instance of the American consul. I rather take it, that the only ground for withholding them is, that it may damage the case of the claimants. It is the barest case of confidentiality that I ever heard pleaded; because many of the documents which we seek are documents furnished by a sheriff-officer to the American consul, relating to a private inquiry which he was engaged in making. These are not confidential communications between a party and his law-agent; they are not precognitions got up for the conduct of any particular case, and I submit to your Lordship that I am entitled to these. Then, under the call addressed to Mr. Paterson, it appears that he has documents addressed to him by the American consul, and it may be that these stand in a different position from the letters and memoranda on the subject of this vessel addressed by Miller to the consul, or to Mr. Paterson as representing him. Of course I can only speak of these documents in the most general terms, in consequence of the very general terms of the haver's deposition; but it clearly appears from the deposition of Mr. Paterson, that these are documents which bear directly upon the construction, equipment, and destination of the 'Pampero,' and these are precisely the documents which we seek to recover, and which clearly fall under the call. I don't ask these documents if they are not within the call, but so far as within the call, I ask your Lordship to give me these documents, on the ground that the plea of confidentiality is not well founded. I don't know any gentleman better informed on the subject of confidentiality than the haver who is in possession of these documents, and he declines to produce them on the ground of confidentiality, and of the duty which he owes to his client; but he says,—'Provided he authorizes 'me to do so, I shall produce or exhibit said documents, or such of 'them as come within the terms of the specification.' He does not put it on the ground that any proceedings were contemplated, or that the communications which passed between him and the consul related to a matter connected with the present suit. And although, for his own protection, and perhaps very properly, he has declined to produce, I think your Lordship will give me these documents without hesitation, as they are documents clearly falling under the call, and passing between the consul and Mr. Paterson in the course of inquiries as to the construction, equipment, or destination of the vessel,—inquiries which have no connexion with the Crown or the Crown proceedings, and which, therefore, in a question between the Crown and me, are not confidential. There are also two other documents falling under this, viz., a letter by Mr. Hart to Mr. Miller, and a note by the consul to Mr. Miller, and these have been sealed up. So that Mr. Miller and Mr. Paterson between them, have got the following documents:—Mr. Miller has copies of all the communications addressed by him to Mr. Paterson and the consul, and Mr. Paterson has the greater part of the principals of these copies.

Lord Ormidale.—Has Miller produced copies?

Mr. Watson.—Yes, he produces his private letter-book. Mr. Miller has also a note from Mr. Hart, and a note from the American consul, which are produced. Then Mr. Paterson has the greater part of the communications, memoranda, &c., relative to the vessel, her construction, and equipment, addressed by Mr. Miller to him and to the American consul, and he has also letters, and copies of letters passing between himself and the American consul, and he declines to part with them, or with copies of them, and he declines even to commit them to the judgment of the Court. I now pass to Mr. Hart's objections. His deposition is, 'I have in my possession some letters and other documents—(*Reads to*)—from the claimant Mr. Galbraith;' and he produces the letter addressed to him before the date of the seizure by Mr. Galbraith, one of the owners, by Mr. Thomson, one of the builders, and by Mr. Stevenson, agent for Mr. Thomson; he makes that concession, as we were in possession of copies to produce, failing the principals; 'and the call, &c., having been repeated—(*Reads to*)—disposal of the Court.' The ground upon which he declines, is because the documents have came into his custody in the course of an investigation at his instance, as Procurator-Fiscal. I am quite aware of the privilege which the Crown, even through its Procurators-Fiscal, is entitled, to a certain extent, to plead. On this subject I refer your Lordship to the law as laid down by Mr. Dickson, in his book on Evidence, from p. 918 to 922 inclusive. I think he very fairly explains the ground on which this privilege of the Crown rests. Of course the privilege is pleadable in a greater or less degree according to the nature of the investigation, and the party pleading it. I don't think an inferior official, such as the fiscal of a county, is entitled to carry the plea of privilege to the same extent as one of the Privy Council, or as one of the Secretaries of State.

Lord Ormidale.—Has the fiscal not precisely the same privilege *in criminalibus* as the Lord Advocate? I should think he has. It is rather a duty than a privilege.

Mr. Watson.—I shall inquire how far that duty or privilege extends. Mr. Dickson at page 918 says, 'Reasons of public policy 'require—(*reads to*)—officers under his authority;' and then, 'On 'the same grounds of public policy—(*reads to*)—had to be divulged.'

Lord Ormidale.—Then it comes to this, that the Lord Advocate's statement is enough.

Mr. Watson.—In the case of Henderson and Robertson in 1818 it was so held.

Lord Ormidale.—There is, I think, a much more recent case, in which the late Lord Justice-Clerk Hope was much opposed to asking the Lord Advocate to produce what he said or thought should not be produced, and he was supported to the fullest extent by Lord Cockburn.

Mr. Watson.—I think that is the case of Donald *v.* Hart; but that referred to the result of investigations made by the Lord Advocate. But I am not insisting against the privilege of the Crown to get such documents as these. I ask your Lordship on this point to take a note of sections 1851 and 1852 of Mr. Dickson's book.

Lord Ormidale.—Of course I cannot take what Mr. Dickson says is the state of the law without looking into the authorities cited by him.

Mr. Watson.—I merely refer to it generally, because I don't intend to maintain that the law is not well laid down in favour of the Crown, or that, if the Lord Advocate says that from any reasons of state policy it would be dangerous to make production, I am entitled to have production in the face of such a statement. But the question is, whether, whenever the Procurator-fiscal is called as a haver in any civil, or partly civil and partly criminal cause, depending before the Court of Exchequer in a suit between the Crown and the parties calling for production, he is entitled to take the ground which the Fiscal has taken in this case, and to decline to produce, because the documents have come into his possession in the course of an investigation at his instance as Procurator-fiscal. That is a ground which would extend the Lord Advocate's privilege far beyond anything that has yet been decided in his favour. Wherever the Crown receives communications in regard to an offence, and when they are making an investigation with a view to ulterior proceedings, whether these proceedings be adopted or not, I am quite aware that it is the privilege of the public prosecutor to refuse to part with these documents. Still there are circumstances in which it may be allowable to recover them, and in which the Court will only refrain from granting diligence for their recovery upon the statement of the Lord Advocate, that the production of them would be damaging to the State. But the privilege which Mr. Hart pleads goes to this,—the documents may have no connexion with the Crown, the documents may be the fairest and best and most competent evidence in the cause, but if the procurator-fiscal has once laid his clutches on them, he is not bound to give them up.

Lord Ormidale.—If documents come into his possession as procurator-fiscal, they are Crown documents. It is the possession of the Crown, and not his own possession.

Mr. Watson.—The same question might be raised in other circumstances to the detriment of the subject, if this point of privilege was conceded by the Court. I shall take a case which actually did occur—a case where an Information having been lodged of bigamy, the fiscal took possession, in the private repositories of the accused, of the whole letters written to him by the person accusing him of bigamy, and the proceedings at the instance of the Crown, which ultimately proved abortive, were very shortly followed by a declarator in the Court of Session, and of course the best material which the defender in the civil suit could have for conducting his defence to the civil action, was the letters which had been taken from his possession by the public prosecutor. The officials of the Crown, when called upon to produce them, gave the answer which Mr. Hart has here done. But would the Civil Court stand by, and simply because the fiscal declines to say what documents he has, or to produce them, refuse to allow the parties to the civil suit to recover them? There can be no pretext of reasons of state policy in regard to such documents, and it would be the grossest injustice to hold that whenever documents came into the hands of the fiscal, the effect was to destroy them as evidence in all civil suits. If the declinature of the fiscal was confined to documents or communications received by the Crown, the result of inquiries made by the Crown, or precognitions taken by or for the Crown, I could quite understand it; but if the present contention of the fiscal were given effect to, it would be pushing the privilege to an extent for which I can find no warrant in principle or precedent, and certainly none in common justice.

Lord Ormidale.—Are the documents in Mr. Hart's possession documents addressed to him as part of his investigation; or were they seized by him?

Mr. Watson.—He declines to say what they are.

Lord Ormidale.—Did you ask him that?

Mr. Watson.—He says, 'I decline to state the nature of such 'documents.'

Lord Ormidale.—That means their contents.

Mr. Rutherfurd.—I may state that Mr. Hart is quite prepared to say that there was no seizure of any such documents. Does my learned friend press no objection against the non-production by Mr. Murray as Crown Agent, or by Sir Archibald Alison?

Mr. Watson.—No. Sir Archibald has distinguished between the confidential and non-confidential, and given us the benefit of the latter. To that I can have no objection.

Mr. Rutherfurd.—Then, as the objections against the Crown agent and against Sir A. Alison are not supported, and as I intend to offer no argument with reference to the objections stated by Mr. Miller and Mr. Paterson, I shall be very short in answer to my learned friend.

Lord Ormidale.—Who are you for?

Mr. Rutherfurd.—For the Crown,—for the pursuer.

Lord Ormidale.—And the pursuer alone?

Mr. Rutherfurd.—Yes, and I intend to support the objection to produce which has been stated by the Procurator-fiscal Mr. Hart.

Lord Ormidale.—If you appear for the pursuer alone, and if you admit that the documents fall under the call, what right have you to support the objection of Mr. Hart? If you appeared separately for the Lord Advocate, that might be a different matter. But this is a very important point, and I expected it to be argued fully by senior counsel. It appears to me that the plea of confidentiality stated by a haver, a professional man, who says that the writings called for came into his hands as professional adviser of his client, is a plea that is only available, and can only be supported by the haver himself or his employer, and not by the other party at all.

Mr. Rutherfurd.—I appear for the employer of Mr. Hart.

Lord Ormidale.—Who is he?

Mr. Rutherfurd.—The Lord Advocate.

Lord Ormidale.—Then you don't appear for the Lord Advocate merely in his character of pursuer of this action?

Mr. Rutherfurd.—No.

Lord Ormidale.—But you appear for the Lord Advocate in his official character?

Mr. Rutherfurd.—Certainly. The sole question to which I have to address myself is the objection taken by Mr. Hart. (*Reads from Mr. Hart's deposition*). The investigation here referred to is an investigation at the instance of the Crown against certain parties under the Foreign Enlistment Act as for a misdemeanour, some of these parties being mentioned in the Information in the case of the seizure of the vessel. The Foreign Enlistment Act not only authorizes seizure of the ship, but it also creates a misdemeanour which may be tried in the Criminal Court; and an investigation is still going on at the instance of the Crown against certain parties as for that misdemeanour.

Mr. Watson.—Then your statement is, that the investigation referred to is the investigation for criminal purposes?

Mr. Rutherfurd.—It is an investigation with reference to the criminal charge under the Statute.

Mr. Watson.—Then is my learned friend going to give us the documents coming under Mr. Hart's investigation for civil purposes?

Mr. Rutherfurd.—The only procedure for civil purposes that I know of is the procedure for seizure of the vessel. But the objection taken by Mr. Hart is, I submit, perfectly sound. In Mr. Dickson's work, we have the reason very correctly stated why public policy requires that evidence should be excluded in matters the disclosure of which would be prejudicial to the public service. I submit that that applies to all criminal investigations at the instance of the Crown, and although a distinction is taken in some cases where documents coming into the hands of the Crown officials, in the course of a criminal investigation, may be ordered to be produced by the Crown, still that is an exceptional case, which can only occur where special cause is shown by the party, and where the Lord Advocate does not appear and state that the production of such documents would be prejudicial to the public interest. Now, with regard to the cases mentioned by Mr. Dickson in support of his statement at p. 918, that the divulgence of such matters would frustrate criminal investigations; I refer first to the case of Donald *v.* Hart, 6th July 1844, 6 D. 1255; that was an action of damages against the Procurator-fiscal, arising out of an inquiry made by him, and the Court refused to allow the precognition to be obtained on grounds of public policy, an objection having been taken by the Lord Advocate, who appeared, and refused to produce, and also because no sufficient cause for the production was shown. Then there is the case of Hill *v.* Fletcher, 12th November 1847, 10 D. 37. This was an action of damages arising out of an abortive criminal prosecution for a rape; the proceedings against the accused had failed, and the woman raised a civil action, and that was a stronger case for producing the documents than we have here, because she stated that her action could not proceed without the evidence which had been obtained by the Procurator-fiscal.

Lord Ormidale.—Could the parties not have made a precognition for themselves?

Mr. Rutherfurd.—But there were a declaration and medical certificates, which to be worth anything, must be the certificates made at the time. The application for the documents, which were particularly specified, was refused, though the printed indictment was allowed to be given up. Then, in Earl *v.* Vass, House of Lords, 1822, 1 Shaw's Appeals, 229, the judgment of the Court of Session was reversed, and the House of Lords held that communications to a public official, referring to the conduct of a party in a public employment, or applying for a public office, should not be given up, on the broad principle that reasons of public policy required that public officers and public boards should not be compelled to disclose communications falling into their hands in their official capacity. These are stronger cases than the present, because there the parties ran great risk that their case would fail without the documents called for. But we have no special cause shown for the production of the documents here; and therefore I submit that these cases are *a fortiori* of the present. In the case of Little *v.* Smith, 8 D. 265, and 9 D. 743, which is the case referred to by your Lordship in the course of my friend's argument, we have the opinion of Lord Cockburn, very strongly supporting that of the Lord Justice-Clerk Hope, to the effect that a declaration made in the course of a criminal investigation, at the instance of a procurator-fiscal, was the property of the Crown, and that the Crown could not be compelled to produce it, although the Lord Advocate did not appear and object. Lord Cockburn says,—'The only case I 'recollect of in which a precognition was properly allowed to be pro-'duced, was in the case of Harper, which was an action of damages 'against a magistrate for taking a precognition unfairly, and it was 'therefore necessary to see what the precognition contained.' It is said that this objection cannot be taken by the Procurator-fiscal, but I submit it is the duty of the Procurator-fiscal, as a subordinate official under the Lord Advocate, to take the objection. He could not waive the objection as long as his principal, the Lord Advocate, had not waived it; and the Lord Advocate was not cited as a party, nor was any question put either to the Lord Advocate or to Mr. Hart, whether the production of these documents would be injurious to the public service or not. But I submit that the general rule is, that communications made to a public official in the position of the Procurator-fiscal, are privileged communications, which cannot, in the general case, be recovered, although I don't dispute that, on a special cause shown, they may be recovered, provided that the public service be not prejudiced by their production.

Lord Ormidale.—Probably the general principle which you state is correct, but there is a little difficulty in applying it to the documents here, from not knowing what they are, from not knowing whether they are of the nature of precognitions or communications by the Fiscal himself to his agents, or persons acting for him, or documents seized or taken possession of by him. I cannot comprehend at present how any precognition taken by Mr. Hart, or any letter written by him or his subordinates, can by possibility be matter of evidence in this case.

Mr. Watson.—I don't ask any precognition taken by Mr. Hart for the Crown, or any letters written by him in the course of his investigation as Fiscal.

Mr. Rutherfurd.—But Mr. Hart says that the only documents in his possession are those which came into his possession in the course of his investigations, and I am authorized to state that no such documents have come into his possession by seizure, that they are merely letters and other documents addressed to him upon the public service, and Mr. Hart, if necessary, will amend his deposition to that effect. I should object to Mr. Hart making any statement as to the nature of the documents in his possession, or from whom he got them, because if Mr. Hart was compelled to give the names of the persons from whom he received letters, or to whom he wrote in the course of his investigation, he would be destroying his own plea of confidentiality. It would be giving the parties a clue to where they might get evidence falling under this call from third parties other than Mr. Hart, and these third parties could not take up the same ground of confidentiality, and might be compelled to produce them, just doing the very harm to the public service which Mr. Hart's objection is intended to obviate. Therefore, I say it was the duty of Mr. Hart to decline to produce these documents, because he could not waive an objection which had not been waived by the Lord Advocate. If the parties had shown special cause,—if they had cited the Lord Advocate and asked him whether the production of such documents would be injurious to the public service, and the Crown had not objected, or stated that their production would be injurious, I think the parties might have been entitled to recover them. But they have not done so, and no special cause has been shown. My learned friend referred to the Yelverton case, and said that the party in such a case would not be able to recover letters for the proof in a declarator, if this objection were well founded. But that case might just be one of the exceptions to the rule which I have stated. If a party raises a declarator of marriage, what stronger special cause could be stated for the recovery of the letters which may have formed part of the productions in the criminal process? Moreover, they would be able to specify exactly what they wanted, and it would not be the very general specification which we have here. In the case of Craig *v.* Marjoribanks, 3 *Murray*, 343, an action against a Justice of Peace, on the ground of a criminal inquiry having been sanctioned by him upon improper grounds, where the Lord Chief Commissioner refused to order production of the precognitions and letters, transmitting them to the Lord Advocate, because the precognitions had been followed by a trial before the Sheriff, and a verdict of guilty, and he says, that even if the question had been of a different nature, the writings must have been specified much more particularly.

Lord Ormidale.—There is a complete and manifest distinction between documents that existed long prior to the Fiscal's proceedings, and which did not arise at his instance, or in answer to inquiries of his, and letters written by him, or documents of the nature of precognitions.

Mr. Watson.—I don't ask the one, and I ask the other; but the Crown say that whatever is in the hands of the Fiscal is not available.

Lord Ormidale.—I understand Mr. Rutherfurd to say that the Fiscal is ready to amend his deposition to the effect of stating that the documents which he holds are of the nature of inquiries and answers to inquiries in regard to a contemplated prosecution by him as procurator-fiscal, or in contemplation of a criminal prosecution at the instance of the Crown.

Mr. Rutherfurd.—Yes; and communications made to him.

Lord Ormidale.—Of the nature of inquiries and answers to inquiries in regard to a contemplated criminal prosecution.

Mr. Rutherfurd.—He would include communications addressed to him, whether in answer to inquiries or not.

Lord Ormidale.—Then if Mr. Watson gets a written statement that what the Fiscal holds is nothing more than Mr. Rutherfurd states, there is an end of the question.

Mr. Rutherfurd.—I shall only say farther that Mr. Miller in his deposition says, that he has copies of letters addressed to the Fiscal. Of course, if the principals cannot be produced in evidence, the copies could not be produced.

Mr. Watson.—We are not to be shut out from copies of everything, because the Crown choose to keep the principals.

Lord Ormidale.—But it is not only the privilege of the Fiscal, it is his duty to withhold a certain class of documents.

Mr. Gifford.—I understand my friend now to state that he does not ask any letters written by or to the Fiscal as Fiscal.

Lord Ormidale.—As Fiscal with reference to his public duty.

Mr. Watson.—And in the course of his investigations.

Mr. Gifford.—Then my friend must no longer make a general call.

Lord Ormidale.—Mr. Watson is perfectly safe in giving up the point if your statement is correct, because it is manifest that no communication of the nature referred to can be evidence in the cause.

Mr. Watson.—Then my learned friend will communicate to us the amendment which he proposes on the Fiscal's deposition.

Lord Ormidale.—Has any notice of this discussion been given to Mr. Paterson, Mr. Miller, or the American consul?

Mr. Watson.—I understand not.

Lord Ormidale.—That is very important, because properly speaking the objection of confidentiality is an objection that the haver and his employer have alone a right to maintain. If they choose to yield it, the parties have no right to take it. Before I would ordain these productions to be made, I would require very special notice to Mr. Paterson and Mr. Miller, and also to their alleged employer, Mr. Underwood, the American consul, to give them an opportunity of appearing before me, and, if they please, of supporting the objection they have taken, and perhaps with certification that if they don't appear, I will hold that they have departed from it.

Mr. Rutherfurd.—Our statement is that Mr. Hart has no documents in his possession except such as he has received in his public capacity as Procurator-fiscal, being of the nature of affidavits, precognitions, letters, and other communications to him, or copies of letters addressed by him to other parties in reference to the criminal investigation.

Lord Ormidale.—I shall pronounce an interlocutor appointing notice to be given to these gentlemen, that they may, if they think proper, appear before me on a certain day to support their objection. I think it would also be advisable to put into the interlocutor a recommendation that Mr. Paterson should bring the documents with him, because I may require to examine them before disposing of the objection. If the statement made by Mr. Rutherfurd as to the documents in Mr. Hart's possession is put in, there is an end to the case as regards the Fiscal.

Mr. Watson.—Yes.

Lord Ormidale.—And it is quite clear that such communications could not be evidence. If that is understood, the intimation need not be made to the Fiscal nor to Sir Archibald Alison, or Mr. Murray, against whom the objection is given up; but the intimation must be made to Mr. Paterson, Mr. Miller, and the American Consul.

Monday, at eleven o'clock, at his Lordship's Bar, was then appointed for farther proceeding in the case.

Monday, 4th April.

Lord Ormidale.—Is the matter as to Mr. Hart, the Fiscal, finally arranged?

Mr. Clark.—I understand that no statement has been furnished to us yet.

Solicitor-General.—The statement which Mr. Rutherfurd made at the bar the other day is, we understand, exactly in accordance with the fact. If my learned friends are not satisfied with that, they are entitled to examine Mr. Hart farther.

Mr. Clark.—The statement we have received, as I understand, is not conform to that statement at the bar.

Solicitor-General.—I understand it is exactly in accordance with the truth. If you are not satisfied with it, you must just examine him.

Mr. Clark.—Then we must just examine Mr. Hart and Mr. Murray.

Solicitor-General.—As regards Mr. Murray, it was abandoned.

Mr. Clark.—Will you give us the same statement as to Mr. Murray?

Lord Advocate.—My impression is, that my instructions to Mr. Murray would be to decline answering any questions upon the subject.

Mr. Clark.—That is what he has done, and the question is, whether Mr. Murray is entitled to make that absolute declinature. We do not want confidential documents, but the question is what he is entitled to withhold.

Lord Advocate.—He is quite ready to say that he has nothing in his hands that is not confidential, and which did not come into his hands as Crown agent, but beyond that he can make no statement.

Lord Ormidale.—Is not that quite sufficient?

Mr. Clark.—It does not follow that everything of that kind is confidential. (*Reads from Mr. Murray's deposition*). Now, any letters which Mr. Murray writes to another person conducting this litigation upon the part of the Crown and with reference to that litigation I admit are privileged; and any letters which he receives in answer to those letters which he so writes as agent for the Crown, I also admit are privileged; but it does not follow that all letters or all documents which he has received since he became agent in this matter are privileged; and that is the extent to which Mr. Murray pleads privilege. No matter what was the date of the document, no matter from whom he received it, simply because he received it since he became agent in this cause for the Crown, and with reference to these proceedings, he says it is privileged. Now, I take it that the plea of confidentiality does not cover all documents or things which he may recover with reference to a particular trial, but can only be extended to his own communications to parties in connexion with the trial or for the purposes of the trial, and the answers he receives from those parties. But if he receives a document which may be of use to us, and which was in existence it may be before this trial ever was thought of, is that to be a privileged document? That is the extent to which Mr. Murray pleads his privilege. If he will say that he has no documents in his possession except documents which he has received in answer to communications of his own, or communications made with reference to this case, I shall admit the privilege.

Lord Ormidale.—Upon his statement?

Mr. Clark.—Of course.

Lord Ormidale.—You might not unfairly say that you would not take Mr. Murray's statement, but that you would require that I should examine the documents myself, and admit the plea if I found it applicable.

Mr. Clark.—That would probably be the more regular course, and I don't say that I may not find it necessary to follow that course, but meantime I don't think I shall require to do so. My objection is, that Mr. Murray states the plea of confidentiality too broadly. He may have in his possession a great variety of documents which came into existence long before these proceedings commenced, and he says, 'Because I am Crown Agent conducting 'these proceedings, I shall give you no information as to the source 'from which I received them; I shall not state the character of 'the documents, but I say I am protected by the plea of confiden'tiality as regards the whole documents I have received.' Mr. Murray is merely agent for the common informer, because the Lord Advocate has no higher character in this case. The same proceedings might have been taken by any person, and therefore I say Mr. Murray has no privilege whatever as being Crown Agent. He is merely the agent of the pursuer of this action; and I am entitled to examine the pursuer's agent, and to make him produce any documents he has which do not relate to this prosecution, and which came into existence before this prosecution ever was thought of.

Lord Advocate.—Such a contention is utterly absurd. I deny that I appear here as a common informer. But Mr. Murray does not plead his privilege merely as agent in the cause. On the contrary, he pleads this, that he has nothing in his possession that he has not obtained as acting for the Government of the country in this matter; and the contention that he shall produce the documents which he may have received, or the correspondence which has come into his hands as acting on the part of the Government, is a contention that does not require argument. Mr. Murray is quite ready to say that he has no documents that came into his possession otherwise than as my hand in this matter.

Lord Ormidale.—In criminal cases there is plenty of authority to the effect that he would not be bound to give such documents up.

Lord Advocate.—But this is much higher.

Lord Ormidale.—Is it not just a civil suit?

Lord Advocate.—No. I shall assume that these are documents which are the property of the Government; if they were asked for even in Parliament, and Government said, It is contrary to the public service to produce them, the House of Commons never would dream of even voting upon it; much more are they privileged in a Court of Justice.

Lord Ormidale.—I should like to have some authority upon that point; I don't think it is very clear. Suppose that there had come into the hands of Mr. Hart a model or sketch of the vessel to be constructed, furnished by the parties who originally gave the order for the construction of the vessel, and which would show very distinctly the sort of vessel it was to be, are the defenders in this case to be precluded from the evidence of that plan or model, which may be very favourable for them, merely because it has got into the hands of a public officer?

Lord Advocate.—But suppose Government receive a communication from a third party in relation to this vessel, and that they confidentially transmit it to me for inquiry, and I give it into the hands of the Crown agent, is my learned friend entitled to recover that?

Lord Ormidale.—No; very likely not. But is it to be assumed because the Lord Advocate says so,—no doubt he has very high powers and privileges,—but is it sufficient that the Lord Advocate here says all the documents called for in the hands of Mr. Murray are of that description?

Lord Advocate.—I am quite prepared to say that he has nothing that does not fall distinctly under that category.

Lord Ormidale.—Supposing that to be stated, would that not be satisfactory?

Mr. Clark.—This has been recognised as a civil proceeding; it is not a criminal proceeding; and I don't know that the Crown, suing in a civil Court, is entitled to any higher privilege than any other party suing in a civil Court.

Lord Ormidale.—The privilege of the Crown was well elicited in the case of Leven *v.* Young about 1815, where this principle was authoritatively settled in the House of Lords, that every information or communication made to the Government of the country, or any of its officers, was privileged and protected.

Mr. Clark.—And if Mr. Murray, when examined, had said: 'I 'have nothing in my hands except communications made to 'Government, and which have come into my hands as agent in this 'cause,' there would then have been an opportunity of raising the question which the Lord Advocate desires to raise. But all that Mr. Murray, acting under the instructions of the Lord Advocate, says, is: 'I have no information, and I have no documents except 'what I have received or written as Crown Agent.' Now, for all I know, these documents may not have been received by Mr. Murray or the Lord Advocate as a Government official at all.

Lord Ormidale.—It has been stated now by the Lord Advocate—

Mr. Clark.—But I am entitled to ask Mr. Murray. I can imagine that there are some documents which have been received by him as Crown Agent, since this case commenced, which I am not entitled to recover; but the Crown says that all documents received by him as Crown Agent since the commencement of these proceedings, and which have been received by him as agent in this cause, are privileged. If Mr. Murray had made on oath the statement which the Lord Advocate has now made, we might never have raised this question, but the only answer which he gives is that which I have already read.

Solicitor-General.—There is another view of this matter which appears to me worthy of consideration. The Crown Agent appears to be examined as a haver in form, but in truth as on precognition. He is examined not for the purpose of getting any individual thing, the existence of which is known, but for the purpose of ascertaining whether such and such things do exist to his knowledge or no. Now, to call your adversary's agent, who, at your adversary's expense and for his interest, has made investigations and obtained information, and to ask him to give you the result of that, is, I think, unprecedented, and fraught with the most dangerous consequences. You call the agent for the Crown here, and ask him not if he has got a particular letter or document, being plainly of a description which you are entitled to get as evidence whether it is in his hands or no; but you ask him, Have you ascertained, as agent for the Crown and at the expense of the Crown, the existence of any documents with reference to this vessel? The answer is, I shall not tell you what I have ascertained the existence of, or what I have recovered for my client; if you want a particular letter, I will tell you whether I have it or not, but I shan't tell you in this general way whether I have any memoranda or orders or documents in regard to the ship. And if you may examine an agent in this way, you may examine a counsel. Now I think it is in accordance with practice and policy, that when you are to examine your adversary's agent, you must be precise and specific in your demand; you are not to fish him,—to call on him for information as to the existence or non-existence of things, or as to his knowledge on that subject.

Lord Ormidale.—You may, except when it is protected; and that is the whole question.

Mr. Clark.—The defenders were examined by the Crown upon the very same article of the specification, upon the very same call.

Solicitor-General.—That is a party, and a party is quite another thing.

Lord Ormidale.—The answer may be conclusive that it is protected by confidentiality, and that must also apply to any inquiry as to where the thing is. But the whole question is this, Is it enough for the haver to say, 'It is all protected, and I will neither 'show it, because I say it is protected, nor will I answer a single 'question about it?' As I understand, Lord Advocate, your plea is not intended to apply to things that had their existence before this action was contemplated.

Lord Advocate.—Certainly not. Mr. Murray has nothing that he did not get from one or other of the Government officers employed in this matter with special reference to this case.

Lord Ormidale.—And which had not an existence before.

Lord Advocate.—Certainly not.

Mr. Clark.—If your Lordship takes our view, you would repel the objection stated by the haver, with such qualifications as your Lordship might think proper.

Lord Ormidale.—If I took your view I would do that, or I might make the qualification that I would examine in the first place the documents myself. I would only dismiss your appeal in respect of the statement now made by the Lord Advocate.

Mr. Clark.—Your Lordship will keep in view that we object to take any statement of the Lord Advocate. We must have the statement upon oath of the haver in common form.

Lord Ormidale.—There are cases, of which Donald *v.* Hart, for example, was one, where the statement of the Lord Advocate was taken. The whole of this matter is attended with a great deal of delicacy, and we must conform to precedent.

Lord Advocate.—Your Lordship will also keep in mind that though this is a civil prosecution, that is, an information of seizure in the Court of Exchequer, it proceeds on the commission of a misdemeanour.

Lord Ormidale.—An action of damages for assault is a civil suit, though it proceeds on the footing that there has been a crime.

Lord Advocate.—But the Statute makes the offence, and this is simply the result in Exchequer of the commission of the offence.

Mr. Gordon.—I ask your Lordship to notice that the call is for documents furnished by Henry Miller to Mr. Paterson or Mr. Underwood. It is not for documents furnished to the Fiscal or the Lord Advocate or the Crown Agent.

Lord Advocate.—They may have been furnished to Mr. Paterson or Mr. Underwood, but it does not follow that they may not have come into Mr. Murray's hands precisely in the way I have stated.

Mr. Clark.—In the case of Donald *v.* Hart, the order asked was for the recovery of a precognition.

Lord Ormidale.—I was not talking of the particular thing asked there, but I think in that case and some others the Lord Advocate's statement was taken.

Mr. Clark.—But you would ascertain before that the character of the document sought to be recovered.

Lord Advocate.—Suppose it had relation to a trial for sedition or treason, out of which an Exchequer case arose; there might be communications passing among the humblest individuals, showing not merely sedition in this country, but an intended invasion, or some matter of the deepest public moment. This might have been forwarded to Government, and put into the hands of the executive officers. Is it not perfectly plain that the same rule would apply?

Mr. Gordon.—But there is a distinction between the two cases, because there the Lord Advocate is a neutral party, while here he is engaged in a civil prosecution, and therefore we are entitled to have a more minute examination as to the nature of the documents which have come into his possession. If it is said they were documents connected with a criminal matter, anything done by the Fiscal or any communication made to the Fiscal, that is quite different.

Lord Ormidale.—But the Lord Advocate has stated that Mr. Murray holds nothing, and knows about nothing, except the communications which have been made to him with reference to the public service. Now, you will find that the privilege of Government goes that length, and that is not the privilege of the Crown alone, but of every officer of the Government. The only difficulty that occurs to my mind just now is, as to whether the Court has not the right to see the documents in the first place, and be satisfied that they are of that nature. Do you say that the Court cannot examine the documents ?

Lord Advocate.—I think the privilege is to be pleaded as high as that.

Lord Ormidale.—That the Government officer's statement must be taken ?

Lord Advocate.—I think so.

Mr. Gordon.—I am not aware that that has ever been held where the Lord Advocate is the party suing.

Lord Advocate.—It is just where he is the party suing that his statement is taken ; and if I were to plead this on the ground that all these documents were obtained with a view to a criminal prosecution, I should be quite well founded ; though I think that is lower ground than I am taking, because every one of these documents came into my hands in regard to a matter which has been made the subject of criminal prosecution.

Lord Ormidale.—I am glad that that statement has been made, because it may be enough for you here.

Mr. Clark.—Our wish is to get that statement recorded in the usual way by the haver.

Lord Ormidale.—I shall look into the authorities on the subject, and if I find that the mere statement of the Lord Advocate is not enough, and that that statement must be made by the haver on oath, I shall give effect to that view. If, on the other hand, I shall find, as I expect to find according to my recollection and impression, that the statement of the Lord Advocate is enough, then of course the statement that has been made here is conclusive.

Mr. Gordon.—In the Yelverton case, documents were recovered which had come into the possession of the Fiscal.

Lord Advocate.—That was a special call for special letters belonging to the party who asked for them.

Lord Ormidale.—Where is that reported ?

Mr. Gordon.—I don't know that it is specially reported on that point.

Lord Advocate.—In the case of Henderson *v.* Robertson, 15 D. 292, it was considered a material circumstance that the Lord Advocate did not state that the public service would suffer any injury.

Mr. Clark.—It was the information that was sought there, which undoubtedly is a privileged document.

Lord Ormidale.—The question I have to decide is whether the Lord Advocate's statement may be taken in regard to all documents, without it being known to the Court or anybody but himself what their character is.

Mr. Clark.—Whenever we know that the document is in itself of a privileged kind, such as a precognition or a criminal information lodged with the Fiscal, or it may be communications made to Government, then will arise the question whether or not the Lord Advocate's statement is to be taken as sufficient that the public service would be injured by the production of these documents. But till we ascertain the character of the document, your Lordship is not in a position to take the Lord Advocate's word in the matter. We may examine the Lord Advocate as a haver.

Lord Advocate.—My learned friends would be in a better position for saying what they now say if they made a special call for special documents. They want an examination at large, and I say they cannot have that without injury to the public service, because in that way Mr. Murray would be obliged to make statements regarding documents which, when they were made, they must see they could not recover. If they want anything special from Mr. Murray or the Lord Advocate, let them state it.

Mr. Clark.—We ask for documents or letters written by Henry Miller to Adam Paterson, neither of whom, so far as we are aware, hold any position under the Crown at all.

Lord Advocate.—Certainly not.

Mr. Clark.—What we want is to have these documents recovered, or a statement by Mr. Murray that any such documents came into his possession simply as the officer of the Crown, and as part of a communication made to Government?

Mr. Gordon.—In the case of Robertson *v.* Henderson, the Court found it unnecessary to give any opinion upon the point, whether any statement that a disclosure would prejudice the public interest would be sufficient to protect the informant in the case of an ordinary claim, where such information was said to be made maliciously and without probable cause; and Lord Cockburn goes this length, 'I always understood that the Lord Advocate is bound to 'tell the name of his informer, and produce his information.'

Lord Ormidale.—That is to enable the party injured to bring his action of damages.

Lord Advocate.—But all these cases are after the information has served its purpose in the Lord Advocate's hands; but as to producing an information in the middle of the inquiry, such a thing never was heard of.

Lord Ormidale.—It is not disputed that all information coming into the hands of the public prosecutor in regard to the public service, and every information coming into his hands which had not an existence previous to the action being contemplated, are protected, and the defenders say they are ready to give effect to that plea, if Mr. Murray will state so as a haver on oath. The question then is narrowed very much to this, Ought Mr. Murray to be called on to depone as the Lord Advocate has now stated, since that would be satisfactory to the other party. It would certainly be a very serious matter to infringe upon the rights of the Lord Advocate, that is, upon the rights of the Government of the country; on the other hand there is some risk of the ends of justice being defeated, and the defenders being seriously prejudiced if I don't allow them at all events to get the oath of the haver to that effect.

Lord Advocate.—I suppose my learned friends want something practical. Mr. Murray has nothing whatever in his possession that he did not receive either from myself, or from the Fiscal, or from the collector of customs, who is as much the head of a Government department as I am.

Lord Ormidale.—And with reference to this prosecution.

Lord Advocate.—Yes.

Lord Ormidale.—And none of these things that he has so received had their existence before this action was contemplated.

Lord Advocate.—Before this inquiry was contemplated.

Mr. Clark.—We ask for communications by Henry Miller to Adam Paterson.

Lord Advocate.—Suppose they were that Henry Miller writes to Adam Paterson to say that he has been employed by the parties in this case, for the express purpose of recruiting soldiers and getting up arms, or giving orders for armament for the 'Pampero;' suppose this, though it is not the case in point of fact,—suppose the state of it were that Adam Paterson, having got this information, immediately transmits it to Her Majesty's Government, and Her Majesty's Goverment send it to me, does my learned friend say that that is not as much a part of our confidential communications as any of the rest of them, in this inquiry?

Mr. Gordon.—In such a case we would have Henry Miller's communications, because the probability is, that he would be a witness in such a case against me.

Lord Advocate.—And you want his precognition.

Mr. Gordon.—No; but I want to see what he has stated in writing, not to the Crown, but to Mr. Paterson, who is not connected with the Crown.

Lord Ormidale.—It is very possible that, in the circumstances of this case, I may allow the haver to be farther examined; not with a view of his producing these things, but for the purpose of his making, on oath, the statement which has been made by the Lord Advocate, which I understand is satisfactory to the other parties.

Lord Advocate.—My learned friends know perfectly well, that Mr. Murray gave his answer under instructions. Undoubtedly my learned friend reads the answer more narrowly than it was intended, because it was intended to express all that I have said to-day; but if my learned friends want it more distinctly expressed on oath, I have not the slightest objection.

Mr. Clark.—I think we are entitled to put it in this way—'Have 'you any letters from Henry Miller to Adam Paterson?' and I think Mr. Murray is bound to say, Yes.

Lord Ormidale.—I don't know that.

Lord Advocate.—Mr. Murray will not say whether he has them or not, and he is not bound to do so.

Mr. Clark.—He is bound to tell us what letters he has.

Lord Advocate.—No.

Mr. Clark.—Unless Mr. Miller or Mr. Paterson were employed by the Crown, I have a right to recover all letters which passed between Mr. Miller and Mr. Paterson relative to the Pampero.

Lord Advocate.—If my learned friend is entitled to make Mr. Murray answer whether he has these, he is entitled to make him answer as to everything else.

Lord Ormidale.—The further we proceed in this discussion, the more seems to be wanted. Last week, I understood that everything on this point had been arranged, and it was stated by the counsel for the defenders that the statement of the Lord Advocate, or Mr. Murray himself, without any oath, was quite sufficient. But as the Lord Advocate now, for the purpose of saving discussion, and saving the determination of the very important question which has been raised, has conceded that Mr. Murray may be further cited as a haver, I shall allow that to be done, and then we will see what questions arise. It was stated that that was all the defenders wanted,—the deposition on oath by Mr. Murray to the same effect as the statement of the Lord Advocate.

Mr. Clark.—All I meant to say was, that if, in examining Mr. Murray, he states that he has no letters except those which he received as agent for the Crown, and shows that the letters passing between Henry Miller and Adam Paterson are within that category, I want nothing farther.

Lord Ormidale.—Then I shall make avizandum of this point.

Mr. Clark.—Then Mr. Henry Miller was the first haver examined, and your Lordship appointed intimation to be made to him.

Mr. Burnet, who appeared for Mr. Miller, asked his Lordship to take up first the case of Mr. Underwood and Mr. Paterson, on whose employment Mr. Miller had acted.

Lord Ormidale.—Does any one appear for Mr. Paterson?

Mr. Moncrieff, writer, Glasgow.—I appear for Mr. Paterson.

Lord Ormidale.—A haver must either appear by himself or by counsel. That is a rule of Court which I am not entitled to depart from.

Mr. Moncrieff.—He is my partner.

Lord Ormidale.—Perhaps we may consider ourselves in chambers here. Have you anything to state on behalf of Mr. Paterson?

Mr. Moncrieff.—Nothing more than that he pleads confidentiality.

Lord Ormidale.—Has he not got leave from Mr. Underwood to produce the documents?

Mr. Moncrieff.—He has not.

Mr. Clark stated that Mr. Underwood had been cited to appear before the Commissioner at Glasgow, but had not obeyed the citation, and therefore, of course, he had not been examined. He had been cited again for to-morrow.

Mr. Underwood appeared, and his Lordship explained to him the plea of confidentiality which Mr. Paterson maintained, and stated that he had been cited that he might have an opportunity of intimating whether, as Mr. Paterson's employer, he would waive that plea.

Mr. Underwood, after mentioning that it was his official engagements which had prevented him from obeying the first citation before the Commissioner, and that he intended being present before him to-morrow, said—Mr. Paterson was employed by me to aid and assist me in questions that might possibly arise in reference to the trial connected with the 'Pampero.' These relations are confidential, and I consider myself perfectly justified in relying upon the plea of confidentiality. I have no disposition to excuse Mr. Paterson from that plea, and if I am permitted not to do so, I shall not do so.

Lord Ormidale.—There is another view of it which is frequently taken, that before disposing of the plea of confidentiality, the Court should take an opportunity of breaking the seals of the documents, and examining them for itself, to see how far the plea applies, and if satisfied that the plea is well founded, re-sealing the documents and returning them.

Mr. Underwood.—I am perfectly willing, so far as I am concerned, to submit the question of confidentiality to your Lordship upon an inspection of the papers, and to take your Lordship's opinion whether it applies or not.

Lord Ormidale.—Nothing could be fairer or more satisfactory than that.

Mr. Clark.—Of course your Lordship will understand, and Mr. Underwood will understand, that we maintain that there is no such plea of confidentiality as he states open either to him as American consul, or to Mr. Paterson as his agent, or to Mr. Miller, who was employed by one or other or both.

Lord Ormidale.—The American consul will understand that that is merely the argument of the party. Mr. Underwood is not a party to this cause, and there may be great difficulty in holding that the plea of confidentiality applies where that is the case.

Mr. Clark.—That is just what I was indicating.

Lord Ormidale.—At the same time the plea may apply, though he is not a party to this suit, if the communications in question have passed with reference to a contemplated suit.

Mr. Clark.—At his instance.

Lord Ormidale.—Or where he is likely to be a party.

Mr. Clark.—But we don't understand that that is yet stated. It would be convenient, perhaps, to take this question now, as Mr. Underwood is here.

Mr. Underwood.—I should prefer if it were not taken now, unless there be a necessity for it.

Lord Ormidale.—Perhaps it may be taken as conveniently after Mr. Underwood is examined, and then, if there are any questions arising on his examination, they can be taken together.

Mr. Clark.—From what Mr. Underwood has said, I presume that when he is examined to-morrow, the course to be taken will be, that with whatever explanations he chooses to couple the documents, he will put them under seal, so that they may be transmitted to the Court.

Mr. Underwood.—I do not wish to be misunderstood. I have only spoken with reference to the documents in Mr. Paterson's hands.

Lord Ormidale.—Mr. Underwood is quite entitled to be advised by his agent, or by counsel, on his examination to-morrow, and that may be very desirable, because though he may be acquainted with the general principles of English law, he cannot be expected to know our forms of procedure.

Mr. Clark.—We may take the discussion on the plea of confidentiality, with reference to the documents which Mr. Miller has produced, and he is here represented by counsel.

Mr. Burnet.—I may mention, on behalf of Mr. Miller, that he thought proper, out of respect to the Court, when he was examined as a haver, to hand to the Commissioner, under seal, extracts from his letter-book, containing the letters addressed by him to Mr. Underwood, Mr. Adam Paterson, and Mr. Hart. He also handed to the Commissioner, also under seal, a letter from Mr. Hart, and a memorandum from Mr. Underwood, addressed to himself. The greater part of the letters in Mr. Miller's letter-book were addressed to Mr. Hart, the Procurator-Fiscal, between 24th November and 10th December, to which day the call on Mr. Miller was limited. I understand, from what has passed to-day, that these letters, addressed to Mr. Hart as Procurator-Fiscal, are not insisted for, but whether or not, it is quite clear that if your Lordship does not allow the defenders to recover the principal letters addressed by Mr. Millar to Mr. Hart, you cannot compel Mr. Miller to produce the secondary evidence of these letters which his letter-book affords. As to the letter from Mr. Hart to Mr. Miller, he has no objection to produce it if the Crown don't object; and the letter from Mr. Underwood is in the same position. But until the question is decided as between the American consul and the defenders, he objects to the excerpts from his letter-book being opened and made productions under this commission. There is another objection which Mr. Miller has to the production of these excerpts from his letter-book, which is personal to himself. He is sometimes employed to make very delicate and difficult inquiries, and to communicate in a confidential manner to his employers the information which he obtains for them, and he would be placed in a very delicate position, if your Lordship were to hold that he is bound to produce the letters in his letter-book which he writes to his employers under such confidential employment.

Lord Ormidale.—Who was his employer here?

Mr. Burnet.—Mr. Paterson, as agent for the American consul.

Mr. Clark.—Is there any relation of confidentiality between Mr. Miller and the American consul, because he was his employer as well as Mr. Paterson? I understand that plea is limited to the law adviser.

Lord Ormidale.—I understood that sub-agents were also comprehended in it.

Mr. Burnet.—That is the position Mr. Miller occupied.

Lord Ormidale.—I don't think I ought to dispose of this matter except subject to the arrangement made with Mr. Underwood.

Mr. Clark.—But is Mr. Miller entitled to plead confidentiality because he was employed by Mr. Underwood? Mr. Miller tells us what he was employed to do, viz., to assist Mr. Paterson in making a private inquiry, and in precognoscing witnesses. That won't create confidentiality, unless it is said, which Mr. Miller does not say, that the inquiry was made with reference to this cause, or with reference to a cause which Mr. Underwood was then contemplating to raise in the Courts of Scotland.

Mr. Burnet.—Surely if your Lordship holds that Mr. Underwood is justified in refusing to authorize Mr. Paterson to produce the principal letters in his possession, you will not compel Mr. Miller to produce his letter-book.

Lord Ormidale.—I think the whole matter should be postponed and taken together. It is quite possible that some of the difficulties may be removed, or that matters may appear differently after Mr. Underwood's examination. [To Mr. Underwood]—Then I understand you to say that you have no objections that all the documents called for, if they are covered apparently by the diligence, should be produced under seal, in case I should think it right to examine them before disposing of the question of confidentiality.

Mr. Underwood.—I understand your Lordship's question to apply to documents in Mr. Paterson's hands.

Lord Ormidale.—All I meant in regard to anything you have that may be called for to-morrow, was by way of suggestion, and nothing else. If you see your way with propriety to produce under seal to-morrow, good and well.

Mr. Moncreiff.—I have got all Mr. Paterson's papers with me.

Lord Ormidale.—Then you will probably manage to have them put in the hands of the clerk under seal.

Mr. Moncreiff.—I will put them under seal.

Farther discussion on this point adjourned till Tuesday, 12th April, at eleven o'clock.

Mr. Gifford.—The Lord Advocate has presented an incidental petition in this case, with a view of getting possession for the purpose of evidence at the trial, of various articles, the locality where they are deposited being known to him, but which are withheld by the parties who have possession or custody of them. The things which the Lord Advocate requires possession, or at least exhibition of, fall under three heads,—*1st,* Models of the 'Pampero,' including models of her equipments; *2d,* Equipments or furnishings not seized with the vessel, but prepared elsewhere for use upon the vessel; and *3d,* Furnishings of a different kind, bearing upon the use for which the Crown says the 'Pampero' was intended, and I class these together as uniforms, arms, and accoutrements intended to be used by the marines or seamen who were to be employed on board the vessel. In the Specification originally moved before your Lordship, there was a call made for these articles, and no objection was then taken to the competency of recovering them by diligence. That objection was raised for the first time in the Inner House, and the Court refused to include the models and equipments in a diligence for the recovery of writs, leaving the Lord Advocate to make application for these in some other form. [Mr.

Gifford here quoted from the remarks of the Judges in the Inner House on this point.] It will not be disputed that if there is a model of the 'Pampero' in existence, with guns and all the appliances of a ship of war shown on the model, the Confederate arms emblazoned on it, or the Confederate flag flying on it, that is relevant evidence in this case. So, if I can get equipments—guns or gun-carriages—and prove that these were intended for the 'Pampero,' either by the name being engraved on them or in some other way, that would be relevant; and in like manner, if I can get the officers' uniforms with the Confederate button on them, that also would be relevant evidence in the case. The only question is, whether I am entitled to recover these. (*Reads from Petition*). With reference to the question of the intention with which the ship was fitted out, these articles may be most important. The Petition gives sufficient specification of what the things are, the persons in whose possession they are, are specified, and also the place where they are to be found. It may be said that there is no precedent for this; but I found on the absence of any contrary authority, and on the recovery of models, etc., by diligence where no objection was made to the form thereof. But I don't need to rely on precedents in civil cases, because I think this is a penal procedure, the necessary condition of which is that there shall be an offence proved; and if the analogy of criminal proceedings is to be looked to, we don't require to go far for a precedent, for a search-warrant is granted in every criminal case.

Mr. Clark.—Which part of the prayer of your Petition do you ask?

Mr. Gifford.—I ask either an order on the parties to produce, or a search-warrant to recover. Now, if in criminal cases the prosecutor is entitled to recover articles necessary to prove the case, why should I not have the same facilities here if that is necessary for the ends of justice? I admit it is a matter for the discretion of the Court; but I am surely entitled to these things if they exist, unless the other party can state some very good reason against it. Although there is no direct authority for procedure like this in a civil case, there are cases which bear upon it, and which show the power that the Court has in such matters; for example, where a party has servants or witnesses under his control, whom he puts aside, the Court has ordained him to produce them,—Carnousie *v.* Meldrum, 27th June 1629, 1 Brown Sup., 172; Executors of Earl of Londonderry *v.* Earl of Stair, July 1743, Mor. 16,748. The same principle has been recognised in Newry Railway Company *v.* Graham, 20th Dec. 1851, 14 D. 297. I admit that I have found no case exactly in point, but I submit that it is clearly competent for your Lordship to grant the prayer of our petition.

Lord Ormidale.—I have some doubts whether I could grant both alternatives of the prayer.

Mr. Gifford.—If there is any technical difficulty, the prayer may be amended.

Mr. Shand.—This application refers to three classes of articles, —1*st*, Models; 2*d*, Equipments; and 3*d*, Uniforms, arms, and accoutrements. Now, as to the first two, the Inner House having refused the application to recover them in the ordinary way in which the Court recognise the right of a party to recover subjects which may be made evidence, I submit you cannot grant an authority in this irregular and unusual and unprecedented way to recover the very same things.

Lord Ormidale.—I think all the Court decided was, that they could not be recovered in the form of commission and diligence.

Mr. Shand.—It appears to me that that is the only form in which they can competently recover evidence to be used at the trial. But look at the way in which this application is presented. There are two modes suggested by which the articles are to be made available; 1*st*, that your Lordship shall appoint certain parties to produce and deliver over the articles; but then if my learned friend does not recover from them, he asks authority to use this as a means of groping for evidence in other quarters.

Lord Ormidale.—In an ordinary case of diligence against havers, you don't name the havers. You may go searching about everywhere, provided you have authority to get the things.

Mr. Shand.—But the Court has decided that the articles cannot be recovered under a diligence against havers; and I may state what the argument was, because I repeat the argument on the merits of the question. It was maintained in the Inner House by the respondents, that it was a right and proper thing that documents should be recovered and put into process, because they must be put before the jury and before the Court, if they are to be used in evidence. Documents are the best, and indeed the only evidence of their contents, and must be put in process before they can be made available. But it is totally different with reference to articles of the nature here called for. As to material objects, you may have any amount of evidence of witnesses who can speak to their existence and character, and the purpose for which they were intended.

Lord Ormidale.—Suppose one witness should say that they bore the Confederate arms, and another that they bore the United States arms, the Court and the Jury would be very apt to ask why the articles had not been got.

Mr. Shand.—That observation would apply to every case in which witnesses differ as to their description of a material object. Now, one of two things is here asked, and either I think objectionable. My learned friend's first alternative proposal is, to call on the custodiers of certain articles, and to ask them in their deposition to state the intent with which they were held.

Lord Ormidale.—Could he in substance and reality distinguish the first alternative prayer from a commission and diligence? I think it is substantially the same.

Mr. Gifford.—It has the same object.

Lord Ormidale.—And, therefore, the decision of the Inner House would strike against you there.

Mr. Shand.—And asking witnesses to bring certain things which were intended for a certain purpose, is practically taking a precognition on oath. You ask not for a certain quantity of grey cloth, but for a certain quantity of grey cloth cut and made up into uniforms, with intent to be used on board the 'Pampero;' and so you ask for gun-carriages intended to be put on board the 'Pampero,'—is not that taking a precognition on oath to enable the Crown to get up a case against the defenders? And can anything be more detrimental to the interests of justice? There is also this objection, that in substance it is impossible to distinguish between this and an examination of havers upon oath. Take the case of John Macfarlane &. Co.,—where is the distinction between their position under what is proposed under the first alternative, and a citation to them to appear as havers before the commissioner? And the Court has refused that. The second alternative is equally objectionable. It is a search-warrant in a civil proceeding. Mr. Gifford cited two old cases which are unparalleled, and which certainly would be no authority now for similar proceedings. Did your Lordship ever hear of a search-warrant to entitle officers to go and break open doors and lock-fast places, to put into process material objects? My friend concedes that he has no authority to entitle him to ask that; and is your Lordship to be the first to grant a warrant of this kind in a case not in the least degree peculiar as requiring production of physical objects? There have been many patent cases and cases of contravention of trade-marks; the pursuer there must get his evidence extrajudicially; he is not entitled to ask the Court for a warrant to search his adversary's lock-fast drawers. Such a warrant is unprecedented, and I submit your Lordship cannot grant it. It is nothing to the purpose to say that search-warrants have been granted in criminal cases. We are here in a civil proceeding, which might have been taken by any private individual as well as by the Lord Advocate, and there is nothing peculiar in this case to take it out of the ordinary rule of a civil action.

Mr. Gifford.—My friend objects to both alternatives—to being asked to produce these things himself, or to allowing any warrant to go out for their recovery; but he has not said a word against the relevancy or importance of them as evidence, nor has he stated the least prejudice which his clients would sustain from the things being recovered and made evidence.

Lord Ormidale.—He said there would be prejudice in regard to the depositions; but the answer to that is, that any such deposition would not be evidence.

Mr. Shand.—It is a valuable precognition.

Mr. Gifford.—So is every examination of a haver under a diligence. My friend's first objection to the first part of the prayer is, that it is practically a diligence, and your Lordship suggested that it was another form of getting at the thing. I admit that, but did not the Court say that we would get it in another form? Though the object and result is the same, it surely cannot be said that because we cannot get it in the form of a diligence, we are not to get it in any other form? Lord Ardmillan expressly said that the Lord Advocate was 'entitled to any form of warrant by which he' 'can be aided in procuring the equipments of the "Pampero."' All that the other Judges said was, that the form of diligence was not the proper form for recovering them. Therefore, it is no objection to say that the object is to get the same thing in another form. That is our purpose, but the virtue of our present application is that it is in another form. My learned friend says it is unprecedented in civil proceedings. I don't know that it is, although there may be no express decision on the point. Have warrants not been granted in patent cases for the inspection of manufactories, where it was alleged that the patent process was going on?

Mr. Shand.—Not where it was resisted.

Lord Ormidale.—My impression is that the Lord Ordinary in the Bill-Chamber has granted warrant for inspection in patent cases, where the question was about granting an interdict, but then it was confined entirely to the party; and there could be nothing but inspection in such a case, because the building and machinery could not be brought into Court. Besides, in patent cases, it might be very important to ascertain distinctly the process followed, because a very little change afterwards might make all the difference between infringement and no infringement.

Mr. Gifford.—I think it is a very common practice to have an inspection in such cases.

Lord Ormidale.—I think Mr. Clark was counsel in a case which came before me in the Bill-Chamber as to patent iron-pillars. I have a strong impression that I granted an order for inspection there.

Mr. Clark.—It was an order, of consent, to produce some of the pillars.

Mr. Gifford.—But I found on its being of consent, because if it could be resisted in these patent cases, the defenders would resist it.

Lord Ormidale.—According to my impression, it might be said that it is the established practice in patent cases, which is better than particular precedent.

Mr. Gifford.—My friend's objection to the search-warrant is, that such a thing is not known in a civil proceeding, which he says this is. Now, I cannot conceive anything more strongly criminal in its nature than the offence created by this Statute, and the proceedings authorized to repress it. It is a statutory offence, and in point of fact proper criminal proceedings have been commenced. There is a warrant out (or at all events a warrant has been applied for) for the apprehension of Captain North and Captain Sinclair for contravention of the Statute as criminals; but whether that is done or not it is undoubtedly competent, and the offence is punishable by fine and imprisonment. But does it cease to be criminal when forfeiture of the vessel is all that is concluded for?

Lord Ormidale.—But it is civil procedure that is applicable to this case.

Mr. Gifford.—But if the case involves criminal elements, I think I am entitled to criminal remedies. My friend does not take the least benefit by saying that any person may be the informer here;

for that just the more strongly indicates its criminal character. A civil suit can only be instituted by the private party interested; a criminal proceeding can be taken up by anybody. That just stamps its criminal character upon it, and as undoubtedly it will be penal in its results, I don't know why the admitted practice in criminal causes should not be applicable here. If it is necessary in a case of assault to get a search-warrant, is it to be refused in a case where an offence has been committed which tends to endanger the peace of the realm? I submit, therefore, that a search-warrant is the appropriate remedy, and that there is nothing incompetent in it. I ask your Lordship to grant one or both of the remedies asked.

Mr. Clark.—I don't dispute that if a model were found, such as that which Mr. Gifford so poetically described, of the ship 'Pampero' with the Confederate flag flying, and her guns firing, and a Federal ship sinking in the distance, it might be somewhat important evidence for the purposes of this action; but such a model has not yet been discovered, though my friends have had the most ample opportunities of searching over the whole premises of my clients, the Messrs. Thomson. But there is one view of this case which seems to me conclusive of the first part of the prayer of the petition. My friend says this is a criminal proceeding; and so far as regards that first part of the prayer, I am willing to accept that definition of these proceedings, but I am very much surprised to find them so represented when my friends have not thought it improper to examine upon oath the parties to this criminal suit! I thought it was in respect that this was a civil suit as contradistinguished from a criminal suit, that it was competent for the Lord Advocate to apply for a commission and diligence, and to examine the different defenders upon oath as to what writings they had in their custody, with the view of obtaining documents which might be used in evidence against them at the trial. But this is plainly a civil suit, brought no doubt at the instance of the Lord Advocate, but at the same time one which might be brought by any common informer whatever. Mr. Gifford said it was one of the indications of a criminal proceeding that it could be brought at the instance of a common informer; but I thought it was one characteristic of our procedure in Scotland, that no criminal process whatever could be originated by a common informer, and that no criminal procedure could be originated even by the party injured, unless he obtained the concurrence of the Lord Advocate. If the test of my friend is good, it is in my favour, because the proceedings here might originate by an Information at the instance of any one not having interest in the matter, but choosing to inform the Court in regard to it. I think, therefore, it is perfectly out of the question to say that the Crown is entitled to deal with this as a criminal process, and I have, therefore, to consider what is their right under a civil process. In the first part of the prayer, my friend asks for the production of certain articles which he is not entitled to obtain by means of a commission and diligence. What he asks is, that the defenders and the parties mentioned in the petition, shall be ordered to compear on a certain day for the purpose of being examined on oath, in order to produce certain articles which, it is said, they possess. Now, if there is any distinction between that and an ordinary commission and diligence to recover documents, my friend ought to have pointed it out, for I don't see any; and that has already been found by the Court incompetent for the purpose of recovering articles of this kind. The purpose and effect of it really would be to put the defenders on oath for the purpose of precognoscing them as to what they intended to put on board the 'Pampero,' and that, I submit, to be out of the question. As regards the other matter, my friend can only justify it on the ground of this being a criminal proceeding. The cases of patents are not in the least like it. What is sought there is the recovery of certain special articles in the hands of the defenders with reference to the process he is said to be carrying on; but what is asked here is a general warrant to recover articles not in the hands of the defenders alone, but in the hands of a great many other parties, and to be carried out just like a criminal warrant. I have already said this is not a criminal proceeding, and on the whole matter I submit that your Lordship should not grant the prayer of this petition.

His Lordship then took this point to avizandum.

Lord Ormidale [to Mr. Clark].—I shall probably allow your appeal to the effect of permitting Mr. Murray to be further examined as a haver, and supposing Mr. Murray on oath depones to the effect stated by the Lord Advocate, I understood you to say that it would be satisfactory except in one particular.

Mr. Clark.—If Mr. Murray will answer the question we put to him, and bring out in his answer what the documents are, and if he says that these documents he received as agent in the cause, then the question will arise whether these documents are privileged or not, and whether the statement of the Lord Advocate, that they cannot be given up from considerations relating to the public service, is sufficient. Suppose, for instance, Mr. Murray said: 'I 'received such and such a letter from an officer of the Government 'in reference to this matter,' I would at once admit that this is undoubtedly a privileged document, for example, the Secretary of State writing to him or to the Lord Advocate; but it does not follow, because Mr. Murray received these letters, passing between Miller and Paterson and Underwood, through an officer of the Government, or through the Lord Advocate, that they are necessarily privileged in this case. We want to know what the documents are,—their general character, of course,—in order that we may raise the question before your Lordship whether they are or are not privileged.

Lord Ormidale.—What is to be said about Mr. Hart and Sir Archibald Alison?

Mr. Clark.—We are to examine them again.

Lord Ormidale.—Do I require to pronounce anything as to them?

Mr. Clark.—No.

Lord Ormidale.—I took a note that Sir Archibald Alison was out of the case.

Mr. Gifford.—I thought the same with regard to Mr. Murray.

Mr. Clark.—Sir Archibald Alison's name was not mentioned to-day, and therefore I say nothing about him one way or other. As regards Mr. Hart, we shall probably examine him again.

Lord Ormidale.—Then I shall note that I was not asked to pronounce as to him.

Mr. Clark.—I think not, because we left that part of the case with the impression that Mr. Hart was to be re-examined. Nothing is given up as to him.

Lord Ormidale.—Then I shall note that, as regards Sir Archibald Alison, there is to be no farther discussion.

Mr. Clark.—I have not raised anything as to him.

[An arrangement having been come to between the parties, his Lordship was made aware that it was unnecessary to pronounce judgment on the matters discussed at this hearing.]

Thursday, 5th May 1864.

(*Before* LORD ORMIDALE *in Chambers.*)

Present.—Mr. Gifford and Mr. Rutherfurd, with Mr. Murray, Crown Agent; Mr. J. C. Brodie for the defenders, Messrs. Fleming; Mr. Webster for the defenders, Messrs J. and G. Thomson.

Mr. Gifford.—Three minutes have been signed and put in process, and it occurs to me that the proper course will be to pronounce a separate interlocutor in regard to each. The first minute is as follows:—

'Minute for Messrs. James and George Thomson, engineers and 'shipbuilders in Glasgow, *Claimants*, in the Information of Seizure 'of the vessel "Pampero," at the instance of the Lord Advocate 'against John Fleming and Others.

'*Shand* stated that the said James and George Thomson had 'received a satisfactory undertaking from or on behalf of the 'owners of the "Pampero," in consequence whereof he craved 'leave to withdraw and now hereby withdraws the Claim and Pleas 'for the said James and George Thomson, and that upon the foot- 'ing that they are not to be found liable in any costs in the suit. '—In respect whereof, &c.' (Signed) 'ALEXANDER BURNS SHAND.' The Crown have no objection to that, and the first interlocutor will be allowing the minute to be received, and in terms thereof, and of consent of the Crown, holding Messrs. Thomson as withdrawn from the process, finding no expenses due to either party. I suppose that meets Mr. Webster's views.

Mr. Webster.—Entirely.

Mr. Gifford.—The next minute is a minute for Messrs. John Fleming and Co.:—

'Minute for John Fleming of London for himself and the other 'partners of the firm of Smith, Fleming, and Co. of London, 'Robert Simpson of London, Edgar Pinchback Stringer of London, 'Alexander Collie of Manchester, Thomas Dunlop Finlay of Glas-'gow, Peter Denny of Dumbarton, and James Galbraith of Glas-'gow, owners of the ship or vessel "Pampero," in Information of 'Seizure of said vessel at the instance of the Right Honourable 'James Moncrieff, Her Majesty's Advocate, on behalf of Her 'Majesty, *Pursuer*, against the said John Fleming and Others, '*Defenders*,

'*Clark* for the minuters, the said John Fleming and Others, re-'spectfully stated to the Court that they adhere to the statement 'in their pleas, to the effect that in so far as they are concerned, 'all of the counts of the Information are unfounded in fact; but 'having ascertained that the defendant, George T. Sinclair, did at-'tempt and endeavour to furnish the said ship or vessel with the 'intent mentioned in the 37th of the said counts, and being advised 'that the said ship or vessel may therefore be legally liable to 'seizure, even though her owners have not themselves infringed the 'Statute, they had entered into an agreement with the pursuer for 'the settlement of this case; and in pursuance of that agreement, 'the Joint Minute herewith produced had been signed by the parties. '(Signed) And. R. Clark.'

This Minute is of the nature of a protest that these parties are not guilty of the constructive crime which the Statute creates. The Crown are no parties to this Minute, but they have no objection to its being lodged. It is not intended that anything should follow upon it; it merely states the reason why they have consented to the third Minute, which I am going to read; still, as they wish this Minute in, I would suggest that an interlocutor, allowing it to be received, should be pronounced. Then follows what completes the case, viz., a Joint Minute for the Lord Advocate and for Messrs. Fleming:—

'Joint Minute for the Right Honourable James Moncreiff, Her 'Majesty's Advocate, on the behalf of Her Majesty, and for John 'Fleming of London, for himself and the other partners of the firm 'of Smith, Fleming, and Company of London, Robert Simpson of 'London, Edgar Pinchback Stringer of London, Alexander Collie 'of Manchester, Thomas Dunlop Finlay of Glasgow, Peter Denny 'of Dumbarton, and James Galbraith of Glasgow, owners of the 'ship or vessel "Pampero," in Information of Seizure of said vessel 'at the instance of the Right Honourable James Moncreiff, Her 'Majesty's Advocate, on behalf of Her Majesty, *Pursuer*, against 'the said John Fleming and Others, *Defenders*.

'*Rutherfurd* for the pursuer, and *Clark* for the said John Flem-'ing and others, defenders, stated that an agreement had been en-'tered into between them, by which it had been *inter alia* arranged 'as follows, viz.:—

'1. That the said John Fleming and others, defenders, shall consent to a verdict being entered for the Crown, without the intervention of a jury, on the 37th count of the Information, but this on the footing that no liability is incurred by the said defenders to Her Majesty's Advocate, or to any of the officers of the Crown, in their capacity of informers.

'2. That on the application of the said verdict, no expenses shall be found due by either party in this suit. (Signed) AND. RUTHERFURD, *for the pursuer.* AND. R. CLARK, *for Fleming and others.*'

Upon that minute, I think, a third interlocutor should be pronounced, finding in terms of the Minute and of consent a verdict for the Crown on the 37th count, and of consent finding that no liability is incurred by the defenders to Her Majesty's Advocate, or to any of the officers of the Crown in their capacity of informers, and finding no expenses due by either party. I think that exhausts the case.

Mr. Brodie.—I am sorry that we should have had the trouble of coming here to-night since this is the result of it; but I may mention in explanation, that an agreement was entered into by the Lord Advocate, and the parties in this cause, one clause of which was 'that the said second parties shall be entitled to make a statement by judicial minute or otherwise, to the effect that though said ship or vessel is legally liable to seizure, they have not themselves knowingly infringed the law.' That was a stipulation of the agreement on which all this proceeds that is now before your Lordship. The Crown-agent sent me the draft of an interlocutor which he proposed your Lordship should pronounce, in which no reference whatever was made to this Minute. I then proposed to him that reference should be made to the Minute in the Interlocutor, but to that he strongly objected, for what reason I was unable to divine. Of course it is perfectly immaterial to me whether, if reference be made to it, it be made in one interlocutor or in three interlocutors, but what I objected to was, that no reference should be made in your Lordship's interlocutor to that Minute which we distinctly stipulated with the Crown should be given in.

Mr. Gifford.—There has been some misunderstanding. Mr. Murray thought you were stipulating for it in the final verdict. But you have no objection to the course now proposed?

Mr. Brodie.—No objection.

Lord Ormidale.—The Minute proceeds on the footing that I am to pronounce a verdict, and I assumed that there was to be a Jury.

Mr. Gifford suggested that the judgment should run, 'Finds for the Queen on the 37th Count, in terms of the Minute.'

The following interlocutors were then pronounced:—

'The Lord Ordinary in Exchequer Causes having heard parties' procurators, allows the Minute for Messrs. James and George Thomson, No. 36 of Process, to be received, and in terms thereof, and of consent of parties, allows the said James and George Thom-

'son to withdraw their Claim and Pleas, Nos. 5 and 9 of Process, 'and holds the same to be withdrawn accordingly, in terms of 'said Minute, and decerns.'

'The Lord Ordinary in Exchequer Causes having heard parties' 'procurators, allows the Minute for Messrs. John Fleming and 'Others, No. 37 of Process, to be received.'

'The Lord Ordinary in Exchequer Causes, having considered the 'Joint-Minute for the parties, No. 38 of Process, and heard parties' 'procurators, of consent finds for the Queen on the 37th Count of 'the Information; further, of consent finds that no liability is in-'curred by the defenders to Her Majesty's Advocate, or to any of 'the officers of the Crown in their capacity of Informers, and finds 'no expenses due to or by any of the parties in the cause, all in 'terms of the said Minute, and decerns.'

APPENDIX.

I.—APPRAISEMENT BY COLLECTOR OF CUSTOMS, GLASGOW.

Call per ADVOCATUM, SOLICITOR-GENERAL, GIFFORD, *et* RUTHERFURD.
ANDREW MURRAY, Jr., W.S., *Agent.*

APPRAISEMENT OF SEIZURE of the Ship or Vessel 'Pampero,' with her Tackle, Apparel, and Furniture, as she now lies seized at Glasgow Harbour, in the County of Lanark, on the 10th day of December 1863, by Frederick William Trevor, Collector of Customs, Glasgow, for being equipped, furnished, and fitted out, with intent to be employed in the service of persons exercising, or assuming to exercise, the powers of Government in and over a Foreign State, Colony, Province, or People, viz., the so-called Confederate States of America, to commit hostilities against the United States of America, with which Her Majesty was not at war, in contravention of the Act Fifty-nine George Third, chapter sixty-nine, section seven.

APPRAISEMENT OF SEIZURE.

Date of Seizure.	Officer's Name by whom Seized.	Where Seized.	For what cause Seized.	Species and Quantity of Goods Seized.	Value appraised.
1863. 10th December.	Frederick William Trevor, Collector of Customs, Glasgow.	Glasgow Harbour.	For being equipped, furnished, and fitted out, with intent to be employed in the service of persons exercising, or assuming to exercise, the powers of government, in and over a foreign state, colony, province, or people, viz., the so-called Confederate States of America, to commit hostilities against the United States of America, with which Her Majesty was not at war, in contravention of the Act 59 Geo. III. cap. 69, s. 7.	The ship or vessel 'Pampero,' with her tackle, apparel, and furniture, except sails, .	£20,000 0 0
				Engines, boilers, and machinery, with spare machinery, .	12,000 0 0
				TOTAL,	£32,000 0 0

I, Frederick William Trevor, Collector of Her Majesty's Customs at Glasgow, hereby certify, that the foregoing Appraisement made by me in order to be returned to the Court of Session as the Court of Exchequer in Scotland, is just and true as to the quantity, quality, and value of the articles therein stated, and in all other particulars, to the best of my knowledge.

Dated at Glasgow this 16th day of December 1863.

FRED. W. TREVOR.

II.

ABSTRACT OF INFORMATION OF SEIZURE, *in Causa*, THE LORD ADVOCATE against JOHN FLEMING and OTHERS, claiming the Vessel 'Pampero,' seized under the Foreign Enlistment Act (59 Geo. III. c. 69.) In the COURT OF EXCHEQUER in Scotland, sitting at Edinburgh, the twenty-eighth day of January in the year of our Lord One thousand eight hundred and sixty-four;

I, The Right Honourable JAMES MONCREIFF, Her Majesty's Advocate on the behalf of Her Majesty, inform the Court that heretofore and after the third day of July in the year of our Lord one thousand eight hundred and nineteen, and before this twenty-eighth day of January in the year of our Lord one thousand eight hundred and sixty-four, to wit, on the tenth day of December in the year of our Lord one thousand eight hundred and sixty-three, to wit, at Glasgow, in the county of Lanark, a certain officer of Her Majesty's Customs, to wit, Frederick William Trevor, then by law empowered so to do, did seize and arrest to the use of Her Majesty, as forfeited, a certain ship or vessel called the 'Pampero,' together with the furniture, tackle, and apparel belonging to and on board the said ship or vessel:

1ST COUNT. For that certain persons, to wit, John Fleming of London, for himself, and also as representing the other partner or partners, if any, of the firm of Smith, Fleming, and Company of London, who are or may be interested along with him in the 'Pampero,' Robert Simpson of London, Edgar Pinchback Stringer of London, Alexander Collie of Manchester, Thomas Dunlop Finlay of Glasgow, Peter Denny of Dumbarton, and James Galbraith of Glasgow, George T Sinclair, and other persons whose names are to me, Her Majesty's said Advocate, at present unknown, heretofore, and before the making of the said seizure, and after the third day of July in the year of our Lord one thousand eight hundred and nineteen, and before this twenty-eighth day of January in the year of our Lord one thousand eight hundred and sixty-four, to wit, on the tenth day of December in the year of our Lord one thousand eight hundred and sixty-three, within a certain part of the United Kingdom, to wit, Glasgow, in the county of Lanark, without any leave or license of Her Majesty for that purpose first had and obtained, did equip the said ship or vessel with intent and in order that such ship or vessel should be employed in the service of certain foreign states styling themselves the Confederate States of America, with intent to cruise and commit hostilities against a certain foreign state with which Her Majesty was not then, to wit, on the day and year last aforesaid, at war, to wit, the Republic of the United States of America, contrary to the form of the Statute in such case made and provided, whereby, and by force of the Statute in that case made and provided, the said ship or vessel, together with the said tackle, apparel, and furniture, became and was forfeited.

2D COUNT. And also for that certain persons, to wit, John Fleming of London, for himself, and also as representing the other partner or partners, if any, of the firm of Smith, Fleming, and Company of London, who are or may be interested along with him in the 'Pampero,' Robert Simpson of London, Edgar Pinchback Stringer of London, Alexander Collie of Manchester, Thomas Dunlop Finlay of Glasgow, Peter Denny of Dumbarton, and James Galbraith of Glasgow, George T Sinclair, and other persons whose names are to me, Her Majesty's said Advocate, at present unknown, heretofore, and before the making of the said seizure, and after the third day of July in the year of our Lord one thousand eight hundred and nineteen, and before this twenty-eighth day of January in the year of our Lord one thousand eight hundred and sixty-four, to wit, on the day and year last aforesaid, within a certain part of the United Kingdom, to wit, Glasgow, in the county of Lanark, without any leave or license of Her Majesty for that purpose first had and obtained, did equip the said ship or vessel, with intent and in order that such ship or vessel should be employed in the service of certain foreign states, styling themselves the Confederate States of America, with intent to cruise and commit hostilities against citizens of a certain foreign state, with whom and with which respectively Her Majesty was not then, to wit, on the day and year last aforesaid, at war, to wit, citizens of the Republic of the United States of America, contrary to the form of the Statute in such case made and provided, whereby, and by force of the Statute in that case made and provided, the said ship or vessel, together with the said tackle, apparel, and furniture, became and was forfeited.

3D COUNT. And also for that certain persons, to wit, John Fleming of London, for himself, and also as representing the other partner or partners, if any, of the firm of Smith, Fleming, and Company of London, who are or may be interested along with him in the 'Pampero,' Robert Simpson of London, Edgar Pinchback Stringer of London, Alexander Collie of Manchester, Thomas Dunlop Finlay of Glasgow, Peter Denny of Dumbarton, and James Galbraith of Glasgow, George T Sinclair and other persons whose names are to me, Her Majesty's said Advocate, at present unknown, heretofore, and before the making of the said seizure, and after the third day of July in the year of our Lord one thousand eight hundred and nineteen, and before this twenty-eighth day of January in the year of our Lord one thousand eight hundred and sixty-four, to wit, on the day and year last aforesaid, within a certain part of the United Kingdom, to wit, Glasgow, in the county of Lanark, without any leave or license of Her Majesty for that purpose first had and obtained, did equip the said ship or vessel, with intent to cruise and commit hostilities against a certain foreign state, with which Her Majesty was not then, to wit, on the day and year last aforesaid, at war, to wit, the Republic of the United States of America, contrary to the form of the Statute in such case made and provided, whereby, and by force of the Statute in that case made and provided, the said ship or vessel, together with the said tackle, apparel, and furniture, became and was forfeited.

4TH COUNT. And also for that certain persons, to wit, John Fleming of London, for himself, and also as representing the other partner or partners, if any, of the firm of Smith, Fleming, and Company of London, who are or may be interested along with him in the 'Pampero,' Robert Simpson of London, Edgar Pinchback Stringer of London, Alexander Collie of Manchester, Thomas Dunlop Finlay of Glasgow, Peter Denny of Dumbarton, and James Galbraith of Glasgow, George T Sinclair, and other persons whose names are to me, Her Majesty's said Advocate, at present unknown, heretofore, and before the making of the said seizure, and after the third day of July in the year of our Lord one thousand eight hundred and nineteen, and before this twenty-eighth day of January in the year of our Lord one thousand eight hundred and sixty-four, to wit, on the day and year last aforesaid, within a certain part of the United Kingdom, to wit, at Glasgow, in the county of Lanark, without the leave or license of Her Majesty for that purpose first had and obtained, did equip the said ship or vessel with intent to cruise and commit hostilities against citizens of a certain foreign state, with whom and with which respectively Her Majesty was not then, to wit, on the day and year last aforesaid, at war, to wit, citizens of the Republic of the United States of America, contrary to the form of the Statute in such case made and provided, whereby, and by force of the Statute in that case made and provided, the said ship or vessel, together with the said tackle, apparel, and furniture, became and was forfeited.

5th Count. And also for that certain persons, to wit, John Fleming of London, for himself, and also as representing the other partner or partners, if any, of the firm of Smith, Fleming, and Company of London, who are or may be interested along with him in the 'Pampero,' Robert Simpson of London, Edgar Pinchback Stringer of London, Alexander Collie of Manchester, Thomas Dunlop Finlay of Glasgow, Peter Denny of Dumbarton, and James Galbraith of Glasgow, George T Sinclair, and other persons whose names are to me, Her Majesty's said Advocate, at present unknown, heretofore, and before the making of the said seizure, and after the third day of July in the year of our Lord one thousand eight hundred and nineteen, and before this twenty-eighth day of January in the year of our Lord one thousand eight hundred and sixty-four, to wit, on the day and year last aforesaid, within a certain part of the United Kingdom, to wit, Glasgow, in the county of Lanark, without any leave or license of Her Majesty for that purpose first had and obtained, did equip the said ship or vessel, with intent and in order that such ship or vessel should be employed in the service of divers and very many persons exercising the powers of government in and over certain foreign states, styling themselves the Confederate States of America, with intent to cruise and commit hostilities against a certain foreign state with which Her Majesty was not then, to wit, on the day and year last aforesaid, at war, to wit, the Republic of the United States of America, contrary to the form of the Statute in such case made and provided, whereby, and by force of the Statute in that case made and provided, the said ship or vessel, together with the said tackle, apparel, and furniture, became and was forfeited.

6th Count. And also for that certain persons, to wit, John Fleming of London, for himself, and also as representing the other partner or partners, if any, of the firm of Smith, Fleming, and Company of London, who are or may be interested along with him in the 'Pampero,' Robert Simpson of London, Edgar Pinchback Stringer of London, Alexander Collie of Manchester, Thomas Dunlop Finlay of Glasgow, Peter Denny of Dumbarton, and James Galbraith of Glasgow, George T Sinclair, and other persons whose names are to me, Her Majesty's said

Advocate, at present unknown, heretofore, and before the making of the said seizure, and after the third day of July in the year of our Lord one thousand eight hundred and nineteen, and before this twenty-eighth day of January in the year of our Lord one thousand eight hundred and sixty-four, to wit, on the day and year last aforesaid, within a certain part of the United Kingdom, to wit, Glasgow, in the county of Lanark, without any leave or license of Her Majesty for that purpose first had and obtained, did equip the said ship or vessel, with intent and in order that such ship or vessel should be employed in the service of divers and very many persons exercising the powers of government in and over certain foreign states, styling themselves the Confederate States of America, with intent to cruise and commit hostilities against citizens of a certain foreign state, with whom and with which respectively Her Majesty was not then, to wit, on the day and year last aforesaid, at war, to wit, citizens of the Republic of the United States of America, contrary to the form of the Statute in such case made and provided, whereby, and by force of the Statute in that case made and provided, the said ship or vessel, together with the said tackle, apparel, and furniture, became and was forfeited.

7TH COUNT. And also for that certain persons, to wit, John Fleming of London, for himself, and also as representing the other partner or partners, if any, of the firm of Smith, Fleming, and Company of London, who are or may be interested along with him in the 'Pampero,' Robert Simpson of London, Edgar Pinchback Stringer of London, Alexander Collie of Manchester, Thomas Dunlop Finlay of Glasgow, Peter Denny of Dumbarton, and James Galbraith of Glasgow, George T Sinclair, and other persons whose names are to me, Her Majesty's said Advocate, at present unknown, heretofore, and before the making of the said seizure, and after the third day of July in the year of our Lord one thousand eight hundred and nineteen, and before this twenty-eighth day of January in the year of our Lord one thousand eight hundred and sixty-four, to wit, on the day and year last aforesaid, within a certain part of the United Kingdom, to wit, Glasgow, in the county of Lanark, without any leave or license of Her Majesty for that purpose first had and obtained, did equip the said ship or vessel with intent and in order that such ship or vessel should be employed in the service of divers and very many persons exercising the powers of government over part of a certain foreign people, to wit, part of the people of the United States of America, with intent to cruise and commit hostilities against a certain foreign state with which Her Majesty was not then, to wit, on the day and year last aforesaid, at war, to wit, the Republic of the United States of America, contrary to the form of the Statute in such case made and provided, whereby, and by force of the Statute in that case made and provided, the said ship or vessel, together with the said tackle, apparel, and furniture, became and was forfeited.

8TH COUNT. And also for that certain persons, to wit, John Fleming of London, for himself, and also as representing the other partner or partners, if any, of the firm of Smith, Fleming, and Company of London, who are or may be interested along with him in the 'Pampero,' Robert Simpson of London, Edgar Pinchback Stringer of London, Alexander Collie of Manchester, Thomas Dunlop Finlay of Glasgow, Peter Denny of Dumbarton, and James Galbraith of Glasgow, George T Sinclair, and other Persons whose names are to me, Her Majesty's Advocate, at present unknown, heretofore, and before the making of the said seizure, and after the third day of July in the year of our Lord one thousand eight hundred and nineteen, and before this twenty-eighth day of January, in the year of our Lord one thousand eight hundred and sixty-four, to wit, on the day and year last aforesaid, within a certain part of the United Kingdom, to wit, Glasgow, in the county of Lanark, without any leave or license of Her Majesty for that purpose first had and obtained, did equip the said ship or vessel with intent and in order that such ship or vessel should be employed in the service of divers and very many persons exercising the powers of government over part of a certain foreign people, to wit, part of the people of the United States of America, with intent to cruise and commit hostilities against citizens of a certain foreign state with whom and with which respectively Her Majesty was not then, to wit, on the day and year last aforesaid, at war, to wit, citizens of the Republic of the United States of America, contrary to the form of the Statute in such case made and provided, whereby, and by force of the Statute in that case made and provided, the said ship or vessel, together with the said tackle, apparel, and furniture, became and was forfeited.

9th Count,	same as	1st Count,		Substituting 'did furnish' for 'did equip.'	
10th	”	2d	”	”	”
11th	”	3d	”	”	”
12th	”	4th	”	”	”
13th	”	5th	”	”	”
14th	”	6th	”	”	”
15th	”	7th	”	”	”
16th	”	8th	”	”	”
17th Count	same as	1st Count,		Substituting 'did fit out' for 'did equip.''	
18th	”	2d	”	”	”
19th	”	3d	”	”	”
20th	”	4th	”	”	”
21st	”	5th	”	”	”
22d	”	6th	”	”	”
23d	”	7th	”	”	”
24th	”	8th	”	”	”
25th Count	same as	1st Count,		Substituting 'did attempt and endeavour to equip,' for 'did equip.'	
26th	”	2d	”	”	”
27th	”	3d	”	”	”
28th	”	4th	”	”	”
29th	”	5th	”	”	”
30th	”	6th	”	”	”
31st	”	7th	”	”	”
32d	”	8th	”	”	”
33d Count	same as	1st Count,		Substituting 'did attempt and endeavour to furnish,' for 'did equip.'	
34th	”	2d	”	”	”
35th	”	3d	”	”	”
36th	”	4th	”	”	”
37th	”	5th	”	”	”
38th	”	6th	”	”	”
39th	”	7th	”	”	”
40th	”	8th	”	”	”

41st Count same as	1st Count,		Substituting 'did attempt and endeavour to fit out,' for 'did epuip.'	
42d	”	2d ”	”	”
43d	”	3d ”	”	”
44th	”	4th ”	”	”
45th	”	5th ”	”	”
46th	”	6th ”	”	”
47th	”	7th ”	”	”
48th	”	8th ”	”	”
49th Count same as	1st Count,		Substituting 'did procure to be equipped' for 'did equip.'	
50th	”	2d ”	”	”
51st	”	3d ”	”	”
52d	”	4th ”	”	”
53d	”	5th ”	”	”
54th	”	6th ”	”	”
55th	”	7th ”	”	”
56th	”	8th ”	”	”
57th Count same as	1st Count,		Substituting 'did procure to be furnished' for 'did equip.'	
58th	”	2d ”	”	”
59th	”	3d ”	”	”
60th	”	4th ”	”	”
61st	”	5th ”	”	”
62d	”	6th ”	”	”
63d	”	7th ”	”	”
64th	”	8th ”	”	”
65th Count same as	1st Count,		Substituting 'did procure to be fitted out' for 'did equip.'	
66th	”	2d ”	”	”
67th	”	3d ”	”	”
68th	”	4th ”	”	”
69th	”	5th ”	”	”
70th	”	6th ”	”	”
71st	”	7th ”	”	”
72d	”	8th ”	”	”
73d Count same as	1st Count,		Substituting 'did knowingly aid, assist, and be concerned in equipping' for 'did equip.'	
74th	”	2d ”	”	”
75th	”	3d ”	”	”
76th	”	4th ”	”	”
77th	”	5th ”	”	”
78th	”	6th ”	”	”
79th	”	7th ”	”	”
80th	”	8th ”	”	”
81st Count same as	1st Count,		Substituting 'did knowingly aid, assist, and be concerned in furnishing' for 'did oquip.'	
82d	”	2d ”	”	”
83d	”	3d ”	”	”
84th	”	4th ”	”	”
85th	”	5th ”	”	”
86th	”	6th ”	”	”
87th	”	7th ”	”	”
88th	”	8th ”	”	”

89th Count	same as	1st Count,	Substituting 'did knowingly aid, assist, and be concerned in furnishing' for 'did equip.
90th	"	2d "	" "
91st	"	3d "	" "
92d	"	4th "	" "
93d	"	5th "	" "
94th	"	6th "	" "
95th	"	7th "	" "
96th	"	8th "	" "

97TH COUNT. And also for that certain persons, to wit, John Fleming of London, for himself, and also as representing the other partner or partners, if any, of the firm of Smith, Fleming, and Company of London, who are or may be interested along with him in the 'Pampero,' Robert Simpson of London, Edgar Pinchback Stringer of London, Alexander Collie of Manchester, Thomas Dunlop Finlay of Glasgow, Peter Denny of Dumbarton, and James Galbraith of Glasgow, George T   Sinclair, and other persons whose names are to me, Her Majesty's said Advocate, at present unknown, heretofore, and before the making of the said seizure, and after the third day of July in the year of our Lord one thousand eight hundred and nineteen, and before this twenty-eighth day of January in the year of our Lord one thousand eight hundred and sixty-four, to wit, on the day and year last aforesaid, within a certain part of the United Kingdom, to wit, Glasgow, in the county of Lanark, without any leave or license of Her Majesty for that purpose first had or obtained, did attempt to fit out the said ship or vessel, with intent and in order that such ship or vessel should be employed in the service of divers and very many persons exercising the powers of government over part of a certain foreign people, to wit, part of the people of the United States of America, as a transport or store-ship against a certain foreign state with which Her Majesty was not then, to wit, on the day and year aforesaid, at war, to wit, the Republic of the United States of America, contrary to the form of the Statute in such case made and provided, whereby, and by force of the Statute in that case made and provided, the said ship or vessel, together with the said tackle, apparel, and furniture, became and was forfeited.

98TH COUNT. And also for that certain persons, to wit, John Fleming of London, for himself, and also as representing the other partner or partners, if any, of the firm of Smith, Fleming, and Company of London, who are or may be interested along with him in the 'Pampero,' Robert Simpson of London, Edgar Pinchback Stringer of London, Alexander Collie of Manchester, Thomas Dunlop Finlay of Glasgow, Peter Denny of Dumbarton, and James Galbraith of Glasgow, George T   Sinclair, and other persons whose names are to me, Her Majesty's said Advocate, at present unknown, heretofore, and before the making of the said seizure, and after the third day of July in the year of our Lord one thousand eight hundred and nineteen, and before this twenty-eighth day of January in the year of our Lord one thousand eight hundred and sixty-four, to wit, on the day and year last aforesaid, within a certain part of the United Kingdom, to wit, Glasgow, in the county of Lanark, without any leave or license of Her Majesty for that purpose first had or obtained, did equip, furnish, and fit out, and did attempt and endeavour to equip, furnish, and fit out, and did procure to be equipped, furnished, and fitted out, and did knowingly aid, assist, and be concerned in the equipping, furnishing, and fitting out of the said ship or vessel, with intent and in order that such ship or vessel should be employed in the service of certain foreign states, styling themselves the Confederate States of America, and in the service of divers and very many persons exercising and assuming to exercise the powers of government in and over certain foreign states, styling themselves the Confederate States of America, and in the service of divers and very many persons exercising and assuming to exercise powers of government over part of a certain foreign people, to wit, part of the people of the United States of America, as a transport or store-ship, against, and with intent to cruise and commit hostilities against a certain foreign state, with which Her Majesty was not then, to wit, on the day and year last aforesaid, at war, to wit, the Republic of the United States of America, and against citizens of a certain foreign state, with whom and with which respectively Her Majesty was not then at war, to wit, citizens of the Republic of the United States of America, contrary to the form of the Statute in such case made and provided, whereby, and by force of the Statute in that case made and provided, the said ship or vessel, together with the said tackle, apparel, and furniture, and the materials, arms, ammunitions, and stores, belonging to and on board the said ship or vessel, became and were forfeited.

Wherefore I, Her Majesty's said Advocate, on behalf of Her Majesty, pray the consideration of the Court in the premises, and that the said ship or vessel, together with her said furniture, tackle, and apparel, may, for the respective reasons aforesaid, severally remain forfeited.

J. MONCREIFF.

III.—CLAIM FOR THE OWNERS.

CLAIM for the ship or vessel 'Pampero,' with her Tackle, Apparel, and Furniture, as she now lies seized by FREDERICK WILLIAM TREVOR, Collector of Customs, Glasgow, at Glasgow Harbour, in the County of Lanark.

We, Messrs. Smith Fleming and Company, merchants in London, and John Fleming, merchant in London, acting partner of said firm, Robert Simpson, merchant in London, Edgar Pinchback Stringer, merchant in London, Alexander Collie, merchant in Manchester, Thomas Dunlop Finlay, merchant in Glasgow, Peter Denny, shipbuilder, Dumbarton, and James Galbraith, merchant in Glasgow, Declare that we are the owners of the ship or vessel 'Pampero,' with her tackle, apparel, and furniture (except sails), and her engines, boilers, and machinery, with spare machinery contained in the appraisement made by Frederick William Trevor, Collector of Customs, Glasgow, dated the 16th day of December 1863, and we claim the same.

JAS. GALBRAITH,
for self and other Claimants.
WM. WATSON, *Counsel for the Claimants.*

IV.—CLAIM FOR THE BUILDERS.

CLAIM for the ship or vessel 'Pampero,' or Goods seized by FREDERICK WILLIAM TREVOR, Collector of Customs, Glasgow.

On behalf of Messrs J. and G. Thomson, shipbuilders in Glasgow, I, James Webster, S.S.C., declare, that they have a right of lien or retention over the vessel or goods, contained in the appraisement made by the said Frederick William Trevor, dated the 16th day of December 1863, for £16,000, due to the claimants as builders of the said vessel, and interest thereon, and I claim a right to retain the vessel in security thereof, or otherwise to have the vessel restored to the possession of the claimants, in whose possession the said vessel was at the date of the said seizure.

JAMES WEBSTER.

Edinburgh, 21*st January* 1864.

V.—PLEAS FOR THE OWNERS.

PLEAS for JOHN FLEMING of London, for himself and the other Partners of the Firm of SMITH, FLEMING, and COMPANY of London, ROBERT SIMPSON of London, EDGAR PINCHBACK STRINGER of London, ALEXANDER COLLIE of Manchester, THOMAS DUNLOP FINLAY of Glasgow, PETER DENNY of Dumbarton, and JAMES GALBRAITH of Glasgow, claiming the property of the ship or vessel called the 'Pampero,' together with the Furniture, Tackle, and Apparel belonging to and on board the said ship or vessel, to THE INFORMATION OF SEIZURE, *in causa*, HER MAJESTY'S ADVOCATE against the said JOHN FLEMING and Others claiming the said vessel 'Pampero,' seized under the Foreign Enlistment Act (59 Geo. III. cap. 69).

For plea to the said Information, the said John Fleming for himself, and also as representing the firm of Smith, Fleming, and Company of London, Robert Simpson of London, Edgar Pinchback Stringer of London, Alexander Collie of Manchester, Thomas Dunlop Finlay of Glasgow, Peter Denny of Dumbarton, and James Galbraith of Glasgow, claiming the property of the said ship or vessel called the 'Pampero,' together with the furniture, tackle, and apparel on board the said ship or vessel, do say that the said ship or vessel, furniture, tackle, and apparel did not, nor did any or either of them, or any part thereof, become, nor are, nor is the same, or any or either of them, or any part thereof, forfeited for the several supposed causes in the said Information mentioned, or for any or either of them, in manner of form as by the said Information is charged.

And for a farther plea they do say that each and all of the counts in said Information are bad in law.

And for a farther plea they do say that each and all of said counts are unfounded in fact.

(Signed) WM. WATSON.

VI.—PLEAS FOR THE BUILDERS.

PLEA for Messrs. J. and G. THOMSON, Shipbuilders, Glasgow, Claimants.

For plea to the Information lodged by Her Majesty's Advocate, the claimants say that the said ship or vessel called the 'Pampero,' together with the furniture, tackle, and apparel belonging to and on board the said ship or vessel, did not, nor did any or either of them, or any part thereof, become, nor are, nor is the same, or any or either of them, or any part thereof, forfeited for the several supposed causes in the said Information mentioned, or for any or either of them, in manner and form as by the said Information is charged: And for a further plea the said claimants say that the statements in the several counts in said Information are untrue in fact, and that the said counts are bad in law.

(Signed) ALEX. BURNS SHAND.

VII.—SPECIFICATION OF WRITS, &c.

1. Missive offer by Messrs. James and George Thomson, shipbuilders, Clyde Bank Foundry, Glasgow, to Edward Pembroke, Esq., Austin Friars, London, to construct a first-class screw-steamer (afterwards called the 'Canton' or 'Pampero'), dated 10th October 1862.

2. Letter by Mr. Pembroke to Messrs. J. & G. Thomson, accepting of said offer, dated 17th October 1862.

3. Contract between the said James and George Thomson, and Edward Pembroke, for the construction of the said vessel, or of a first-class screw-steamer (afterwards called the 'Canton' or 'Pampero'), dated 12th and 22d November 1862, and relative specification.

4. Memorandum of agreement between the said Edward Pembroke and George T Sinclair, Esquire, therein designed as 'presently residing in London,' dated 17th October 1862, relative to the sale of a screw-steamer (afterwards called the 'Canton' or 'Pampero').

5. Specification docqueted as relative to said agreement.

6. Transfer by the said Edward Pembroke to Messrs. Smith, Fleming, & Co. of London, and others, dated 17th October 1862, of his interest in the said contract and agreement.

7. All letters, or copies of letters, dated on or before the 10th day of December 1863, from any of the parties named in the said Information, or from the said James and George Thomson as a company or individual partners, or from the said Edward Pembroke, to the said George T

Sinclair, or to each other, in regard to the said missive offer, acceptance, contract, memorandum of agreement, specification and transfer, or either of them, or in regard to the building or construction of the said screw-steamer, or to any of her fittings or furnishings.

8. All drawings, sketches, or plans of the said ship or vessel, or of any of her equipments, fittings, or furnishings, or intended fittings or furnishings.

9. All orders, letters, or memoranda, or copies of orders, letters, or memoranda, in regard to the said ship or vessel, or the construction, sale, or use thereof, or of any of her equipments, fittings, or furnishings, dated on or before the 10th day of December 1863.

10. The letter-books, business and other books of any of the parties above named, that certified copies or excerpts may be taken therefrom, at the sight of the Commissioner, of any of the documents specified in any of the foregoing articles.

11. All drafts of the writs mentioned in the first six heads of the specification.

VIII.—INTERLOCUTORS.

26*th January* 1864.—LORD ORMIDALE.—*Act.* RUTHERFURD—*Alt.* SHAND.—The Lord Ordinary in Exchequer Causes appoints the Lord Advocate to lodge an Information of seizure on the behalf of Her Majesty within ten days from this date. R. MACFARLANE.

4*th February* 1864.—LORD ORMIDALE.—*Act.* RUTHERFURD—*Alt.* .—The Lord Ordinary in Exchequer Causes appoints parties' procurators to be heard upon the Information, No. 7 of Process, on Thursday next. R. MACFARLANE.

13*th February* 1864.—LORD ORMIDALE.—*Act. Advocatum,* SOLICITOR-GENERAL, GIFFORD, *et* RUTHERFURD—*Alt.* COOK, GORDON, SHAND, WATSON, *et* ANDERSON.—The Lord Ordinary in Exchequer Causes allows the pleas for the claimants now tendered to be received. R. MACFARLANE.

16*th February* 1864.—LORD ORMIDALE.—*Act.* SOLICITOR-GENERAL, GIFFORD, *et* RUTHERFURD—*Alt.* COOK, GORDON, CLARK, WATSON, *et* ANDERSON.—The Lord Ordinary in Exchequer Causes allows the Information to be amended by the deletion in the 9th count of the words 'fifth day of April,' and the substitution therefor of the words 'tenth day of December;' and in the 74th count by the insertion of the word 'aid' after the word 'knowingly,' and before the word 'assist;' and in the 98th count by the insertion of the word 'aid' after the word 'knowingly,' and before the word 'assist.' R. MACFARLANE.

23*d February* 1864.—LORD ORMIDALE.—*Act.* SOLICITOR-GENERAL, GIFFORD, *et* RUTHERFURD—*Alt.* COOK, GORDON, CLARK, SHAND, WATSON, *et* ANDERSON.—The Lord Ordinary in Exchequer Causes having heard counsel for the parties, and considered the argument, the Information, and other proceedings, appoints Tuesday, the 5th day of April next (1864), at ten o'clock forenoon, within the Parliament House, Edinburgh, for trying the matters put in issue by said Information.

R. MACFARLANE.

Note.—The defenders, in the course of their argument, raised various questions of law and relevancy, in respect of which they maintained that the Information was, except to a very limited extent, untenable under the Statute upon which it is laid, and they asked the Lord Ordinary to decide these questions of law and relevancy before trial.

It appears to the Lord Ordinary that it is unnecessary and inexpedient in this case to dispose of any question of law and relevancy before trial, and accordingly he has followed the course which was adopted in the similar case of the 'Alexandra' in England.

So far as the Lord Ordinary can judge at present, the defenders will not be precluded merely by the case being appointed to be tried, from afterwards availing themselves of every plea in law or of relevancy which is in itself well founded; but as the Lord Ordinary cannot prejudge any matter whatever, so he can give no assurance on the subject.

The Lord Ordinary is not to be understood as holding that cases may not occur where it would be proper as well as competent to dispose of questions of law and relevancy before trial, although it must always be desirable to avoid, where it can be done with a due regard to the interests of the parties and the ends of justice, a double course of litigation, with its attendant evils of expense and delay.

In regard to the expediency in the present case of not disposing of the questions of law and relevancy which have been raised by the defenders, there can be little doubt. According to the defenders' own showing, the Information is not wholly irrelevant; and even as regards those parts of it to which the defenders' objections, as stated to the Lord Ordinary, apply, they, or at least some of them, may be affected by the evidence at the trial. The defenders' argument on relevancy may possibly also be superseded by the course which the case may take at the trial. Until, then, the whole facts and circumstances of the case have been fully disclosed at the trial, it would be unsafe, if not impossible, to decide how far the Information is or is not maintainable under the Statute on which it is laid.

The competency of the course which has been taken cannot, it is thought, be reasonably questioned. By the 6th section of the Court of Exchequer (Scotland) Act, 19 & 20 Vict. cap. 56, it is enacted, that where, as in the present instance, the defender shall appear and shall not admit the truth of the Information, 'the Lord Ordinary shall appoint a day for hearing the parties upon such Information where this may appear to him to be necessary, or shall appoint a day for trying the matters put in issue by such Information without any adjustment of any separate issue or issues, or shall take such other course as to him shall seem proper.'

On the assumption that the Lord Ordinary is right in appointing the case to be tried before disposing of any questions of law or relevancy, the day which has been appointed by the Lord Ordinary for the trial was that which was suggested as likely to be suitable for both parties; although, as the defenders mention, a change of the day for trial might possibly yet become necessary, in consequence of intervening circumstances. (Initd.) R. M'F.

23*d* *February* 1864.—Lord Ormidale.—*Act.* Solicitor-General, Gifford, *et* Rutherfurd—*Alt.* Cook, Gordon, Clark, Shand, Watson, *et* Anderson.—The Lord Ordinary in Exchequer Causes grants diligence at the instance of the pursuer against havers for recovery of the writings, books, models, drawings, sketches, plans, equipments, fittings, and furnishings, or other articles mentioned in the specification No. 11 of

Process, and grants commission to Mr. Alexander Smith Kinnear, advocate, whom failing, to Mr. John Pettigrew Wilson, advocate, to take the depositions of the havers in Scotland, and to receive their productions and exhibits, and to Mr. William Robertson, junior, Parliamentary Solicitor, Westminster, whom failing, to Mr. J. Boyd Kinnear, Barrister-at-Law, Lincoln's Inn, London, to take the depositions of the havers at London, and to receive their productions and exhibits, and appoints the same to be reported *quam primum*. R. MACFARLANE.

Edinburgh, 19*th March* 1864.—The Lords having considered the Reclaiming Note for John Fleming and others, No. 12 of Process, and heard counsel on the objections argued by the defenders against the relevancy of the Information,—Recal the interlocutor of the Lord Ordinary reclaimed against; and the Lord Advocate having withdrawn the twenty-five counts, numbered respectively 3, 4, 11, 12, 19, 20, 27, 28, 35, 36, 43, 44, 51, 52, 59, 60, 67, 68, 75, 76, 83, 84, 91, 92, 98, find as follows:—I. As regards the objections urged against the relevancy of the count, No. 1, and all the other counts now remaining, except No. 97, on the ground that the matters therein set forth do not amount to a contravention of the Statute, inasmuch as the allegation against the defenders set forth in these counts is not that they did equip, or attempt to equip the vessel with intent to cruise and commit hostilities, but is that they did equip, or attempt to equip the vessel with intent and in order that such vessel should be employed in the service of certain foreign states with intent to cruise and commit hostilities; Find that said objection is not well founded, and repel the same: II. As regards the objection urged against the relevancy of the same counts, on the ground that arming is not alleged *in terminis*, and that the terms 'equip,' 'furnish,' 'fit out,' used in the Information, cannot be held to include arming; Find that said objection is not woll founded, and repel the same: Appoint Thursday, the 5th day of May next, at 10 o'clock forenoon, within the Parliament House, Edinburgh, for trying the matters put in issue by the said Information: Grant diligence at the instance of the pursuer against havers for recovery of the writings and others mentioned in the specification, No. 11 of Process, as this day amended, and diligence at the instance of the defenders for recovery of the writings mentioned in article 9 of the said specification; and grant commission to Mr. Alexander Smith Kinnear, Advocate, whom failing, to Mr. John Pettigrew Wilson, Advocate, to take the depositions of the havers in Scotland, or elsewhere, except in London, and to receive their productions and exhibits; and to Mr. John Boyd Kinnear, Barrister-at-Law, Lincoln's Inn, London, whom failing, to Mr. William Robertson, Parliamentary Solicitor, Westminster, to take the depositions of the havers at London, and to receive their productions and exhibits, with power to the respective commissioners to take excerpts from the writings, and appoint the same to be reported *quam primum;* and remit to the Lord Ordinary to proceed with the cause.

(Signed) DUN. M'NEILL, *I.P.D.*

IX.

FOREIGN ENLISTMENT ACT.

ANNO QUINQUAGESIMO NONO

GEORGII III. REGIS.

CAP. LXIX.

An Act to prevent the Enlisting or Engagement of His Majesty's Subjects to serve in Foreign Service, and the fitting out or equipping, in His Majesty's Dominions, Vessels for Warlike Purposes, without His Majesty's Licence. [3*d July* 1819.]

WHEREAS the Enlistment or Engagement of His Majesty's Subjects, to serve in War in Foreign Service, without His Majesty's Licence, and the fitting out and equipping and arming of Vessels by His Majesty's Subjects, without His Majesty's Licence, for Warlike Operations in or against the Dominions or Territories of any Foreign Prince, State, Potentate, or Persons exercising or assuming to exercise the Powers of Government in or over any Foreign Country, Colony, Province, or Part of any Province, or against the Ships, Goods, or Merchandise of any Foreign Prince, State, Potentate, or Persons as aforesaid, or their Subjects, may be prejudicial to and tend to endanger the Peace and Welfare of this Kingdom: And whereas the Laws in force are not sufficiently effectual for preventing the same: Be it therefore enacted by the King's most Excellent Majesty, by and with the Advice and Consent of the Lords Spiritual and Temporal, and Commons, in this present Parliament assembled, and by the Authority of the same, That from and after the passing of this Act, an Act passed in the Ninth Year of the Reign of His late Majesty King *George* the Second, intituled *An Act to prevent the listing His Majesty's Subjects to serve as Soldiers without His Majesty's Licence;* 9 G. 2. c. 30. and also an Act passed in the Twenty-ninth Year of the Reign of His said late Majesty King *George* the Second, intituled *An Act to prevent His Majesty's Subjects from serving as Officers under the* French *King; and for better enforcing an Act passed in the Ninth Year of His present Majesty's Reign, to prevent the enlisting His Majesty's Subjects to serve as Soldiers without His Majesty's Licence; and for obliging such of His Majesty's Subjects as shall accept Commissions in the* Scotch *Brigade in the Service of the States General of the United Provinces, to take the Oaths of Allegiance and Abjuration;* 29 G. 2. c. 17. and also an Act passed in *Ireland* in the Eleventh Year of the Reign of His said late Majesty King *George* the Second, intituled *An Act for the more effectual preventing the enlisting of His Majesty's Subjects to serve as Soldiers in Foreign Service with-* Irish Act, 11 G. 2.

out His Majesty's Licence; and also an Act passed in *Ireland* in the Nineteenth Year of the Reign of His said late Majesty King *George* the Second, intituled *An Act for the more effectual preventing His Majesty's Subjects from entering into Foreign Service, and for publishing an Act of the Seventh Year of King* William *the Third, intituled 'An Act to prevent 'Foreign Education;'* and all and every the Clauses and Provisions in the said several Acts contained, shall be and the same are hereby repealed.

Irish Act, 19 G. 2.

Recited Acts repealed.

Subjects enlisting or engaging to enlist or serve in Foreign Service, military or naval, guilty of Misdemeanor.

II. And be it further declared and enacted, That if any natural-born Subject of His Majesty, His Heirs and Successors, without the Leave or Licence of His Majesty, His Heirs or Successors, for that Purpose first had and obtained, under the Sign Manual of His Majesty, His Heirs or Successors, or signified by Order in Council, or by Proclamation of His Majesty, His Heirs or Successors, shall take or accept, or shall agree to take or accept, any Military Commission, or shall otherwise enter into the Military Service as a Commissioned or Non-Commissioned Officer, or shall enlist or enter himself to enlist, or shall agree to enlist or to enter himself to serve as a Soldier, or to be employed or shall serve in any Warlike or Military Operation, in the Service of or for or under or in Aid of any Foreign Prince, State, Potentate, Colony, Province, or Part of any Province or People, or of any Person or Persons exercising or assuming to exercise the Powers of Government in or over any Foreign Country, Colony, Province, or Part of any Province or People, either as an Officer or Soldier, or in any other Military Capacity; or if any natural-born Subject of His Majesty shall, without such Leave or Licence as aforesaid, accept, or agree to take or accept, any Commission, Warrant, or Appointment as an Officer, or shall enlist or enter himself, or shall agree to enlist or enter himself, to serve as a Sailor or Marine, or to be employed, or engaged, or shall serve in and on board any Ship or Vessel of War, or in and on board any Ship or Vessel used or fitted out, or equipped or intended to be used for any Warlike Purpose, in the Service of or for or under or in Aid of any Foreign Power, Prince, State, Potentate, Colony, Province, or Part of any Province or People, or of any Person or Persons exercising or assuming to exercise the Powers of Government in or over any Foreign Country, Colony, Province, or Part of any Province or People; or if any natural-born Subject of His Majesty shall, without such Leave and Licence as aforesaid, engage, contract, or agree to go, or shall go to any Foreign State, Country, Colony, Province, or Part of any Province, or to any Place beyond the Seas, with an Intent or in order to enlist or enter himself to serve, or with Intent to serve in any Warlike or Military Operation whatever, whether by Land or by Sea, in the Service of or for or under or in Aid of any Foreign Prince, State, Potentate, Colony, Province, or Part of any Province or People, or in the Service of or for or under or in Aid of any Person or Persons exercising or assuming to exercise the Powers of Government in or over any Foreign Country, Colony, Province, or Part of any Province or People, either as an Officer or a Soldier, or in any other Military Capacity, or as an Officer or Sailor, or Marine, in any such Ship or Vessel as aforesaid, although no enlisting Money or Pay or Reward shall have been or shall be in any or either of the Cases aforesaid actually paid to or received by him, or by any Person to or for his Use or Benefit; or if any Person whatever, within the United Kingdom of *Great Britain* and *Ireland*, or in any Part of His Majesty's Dominions elsewhere, or in any Country, Colony, Settlement, Island, or Place belonging to or subject to His Majesty, shall hire, retain,

All Persons retaining or procuring others to enlist, guilty of the like Offence.

engage, or procure, or shall attempt or endeavour to hire, retain, engage, or procure, any Person or Persons whatever to enlist, or to enter or engage to enlist, or to serve or to be employed in any such Service or Employment as aforesaid, as an Officer, Soldier, Sailor, or Marine, either in Land or Sea Service, for or under or in Aid of any Foreign Prince, State, Potentate, Colony, Province, or Part of any Province or People, or for or under or in Aid of any Person or Persons exercising or assuming to exercise any Powers of Government as aforesaid, or to go or to agree to go or embark from any Part of His Majesty's Dominions, for the Purpose or with Intent to be so enlisted, entered, engaged, or employed as aforesaid, whether any enlisting Money, Pay, or Reward shall have been or shall be actually given or received, or not; in any or either of such Cases, every Person so offending shall be deemed guilty of a Misdemeanor, and upon being convicted thereof, upon any Information or Indictment, shall be punishable by Fine and Imprisonment, or either of them, at the Discretion of the Court before which such Offender shall be convicted.

Act not to extend to Persons enlisted or serving before the Times herein specified.

III. Provided always, and be it enacted, That nothing in this Act contained shall extend or be construed to extend to render any Person or Persons liable to any Punishment or Penalty under this Act, who at any Time before the First Day of *August* One thousand eight hundred and nineteen, within any Part of the United Kingdom, or of the Islands of *Jersey, Guernsey, Alderney*, or *Sark*, or at any Time before the First Day of *November* One thousand eight hundred and nineteen, in any Part or Place out of the United Kingdom, or of the said Islands, shall have taken or accepted, or agreed to take or accept any Military Commission, or shall have otherwise enlisted into any Military Service as a Commissioned or Non-commissioned Officer, or shall have enlisted, or entered himself to enlist, or shall have agreed to enlist or to enter himself to serve as a Soldier, or shall have served, or having so served shall, after the said First Day of *August* One thousand eight hundred and nineteen, continue to serve in any Warlike or Military Operation, either as an Officer or Soldier, or in any other Military Capacity, or shall have accepted, or agreed to take or accept any Commission, Warrant, or Appointment as an Officer, or shall have enlisted or entered himself to serve, or shall have served, or having so served shall continue to serve as a Sailor, or Marine, or shall have been employed or engaged, or shall have served, or having so served shall, after the said First Day of *August*, continue to serve in and on board any Ship or Vessel of War, used or fitted out, or equipped or intended for any Warlike Purpose; or shall have engaged, or contracted or agreed to go, or shall have gone to, or having so gone to shall, after the said First Day of *August*, continue in any Foreign State, Country, Colony, Province, or Part of a Province, or to or in any Place beyond the Seas, unless such Person or Persons shall embark at or proceed from some Port or Place within the United Kingdom, or the Islands of *Jersey, Guernsey, Alderney*, or *Sark*, with Intent to serve as an Officer, Soldier, Sailor, or Marine, contrary to the Provisions of this Act, after the said First Day of *August*, or shall embark or proceed from some Port or Place out of the United Kingdom, or the Islands of *Jersey, Guernsey, Alderney*, or *Sark*, with such Intent as aforesaid, after the said First Day of *November*, or who shall, before the passing of this Act, and within the said United Kingdom, or the said Islands, or before the First Day of *November* One thousand eight hundred and nineteen, in any Port or Place out of the said United Kingdom, or the said Islands, have hired, retained, engaged, or procured, or attempted or endeavoured to hire, retain, engage, or procure, any person or Persons whatever, to enlist or to enter, or to engage to enlist or to serve, or be employed in any such Service or Employment as aforesaid, as an Officer, Soldier, Sailor, or Marine, either in Land or Sea Service, or to go, or agree to go or embark for the Purpose or with the Intent to be so enlisted, entered, or engaged, or employed, contrary to the Prohibitions respectively in this Act contained, anything in this Act contained to the contrary in anywise notwithstanding; but that all and every such Persons and Person shall be in such State and Condition, and no other, and shall be liable to such Fines, Penalties, Forfeitures, and Disabilities, and none other, as such Persons or Person was or were liable and subject to before the passing of this Act, and as such Person or Persons would have been in, and been liable and subject to, in case this Act and the said recited Acts by this Act repealed had not been passed or made.

Justices to issue Warrants for the Apprehension of Offenders.

IV. And be it further enacted, That it shall and may be lawful for any Justice of the Peace residing at or near to any Port or Place within the United Kingdom of *Great Britain* and *Ireland*, where any Offence made punishable by this Act as a Misdemeanor shall be committed, on Information on Oath of any such Offence, to issue his Warrant for the Apprehension of the Offender, and to cause him to be brought before such Justice, or any Justice of the Peace; and it shall be lawful for the Justice of the Peace before whom such Offender shall be brought, to examine into the Nature of the Offence upon Oath, and to commit such Person to Gaol, there to remain until delivered by due Course of Law, unless such Offender shall give Bail, to the Satisfaction of the said Justice, to appear and answer to any Information or Indictment to be preferred against him, according to Law, for the said Offence; and that all such Offences which shall be committed within that Part of the United Kingdom called *England*, shall and may be proceeded and tried in His Majesty's Court of King's Bench at *Westminster*, and the Venue in such Case laid at *Westminster*, or at the Assizes or Session of Oyer and Terminer and Gaol Delivery, or at any Quarter or General Sessions of the Peace in and for the County or Place where such Offence was committed; and that all such Offences which shall be committed within that Part of the United Kingdom called *Ireland*, shall and may be prosecuted in His Majesty's Court of King's Bench at *Dublin*, and the Venue be laid at *Dublin*, or at any Assizes or Session of Oyer and Terminer and Gaol Delivery, or at any Quarter or General Sessions of the Peace in and for the County or Place where such Offence was committed; and all such Offences as shall be committed in *Scotland*, shall and may be prosecuted in the Court of Justiciary in *Scotland*, or any other Court competent to try Criminal Offences committed within the County, Shire, or Stewartry within which such Offence was committed; and where any Offence made punishable by this Act as a Misdemeanor shall be committed out of the said United Kingdom, it shall be lawful for any Justice of the Peace residing near to the Port or Place where such Offence shall be committed, on Information on Oath of any such Offence, to issue his Warrant for the Apprehension of the Offender, and to cause him to be brought before such Justice, or any other Justice of the Peace for such Place; and it shall be lawful for the Justice of the Peace before whom such Offender shall be brought, to examine into the Nature of the Offence upon Oath, and to commit such Person to Gaol, there to remain till delivered by due Course of Law, or otherwise to hold such Offender to Bail to answer for such Offence in the Superior Court competent to try and having Jurisdiction to try Criminal

Where Offences shall be tried.

Offences committed in such Port or Place; and all such Offences committed at any Place out of the said United Kingdom shall and may be prosecuted and tried in any Superior Court of His Majesty's Dominions competent to try, and having Jurisdiction to try Criminal Offences committed at the Place where such Offence shall be committed.

V. And be it further enacted, That in case any Ship or Vessel in any Port or Place within His Majesty's Dominions shall have on board any such Person or Persons who shall have been enlisted or entered to serve, or shall have engaged or agreed or been procured to enlist or enter or serve, or who shall be departing from His Majesty's Dominions for the Purpose and with the Intent of enlisting or entering to serve, or to be employed, or of serving or being engaged or employed in the Service of any Foreign Prince, State, or Potentate, Colony, Province, or Part of any Province or People, or of any Person or Persons exercising or assuming to exercise the Powers of Government in or over any Foreign Colony, Province, or Part of any Province or People, either as an Officer, Soldier, Sailor, or Marine, contrary to the Provisions of this Act, it shall be lawful for any of the principal Officers of His Majesty's Customs, where any such Officers of the Customs shall be, and in any Part of His Majesty's Dominions in which there are no Officers of His Majesty's Customs, for any Governor or Persons having the Chief Civil Command, upon Information on Oath given before them respectively, which Oath they are hereby respectively authorized and empowered to administer, that such Person or Persons as aforesaid is or are on board such Ship or Vessel, to detain and prevent any such Ship or Vessel, or to cause such Ship or Vessel to be detained and prevented from proceeding to Sea on her Voyage with such Persons as aforesaid on board: Provided, nevertheless, that no principal Officer, Governor, or Person shall act as aforesaid, upon such Information upon Oath as aforesaid, unless the Party so informing shall not only have deposed in such Information that the Person or Persons on board such Ship or Vessel hath or have been enlisted or entered to serve, or hath or have engaged or agreed or been procured to enlist or enter or serve, or is or are departing as aforesaid, for the Purpose and with the Intent of enlisting or entering to serve or to be employed, or of serving, or being engaged or employed in such Service as aforesaid, but shall also have set forth in such Information upon Oath, the Facts or Circumstances upon which he forms his Knowledge or Belief, enabling him to give such Information upon Oath; and that all and every Person and Persons convicted of wilfully false swearing in any such Information upon Oath, shall be deemed guilty of and suffer the Penalties on Persons convicted of wilful and corrupt Perjury.

Vessels with Persons on board engaged in Foreign Service, may be detained at any Port in His Majesty's Dominions.

Oath to be made as to Facts and Circumstances.

VI. And be it further enacted, That if any Master or other Person having or taking the Charge or Command of any Ship or Vessel, in any Part of the United Kingdom of *Great Britain and Ireland*, or in any Part of His Majesty's Dominions beyond the Seas, shall knowingly and willingly take on board, or if such Master or other Person having the Command of any such Ship or Vessel, or any Owner or Owners of any such Ship or Vessel, shall knowingly engage to take on board any Person or Persons who shall have been enlisted or entered to serve, or shall have engaged or agreed or been procured to enlist or enter or serve, or who shall be departing from His Majesty's Dominions for the Purpose and with the Intent of enlisting or entering to serve, or to be employed, or of serving, or being engaged or employed in any Naval or Military Service,

Penalty on Masters of Ships, &c. taking on board Persons enlisted contrary to this Act, £50 for each Person.

contrary to the Provisions of this Act, such Master or Owner or other Person as aforesaid shall forfeit and pay the Sum of Fifty Pounds for each and every such Person so taken or engaged to be taken on board; and moreover every such Ship or Vessel, so having on board, conveying, carrying, or transporting any such Person or Persons, shall and may be seized and detained by the Collector, Comptroller, Surveyor, or other Officer of the Customs, until such Penalty or Penalties shall be satisfied and paid, or until such Master or Person, or the Owner or Owners of such Ship or Vessel, shall give good and sufficient Bail, by Recognizance before one of His Majesty's Justices of the Peace, for the Payment of such Penalty or Penalties.

Penalty on Persons fitting out armed Vessels to aid in Military Operations with any Foreign Powers without Licence;

VII. And be it further enacted, That if any Person, within any Part of the United Kingdom, or in any Part of His Majesty's Dominions beyond the Seas, shall, without the Leave and Licence of His Majesty for that Purpose first had and obtained as aforesaid, equip, furnish, fit out, or arm, or attempt or endeavour to equip, furnish, fit out, or arm, or procure to be equipped, furnished, fitted out, or armed, or shall knowingly aid, assist, or be concerned in the equipping, furnishing, fitting out, or arming of any Ship or Vessel, with Intent or in order that such Ship or Vessel shall be employed in the Service of any Foreign Prince, State, or Potentate, or of any Foreign Colony, Province, or Part of any Province or People, or of any Person or Persons exercising or assuming to exercise any Powers of Government in or over any Foreign State, Colony, Province, or Part of any Province or People, as a Transport or Store Ship, or with Intent to cruize or commit Hostilities against any Prince, State, or Potentate, or against the Subjects or Citizens of any Prince, State, or Potentate, or against the Persons exercising or assuming to exercise the Powers of Government in any Colony, Province, or Part of any Province or Country, or against the Inhabitants of any Foreign Colony, Province, or Part of any Province or Country, with whom His Majesty shall not then be at War; or shall, within the United Kingdom, or any of His Majesty's Dominions, or in any Settlement, Colony, Territory, Island, or Place belonging or subject to His Majesty, issue, or deliver any Commission for any Ship or Vessel, to the Intent that such Ship or Vessel shall be employed as aforesaid, every such Person so offending shall be deemed guilty of a Misdemeanor, and shall, upon Conviction thereof, upon any Information or Indictment, be punished by Fine and Imprisonment, or either of them, at the Discretion of the Court in which such Offender shall be convicted; and every such Ship or Vessel, with the Tackle, Apparel, and Furniture, together with all the Materials, Arms, Ammunition, and Stores, which may belong to or be on board of any such Ship or Vessel, shall be forfeited; and it shall be lawful for any Officer of His Majesty's Customs or Excise, or any Officer of His Majesty's Navy, who is by Law empowered to make Seizures, for any Forfeiture incurred under any of the Laws of Customs or Excise, or the Laws of Trade and Navigation, to seize such Ships and Vessels aforesaid, and in such Places and in such Manner in which the Officers of His Majesty's Customs or Excise and the Officers of His Majesty's Navy are empowered respectively to make Seizures under the Laws of Customs and Excise, or under the Laws of Trade and Navigation; and that every such Ship and Vessel, with the Tackle, Apparel, and Furniture, together with all the Materials, Arms, Ammunition, and Stores which may belong to or be on board of such Ship or Vessel, may be prosecuted and condemned in the like Manner, and in such Courts as Ships or Vessels may be prosecuted and condemned

or issuing Commissions or Ships.

for any Breach of the Laws made for the Protection of the Revenues of Customs and Excise, or of the Laws of Trade and Navigation.

Penalty for aiding the Warlike Equipment of Vessels of Foreign States, &c.

VIII. And be it further enacted, That if any Person in any Part of the United Kingdom of *Great Britain* and *Ireland*, or in any Part of His Majesty's Dominions beyond the Seas, without the Leave and Licence of His Majesty for that Purpose first had and obtained as aforesaid, shall, by adding to the Number of the Guns of such Vessel, or by changing those on board for other Guns, or by the Addition of any Equipment for War, increase or augment, or procure to be increased or augmented, or shall be knowingly concerned in increasing or augmenting the Warlike Force of any Ship or Vessel of War, or Cruizer, or other armed Vessel which at the Time of her Arrival in any Part of the United Kingdom, or any of His Majesty's Dominions, was a Ship of War, Cruizer, or armed Vessel in the Service of any Foreign Prince, State, or Potentate, or of any Person or Persons exercising or assuming to exercise any Powers of Government in or over any Colony, Province, or Part of any Province or People belonging to the Subjects of any such Prince, State, or Potentate, or to the Inhabitants of any Colony, Province, or Part of any Province or Country under the Control of any Person or Persons so exercising or assuming to exercise the Powers of Government, every such Person so offending shall be deemed guilty of a Misdemeanor, and shall, upon being convicted thereof, upon any Information or Indictment, be punished by Fine and Imprisonment, or either of them, at the Discretion of the Court before which such Offender shall be convicted.

Offences committed out of the Kingdom may be tried at Westminster.

IX. And be it further enacted, That Offences made punishable by the Provisions of this Act, committed out of the United Kingdom, may be prosecuted and tried in His Majesty's Court of King's Bench at *Westminster*, and the Venue in such case laid at *Westminster*, in the County of *Middlesex*.

How Penalties shall be sued for and recovered.

X. And be it further enacted, That any Penalty or Forfeiture inflicted by this Act may be prosecuted, sued for, and recovered, by Action of Debt, Bill, Plaint, or Information, in any of His Majesty's Courts of Record at *Westminster* or *Dublin*, or in the Court of Exchequer, or in the Court of Session in *Scotland*, in the Name of His Majesty's Attorney-General for *England* or *Ireland*, or His Majesty's Advocate for *Scotland* respectively, or in the Name of any Person or Persons whatsoever; wherein no Essoign, Protection, Privilege, Wager of Law, nor more than One Imparlance shall be allowed; and in every Action or Suit the Person against whom Judgment shall be given for any Penalty or Forfeiture under this Act shall pay Double Costs of Suit; and every such Action or Suit shall and may be brought at any Time within Twelve Months after the Offence committed, and not afterwards; and One Moiety of every Penalty to be recovered by virtue of this Act shall go and be applied to His Majesty, His Heirs or Successors, and the other Moiety to the Use of such Person or Persons as shall first sue for the same, after deducting the Charges of Prosecution from the whole.

Double Costs.

Limitation of Actions.

Former Rules established by Law to be applied to Actions commenced in pursuance of this Act.

XI. And be it further enacted, That if any Action or Suit shall be commenced, either in *Great Britain* or elsewhere, against any Person or Persons for anything done in pursuance of this Act, all Rules and Regulations, Privileges and Protections, as to maintaining or defending any Suit or Action, and pleading therein, or any Costs thereon, in relation to any Acts, Matters, or Things done, or that may be done by any Officer of Customs or Excise, or by any Officer of His Majesty's Navy, under any Act of Parliament in force on or immediately before the passing of this Act, for the Protection of the Revenues of Customs and Excise, or Prevention of Smuggling, shall apply and be in full Force in any such Action or Suit as shall be brought for anything done in pursuance of this Act, in as full and ample a Manner to all Intents and Purposes as if the same Privileges and Protections were repeated and re-enacted in this Act.

Penalties not to extend to Persons entering into Military Service in Asia.

XII. Provided always and be it further enacted, That nothing in this Act contained shall extend, or be construed to extend, to subject to any Penalty any Person who shall enter into the Military Service of any Prince, State, or Potentate in *Asia*, with Leave or License, signified in the usual Manner, from the Governor-General in Council, or Vice-President in Council of *Fort-William*, in *Bengal*, or in conformity with any Orders or Regulations issued or sanctioned by such Governor-General or Vice-President in Council.

Y.

CPSIA information can be obtained
at www.ICGtesting.com
Printed in the USA
LVHW100514130422
716029LV00002B/111

9 783752 592757